# MURDER LIGHT
## One Murder, Endless Humor

Hugh McClintock

Preliminary, first-person versions of
*Murder Light* were published as *After All,
Murder is Murder (2009)* and *TWIST (2011).*

# Dallas, Texas, 1980 . . .

The thirty-six-year-old founder of Edgecom Data Company dies in the hospital the day after undergoing successful surgery.

His doctors dismiss the founder's death as a random event, one that is not singularly exceptional.

The founder's close friend, A. J., an Edgecom executive, believes unreservedly that his friend was murdered. Convincing a comely City-of-Dallas detective to support his stealth investigation, they couple, rock, roll, and zigzag their way through Edgecom's vigorous personal computer business – to the bombshell discovery that the founder was indeed murdered.

Their digging ultimately overturns a jury's wrongful death-sentence, the would-be conviction of an innocent man, and uncovers the true facts of the utterly improbable homocide.

Episodes during the early years of the personal computer industry accent the plot and setup numerous incidents of humor

# Prologue

November had all but slipped away before A. J.'s suspicion finally coalesced into the grim certainty that his friend and boss, Edgecom's incandescent, thirty-six year old founder, had been murdered.

When he arrived at the police station, a lone sergeant, hunched over the counter, was sullenly thumbing through a stack of documents. Intent on scrutinizing every sentence, the sergeant's bald head all but glowed. A. J. waited in front of the counter a good five seconds before politely asking to talk to a detective.

The sergeant did not look up. "About *what*? Domestic violence? High-Seas piracy? I can't read your mind, Pal."

"Uh, homicide . . . I guess."

The sergeant's head slowly came up. "Homicide, you *guess*. It's not something I'd be guessing about."

"Well . . . my case may not seem to be airtight, but–"

"You knew the . . . victim?"

"He was my boss. And a friend."

The sergeant was unsympathetic. "Where'd this, uh, alleged murder take place?"

"At Medical City Hospital."

"*Inside* Med City?"

A. J. resisted appropriating his asshole attitude. "Yes sir, inside, only it wasn't–"

"What's your name?"

". . . a, uh, violent attack. MacRae. Alan MacRae."

The sergeant studied A. J.'s face a moment, scribbled letters on a Post-it, and then waved toward an empty bench snug against the front wall near the room's entrance.

The room where the sergeant, among other duties, received walk-in complainants was windowless but radiant with fluorescent lighting. Standing to the left of his station was a grungy oak table offering visitors summaries of ordinances on illicit behavior. The building's air-conditioning system had to be first rate: the coolness of the room reminded A. J. of the bland, windowless, three-story, yellow-brick building in Oak Cliff where his mother cached her mink furs in the summer. It was warm outdoors, for late November, but not that warm.

"Lennie," A. J. heard the sergeant say as he walked toward one of the benches at which the Sergeant had gestured. "You have a customer . . . *another* malice aforethought . . . male."

The sergeants voice, A. J. noticed, had become gentle and less seasoned.

A scratchy acknowledgement crackled over the telephone intercom, and a minute later a thirtyish woman wearing a silver-and-blue Dallas Cowboys warm-up jacket, a dark-blue denim skirt, and western-tooled, mahogany-colored cowboy boots, opened a door in the room's back wall. Her eyes fast on the sergeant, she beckoned to A. J. with a quick nod and disappeared back inside the building.

A. J. caught up with her in a room sparingly furnished with four scuffed and stained dark wooden desks and a six- to eight-foot, wall-mounted blackboard. Every desk was cluttered with what appeared to be the residue of interrupted paper work activity; the blackboard was lined with scripts of crime-related reminders. A tall, jacketless, burr-headed man holding a phone to his ear was standing between the two back desks. A. J. figured the man to be his age, forty-two. Listening intently to the voice on the line, burr head was slowly, mindlessly, removing an empty shoulder holster with his free hand.

The woman summoned by the desk sergeant – Lennie he called her – gestured  at a chair positioned backwards alongside the desk situated nearest to the room's doorway, nodded at the man on the telephone, and continued briskly on toward a door leading deeper into the building. The burr-headed man's eyes panned down from her butt to the tops of her cowboy boots.

A. J. sat down in the chair by the side of the desk, mentally reviewed his argument for a charge of murder, and furtively watched the detective – A. J. presumed he was a detective – for signs he was winding up his telephone call.

Shortly, Lennie returned. "I'm Detective Deemer," she said, settling into the chair behind the desk next to where A. J. was waiting. Laying a tablet on the top of the desk, she added, briskly, "You're here to report a murder?" A scribbled note that A. J. couldn't make out was written across the top edge of the top sheet of her tablet.

Having initially assumed that the woman wearing the Dallas Cowboys jacket was only office help, A. J. had to overcome a moment of surprise. "How do you do," he said witlessly.

A. J. was a kid the last time he had used that wordy greeting – urged to do so by his mother.

"I've been a Dallas police officer for seven years," Detective Deemer said coolly. She looked up from her tablet, her eyes boring into A. J.'s. "The last three as a lead-detective investigating crimes against persons."

Knocked down a peg, A. J. tried not to simper stupidly. "I see," he nodded.

Detective Deemer's next remark, "I'm trolling," was apparently induced by A. J.'s obvious miscalculation of her vocational status, which he compounded by his openly uncertain appraisal of her sporty western outfit.

Lennie looked away, left it to A. J. to guess what she meant by "trolling." A. J. decided that she was dressed to snatch-hook men looking for a quick skinny-dip in a guest room at a cheap, compliant motel.

"The sergeant used the name Lennie," A. J. said, finally. "I assumed . . . you'd be a man. You know, that I'd be talking to, ah, a Detective Leonard . . . somebody . . . different."

The woman shook her head. "Lenore."

Lenore, or Detective Deemer, A. J. decided, was not out-and-out beautiful, but she wasn't bad-looking, either.

After poorly expressing the situation under pinning his boss's " passing" – A. J. called it passing, with reservations – he spent the next five minutes trying hard to make his case.

When A. J. finished, Detective Lennie, after sitting back and loosely crossing her arms, expressed a judgment that A. J. was hoping not to hear: "My advice to you, Mister"– she glanced at her tablet –"MacRae, is to drop the whole matter. Your evidence – she again consulted her tablet – "relative to the death of Mister Degeorge, simply, is . . . too thin, certainly not enough for a *murder*." As if perplexed, if not irreversibly confused, she skeptically shook her head.

A. J. sat motionless for several seconds. Nodding compliantly, but certain in his heart that Detective Deemer had made a bad call, he slowly stood up.

"Thank you, anyway," he mumbled.

A. J.'s mind, however, was elsewhere: My evidence is too thin? Was not enough to justify a police investigation. A spirited, ever-bustling, thirty-six-year-old man peacefully convalescing in a hospital from serious but common surgery suddenly dies? What exactly does that scene add up to, Detective? Some squirrely epiphany on my part?

A. J. glumly answered his own question: *"It adds up to more digging."*

# [1]

In 1976, Peter Francis Degeorge – Fran, as he insisted on being called – founded Edgecom Data Company in a small, pre-fabbed barn in his backyard. Delivered in sections on a horse-drawn wagon, the barn was put up by an Amish man and his two sons on the lawn behind Fran's home in Richardson, Texas. At the time, Richardson, a moderately upscale suburb of Dallas, was home to some forty-thousand upper, middle-income residents. Nearby, Texas Instruments Corporation, where Fran first worked after graduating from Arkansas State University's Engineering School in 1968, was also growing at a good clip. The world was Fran's oyster.

The job of relocating the neonate firm of Edgecom Data Company amounted to furbishing the new little backyard barn with an oscilloscope, a hand-held multi-meter, two DC power supplies, a two-drawer metal filing cabinet, a work-bench stool, and a work bench. Together, the furniture had taken up a back corner in the cellar of the Degeorge home. Every item, including the thick-legged, six-foot-long work bench, was hauled to the barn by Fran and his wife – who had to have struggled mightily to climb the cellar stairs while hefting one end of the work bench.

Fran, on that cellar bench, had autonomously fashioned a modular, plug-in electronic circuit board that connected a hand-held audio cassette to a personal computer – to a microcomputer, as tiny, home computers were universally called before IBM introduced its PC in 1981. In the 1970s and early 1980s audio cassettes served computer junkies as cheap – albeit glacially slow – off-line units for magnetically storing masses of data. Fran's novel design kick-started Edgecom. At roughly the same time, IBM introduced its PC, which finally awakened the media to the fact that personal computers were not just a transitory, niche market novelty.

In the late 1970s, the home computer market "exploded," as newspaper journalists were inclined to characterize its sudden relentless expansion, and Edgecom synchronously kept pace. Fran moved his company into larger quarters twice, the last into a leased, 18,000-square-foot building in a new industrial park situated in the northeast corner of the city of Dallas.

Two weeks later Fran died in the hospital of heart failure. The morning that A. J. and the rest of the Edgecom employees heard the horrific news was the beginning of a Dallas, June, scorching-hot day: the sky was a shimmering blue and the temperature was barreling toward the one-hundred degree mark. "Foreboding," A. J. would later characterize the morning, although weather-wise it was no different from the other twenty-nine mornings, showers or no, that torridly heated Dallas that June.

Fran – heart, soul, sinewy muscle, omnipresent and ever-haunting spirit – *was* Edgecom Data Company. He and A. J. went back six years to when they worked together at Texas Instruments. They knew each other well enough that Fran once confided to A. J. the reason why he insisted on being called Fran instead of Pete: as her youngest child, and smallish, his Mother always called him "Little Peter." And A. J. told Fran why his marriage was in the crapper: explained that his wife, Allison, among other equally fossilized notions, imagined her vaginal orifice to be the consecrated entrance to a vault of sacred gem stones.

Fran was short, just over five-feet-six-inches tall, but he was husky and self-sufficient – to where he serviced most of his own needs, personal or technical. His self-reliance probably accounted for his often stoic attitude.

Fran was a degreed engineer. Many formally educated engineers are desk jockeys. Not Fran. He manipulated *things*, not words. Still, he instinctively understood the importance of advertising; many engineers conclude that a technically well-designed, commercially intended product would sell itself. Fran

3

knew better, and he always gave the text of the news releases and promo ads created by A. J. an exhaustive wringing out. He barely looked at A. J.'s self-acclaiming Edgecom stuff, however.

As for the computing business itself, A. J. doubted that Fran discussed his notion of future, home-computer commerce with any other employee except me – possibly with his wife, Jo Ellen, who was pretty, sweet, dedicated to an enduring, cohesive marriage, but as mentally agile as an arthritic armadillo. To be honest, however, Fran enjoyed explicitly verbalizing his notion of home computer market projections as much as enlightening A. J. on his marketing strategies.

A. J. was nominally second in command at Edgecom. He did not have a title, but when Fran left Dallas to work a trade show he ordered his department heads to run all important decisions past A. J. especially matters that might backhoe Edgecom finances to below minimal depth. Otherwise, A. J. wrote the copy for Edgecom's magazine ads, ginned up press releases, and fought with Edgecom technicians over the techno-babble they infernally worked into the company's product user manuals, which A. J. also edited and put together for commercial printing.

# [2]

The conference room where Sherman "Nick" Nickerson, Edgecom's brainy, twenty-six-year-old Chief Engineer, presented the "Doubler" to Marketing was uncomfortably warm – forebodingly warm A. J. would subsequently characterize it – on the horrible morning of Fran's death. Anything but a gimmick, the Doubler, a plug-in printed-circuit board literally doubled the data storage capacity of a Tandy Radio Shack, TRS-80, personal-computer disk storage system. Electronically – and provably – it allowed an x gallon word bucket to hold 2x gallons of words.

Once Nick finished his talk, Edgecom's two telephone sales reps, as they usually did, hurried to the podium and launched their queries, their questions centering on the new product's chief selling points. Unmarried, in their early twenties, not especially pretty but conspicuously full-chested and round-bottomed, they had quarried their prey and were relentlessly attacking. Nick, single himself, incessantly welcomed their questions.

A. J. watched for five minutes from his seat at the opposite end of the conference-room table. By then, both women were gushing. He was personally enjoying what could have been the focus of a Vargas Girl pin-up painting: two young women's spring-tensioned fannies thinly lacquered in tautly stretched, summer-weight slacks.

After coughing out a sharp, attention-catching, "Ahem," A. J. barked at Nick, "My office."

Donna, the brassier of the two young women, hooked the thumb of her right hand inside the back waistband of her slacks and pointed her middle finger at the floor. Rising, A. J. said offhandedly to Nick, "Donna seems to think she's number one."

Unaware of Donna's salutary one-finger assessment of A. J.'s mock strict order, Nick slightly nodded. A. J. left the room.

Two hours later, Nick and Edgecom's Director of Marketing were duking it out in the Director's office, where they and A. J. had met to review A. J.'s draft of the Doubler introductory news release. Nick started it. Twenty-six-year-old engineers do socially dumb things – like sarcastically faulting the vacuous pronouncements of blowhard marketing types. And the age-old fight between Sales and Engineering was on – in real time and real fisticuffs. The head of Production, who, on his way to discuss a component need with Sandy, walked by the Director's office and broke up the fight, which was fast becoming a shellacking of

Nickerson. Jennerette's fortuitous arrival ensured that Nickerson would survive to enjoy another captivating, multi-layered, multi-tinted sunset enlivening the western margin of Ft. Worth.

A. J. allowed a half-hour for the dust of Nick's nascent mauling to settle and then headed for his office. Selig Hildreth, Nick's lead technician, had arrived earlier. Knocking lightly on the door jamb, A. J. angled past Sel and plopped into Nick's desk chair. Sel and Knick were arguing the heat-radiating capability of an integrated-circuit add-on heat sink; A. J. fought dozing off into terminus extremity.

Tall, blond, and patchily bearded, Nickerson had a farmer's broad shoulders and big, plentifully nicked hands. He loped when he walked, bounced along as if he were crossing a newly ploughed field, as no doubt he had done through many a Spring and Summer while growing up in Iowa. A. J. remembered him as much for his bobbing gait as for his relentlessly logical mind.

The two men resolved their differences over the utility of the heat sink, and Sel, his brow wrinkled in thought, pensively left the room.

Nick closed his office door. "No," he volunteered, "Sel didn't know about me and Dornhoffer . . . doing our little . . . slam-dance. Hell, my shirttail's always out anyway."

A. J. nodded earnestly. "Cheap shirts do that."

Frowning as if he really cared, A. J. asked Knick where he learned to box. Defending himself against

Edgecom's Marketing Manager, Knick's balled hands looked to be better-suited to holding altar candles than to throwing punches.

Knick's answer was a spiteful glance, nasty enough that A. J. changed the subject. "Nice job this morning . . . your presentation."

"It felt okay . . . but, then . . . genius will out."

"So does the ranting of idiot savants," A. J. reminded him.

Someone knocked lightly on the door. Nick glanced uncertainly at A. J. "Shit," he said softly. Slipping from his stool, he shambled toward the entrance. A. J. improved his posture.

Their timid visitor was Patricia Brown, Fran's pint-sized, ever-perky secretary. Her eyes were watery and her usually sanguine face was closer to a shade of gray pewter. Her auburn-tinted hair, always nappy, appeared, at best, to have been smoothed down with a cooking spatula.

"I just got a telephone call," she said, singling A. J. out, her words barely audible. "From a Doctor Gruenthal. It was about . . . Francis. He . . . God took him last night." Her grief erupted. "At the hospital!"

Having tearfully stammered out that horrible message, Pat fell against A. J. and continued sobbing uninhibitedly. Nick and A. J., stunned and voiceless, stared drop-jawed at each other. Pat began another sentence; her grief interposed, however, and her sobbing resumed.

Fran had told A. J. the day before his hospitalization that his heart itself was healthy, that it had not yet been dangerously oxygen-deprived by the arterial blockages foretold by his shortness of breath and the sometimes repetitious dull pain in his left arm. Fran scoffed impudently at his upcoming hospitalization. The possibility of this young dynamo, his boss, not surviving the operation was not even a stray, weakly flickering blip on A. J.'s search radar.

"I'll tell Marketing," A. J. finally said to Pat. To Nick he said, "Would you please tell Production? I mean, tell Jesse. Personally."

Before Nick answered, Pat, dabbing alternately at one eye and then the other, said she would tell Martha her office pal, Edgecom's sixty-something-year-old lead bookkeeper.

Nick, given a moment to think over A. J.'s question, declined the hapless task of telling Jesse Jennerette that, their boss, Edgecom's galvanic young founder had died only hours ago.

Someone, it flashed through A. J.'s mind, should tell Edgecom's purchasing agent, Sandy Welcheck, the woman who had the onerous job of efficiently buying the parts that Jennerette's five dozen assemblers soldered onto printed-circuit boards. A woman of easy virtue (a gross understatement), divorced from her second husband or maybe her third, and relentlessly on the make, A. J. figured Sandy was likely steering one of the many handsome salesmen, who called on her, to a nooner. Anyway, A. J. did not mention her name.

A. J.'s sense that Fran's untimely death was not a random, unforeseeable happening – as his doctors irrepressibly thought – took seed that afternoon. After all, Fran was only thirty-six, never stopped working – never even slowed down.

Under the right conditions, even the tiniest, least viable seedling will grow into strapping herbage, and the thought of Fran's incessant, non-stop energy, germinated A. J.'s kernel of suspicion. It was months later, however – the Black Friday after Thanksgiving Day – before A. J. finally, confidently took his case to the police.

# [3]

Jesse Jennerette, Edgecom's Manager of Production, worked out of the middle of three side-by-side offices that opened onto the spacious Edgecom Manufacturing bay. Ten office rooms, counting the three counter-situated rooms, were located in the front third of the Edgecom building, where they encircled a skimpily furnished "bullpen" that was some twenty-five feet deep by forty feet wide. Two rooms astraddle the twelve-o'clock position were reserved for Fran and a vice-president, a position still unfilled when he died. A cove, accommodating a secretary's desk, Pat Brown's, and a bank of dark-gray, four-drawer filing cabinets separated the president's and the vice-president's offices.

A. J. signaled Jesse from the doorway of Jesse's office. A huge, native Texan, Jesse, 57, indifferently referred to himself as Production's "Head Nigger." Chiseled in stone was his utter conviction that Negroes and Hispanics were congenitally dumber than whites. He used the words "nigger' and "Spic" discerningly, however, and never, A. J. noticed, when Degeorge was nearby.

Jesse slowly drew away from a table surrounded by ten or so of his six dozen assemblers where he had been gesturing at a schematic taped to a home-movies projection screen. Lumbering into his office, a red, three-inch "Democrats-for-Reagan" badge pinned to a front belt loop, he backed roughly into his desk chair.

"Y'all look like you saw a ghost, Bubba," Jesse said, shaking his head derisively. "Hell that little slam dance 'tween Nick and Dornhoffer didn't 'mount to *nothin'*. You knew it was comin'."

A. J. closed the door, and point-blank told Jesse that Fran had died. Jesse reacted somberly, his solemn frown confirmation of a far deeper hurt than A. J. had expected. Jesse fiercely slapped a ball-point pen off the top of his desk and marched from the room.

Edgecom's Director of Marketing, Karl Dornhoffer, was newly hired. As usual, his office door was barely open. A. J. knocked on a jamb and stepped inside. His welcome was a cowing glare.

Contrary to his North European surname, Karl's roots had to be Mediterranean. Both his hair and his eyes were coal black. His large, overhanging nose begged for rhinoplasty. Hairy, barrel-shaped from shoulders to hips, he was taller than a glance could sustain. A. J. would have wagered a month's pay that Fran had hired him thinking there was a kindred Italian entrenched secretly in a woodpile at the Dornhoffer homestead: Fran's blood name, A. J. knew, was Giordano.

Dornhoffer's scowl vanished. "Our Francis?" he replied to A. J.'s bombshell statement. His shoulders had reflexively rounded forward.

"No, Francis Cardinal Spellman." A. J. nodded.

It was a long second before Karl's next question. "How . . . what in hell happened?"

"His heart stopped."

"His heart?"

A. J. nodded again.

After another long pause Karl said, "Tell my girls, okay."

A. J.  shook his head. "You think they don't already know?"

Karl turned away, began unhooking his suit coat from the back of the office door, and A. J. left the room.

A. J.'s office, one of the ten rooms encircling the office bullpen, was situated two doors past Dornhoffer's office, in a direction away from the front lobby. Undersized, it was positioned between a standard office room and the men's latrine, which served both Office and Manufacturing. A. J. selected that room over Fran's objection, over his predisposition that A. J. should have a bigger office. He did not need the express honor, A. J. argued, nor that much room for his day-to-day grooming of outgoing Edgecom literature.

The wall separating the men's latrine from A. J.'s office had two urinals bolted on the latrine side. When a urinal was flushed, A. J. 's room would all but reverberate from the sound of rushing water, which roared as if he had set up camp near Old Faithful in Yellowstone Park. Nick and his technicians enjoyed dawdling in A. J.'s office pretending to be there on business until "Old Faithful" blew, an event they had always pre-devised.

A. J.'s desk, which supported his disarranged, home-brew computer, one that Fran had lashed together from a half-dozen different makes of electronic equipment, faced the door. Once, returning from a meeting, A. J. found, printed large on a square of cardboard leaning against his computer's video terminal, the admonition: "DON'T STARE! I'm Sensitive."

A. J. closed his office door and dialed home. Before the second ring, Sandy Welcheck pushed clumsily into the room and he hung up the telephone. Sandy suggested that they commiserate over Fran's passing at a nearby Sheraton Hotel bar, her nickel. Up your "festered bucket" she bawled when A. J. curtly refused her invitation. Spinning on her heel, she marched out, caroming off a door jamb on the way.

A. J. dialed home again.

Allison answered.

"It's me," A. J. greeted her cooly.

The night before they had another of their protracted shouting matches, quarreling over whether Danielle, their fifteen-year-old daughter, should be carrying condoms in her little hand purse. A. J. did not know for certain if Danielle was promiscuous, or, for that matter, even a virgin. Of course, he desperately hoped she did not sleep around. A. J. knew this much, however: if she freely bedded her fellow male students, she sure as hell did not inherit that inclination from her mother.

A. J. told Allison about Fran.

"I'm sorry to hear," she said and a breath later added, "Do you plan to stay on at Edgecom?"

Both Allison and A. J. were raised in posh Highland Park, Texas, a tony, self-governing municipality situated near the center of the city of Dallas itself. Allison thought A. J.'s job at Edgecom, and Edgecom itself, for that matter, were beneath his social rank. They argued over that, too.

A. J. exploded at her question about his future plans. "Christ, Allison! Fran's body is not even cold yet! How can you be so goddamn callous? The last thing that I . . . . Oh hell, I'll be late for dinner."

Look for your dinner in the oven Allison said unhesitatingly, "Carolyn is coming by."

She hung up, leaving A. J. to figure out who in the hell Carolyn was and why her visit should compromise their evening meal. A. J. slammed down the receiver and dialed the Degeorge residence.

In the Fall of 1978, Fran moved his family into a new house in the city of Frisco, Texas, which he purchased outright with cash. Located some five miles north of Dallas, Frisco was fast becoming a sizeable bedroom community of modestly upscale homes for Dallas professionals and managers.

The person who answered the telephone had an unfamiliar, throaty voice. A. J. identified himself and asked to speak to Mrs. Degeorge. Father Gallagher asked him to mark time.

A. J. heard the rattle of plastic on wood and Jo Ellen, her voice subdued but steady, greeted him by his nickname, A. J.

"Jo Ellen," A. J. said softly, "How can I help? "What can I–"

"There's just nothing A. J. Not . . . right now."

She said that Betty, her twin sister, and Hummel, Betty's husband, had rushed to her side. Hummel, she said, had graciously taken charge of the dispositioning of Fran's body. Her parents were flying back from their rented condo in Juneau, Alaska. Her two youngsters had temporarily been told that their father was on a long trip. Father Gallagher had broken the sad news to Francis's family in Pennsylvania. Jo Ellen seemed remarkably composed, and it occurred to A. J. that likely she had been medically sedated.

"Please, A.J, you go ahead and run Edgecom. I'm sure that is what Francis would have wanted."

A. J. said that he'd do his best. Jo Ellen said to tell Pat, that she would call her, and then, while A. J. was agreeing to pass her message along, she answered a question posed from someone nearby and broke the connection.

Aimlessly, A. J. walked to Jesse's office. The ceiling light was off, Jesse's way of assuring visitors that he had left for the day; A. J. did not stop.

The production bay, some 70-feet across by 90-feet deep, was dark except for a canopy of florescent light illuminating a twenty-foot-by-twenty-foot front corner. Walled in by six-foot tall, inward-opening, black metal office cabinets, the space, super-lighted, formed a high-tech electronic prototyping lab, a cloistered area of quiet and solitude. The cabinets held electronic gear, parts, supplies, tools, and so forth. A standing drill press stood in one corner; DC power supplies, small vises, and miscellaneous electronic gear sat on each of three work benches. The only sound was the intermittent chatter of fluorescent ceiling lamps and the deep, low-frequency hum of the building's 100-ton, roof-mounted central air unit. One of Jesse's assemblers spontaneously dubbed the prototyping lab the "Bates Motel," and the name stuck.

Norman Israel, Nickerson's only engineer – Engineering consisted of Nickerson, Israel, and four technicians – was sitting on a stool peering at a raft of green, filamentary lines wiggling across the face of an oscilloscope. He looked at A. J., shook his head, and turned back to the oscilloscope.

A. J. said, "The others left, huh?"

Slightly nodding, Israel answered that Nick said it was okay.

A. J. stopped in front of a blackboard standing on the seats of two old, widely separated straight-backed wooden chairs. Leaning against the building's outside concrete-block wall, a chalked schematic of the Doubler's electronics covered most of its surface. Dated 06/17/80, the middle two digits of the date were blurry from erasures – reminders that the schematic itself had been updated many times.

For a few days in May, the blackboard was the medium of an off-color limerick versifying Nick's purported loving devotion to sheep in Iowa:

> Here's to Flora and Fauna
> Who love to bathe nude in a sauna.
> This unsettles boss Nick
> Who is mostly all _____.
> But still true to his ewes in Iowa.

Flora, of course, was the Florence of telephone sales and Fauna was her coworker, Donna. The initials, A. J., penned in Nick's hand, had been printed over the word "Anon," which had been erased from the bottom of the poem but was still discernible. A. J. rubbed away

his initials and ascribed the poem's authorship to
"Homer Nickerson."

Heading to his office, A. J. passed by Nick's room.
The office door was closed, but A. J. could hear
Dornhoffer's self-assured bombast coming from inside.
His pulse raced. After a few seconds, however, he
concluded that it was not an angry exchange, and he
continued walking.

Given Jo Ellen's instruction to run Edgecom, A. J.
decided to begin by holding a meeting at nine the next
morning. He was penning the names on his desk pad of
the persons he would invite when Dornhoffer walked
past his doorway. A. J. called out his name, but he did
not answer.

"*Fuck you*," A. J. thought . . . but then he
reconsidered. When A. J. caught up with Dornhoffer, he
was in his office feeling in his lower outside coat
pockets with both hands. His back was turned to the
doorway,

"I talked to Jo Ellen," A. J. said.

Dornhoffer did not turn around. "How's she taking
it?"

"Who knows. She asked me to run things here. For
now."

Dornhoffer turned my way. Concentrating on an
in-basket on the top of his desk, he centered his necktie.
"Somebody has to."

"I'm calling a meeting for nine tomorrow."

Dornhoffer did not nod, shrug, or otherwise respond, so A. J. returned to his office.

On his way, he decided to visit Nick, *"My chief engineer now,"* A. J. wryly said to himself.

He walked into Nick's office and pulled the door shut. "Earlier I heard Dornhoffer crowing in here."

Nick tilted back in his desk chair and sighed heavily. "Yeah, we kissed and made up. We didn't exactly circle and jerk, but, yeah, we're talking again."

"He's a prick," A. J. said narrowing his eyes provocatively.

Nick shrugged. Opening his one deep desk drawer, Nick began flicking through folders.

"I talked to Jo Ellen," A. J. said. "She put me in charge . . . for now. We'll meet in the morning. At nine."

Knick extracted a folder, studied the contents a second, and returned it. "Nine o'clock," he said, lost in thought.

"Piss on you, Silo," A. J. muttered.

Staring glumly at another folder, Knick weakly flipped A. J. a bird.

The office bay was empty. Even the woman assigned by Dornhoffer to take after-hours West Coast sales calls for the week had left.

A. J. switched the ceiling lights off. For an instant there was blackness, but quickly security lamps flashed on. The room – the whole building in fact – was windowless. The sudden profusion of shadows, of miscellaneously layered trapezoidal shadings, became a sixty-era, three-dimensional op-art mural.

A. J. telephoned Jesse and Martha and told them of his meeting. Neither Pat nor Sandy answered her telephone. A. J. checked the building's side door and rear door, made sure they were secured, and trudged slowly back to his office.

His mind again turned to Edgecom itself: he could not shake the thought that Fran's death was a stake through Edgecom's heart, imagined that six men wearing black business suits were somberly carrying a casket out of the building through the front door.

Nick suddenly appeared in his doorway. "Jesus!" A. J. said, gushing out the name. "Where in the hell'd you come from?"

Nick grinned. "I guess you didn't hear me coming through the other way."

"Hell no, I didn't, Shit-Dick. I thought I was here by myself."

"What do you think?"

"About?"

"About? About panning the Trinity for gold, Pop, what else?"

"I think the fickle finger of fate just reamed Edgecom's asshole, full bore."

Nick shrugged and waited expectantly.

A. J. said, finally, "You think Fran died . . . normally?"

Nick gave A. J. an exaggerated fishy look. "How else?" Shaking his head, he began backing toward the office door.

"My God," A. J. said, "words are your strength, your gift. You must have penned that charming ode about me on the schematic board in the Proto Lab."

Nick ruminated for a second. "I didn't, but it does capture your innate temperament."

A. J. nodded. "*Innately*" he said to himself, and he began to mentally resurrect the circumstances bearing on Fran's death.

# [4]

A. J. parked his car in the back employee parking lot and entered Edgecom through the "people" door, which Jesse, A. J. was certain, had unlocked at exactly one minute before 6:30 a.m. The quiet, intense dedication of Jesse's assemblers was collective deportment that A. J. had paid scant attention to until that Friday morning. Every woman was single-mindedly focused on manually soldering an electronic component into a printed circuit board. The only noise was the low rumble of the 10-ton, roof-mounted air conditioner. Normally, voices and other man-made sounds of equipment and products being moved ricochet off the big room's cinder-block walls like well-stroked tennis balls.

In the summer, on once-a-month-Blue-Jean-Friday – and this was that day – most of Jesse's assemblers, some not altogether slender, boastfully wore the briefest of shorts and the snuggest of tight-fitting tees. Sleeping alone now, A. J. struggled to keep his eyes from locking onto several of those variously hued pairs of semi-well-turned legs and on cleft bosoms striving to escape their thin, deep-cut restraints.

"Nine o'clock," A. J. said loudly to Jesse from the doorway of his office. Standing behind his desk, arms folded across his chest, Jesse glanced up and slightly nodded. The reason for his troubled look were two black, crisscrossed marks roughly inked on two lines of a schematic spread across the top of his desk.

Born and raised in Mesquite, Texas, and still a resident of that solidly red-neck Dallas suburb, Jesse called everybody Bubba – everybody except Fran, whom he unfailingly addressed as Francis. His lips were so thick that they seemed to roll back on themselves. A half-dozen wisps of brown hair spanned his head, ear to ear. Black, horn-rimmed glasses, completely overwhelmed of their cosmetic purpose, exaggerate his ugliness. He always wore a tan, corduroy sports jacket to work, doffed it when he arrived, and slipped it on over a blended, short-sleeved shirt before leaving for home.

Furtively scanning Jesse's minimally clothed assemblers, A. J. strolled to the prototyping lab where Nick's lead technician, Selig Hildreth, assigned that week to support Manufacturing, was standing at his bench probing a circuit board. An ever-reticent person, he did not look around nor did A. J. interrupt him.

A. J. pulled a tablet from the shallow, middle drawer of his desk, printed the date, Friday, June 20, 1980, on the first sheet in the top right-hand corner and began listing topics for his nine-o'clock meeting. Dornhoffer walked briskly past his office doorway and glanced in but did not say a word.

A. J. interrupted his tallying to telephone Pat, who said that she was up to taking the minutes of his meeting. She agreed to tell Miki, our telephone switchboard operator, to watch for Sandy's arrival and to tell her of the meeting. A. J. said that he would tell Miki to be alert for Sandy's arrival. Pat understood, knew A. J. really meant that he would gladly visit the receptionist's station to stealthily ogle Miki. Though marginally competent, Miki, twenty-four, trim, sloe-eyed, and commodiously breasted, was, by the de-facto consensus of Edgecom male-workers, the firm's sexiest employee. Jesse's assemblers called her "Neon Niki."

At one minute before nine, A. J. left his office and walked to the conference room – briskly, A. J. remember, because he had acceded that beginning this day his demeanor mattered.

Dornhoffer, sitting at the head of the conference-room table, was ingesting the scribbling on an open notebook. Jesse, Martha, and Pat were silently watching the doorway. Nick, habitually late for all meetings, had not arrived. Sandy was also a no-show, but A. J. did not much care: he knew her frequent, attention-commanding outbursts would intrude his program.

A. J. eased into a chair at the foot of the table. "We're missing two," he said to Pat. "Let's give 'em another minute."

Dornhoffer stopped reading. "Pat, dear," he said, clasping his hands pontifically on the top of the table, "would you please find Nickerson, and, if you must, *drag* him in here."

Pat looked at A. J. Thus reminded who theoretically was occupying the seat of authority, A. J. was countermanding Dornhoffer's order when Nick sailed into the room. Rounding his shoulders apologetically, he said, "Sorry, Pacific West called."

A. J. looked at Pat and rolled his eyes.

After allowing Nick a few seconds to settle in, A. J. mentioned that yesterday he. had talked to Jo Ellen, Fran's wife. She seemed to be holding up, A. J. explained, and, moreover, she told me to take charge. A. J. did not say that she was calmly indifferent to almost everything A. J. mentioned and that she was likely sedated.

A. J. stared at his list for a few seconds: "Any questions? Before I go down this?"

Dornhoffer had a question. "About our financial situation," he said, addressing Martha Dillbeck. After a long second of pursed, tight-lipped pondering the subject of his own question, he continued. "What, ah, where do we stand in that regard?"

It was Martha's turn to glance uncertainly A J.'s way. Probably in her early sixties, possibly older, Martha wore her graying, wholly un-tinted hair pulled back and gathered into a bun. Glasses dangled from her neck by a black cord intertwined with a shiny silver thread. Her dark linen dress was set-off by a white mother-of-pearl pin and a plain white scarf – embellishments for the occasion, A. J. knew.

Shaking his head, A. J. turned from Martha to Dornhoffer. "We'll go over finances later."

"Besides," Martha chimed in, addressing Dornhoffer, "all I do is post the books. Jack prints trial report runs and then reviews them with Mister Degeorge. He did, I mean. Review them I mean. With Mister Degeorge. My copies are old and so soiled I can hardly decipher them myself."

Martha's inherent loyalty to Degeorge and Edgecom imbued her remark with a cloak of certitude.

Interrupting Dornhoffer, A. J. said that Jack Irickson was the consultant who wrote Edgecom's bookkeeping software. Dornhoffer, the instant A. J. finished, told Martha that he nevertheless would like to "take a peep" at Edgecom's latest financial reports. "It matters, now," he added gravely.

Martha surprised me and probably everybody in the room except her friend Pat. "Well," she said to Dornhoffer, eyes flashing, her chin thrust his way, "you are not going to. As of yesterday morning anything on my desk or in my desk is no one's business except that of the new owner of Edgecom Data Company."

Dornhoffer, unruffled, genially started in again. A. J. interrupted him. They argued over the propriety of reviewing Edgecom's financial situation. Their haggling ended when Jesse had heard enough.

"Dornhoffer," Jesse said, looking past Martha, "Shut the fuck up."

For a few seconds the room was utterly silent.

"Maybe y'all can come back to that one," Jesse finally said, turning to me. "I've got purchase reqs for Sandy to mail that need to be signed off."

"I'll come by your office," A. J. said, thanking him with his eyes for interrupting.

Nick spoke up, said he was waiting for a reply from an engineering student attending Texas Tech University, a senior to whom he had offered employment. "If he calls, should I mention . . . about Fran?"

"Yes. But tactfully," A. J. said sternly. "I'm working up a press release reporting that he died naturally"– A. J. hurriedly scanned the table –"of heart failure."

Dornhoffer nodded heavily. "What else *could* you say?"

A. J. pleaded the importance of retaining key people and at some point favorably remarked on our financial situation. He had hardly finished when Martha spoke up. "About our promotional and staffing efforts, A. J., we'd better not . . . overdo it. I mean. Not . . . make too much of Edgecom's financial . . . condition."

All eyes fell on Martha.

"Meaning what!" Dornhoffer demanded.

As if apologizing, her gaze fixed on A. J., Martha continued. "It's just that . . . we shouldn't imply we're financially all *that* well off."

Dornhoffer scrambled to his feet, and in the same moment A. J. was on his. "Later!" A. J. said to Dornhoffer sharply, holding up a hand. "After I meet with Mrs. Degeorge."

Slamming his notebook shut, Dornhoffer glanced at Jesse and fell back hard into his chair.

I looked around the table. "Anyone else?"

Jesse vaguely raised his hand. "Y'all know," he said to no one in particular, "Blossie Shuttleworth? One of my assemblers? She's a good nigger. Been with Edgecom as long as anyone. Her husband's a preacher boy. He'd like to hold a memorial service tonight."

"Fine by me," A. J. said, polling the table with his eyes.

Everyone nodded. Jesse read aloud the name and address of a church and a starting time for the service. A. J. told Pat to post the word.

A .J. asked for more questions. None were offered. He repeated his warning to forthwith toss in chains any able-bodied seaman teetering on a gunwale of the sloshing Edgecom galleon. He was saying we'd meet again on Monday when Sandy marched importantly into the room.

Her hair newly colored – newly frosted – she loudly informed us that, as always, vendors were mercilessly hounding her for payments. Her wrinkled seersucker slacks were complimented by a silky, beige blouse that buttoned in front. Sandy characteristically padded around the office carpeting in her stocking feet, and when she could not interpret the writing on requisitions for Manufacturing parts she would walk to the edge of the carpeting and yell into the big production bay for Jesse to at once produce his ass. She was wearing sandals on this particular morning.

"What?" she demanded of A. J., did he plan to do about the vendors who were relentlessly chomping on her butt.

"We'll meet later in your office and work it out," A. J. answered stiffly. "Eleven o'clock?"

Sandy shook her head. "Make it ten o'clock. I'm meeting with a vendor. Unless, Sweetie," she added coyly, "*you'd* like to buy me lunch."

Dornhoffer laughed out loud.

A. J. asked Martha to join Sandy and him.

Sandy, at ten o'clock, was her usual brazen, overweening self. She and Martha, virtually indifferent to A. J.'s presence, soon prioritized the current list of noisily chagrinned vendors and calculated the amount of money to apportion to the ones clamoring loudest.

Martha left, and Sandy yelled after her, "Get 'em tiger!" She pushed the list toward me. "Initial it. If you are *the Man*."

"Is that how it works?" A. J. asked.

She shrugged. "Fran always did."

A. J. initialed the sheet. "Happy now?"

She glanced at my signature. "Beside myself with joy. Better than morning sex with a fat-peckered dago. That's what I always told Fran."

"I'll bet."

"Well, guess what, Bucko. You'd lose."

She read my look. "No, Bucko, Fran never poled around in Lake Welcheck. Damn it."

I tried fishing again, hoped to hear her rousingly appraise Fran's vigor. "Didn't have the energy, I suppose?"

"Fran? Shit. It wouldn't have put *him* out any . . . not the way I'd of . . . and so on."

That night, as downhearted as he'd been in a long time, A. J. fell asleep with an encompassing taste of disgust in his mouth. He knew that Fran, ever confident and astonishingly energetic, would have breezed through his meeting as if he were directing a scripted children's play. "*My production*," A. J. decided, "*would have closed in Hartford.*"

# [5]

The church was small and packed. A. J. wedged himself into a pew alongside Nick, who slightly shifted his position and nudged A. J. as he unbuttoned his blazer. Inclining his head toward Hummel Osgood, Nick whispered, "Who is the character wearing the shiny black football helmet?"

A. J. knew that Osgood, whom he had only seen once or twice before, had founded J. Hummel Osgood & Associates, an advertising agency. A. J. knew that the letter J stood for John, and that Fran could not stomach the man, considered him so unconstrainedly full of steer shit that he should not be allowed off the range. Fran's loathing was obsessive, so vengefully Sicilian that A. J. wondered if he suspected Osgood was bonking his wife, Jo Ellen. A. J. personally only knew Osgood as an endlessly self-promoting jerk.

"Him?" A. J. whispered, nodding guardedly at the perfectly coifed Osgood. "One guess."

Nick shrugged.

"Fran's horse-shit brother-in-law," A. J. answered softly from the side of his mouth.

The pianist, a stout black woman wearing a large white, yellow-trimmed hat, began playing. A. J. scanned the gathering – all dolled-up Edgecom employees – but shortly his mind was back on the problem of how in hell to keep Edgecom Data Company from pitching headfirst into one of the endlessly forming seismic chasms of bankruptcy that were fast becoming the landscape of the fledgling personal-computer business – a situation not at all allayed by the rumor that bellwether IBM was on the verge of introducing its own personal computer. A. J. decided to kick it around with Nick in the morning at the plant; A. J. would again touch lightly on the possibility that Fran's death was not an organic washout, nothing more than the result of routine heart failure.

Jesse never worked on Saturday. Nevertheless, he always scheduled overtime for one-third of his assemblers and a supervisor.

Entering through the loading door in the rear of the plant – no doubt unlocked, left opened, and raised by the supervisor working that Saturday – A. J. walked rapidly past a holding area, past several tables of busy assemblers, past the prototyping lab, and into the office bullpen. He slowed long enough to flick on the ceiling lights. Settling into Fran's desk chair, he began shuffling through the papers piled to overflowing in Fran's in-basket.

The heavy door separating Manufacturing from the office area surged open from a hard push, and for a few seconds the sound of manufacturing activity drifted into the office bullpen. Shortly, light was streaming from Nickerson's office doorway. A. J. walked to his room.

"Boo," A. J. said.

"I saw your Caddy," Nick replied evenly, "what's up, Pop?"

"Up to abusing myself," A. J. said.

Fussing at trying to spread a circuit diagram flat on his desk, Nick did not look up. "Allison knows of your Saturday morning habit?"

"Know of it? Shit, she encourages me. Insists that self-abuse is therapeutic."

Nick suddenly marks black X's on two lines coming from a half-inch square identified as I-9, and A. J. realizes that Nick has all but forgotten that he's standing there.

A. J. returned to Fran's office, separated the papers in Fran's in-basket into "Save" and "Discard" stacks, left two notes to himself, and walked to his office to begin a damage-control press release, the well-turned poetry of PR missives. His would all but characterize the untimely death of Edgecom's young founder not only as a natural, albeit unexpected happening, but also – as deferentially as possible – a blessing in disguise.

A. J. wrote and polished a draft and saved two versions on a diskette: DAMCNTR1 and DAMCNTR2. The second version, DAMCNTR2, consisted of provable, factual excerpts of DAMCNTR1. It was a shorter file.

Morning became early afternoon and once again A. J. was mystified at the seeming compressibility of time, the illusion that Professor Einstein had reached down and speeded up the galactic clock. *"Time flies,"* A. J. reminded himself, *"when you love your work."*

It was past two o'clock when he telephoned Betty Osgood, Jo Ellen's sister. He. needed particulars regarding Fran's funeral to pass on to Jesse, Martha, and other Edgecom people.

Dornhoffer irritably answered A. J.'s call. A. J. told him of the funeral arrangements. "We have to work out telephone coverage for sales. You handle it. Okay."

"Me! Tell my girls that some have to work on the day their revered boss is buried? Get real, MacRae."

"Oh balls, Karl. Some of your people won't even *want* to go to the damn funeral."

"To the *what?*" Karl said, emphasizing the word "what" in a way to suggest that A. J. had disrespected the religious propriety of Fran's interment. A. J. could sense that he had turned his head away.

"Screw it," A. J. told him, adding that he would see to the goddamn phone coverage himself.

Fran was buried late in the morning on Tuesday, June 24, 1980. Allison accompanied A. J. to the funeral and to the graveside services. A. J. did not feel like haggling over Danielle's attending so of course she did not go with them.

There was only one mishap: Fran's mother virtually passed out at the grave site. She was wearing a dark suit, likely woolen, and probably her only reasonably formal apparel; it was, A. J. suspected, as much the heat as the grief that caused her to faint. Fran's father had died before A. J. had met Fran.

A. J. saw Betty Osgood single him out to a balding, ruddy-complexioned man his age or possibly a little older. Shortly, the man approached A. J., offered his hand, and introduced himself as Fran's oldest brother, Amelio Degeorge.

"Betty," he said softly, "told me you were Peter's best friend."

Peter, A. J. had to remember, was Fran's given first name. "I guess so," A. J. answered softly.

"What happened?" Amelio asked. "I didn't—"

A. J. interrupted his question. "It was just one of those . . . freak things. The day before he was scheduled for surgery he assured me that his heart was strong, that his cardiologist had said so. We expected him home . . . maybe inside a week. You know how pumped up he always was."

Amelio shook his head slowly, dejectedly. "He was a smart kid. Father was proud of Peter."

"*Very* smart," A. J. said, nodding.

Amelio continued shaking his head: Peter's death was imponderable, as was the understanding of God's hand. At any rate, that is how Amelio's interpretation struck A. J.

A. J. could not help but wonder what Amelio's attitude would have been if he knew that "Fran's best friend" seriously doubted that Fran had died naturally. Still . . . A. J. had no proof that he was killed. If he was murdered, *who* had done it? Who would even want to? Was A. J. going loony? He didn't think so. At any rate, he hoped he wasn't.

# [6]

Pat Brown, early in the morning two days after Fran was buried, marched importantly into A. J.'s office and handed him a stack of envelopes interleaved with wrinkled Post-it messages. "Some are over a week old," she said haughtily. "All are addressed to Fran. So, *get on 'em!*"

A. J. saluted smartly.

"When," Pat asked, still acting high and mighty, "are you moving into the president's office?"

A. J. leaned back and looked past her. "In a couple days," he added pensively, "Soon as I'm up to buffaloing the help."

"A couple of *days*? *Two* whole days for *you* to figure out how to fool the help? You won't need *that* long, Alan."

Pat addressed everyone by their given name. If A. J. was nearby when she referred to Nick as Royce, he would always confidently inform her audience in an aside, "She means, Silo."

Pat handed A. J. the top Post-it. "From Jo Ellen. You're to call her at her home . . . in Frisco."

A. J. nodded. "About what?"

"She didn't say. And I didn't think I should ask her."

A. J. nodded again, slowly. "We haven't talked. You and me."

"I know. I still . . . need time."

"Yeah, me too, I guess. It was so totally out of the blue."

Pat looked away. "I lost my favorite grandfather suddenly. But . . . it wasn't at all the same thing."

"Fran was massively energetic . . . tireless, always busy. It's crazy, I know, but sometimes, I even doubt he truly died naturally, not if—"

"He was angelic," Pat said, her voice petering out."To me."

"I'm sure. Still, I can't help but—"

Pat's eyes bore into the floor. A. J. swore that a cloud formed over her head. Anyway, he stopped his attempt at cross-examining her in the matter of the root cause of Fran's death. After a moment, he said, "Just lay those messages and other stuff on the desk, Dear."

Leaving A. J.'s office, Pat stopped in the doorway and looked back. "And don't forget," she said, high and mighty again, "tomorrow is your birthday."

"Twenty-nine tomorrow" A. J. said, tossing Jo Ellen's scribbled message on top of the others on his desk.

"Me too," Pat said, discrediting his reply with a roll of her eyes.

A. J. sniggered. "Easily."

A. J. turned forty-three on June thirtieth. Norm emceed his birthday luncheon. They celebrated at a Steak & Ale Restaurant situated on LBJ Freeway a half mile south of the Edgecom plant. A. J. rode to the restaurant with Nickerson in his sun-faded, 1972 Chevrolet Nova, the same car that a year earlier he had eased for the first time into a stall at the front of Edgecom's last address on Proctor Street in the Dallas suburb of Garland.

Dust covered the sedan's dash board. "What?" A. J. asked querulously, marking his initials in the dust, "you raising a camel for a pet?" He dragged a finger under his initials. "Abounding, corn-loving Iowa dirt, huh?"

"Exactly," Nick said. "And *don't* contaminate it."

For his birthday, Nick gave A. J. an athletic supporter stitched together – no doubt by Nick's girlfriend – from a SMALL blue-dyed genital cup and a LARGE, fifty- inch, red-dyed waistband: blue and red being SMU's school colors. It looked like genital strapping for a Japanese Sumo wrestler. A. J.'s gifts from Jesse, Norm, and the others were equally demeaning but off-the-shelf ordinary.

Jo Ellen answered the telephone after one ring. Her New Hampshire-like directness surprised A. J. "I'd like to come by tomorrow morning, A. J., and pick up our latest financial summaries. Is nine o'clock too early?"

"No, I'll be here by eight."

"Hummel wants to explain them to me. He is so good that way. Uh, A. J., I'm not thinking. You . . . do you know Hummel?"

"We've talked briefly a couple times. How's his agency doing?"

"Oh, busy, busy. Hummel is a fabulous businessman."

Hummel Osgood, Jo Ellen assured A. J., was more than a fabulous businessman: he was also Fran's best friend, his de facto older sibling, and his mentor of first resort on all matters relating to the woof and warp of Edgecom's business canvass.

*"He's also an asshole,"* A. J. said to himself.

Jo Ellen's request to see Edgecom's financial books was the excuse A. J. needed to open those books to his own reading. He had held off, not because he was troubled by what Martha purported they would show – that Edgecom was slowly bellying up – but in some nutty, self-sanctimonious way, he was concerned about violating an assumed trust that he owed Fran.

They hung up. A. J. dialed Martha's number and told her that Jo Ellen was visiting in the morning to pick up Edgecom's summary financial reports.

"I'll bring you copies," Martha said.

Martha slipped sideways into the chair in front of A. J.'s desk and simultaneously slid a manila folder across the top of the desk. A. J. opened the folder. "I'll have to study these," he said, temporizing. "Do you think Irickson would stop in on short notice?"

"He always has," Martha answered confidently. "He isn't married."

"If you can arrange it, I'll meet him here tonight at say . . . seven."

"I'll call you as soon as I know."

"Good. In your own words Martha, how do we *really* stand financially? I wanted to see you sooner, but . . . ."

"I know. I've seen you flying around here." After a tiny all-is-not-well shake of her head, Martha said, "Not good . . . it's our cash flow. Revenues aren't nearly sufficient to meet expenses. Simply put, A. J., it costs more to run Edgecom than we're taking in. It's not a novel situation . . . not for us. But it's worsening."

The problem, in Martha's cold, bookkeeper-speak, were the liabilities incurred by Edgecom on open credit. In other words, we owed vendors money, a lot for Edgecom's narrow shoulders.

Not smart enough to ask meaningful questions about business finances, A. J. sat quietly and listened. And heard that unless Edgecom somehow pumped up sales, it would take a nuclear-tipped torpedo square amidships before the year was out.

"Couldn't we get a bank loan?" A. J. asked.

Martha shook her head. "We have no collateral. We lease everything."

"But, on our potential?"

"Potential?" Martha shrugged. "I guess not."

"Isn't there a government functionary that subsidizes promising new start-up businesses?"

"Yes, the SBA. The Small Business Administration, sometimes. Actually, Fran was working on an application. There's . . . strings attached."

"Strings?"

Nodding slowly, Martha said, "An applicant must agree to hire a certain percentage of women . . . and minorities."

"Jesus!" A. J. exclaimed, "we meet that requisite in spades."

"Yes, but there's more. A. J., talk to Jack. Frankly, with Fran's passing, I doubt we'd be approved. who'd run Edgecom? And sign the application? You? By what authority. Jo Ellen's?"

"Good questions," A. J. managed to mumble. After a moment he added, "I'll have to get back with you."

Martha left, and for a good ten minutes A. J. sat numbly at his desk wondering where to begin. Then he recalled an article published a week earlier in *The Dallas Morning News*. Titled, "Chrysler's slide into bankruptcy," A. J. knew the article was still lying on top of his filing cabinet among a stack of the *News's* recent business sections.

Chrysler had temporarily suspended payments to its hundreds of suppliers. Defaults, according to the article, were among several symptoms of the giant automaker's money problems. A. J. re-read the article. Finding that Edgecom was an oarsman in a very big lifeboat of troubled business oarsmen, a weight left his shoulders.

Still, how do I deal with a murder that wasn't, with a death that everybody knows God authorized if not approved?

# [7]

The words oozed from the telephone: "Well, my friend, a pleasant hello to you on this delightful, four-leaf-clover, Wednesday afternoon."

The fluting baritone, A. J. knew, belonged to Hummel Osgood. "Hello Hummel," A. J. replied, overcoming a knee-jerk moment of dejection.

Osgood responded blithely as if A. J. had fervidly returned his oily, unctuous greeting. "Big plans for the Fourth? It'll be a scorcher. Hotter'n the inside of a roofer's lunch bucket! Heh?"

"No. No special plans for the Fourth. How's Jo Ellen holding up?"

"Tolerably, my friend, tolerably. All considered. My wife . . . you know Betty, my wife, Jo Ellen's twin sister? She's–"

"Yes. We've met."

". . . staying with Jo Ellen. At the Degeorge home in Frisco. She's comforting that poor dear woman. For now. For not too many more nights, A. J., I hope. I get, ah, lonely."

A. J. glanced at his watch. In two minutes it would be five o'clock. Since the Fourth of July fell on Friday, Edgecom's four-day work break started tomorrow, Thursday.

"They must be close," A. J. said pointlessly. "Being identical twins . . . and all."

"Oh my yes. Of course I stop by Jo Ellen's home, every night. If I can get away by nine. Gracious, but we are busy at my agency."

"I suppose so," A. J. said apathetically. His mind paged quickly through Fran's scathing verbal put-downs of the "shit-ass" married to his wife's twin sister.

"My advertising agency is located in the Kirby Building. You likely know it. Exactly in the center of downtown Dallas. An eleven story landmark."

"Yeah. Akard Street and . . . I've forgotten the cross street."

"Osgood and Associates, takes up the whole top floor. Only thing above us is the elevator motors. Niggers run the elevators. Someday Alan, I'd like to show you my modest little operation. We could—"

"Jo Ellen stopped by the plant yesterday, but we didn't get a chance to talk."

"I know. I carried her there myself. She asked me to go over Edgecom's financial situation with her. I did, happily. She said you'd have reports ready. That dear woman holds you in high regard, my friend. Bottom line, you're tops with her. Hey, how 'bout that one! 'Bottom line, you're tops'"?

"Catchy. I . . . suppose."

"A. J., I'm calling on behalf . . . do you mind, Alan, me calling you A. J.?"

"Everyone does."

"My friends call me, Hummer. I was a fair-to-middlin' fullback in college. Gained eight-hundred yards my senior year . . . all up the middle."

Osgood had the build and countenance of a man who wouldn't know a pigskin from a pig turd without smelling both. Besides, A. J. remembered Fran saying that he had quit college the second semester of his freshman year.

"Eight hundred twenty-six hard yards, to be exact. A. J., I'm calling–"

A. J. knew his claim of being a football player was absolute, total bull shit. "Where at?" he asked.

"Hardin Simmons. The Abilene branch. Uh, A. J. I'm–"

"Hummer it'll be then," A. J. said.

"Great! I'm calling, A. J., on behalf of myself and Jo Ellen. We've struck a deal, and I've decided it'd only be the right and proper thing for me to personally announce the terms at Edgecom. On Monday. Uh, make that on Tuesday morning. You know, go over the touchy, nitty-gritty issues before the rumors start."

"The rumors?"

"The usual . . . crap. Could you set a meeting up for, say, eleven o'clock Tuesday? Jo Ellen will be with me."

"Okay. Uh, who all do you want–"

"The department heads. And yourself."

Osgood's "and yourself" sounded to A. J. like a hurried afterthought. *I'm what? Hierarchically lower than a department head"*?

"Should Pat take the minutes?"

"Pat?"

"Pat Brown. Fran's secretary."

"Um, I think not, A. J. Let's make it strictly a *family* get-together."

A. J. tried drawing him out. "Want me to prepare an agenda?"

"No. Just . . . if you'll but kindly introduce me to the Edgecom higher-ups, I'll wing it. I indeed 'preciate it, A. J. And, ah, A. J., at this time *do not* mention to *anyone* what our little meeting will cover."

"What it will cover?" A. J. murmured feebly.

A. J. agreed not to reveal to anyone what it was that he hadn't even a diaphanous clue about.

Osgood wished him a "delightful" weekend and promised that he and Jo Ellen would arrive Tuesday at eleven o'clock, "straight up."

A. J. dialed Nick's extension and told him there'd be a meeting with Hummel Osgood and Jo Ellen in the Edgecom conference room late Tuesday morning. Nick barely answered: either his mind was on a knotty technical problem or he was hustling a female employee. Then, A. J. remembered it was past five o'clock, and he decided that Nick was almost certainly distracted by an engineering problem.

Jesse had left the plant, which he always did at four o'clock, and A. J. telephoned his home. After A. J. told him of the scheduled meeting, Jesse asked A. J. what he thought Osgood had in mind, and A. J. tossed the question back at him. Jesse did not hesitate. "Sounds to me like we're getting a new boss."

"Yeah," A. J. agreed. "It struck me that way, too."

A. J.'s mood was such that he decided Dornhoffer could go fuck himself, that he would tell Dornhoffer of the meeting on Tuesday morning. Sandy did not answer her telephone.

# [8]

At fourteen minutes after eleven o'clock – A. J.
was checking the time every few seconds – Pat Brown
turned toward me, nodded, and left the conference
room. The chatter stopped abruptly. Jo Ellen, dressed as
if her next perambulation would be on a high fashion
runway at Dallas's downtown Neiman-Marcus
department store, entered first. Though she was Fran's
wife, Jo Ellen seldom visited Edgecom, and her making
an appearance on any day was a red-letter event. Pat
once told me that she was a "good Catholic mother"
meaning, in the vernacular of Pat's upbringing, that Jo
Ellen was a homebody wife.

Fran's father and his father's only brother, Fran's
uncle, of course, both first-generation Italian-
Americans, changed their last names, sometime in their
mid twenties, from Giordano to George and Degeorge.
Not long afterwards, Fran's father began attending a
weekly congregation of Jehovah's Witnesses.

Why he did this was never explained to A. J. or A.
J.'s brother. He eventually joined the Jehovah's

Witnesses, became a ballsy advocate (Fran's characterization) of that creed, married a member, and they raised their kids in that faith. Fran seldom attended services, likely he never cracked a *Watchtower*, and the only time religion came up in a conversation, he always mentioned that faction of Christianity as JWs. One of the large sprays at Fran's funeral was from Dallas' only Jehovah's Witnesses' church.

Osgood, close on Jo Ellen's heels, was wearing a medium gray double-breasted suit, dark gray shirt, and a striped white and light-blue necktie. His salon-sculpted hair was so perfectly coiffed that it truly resembled the football helmet Nick imagined it to be at Reverend Shuttleworth's memorial service.

A. J. remembered bits and pieces of Osgood's bio from Fran's sometime utterances, which were typically underscored with a surly frown and coarse verbal rip-sawing while we heartily quaffed beers in a lounge after a long Saturday of racing to turn a new design over to Manufacturing. After graduating from high school, Osgood enrolled in Theological Studies at Hardin-Simmons University but dropped out his freshman year. In 1970 he opened a one-man advertising agency in Dallas. All but one of his clients was a start-up industrial account. That one account, according to Fran – and Fran never improvised – was a so-called "Massage Parlor," the "Tokyo Spa," or something like that. Situated just outside the northern perimeter of Dallas proper, it paid for Osgood's services with its service, which was some kind of sequential, community oral sex performed by Oriental whores.

Osgood wed Jo Ellen's twin sister, Betty, a year after Fran and Jo Ellen married. Osgood, at the time, was nearly fifty years old – by Fran's measure. He pestered Fran constantly for Edgecom's advertising business. The Osgood's were childless.

A. J. greeted Edgecom's two visitors and gestured at empty chairs that he had positioned near the lectern.

"You all know Hummel," A. J. said, addressing the table. "And Jo Ellen, of course."

There was a collective murmur of affirmation.

A. J. walked to the rear of the room and plunked down in a folding chair, one of two pushed against the back wall.

Osgood's smile was reserved. "Thank you, A. J. I 'preciate it." He repositioned the two empty chairs near the front of the table an immeasurable inch, held one for Jo Ellen, and stepped up to the lectern. He looked at A. J. and nodded toward the door. A. J. got up and closed it.

"Most people," he said, smiling, his eyes sweeping the table, "call me Hummer."

Dornhoffer nodded robustly.

After individually greeting each of Edgecom's three managers, Osgood's eyes found Martha Dillbeck. "Is it . . . Dillard? It's not like me, and I sincerely apologize, Martha, but I've forgotten your last name."

Martha, ramrod thin and always Victorianish in dress, shook her head. "No sir, Mister Osgood. It's Dill*beck*." If Martha was unnerved, even slightly, it wasn't apparent to A. J.

"Anyway," Osgood went on, "it is always nice seeing more than one pretty face"– he winked at Jo Ellen –"in a room full of ugly men."

Nickerson smiled and Jennerette blinked – if that. Dornhoffer stared hard at me, nodded, and laughed heartily.

Osgood patted his hair. His attention back on Martha, he said that he and Jo Ellen, over the "long Fourth of July weekend," had examined Edgecom's financial situation. His gaze circled the table. "And I must tell you – as if you don't already know – that Martha and her charges are doing a terrific job. Outstanding, really."

Osgood spoke admiringly of Martha's "indispensable contribution" to the "demanding job" of "rigorously" keeping the financial books of a "pioneering" electronics company of Edgecom's "high-velocity energy." Fran, he said – after reverently asking "The Heavens" to bless Edgecom's deceased founder – was indeed favored to have an employee of Martha Dillbeck's dedication and ability. Layering his praise, it was a second after he finished before A. J. realized he had slipped in a line inviting Martha to leave the room. Martha, after an awkward moment, rose, glanced confusedly at A. J., and quietly left.

Osgood patted his hair again. He paid homage to Fran, his long-time best friend, the bright kid brother he'd never had, Edgecom's genius architect, the indefatigable begetter of a prospering business. Painting his canvas anecdotally, he turned after each freshet of brush strokes to Jo Ellen, who every time generously smiled and offered a confirming nod.

A. J. thought all along that what they were hearing was well-crafted bullshit, but when Osgood claimed that Fran had asked him to assume a large equity position in Edgecom, and had anointed him to a standing partnership, A. J. knew beyond any question that he was flat-out lying. *Over Fran's dead body*, A. J. thought. It took a second for the literal turn of those words to hit home, and A. J. felt uneasy for casting his thought so loosely.

That queasy feeling was still haunting him when A. J. suddenly realized that Osgood was in the middle of a long pause; Osgood broke the silence by announcing that he was Edgecom's new majority owner.

It did not strike A. J. at that moment, but somehow, in the mysterious way that an individual's clomp of gray matter goes about its background business, his mind laid bare a priceless gem of insight. And by late that evening A. J. was positive, categorically certain, that John Hummel Osgood had murdered Fran. That night, at home, alone, A. J. buffed his gem of insight until it sparkled from any angle.

Dornhoffer jumped to his feet. "Wonderful! Exactly what Edgecom needs is a tough, battle-proven commander. A father-figure, even. No offense, Hummer. Ha ha. Even A. J. would agree as to how–"

"No offense taken, Karl," Osgood interrupted, grinning.

Dornhoffer nodded excitedly. "I'm sure I speak for everyone in this room. "Right, men?"

"Dornhoffer," A. J. said bitingly, before the others had a chance to answer, "you *never* in hell speak for me."

A. J. glared, Karl smiled back, and he handled A. J. with the same lofty aplomb he had used to deflect Martha's anger in A. J.'s meeting on the Friday morning of the day after Fran's passing.

"Well, my goodness," Dornhoffer said to Osgood. "So, A. J. and I don't always see eye-to-eye on every little thing" – he sank back into his chair – "but that's not all bad. We're on the same page when it really matters."

"Shit, Dornhoffer!" A. J. said, spitting the interjection out. "We have never even opened the same book."

Osgood held up a hand, showed Dornhoffer its palm. "Before long, we'll all be reading from the same page of the same book; Budweiser Clydesdales pulling as a harnessed team. Trust me. I'll get it done."

"Not a doubt in my mind," Dornhoffer assured the table.

Osgood nodded. "Spare me a few days. I've been there, friends!"

He patted his hair. "Nick. Your thoughts? Be forthright now. No hemin' and hawin' with me, Pal."

"Sounds to me like a winner," Nick answered breezily.

My seat at the back of the room placed me next in the arc of attendees. "A. J., you'll be my good right arm."

Still focusing on his sudden iridescent insight that pinned Fran's death on Osgood, A. J. managed only a slight nod.

Jesse, in his usual economy of words, allowed that Osgood could count on his support.

Dornhoffer, when Osgood turned his way, jumped to his feet. "Hummer," he said, his manner reverential, "I'd like to say, on behalf of myself and my colleagues, 'Welcome aboard!'"

Osgood humbly smiled.

"I hope," Dornhoffer continued, "I'm not being presumptuous, me welcoming you, Hummer. Only I'm sure you'll come to see how Fran . . . well that Francis didn't back Marketing in the same unbending way he favored Engineering and Manufacturing. It's why he hired me. To hack away the brush surrounding Edgecom's one Amen Corner."

While Osgood nodded approvingly, Dornhoffer continued. "I've been working on a very detailed marketing plan, one that–"

Osgood jabbed the air with an at-a-boy fist. "That's what I like to hear, Karl. But, hold off for now. We'll get together in my office this afternoon, individually, for get-acquainted chats. Okay?"

"Absolutely!"

"Good," Osgood said. "And one more thing. I'm determined to somehow find a way to give you managers a bump in salary." He paused and gave Jo Ellen a sidewise glance. "Only, to be honest we're not in the financial shape Fran seemed to think. A. J. will back me on that."

He waited a moment for A. J. to agree. A. J. did not, however, and Osgood patted his hair.

"A. J." Osgood said, "you stop by my office at one o'clock. Right?"

Slowly, A. J. was beginning to see Osgood in a different light – in black or at best deep ultraviolet. "Fran's old office?" A. J. snapped.

Jesse gave me a slit-eyed cautionary look. A. J. never did know if Osgood answered him, his mind was buffing his gem of insight that irrefutably ascribed Fran's murder to Hummel Osgood.

Osgood gravely warned the table not to mention Edgecom's "enfeebling financial condition" to *anyone,* and then he apportioned his afternoon for the separate interviews.

He turned to Jo Ellen. She had nothing to add except a final generous, smiling nod.

Everybody stood up. Jesse and Nick shambled toward the door. Dornhoffer hurried to where Osgood was helping Jo Ellen from her chair and began pumping his hand. A. J. decided he'd let Dornhoffer walk Osgood and Jo Ellen from the room.

A. J. pulled up to his computer and brought up DAMCNTR1, the draft of his news release reporting the sorrowful death of Edgecom's founder – and, incidentally, announcing Edgecom's fortuitously well-timed sea-change in top management.

A. J. had edited a couple lines when Nick drifted past his doorway. Nick offered to fetch a fire extinguisher, should – as he had "worried fitfully" on other occasions – A. J.'s brisk, uninterrupted key stroking ignite the keyboard. (Cutting-edge wit is not a confidant of engineers.)

The next-to-last paragraph of A. J.'s draft, the one canonizing Edgecom's new owner, needed work. An hour later A. J. had a line in hand: "As a result of Edgecom's current restructuring, J. Hummel Osgood is projected to become president of the four-year-old computer peripherals manufacturer, the position held previously by Degeorge. A successful Dallas businessman, Osgood, the founder of Dallas-based J. Hummel Osgood & Associates, is a microelectronics industry consultant."

A. J. read his effort twice. Bullshit came to mind and then a word A. J. had trouble recalling:

"hagiography." A. J. looked up its meaning and decided bullshit was the word of choice.

By entering the bracketed initials BP from his keyboard, the letter's last sentence, after a one-line space, read: *Founded in 1976, Edgecom Data Company is a leading manufacturer of high-quality peripheral devices for microcomputers.* It was the letter's only sentence that was wholly true. Did A. J. pasture his creation inside the pale of what passed as legitimate PR damage control? Is the Texas King Ranch a large spread?

A. J. printed two copies, all the while thinking that Fran had to be sitting straight up in his grave demanding his head on a platter – or the lid of a garbage can. That image, Fran glaring at him from an open grave persisted. Now mentally closing in on the certainty that Fran had been murdered by Osgood, A. J. was again absorbed by the thought of a preternaturally vigorous thirty-six-year-old dying inexplicably in his hospital room.

# [9]

A. J. followed Osgood into the president's office –
now Osgood's command center. Since twelve fifty, A.
J. had been waiting and fidgeting in the adjacent
unoccupied vice-president's office. Osgood, rounding
Fran's desk, sank hard into the upholstered, high-back,
oak office chair, a birthday gift to Fran from Jo Ellen.
Slouching as if utterly exhausted, he showily drew in
air.

"A client wanted to know how to position"– he
paused and sucked in more air – "their new integrated
check-book pocket-calculator. I conducted a focus
group. Didn't even stop for lunch. It's a neat little
package, but it'll cost too much. Seventy dollars for
punching in withdrawals.  No way. Take a seat, A. J.
You're looking chipper."

A. J.  backed into one of three wooden office chairs
facing Osgood's desk.

"Let's see," Osgood said, straightening. "I want a
modest resume', a bullet or two on your education, past
jobs, uh . . .  a sentence of personal stuff, you know,

your wife and kids' names . . . accomplishments, your address and home telephone number. Tomorrow morning will be fine."

He dispersed a belch of fume with the back of his hand.

"First thing, A. J., is to get out a . . . how shall I put it . . . a *cautiously* worded letter announcing Fran's death."

A. J. slid a copy of DAMCNTR1 across his desk. "I'm still fine tuning," A. J. said ingratiatingly, "but . . . ."

Osgood read for several seconds. "Not *too* bad. Say we punch it up a little and get it out today, okay?"

A. J. thought his writing, if not wholly laudable, was better than "not too bad." He felt blood warming his face, and he leaned back.

Osgood found a tablet and wrote on it for five minutes.

"Here," he said, tearing off two sheets, "make these sentences into the last three paragraphs."

He retrieved A. J.'s draft. "Trash-can your last four grafs. We'll salvage the beginning about Fran dying." He shook his head, "wasn't that a kick in the ass?"

A. J. misunderstood, thought Osgood had hammered his writing.

Osgood caught A. J.'s look: "Fran's passing."

A. J. slowly nodded. "Yeah. That and . . . then some."

Osgood handed A. J. the sheets; A. J. worked them into his breast pocket and stood up. "Who do you want on the contact line?"

"I can tell you who I *don't* want. Me. Give Karl the honor. Let him field the damn calls. Who have you *been* using?"

"Me."

"Okay then. Let Karl answer to the bullshit, and you do the product releases. A square peg in a square hole and a round peg in a round hole. How's that grab you, A. J.?"

"It may work."

Osgood turned away. "We'll need another release in, say, two weeks, explaining our organizational changes. We'll still be covering our ass, but *mainly* we'll be selling Edgecom. Highlight our management upgrade. But, don't break an arm patting ourselves on the back."

A. J. nodded. "Go easy on the brass."

"Exactly. Gold, no brass. You begin it, A. J., and we'll polish it together. Make sense?"

"I guess so."

A. J. turned to leave.

"One more thing, A. J. Ah . . . Edgecom basically makes electronics for the home computer after-market. Right?"

A. J. moved to where he was facing Osgood from behind his chair. He nodded. "Mostly."

"For which ones"– Osgood belched another fume – "for which computers, I. mean? There's a shithouse of them out there."

"The Trash Eighty. Radio Shack's TRS-80. Maybe, oh, fifteen per cent for the SS-50 bus."

"The . . . what bus?"

"The SS-50. It's a . . . standardized fifty-conductor home-computer motherboard. We make a processor card and two interface circuits, one for hooking up a cassette and one for–"

"A processor card?"

"A central processor printed-circuit board. I . . . . Talk to Nick. He's our technical brain."

Osgood did not have a clue, and A. J. did not feel like explaining. *And this guy will be running Edgecom!*

Osgood nodded undecidedly. "Then, when you leave, send Nicholson in."

"Nick? Okay. And about the ode to Edgecom bullshit? Monday?"

Osgood frowned and leaned forward gravely. "Oh goodness no. Friday at the very latest, A. J."

A. J. turned away again. "I'll tell Nick to stop in," he mumbled over his shoulder.

"By the way," Osgood, said his expression wistful. "Say we stop calling Radio Shack's TRS-80 computer the Trash Eighty? Our telephone order girls might pick up on it."

A. J. snorted. "Hell, it's what the Radio Shack people themselves call it."

A. J. left Osgood's in his subjugated new office while he was deciding if Edgecom employees should be allowed to privately denigrate Radio Shack's new home computer.

# [10]

Nick, sitting at his drafting table, was fingering a black, castellated, U-shaped piece of metal with a half-inch square base. When attached to an integrated circuit chip, it would draw off and disperse the circuit's pernicious, self-generated heat.

"For the Doubler?" A. J. asked, backing into Nick's desk chair.

Nick answered without looking up, "Yeah, afraid so. The damn controller chip would heat a dog house in the winter"

Nick's problem was that a big 40-pin integrated circuit, the heart of the Doubler module, began mashing data when the ambient temperature rose above a usually benign eighty degrees Fahrenheit. The only practical solution was to draw off the heat with a bulky metal heat sink, the gadget of Nick's somber examination.

Nick tossed the heat sink onto his drafting table. "We'll have to cut 'em down to fit." He looked at A. J. who infirmly shook his head. "Jesus, I hope not."

"Anyway . . . what'd you get out of the meeting?"

A. J. answered cautiously. "Looks like we have a new owner."

"Nothing gets by you, Pop. What else?"

A. J. pulled the sheet of tablet paper, with Osgood's prose on it, from his pocket. "This is what we're going to tell the world." A. J. read aloud from the sheet:

Alan MacRae, Edgecom's Director of Communications, said that in March, Mr. Degeorge, Edgecom's founder, began restructuring Edgecom in anticipation of its continued rapid growth, and to free himself for related entrepreneurial activity.

As part of the restructuring, which was completed in April, J. Hummel Osgood, hand-picked by Mr. Degeorge to succeed him, was promoted to president of the four-year-old home-computer peripherals manufacturer.

Mr. Osgood, Edgecom's principal stock holder, and a nationally respected Dallas businessman, has been a driving force in the firm since its founding.

"Osgood wrote that?"

A. J. waved the sheet at Nick. "His hand. It's crap, every fuckin' word. Fran hated the pompous bastard. Said he lies like a Persian rug."

"I guess," Nick said, turning away thoughtfully, "He never told Jo Ellen of his snake-belly opinion of Osgood, her own sister's husband. She and Osgood looked to be on *very* good terms this morning."

"He's laying her."

"For sure?"

"Fran thought so."

Nick pushed his office door closed.

"I really don't much give a shit," A. J. said, shaking his head disgustedly.

"You think Osgood really *owns* Edgecom? Or is it still in Jo Ellen's name?"

"Oh, he owns it all right. At least most of the stock. He saw our books, and he's used Martha's financial reports to convince Jo Ellen we're about to belly up. Shit, he stole Edgecom."

"What, exactly, *is* our financial situation?"

A. J. pulled out a bottom desk drawer and rested his feet on its edge. "Well . . . when I first went over the reports with Martha, they scared the shit out of me. But we're not as bad off as we look on paper."

"And . . . how do we look on paper?"

"Well, not great. But we're not dying, either. We're edging through crucial expenses. Except for punctually paying some suppliers. With them it's a damn juggling act. Ever see a man juggle chain saws? They do, you know."

"Borrowing from Peter to pay Paul?"

"No, we're just not paying Paul . . . piecemeal, but not on time, anyway."

A. J. interrupted Nick's next question. "I got nervous after talking to Martha last week, so I called Jack Irickson. And the next day bought him lunch. You remember Irickson, the guy who wrote our bookkeeping software?"

"I know *of* him."

"Well, as it turns out, ol' Irickson's no dummy. He has a Masters in accounting, and he's taught himself how to write computer programs . . . in assembly language, no less. He said, in effect, that we're not all that bad-off financially, that owing a few thousands of bucks to suppliers was no big deal, especially not relative to our potential. He said he'd give odds there's a dozen men living right here in Dallas who'd kill for the chance to lay out a hundred thousand bucks for a finger-nail interest in Edgecom."

Nick shook his head. "But why did Irickson say we're hurting financially if his own conjecturing told him otherwise?"

"Because it *was conjectural.* We're cutting-edge, basically, and . . . hell, he was all over the place. Claimed our financial situation is par for a young, growing electronics firm. That our slow receivables would dematerialize once we shook out our dealer network. Of course his argument was more sophisticated, but–"

"Had to be," Nick said, chuckling at his chance to put A. J. down.

"Like you'd have otherwise understood."

"Does Irickson know that Big Blue's going to churn the micro waters with a big paddle any day now?

Then Edgecom will be playing against the Notre Dame varsity?"

"I'm sure he does. But we'll cross that bridge later."

Nick murmured and shook his head. "When? After the chickens come home to roost? If you're right, A. J., or should I say if Irickson is right, maybe Osgood did steal Edgecom."

"You bet your ass he did. What he didn't steal outright he'll end up buying with Edgecom profits. If we ever make money. Wait and see, Silo."

Nick reflected a moment. "That'd be a neat trick, buy a company with its own money."

"Right. By God, Silo, you're not as slow-witted as our technicians insist. That's exactly what he'd be doing. I didn't tell you this before, but . . . Fran, more than once told me that he thought Osgood was not just a sleazy shit but a fuckin', out-and-out' crook."

"That's . . . a ton, A. J."

"It's why," A. J. said nodding, "I didn't say anything before. Incidentally, our new owner wants to see you. A half-hour ago,"

"Christ. I'm glad you remembered."

Backing toward the door, Nick asked me what I thought Osgood agreed to pay Jo Ellen for his new majority ownership of Edgecom.

"How much for foundering, bankrupt Edgecom? Peanuts. A few bucks and a promise. A percent of the profits. Christ, the way she was dithering around this morning, maybe she screwed him just so's he'd take it off her hands. Who the hell knows?"

She's pretty, isn't she?" Nick offered

"Uh-huh."

"Then, you think it's a done deal?"

"He's protected his ass. Somehow."

Nick left, and A. J.'s mind hiked back to the basic personality of Edgecom's new owner. The bastard, A. J. told himself, may not know a computer from an Ouija board but he's not the moron that A. J. had initially thought. A. J. knew that nailing him for Fran's murder would not be easy. He wondered for a moment if even Osgood's mother loved him. He considered the innately forgiving nature of mothers and decided that she did.

# [11]

It was only eight thirty a.m. so A. J. knew the telephone ring was not a call from Osgood. Or from Nick, for that matter. Maybe, A. J. thought, it's Dornhoffer, "Brasshead" as Norman Israel had discerningly nicknamed Edgecom's marketing director directly after their inaugural fifteen-minute chat.

"MacRae," A. J. brusquely answered, turning from his computer.

"It's me," the caller replied. "Me" was Pat Brown, Fran's secretary until a day or so ago.

"Pat! What's up?"

Born and raised in rural Georgia, closing in on middle-age but still Deep-South cherubic, Pat, sometimes in her down-home patter, still used words like "dogged," "gwine," and "chunk it" (as in darned, going, and toss it). One time, A. J. told her that he wished her name was Rhoda so he could introduce her to people as Tobacco Rhoda. She smiled but clearly had never heard of Erskine Caldwell, her fellow Georgian.

(Or, thankfully, A. J. decided, of the source of his pilfered wit.)

Pat's auburn-tinted hair fell straight down from the scruff of her neck for several inches. Her face, it seemed to A. J. was a skosh wide, especially across the eyes; her nose harmonized comfortably in between. Barely five-feet tall, when she drove a car it appeared from behind that no one was at the wheel. Pat was my age, possibly a few years older. Not her usually bubbly self, she answered in a whisper, "You don't know?"

"I guess not."

"Are you alone?"

"Yes." A. J. wanted to answer, "Yes, sneak on over." But he held back.

"I'll be right there," she said in her lowered voice.

Pat, from her catbird seat as secretary to Edgecom's chief executive, was inescapably abreast of every social happening at the plant. A. J. knew from her manner that on this visit she would not be scurrying over to pass on a juicy rumor of male-female misconduct. She closed A. J.'s office door, skid his visitor's chair to where it faced his desk, and plopped into it. Her face was as colorless as it was on the morning she unhinged Nick and A. J. with the news that Fran had died a few hours earlier.

"It can't be that bad," A. J. said drawing back.

"He fired Martha last night."

A. J. scowled in disbelief. "Osgood fired Martha?"

"Canned her. Just . . . like that!"

"His third day here! Jesus Christ, Pat, are you . . . how do you know?"

"Martha called me from her home. Hummel discharged her. And Dornhoffer marched her out."

"Brasshead in on it, too? He was reading at a desk in the bullpen when I left last night, evidently stationed there by Osgood."

"Osgood wouldn't even let Martha open her desk. She's beside herself."

A. J. shook his head confusedly. "Of all people, why Martha?"

"Exactly, Alan. Why Martha? Believe me, Martha may be getting up in years, but she is still one sharp lady. We're good friends. I *know* her."

"Maybe, Pat . . ." A. J. checked himself long enough to rethink what he was about to say. "I wonder if Karl was just getting even for Martha's all but telling him in my meeting to kiss her you-know-what."

"I doubt it, Alan. She said it was Hummel who unloaded on her. He said she was old and slow and . . . couldn't keep up. It's what she told me he said."

"Fran didn't seem to think she had any shortcomings. At all."

Pat shook her head. "It's chicken . . . manure. We both know it, Alan."

I nodded slowly. "She won't easily find work. How old is Martha?"

Pat waited for voices in the hall to fade. "Sixty-four . . . May eleventh."

"She didn't look it." (Actually, she did "look it," in her face, hair-do, attire, but A. J. was going for pleasantness not honesty.)

"I guess not. I'm worried, Alan."

"It'll take a while. But she'll land on her feet."

"It's not that, Alan. Martha lives alone. She never married. That diamond engagement ring she wears? It was her mother's. But don't say anything."

A. J. nodded solemnly.

"Her Buick is leased. I doubt she has more than . . . two-thousand dollars to her name. Three thousand at most."

"Jesus, that's damn little to fall back on."

"She lives in north Dallas. Addison actually. Her rent is six hundred a month. She'd been drinking . . . wouldn't hear of my driving over. She's flying on Southwest to El Paso this morning."

"I'm surprised to hear that she drank at all."

Pat's facial expression changed from a look of concern to a glance of forgiveness. "Vodka and orange juice. Screwdrivers she called them."

"Southwest to El Paso this morning?"

"She was raised in El Paso."

"Did she leave you a telephone number?"

"No. She said she'd call me. And that also upsets me, Alan. I'm just . . . I don't know what I. should do."

"Hell, Pat, I'd have gotten bagged too. You might have tied one on yourself. I wouldn't worry."

Pat inclined her head and sighed thoughtfully. "Still, A. J. wish I had seen her last night."

"Do her people know?"

"Her girls? She may have called Ducky. I'd better get back."

I dialed Accounting's extension and asked to speak to Martha. Whoever answered said that she was not in. Ducky came on the line and asked if she could be of help.

"It's me, Ducky. I need to look at the Dunn-Marky account. I'll come by. Okay?"

The bookkeeper's room was two-thirds the size of two connected , regular offices. Martha's desk, positioned at the back, set discernibly apart from three others. Two women worked for Martha: Ducky Shreve and a hefty young girl with an odd Spanish first name that I couldn't pronounce and didn't try to remember.

Ducky handed A. J. the Dunn-Marky folder. Smiling deferentially she said, "It's not supposed to leave the room."

"I know," A. J. said." I'll use the spare desk. Has she telephoned?"

Ducky shook her head. "Not yet. She'll be here any minute. She's never late."

"Maybe car trouble?"

Ducky shook her head again. "She'd have telephoned."

Ten minutes passed. Tired of faking it, A. J. was re-assembling the contents of the Dunn-Markey file when Osgood, followed by a trim, chisel-faced man wearing a charcoal-gray suit matching the shade of his short, crinkly hair, walked into the room. His jacket was unbuttoned and his right hand was shoved casually into his front pants pocket. The unbroken, full-length pleats of his trousers would have nicked a bar of steel. The clasps of his attaché case were secured by small imbedded combination locks. A. J figured he had him by five years.

A. J. stood, but Osgood shook his head and waved him back into the chair belonging to the spare desk.

Closing the door, and after recapturing our attention, which had strayed to his companion, Osgood announced that he had discharged Martha. He sadly allowed that it was by far the hardest thing he had ever done. He shook his head downheartedly. Either, he said, it was cashier Martha or let both of his stunned listeners go. Overcoming his all but choked-up grief, which took a long moment, he introduced us to the austere-looking man standing at his side.

Herbert Wickersham, he explained, was a financial wizard, a mathematical genius supremely abreast of the latest accounting practices and rules. As Edgecom's new Chief Financial officer, he would forthwith begin overseeing the already splendid efforts of Edgecom's hard-working, dedicated bookkeepers.

Osgood rattled on and on as he always did. When Wickersham answered that he had nothing to add, Osgood exhaustively praised the women for their "exemplary" contribution to Edgecom's never-ending struggle to make ends meet – when there were, "ha ha, hardly any ends to bring together!" Promising he'd be back to answer questions, Osgood steered Wickersham out of the room.

Watching Osgood's performance that morning – clinically, virtually as an outsider – A. J. came to understand irrevocably that a natural-born sleaze was now running Edgecom.

A. J. passed Jesse on the way to his office. He was no less stunned than A. J. to hear that Martha had been canned and that a man named Wickersham would be overseeing Bookkeeping. Saying he had a minute to spare, Jesse fell in beside me. A. J. pressed him for his take on Osgood.

He shrugged. "I don't know. I've been busy."

We walked into A. J.'s office, and A. J. backed into his desk chair.

Jesse closed the door, leaned back against it, and crossed his arms. "I've only seen him twice. On Monday morning when he told us he'd bought Edgecom and then later when we met for his get-acquainted talk."

"Why do you suppose he canned Martha?"

Jesse was quick to answer. "Wanted his own people. That's the way it works." He righted himself. "I've got to pee."

A. J. said, "I'm going to call Irickson."

"Irickson? Why?"

"To get his measure of Martha. I was under the impression that she was a dammed good bookkeeper."

"Think he'll have heard yet?"

"That she was scrubbed? If he hasn't, he soon will."

"Don't get carried away," Jesse warned.

Pat called A. J. back with Irickson's telephone number. He picked up after one ring, wished me a "Good morning," and tersely asked why I was calling.

"Have you talked to Martha?" A. J. asked him.

"Martha Dillbeck? Today? No."

"She doesn't work at Edgecom anymore."

The line was silent for a long second. "What . . . happened?"

"Osgood sacked her. Brasshead marched her out."

"Who?"

"Dornhoffer."

Irickson couldn't seem to find his tongue. "I'll be damned!" he said finally. "She was *very* good at her job. I don't get it."

It was what A. J. had hoped to hear. "Neither does anyone here *get it.* I thought you'd like to know."

"Yeah," he said, "thanks for the heads-up. Uh, just a minute." A. J. could hear the rustle of papers. "Osgood asked me to meet with him tonight. At Edgecom."

"Something else you should know then. He's hired a guy named Herbert Wickersham to take over Accounting. The name ring a bell?"

"I don't know *anyone* named Wickersham."

"I'm being presumptuous," A. J. said. "But . . . you had better go packing heat."

"Sounds like it," Irickson said, heaving a long sigh.

A. J. offered to spring for lunch. Irickson said he'd take a rain check, that he'd call and we'd get together another day.

"Another day" arrived twenty-four hours later when Irickson telephoned to say he'd like to cash the "rain check," that he had suffered the same fate as Martha. His bookkeeping software, it seemed, was not only rife with programming errors but also fundamentally flawed: the computerization of ancient accounting practices that only straight-lined depreciation and amortization.

"Whatever," A. J. mumbled.

"I've got other clients. I'll survive," Irickson finished quietly.

The following Monday, Herbert Wickersham moved, kit and caboodle, into the room nominally set aside for a financial officer, a room slightly smaller than the office reserved for a vice-president. The room was still vacant because Fran considered entirely dispensable the day-to-day, nuts-and-bolts arithmetic of Edgecom money matters.

The next Monday, in what was to become a daily nine a.m. gathering of officers in Osgood's office, Osgood announced that he had promoted Dornhoffer to vice-president of operations, making him, thereby, theoretically second in command at Edgecom.

Beginning the afternoon of Osgood's announcement, Dornhoffer took to strutting imperiously around the plant, demanding answers to vacuous questions. On his second or third circumnavigation, Israel, caught up in arduously trouble-shooting a balky electronic circuit, told him loudly to fuck off. According to Selig, Dornhoffer's mouth quivered for several seconds but nothing came out. Dornhoffer, thereafter, would no more step into the prototyping lab than he would stride into a smoldering California La Brea tar pit.

Martha Dillbeck and Jack Irickson became the first casualties of Osgood's runaway take-over. A. J. was the third – only his wounding was self-inflicted, more a glancing blow to his pride than a dagger to his heart. Moreover, the laceration healed overnight and did not leave a lasting scar. Besides, convinced that Osgood, even if he somehow endured A J.'s avenging vendetta, would sink Edgecom as it attempted to pull away from its home mooring, A. J. didn't much give a damn.

# [12]

Martha Dillbeck and Jack Irickson were coldly dismissed on the ninth of July. A week later A. J. told Osgood to shove it up his ass and angrily bolted Osgood's office. A. J. returned two days later, however, pacified by a long wheedling telephone call from Osgood that arrived the evening after the day he had stormed out.

Dornhoffer had stolen A. J.'s idea of launching Edgecom into the business of making a utilitarian, inexpensive, no-gingerbread word processor. He heard A. J. pitch his argument to Fran, both the retailing opportunities and Edgecom's ready adaptability, and he presented A. J.'s plan to Osgood as the chimera of his own visionary thinking. A. J. bitterly argued his case. Osgood sided with Dornhoffer and subtly cast A. J. as the imposter. A. J. stormed out of his office.

But then a funny thing happened. The next day Osgood called A. J. at home with an offer that A. J. couldn't refuse, a remunerative raise and other inducements to return to Edgecom as a consultant;

humble forgiveness was the essence of Osgood's demeanor.

A. J.'s "home," at the time was a two-bedroom apartment in Richardson. ("Irreconcilable differences" did not begin to define his frequent shouting matches with Allison.) A. J. had moved into the apartment after a week of living out of boxes and a suitcase in his parent's home in Highland Park. Because his father had not sufficiently recovered from prostate surgery, he and his mother would be weeks late in leaving – to flee the hot summer months of Dallas – for their breezy, ocean-side condominium on the Hawaiian island of Maui. Otherwise, A. J. would have stayed all summer.

Osgood went on and on, as he always did, promising A. J. that when Edgecom committed resources to the development of a word-processing machine A. J. would autonomously manage the project. And the kicker was that he'd be eligible to purchase discounted Edgecom common stock for re-selling "very profitably" in a public offering, an event, the public offering, that he assured A. J. was inevitable. The chance for a financial killing did not turn A. J.'s head, he wasn't poor, but he did crave the prestige of business ownership. Allison, A. J. knew, would have been ecstatic.

Osgood did not rehire A. J. to benefit Edgecom. What happened, in fact, was that he and Wickersham soon realized how an ex-employee, who was once intimately privy to Edgecom's true, uncontaminated financial situation, might suddenly stop circling on LBJ Freeway looking for work and take an off-ramp leading straight to a compensatory pay back. There was never a shred of doubt in A. J.'s mind that that's what happened. At least Osgood's sudden change of heart further opened A. J.'s eyes to the true black-gumbo soul of Edgecom's new owner.

Osgood did not put A. J. in charge of developing Edgecom's first word processor. His promises, as A. J. soon learned, were less substantial than one of the forty-acres-and-a-mule variety, and they were no more meant to hold up than the paper-thin ice atop a Dallas puddle on a winter day. Instead he lured a project engineer named Darren McPherson away from Foster Systems – F-Systems, as it was invariably called by Edgecom technicians – and gave him the job. Osgood had met McPherson through the promotional services provided Foster Systems by his advertising agency.

Darren McPherson was a handsome moron – so good-looking he could have played the romantic lead in a soap opera, but so dumb he couldn't salute the flag without poking a thumb in his eye. A few days after he reported, Edgecom's technicians began furtively calling him "Darren Hysteresis," equating, thereby, Darren's cerebral viscosity with the inherent magnetic friction of iron. Osgood hired McPherson primarily to front the hawking of MaxWriter, not as a working project manager. Likely he did not know that McPherson was hopelessly shallow.

At the program's kick-off meeting Dornhoffer proposed calling Edgecom's word processor "MaxWriter." Osgood, after several pinched-brow nods, said he liked the name. A. J. hated it no less than A. J. loathed Dornhoffer himself, but A. J. had to admit it was catchy and denotative of the machine's capability.

As kids put it, A. J. got screwed by Osgood, but he didn't get kissed. Hell, between Osgood and Wickersham, A. J. got laid weekly – willingly but stupidly – throughout the next year. Laid regularly but unloved, A. J. eventually came to his senses.

By the time of A. J.'s visit with Detective Deemer in November, A. J. was resolutely convinced that Osgood was a greed-driven sleaze bag who had murdered Fran. He worried that proving Osgood's engagement would be Herculean, would amount to tackling the canonization of the Dead Sea Scrolls.

# [13]

A. J. arranged and met Jesse Jeanerette for a beer at the VFW Memorial Post in Mesquite, Texas. It was early-afternoon in mid-August and the bar was unoccupied. Jesse was born and raised in Mesquite. Being a VFW establishment, the City of Mesquite's "Dry" ordinance did not apply. A. J. had hoped that seeing Jesse would bolster an argument he had with himself, a personal agonistes over Osgood's, as yet unproven, collusion in Fran's death. Fran had hardly been lowered into his grave when doubts of the cause of his death began flitting around A. J.'s head like butterflies swarming a buddleia bush. Nick, hearing A. J. out, concluded that he was trying to open a door to Loonyville.

A. J. told Jesse beforehand that he did not have anything particular in mind that he only wanted to palaver a spell. Evidently Jesse knew better because he greeted A. J. as A. J. instead of his usual, put-down nickname, "Bubba."

Jesse had half-smoked a cigarette. His glasses were folded and lying on the bar beside a slightly frothing bottle of beer. Maybe it was only the dim, milieu of the room, but A. J. thought he looked thin and drawn.

"So," A. J. asked Jesse, after they exchanged requisite questions about their families, households, and recent casual activities, "Osgood treating you okay?"

Jesse shrugged. "He hasn't said diddly shit to me."

"*Really*? Does he have a clue? I mean, even the glimmer of a *notion* about how to run Edgecom? And restore its financial health?"

Jesse's smile was ambiguous. He shook his head. "Not that I can tell."

They both took long swigs of their beers.

"It'll work," A. J. said, after setting his glass down, "if he lets you and Nick do your thing."

Jesse shrugged.

A. J. said, conversationally, "I haven't met the new guy, Wickersham."

"Me neither."

"You haven't *met* him?"

"He keeps to himself."

"Doesn't Osgood hold meetings?"

"Almost every morning, but Wickersham's never there."

"I don't know what to make of Osgood," A. J. said, shaking his head. "He's no dummy, but I don't trust the bastard."

Jesse's reply was noncommittal. "No?"

Jesse finished his beer, and A. J. called to the bartender, who was watching TV at the other end of the bar. He ambled toward A. J. , his attention fast on the corner, shelf-mounted TV, and A. J. ordered two more longnecks.

A. J. reopened the conversation. "Osgood's word's no damn good – if you don't already know."

"It isn't?"

The bartender served us our beers and took away our empty bottles.

"I guess you haven't talked to him much?"

"I guess not."

"You know," A. J. said, training his eyes on Jesse's, "that Fran thought he was a prick for all seasons. That's exactly how he put it."

Jesse butted his cigarette. "Look, A. J.," he said, his voice tired but patient. "I know Osgood clobbered you over MaxWriter. At least that's what I heard. But . . . remember, I'm fifty eight, A. J.  I don't have a degree; I scare the shit out of women and children . . . and the pay's not all that bad. Y'all see what I'm saying?"

A. J.'s stomach all but turned at the blunt, clearly expressed truth of his trying to use Jesse. Nodding weakly, A. J. changed the subject to casting for bass. Jesse owned a thousand fishing rods, a million fishing lures, a run-of-the-mill outboard motor boat, and a family-size pontoon boat. And he could talk forever about fishing.

When Jesse and A. J. met that afternoon in August, Osgood had been running Edgecom six weeks. By then A. J. knew damn well Osgood was morally corrupt, that he stacked the deck at every opportunity. Moreover, thoughts of his blatant dishonesty and Fran's strange, unusual way of dying had coalesced in A. J.'s mind into the certainty that Osgood had murdered Edgecom's ever-bustling young founder.

A. J. did not have another person to compare notes with. Nick was a smart engineer, but he wouldn't know a con artist from a conifer tree, wouldn't know if he was being conned or if one of the tree's cones had fallen on his head. And Jesse, understandably, was not about to chance wagering on the wrong horse.

# [14]

Early on a Monday morning, near the end of
August, 1980, Nick burst into A. J.'s provisional office,
his old room next to the men's latrine. Dismay clouded
his face, and he exclaimed breathlessly that Edgecom
was cutting back.. "Osgood called us in yesterday, and
before–"

"On Sunday!" A. J. blurted, interrupting him.

"Yes! Yesterday!"

Nick closed the door and backed into A. J.'s only
visitor's chair. "We're *all* losing people. Jesse, a third of
his assemblers."

"Damn! When?"

"Jesse's telling his people right now."

A. J. slowly shook his head. "You losing any
techs?"

"Greenwood. Billy has the least seniority. He's
only twenty, but he's married, you know, and his wife is
like seven months pregnant. I called him last night."

"How'd he take it?"

Nick shrugged. "Actually, I think he's been looking. I damn near quit myself, but–"

"But, Osgood talked you out of it."

"He said that if I left he might as well close down Engineering and inside a month . . . we'd augur in."

"Well, he's *right*," A. J. said emphatically.

"Osgood said we're up to our eyeballs in red ink and have been for two years. He said . . . ." Nick did not complete his thought.

After a moment, A. J. said, "That's interesting because we're current with vendors again."

"Don't ask me. All I know is what the man said yesterday."

"How'd Jesse take it?"

"Uh, impassively. I'm sure it wasn't the first layoff he's had to weather."

"Yeah, that's Production for you. Dornhoffer?"

"Brasshead's losing Donna."

"Turbo Ass?"

"Yeah, and I hear she's knocked-up."

"That takes my breath away," A. J. observed sardonically.

"Osgood claims that he and Herb beat their brains out for a week, but there wasn't any other way."

"Was Wickersham there?"

"You jest."

"Then, Bookkeeping's safe."

That Monday afternoon, at a gathering of all hands just outside the entrance to the prototyping lab, Osgood, standing on top of a battered Army footlocker that Fran pre-shipped Edgecom products to trade shows in, blamed the layoffs on continued softening of the microcomputer market, a situation further compounded by egregious prior mismanagement of Edgecom's operating cash. He said he abhorred pointing fingers, and promised no more cut-backs, not in the foreseeable future. Four days later, on Friday, he dismissed eleven more of Jesse's assemblers. Wickersham's initial revenue projections were overly optimistic, he explained apologetically to the forty or so surviving employees.

The two mass cutbacks, falling only a week apart, amounted to a fist in the gut of the collective body of Edgecom's long-time, ever loyal employees. ("Time" in the pubescent personal computer business was measured in units of months, the sales of any given product often plunging with the advertising of a cheaper, mail-order facsimile in the latest issue of *Byte* or *Kilobaud* magazine.)

Still, for Nick himself, what happened the Tuesday after the second mass layoff was more like a knee to the groin than a blow to the midsection: Norman Israel gave notice. It was mid-morning when Nick, his expression doleful, trudged into A. J.'s office and told him that Israel had quit.

Israel was Nick's age, give-or-take a few months, and he was just as bright, maybe smarter than Nick. Moreover, the two men had become staunch comradesin-arms about everything, but never more so than in profaning the ideology of political conservatives and especially all stands of Republican politicians. They raged over Ronald Reagan's every utterance – provided Jennerette was not within earshot: Jesse read every piece of conservative literature that he could lay his hands on, and he listened five nights a week to a right-wing radio talk show. Moreover, he debated with a scorched-earth, take-no-prisoners fervor.

A. J. fell back in his chair. "It's a done deal?"

"Cut and dried. He's accepted a written offer from Recognition Systems."

"Damn, I hate hearing that . . . I mean, hearing that Norm's leaving. Besides liking the guy, who'll write our software?"

Nick shrugged. "Me, I guess. And Sel's a fair kitchen-table programmer. But, I swear, Norm was genetically wired to write software code."

"Sel," A. J. said as if surprised. Oh, you mean Mace."

"Oh hell," Nick gushed, ignoring my mention of Hildreth's new but virtually dead nickname, "we're not busy anyway. I'm just screwing the pooch, as we men of the right stuff like to say."

"The right stuff?" A. J. said, smiling. He had read and passed on Tom Wolfe's popular novel, *The Right Stuff* to Nick.

Nick nodded absentmindedly. "McPherson bugs me about MaxWriter now and then, but I've heard he's bringing in his own people."

"He is. Two persons from F-Systems. Why did Norm say he was quitting?"

"Shit, he didn't have to *say*. The handwriting on the wall was neon."

Nick, looked away to avoid A. J.'s stare. After a moment he nodded. "Osgood's offered me shares. Promised I'd make four-hundred-thousand bucks when we go public. I'd have been out of here a long time ago, if . . . do you blame me for sticking around?"

A. J. decided to not tell Nick that he had been offered the same package by Osgood.

"Hell no," A. J. answered. "Only one thing though, have you seen any stock yet?"

"No. Not . . . so far."

"Anything in writing?"

"No, but—"

A. J. was certain of Nick's answer, and he did not wait to hear it: "When's Norm's last day?"

"Two weeks from yesterday. Hell, he can leave tomorrow if he wants. I'd miss him as a friend is all."

A. J. nodded sympathetically. "I know what you mean."

They both listened to what sounded like an open spigot weakly running into a bucket of water – until it sputtered to a stop. Shortly a urinal in the men's john was flushed.

A, J. said, "What about Norman's cannon? You going to be the one to light the touch hole after he's left? Touch holes are right up your alley."

Nick grinned. "Yeah, Norman gave me a diskette with the program code. I'm waiting for just the right time to hook it in . . . to wheel Norm's cannon out of mothballs. So to speak."

Nick tried to laugh in a sinister way, and A. J. told him, "You're about as diabolic as Casper the Friendly Ghost, Silo."

"I was trying for *scary*, Pop."

"Hey," A. J. said, "Don't let Norm leave until he comes up with a nickname for Osgood."

"You haven't heard?"

"Heard what?"

"It's 'Cheeks.'"

A. J. leaned back and crossed his arms. "We're going to miss that boy."

# [15]

A. J. bought Jack Irickson lunch two days after Irickson was dismissed by Osgood. They hit it off and began regularly eating together at the Chop House on Coit Road in Richardson.

Jack was A. J.'s age, only he had substantially more hair – thick and heavy over the nape. He was more upbeat than A. J. had anticipated.

"Something's bugging me, Jack," A. J. said, while they waited to be shown a table. "Business is way off. Yet, we're paying our bills. We even seem to have amended our vendor accounts. I talked to Sandy."

Jack stopped appraising a waitress. "Sandy?"

"Sandy Welcheck, our buyer."

The hostess returned, led us to a four-place table, and we settled into opposing chairs.

"This, ah, *Sandy* told you that Edgecom is current with vendors?"

A. J. grinned. "Not exactly. But . . . she's getting nooners regularly again. Or, giving them. Whatever."

Jack inclined his head uncertainly.

A. J. smirked. "Sandy has many boyfriends. All salesmen. They – Sandy and the drummers – take long lunches together. *Very* long lunches. Sometimes, all-afternoon long."

Jack shifted his eyes. "Hell A. J., I should be dining with Sandy, not you."

"Yeah. What's going on, Jack? I mean, Edgecom's sales didn't suddenly skyrocket."

The waitress brought wine drinks. Irickson sampled his and slowly set the goblet down. "It could be Osgood's own money but I doubt it. More likely he has arranged with a bank for a debt-consolidation loan."

Jack sipped his drink. "You want me to connect the dots, huh?"

A. J. nodded. "From the top of your head Jack, what would . . . say, Mission Savings, charge for such a loan?"

"Mission? At today's rates? Eighteen, nineteen percent. Thanks to Georgia Boy."

Loan rates were not something A. J. kept track of, but Jack's numbers seemed awfully high. "Are you serious?"

Jack tittered. "Am I the Dog Star? Yes, I'm serious. It's either nineteen per cent, or fifty per cent a *week*. Default and you can kiss your knee caps goodbye. And sulfuric acid, I've heard, is a nasty eye wash."

"Some choice. Still, if he's taking Edgecom public, like you . . . ."

The waitress brought our salads, and Jack passed me the pepper mill.

"Oh he's going public all right. Trust me, A. J. What he'll–"

"Still, Osgood sure as hell wouldn't want investors seeing a big loan on the books. Would he?"

"Hell no. Obviously not. And they won't. What he'll do . . . anyway here's how I'd work it. The loan will be drafted to his advertising agency. He'll have to personally . . . or to somehow secure it, of course. Does he have a partner?"

"Not that I know of."

"Okay, forget that. Anyway, the money will be bootlegged into Edgecom and booked as sales revenue."

"But not legally of course."

Jack snorted. "Christ no, not legally."

"How does he do that, Jack? Paper over the shortfalls? I'm way out of my pay scale."

"Easy. He'll make up phony invoices, upgrade some old ones. You know, of course, anyone with supervisory access to Edgesales can edit an invoice."

Edgesales was a rudimentary version of a data processing system that later in the 1980's became popularly marketed as "local area networks," or LANs. Some four months after Norman Israel hired in, he and Nick, working evenings and weekends on their own, had developed Edgesales for the express purpose of computerizing Edgecom sales activity. Edgesales allowed multiple users to share the same mass data storage unit and same high-quality printer.

"No, I didn't know. I should have."

Jack noticed A. J.'s pained expression. "Initially Fran only wanted the two of us, him and me, on the supervisory list."

A. J. shrugged, let on it didn't matter that Fran had not allowed him the privilege of rooting around in Edgecom's sales numbers. In truth, A. J. *was* hurt.

Jack continued. "He'll doctor"– Jack's fingers set the word doctor in quote marks – "several hundred invoices. Probably do it himself. What does Edgecom charge for a one-drive add-on?"

"Four hundred bucks."

"And for a two-drive package?"

"Eight hundred. Give or take."

"There you have it. Osgood changes selected Edgesales invoices for one-drive units to two-drive units. Do the math, A. J. Four hundred dollars into, oh, two hundred thousand dollars, accretes to, what? Five hundred invoices? Two day's work. If that."

A. J. fell back in his chair. "*Two* day's work?"

"Sure. Change the one to a two in the quantity column of an invoice, and you've nailed it. Edgesales itself extends prices, re-computes the sales tax, if any, and . . . so on."

"You would know," A. J. mumbled. "Still . . . I mean there's got to be more to it."

Jack shrugged. "Bringing up an invoice would take a few seconds. After you'd massaged . . . five hundred . . . did I say, you'd run the Ledger and Journal programs against the updated sales data base and voila, you have a new set of books . . . mainly a spanking-new income statement and a new balance sheet, all purporting that Edgecom is ass-deep in black ink."

The waitress brought their steak sandwiches. Jack stopped her from removing his salad, which he had hardly touched, and they began eating.

A. J. hesitantly broke the silence, asked timorously if the deception would survive an audit.

"Oh hell no," Jack snapped. "But let's back up, A. J. Osgood will have to arrange a private placement before he goes public, if for no reason except to fund it. Which can't be done on the cheap."

"Phase one?"

"Yeah," Jack said loosely. "And those first investors, they won't do any serious digging. One of them pull the ring on a hand grenade sharing the pocket holding his billfold? The guy would have to be a nuthouse doofus."

"Have to be," A. J. said grinning at Jack's definition of a financial moron.

"The sizzle sells the steak."

"Uh-huh," Jack said uncertainly. "And in this case the steak is a nifty little computer company that . . . if you gnaw off a bite you land on your ass. The hiss and crackle . . . and aroma won't tell you doodoo about the meat itself."

Diners began leaving, including two thirtyish women snugly sheathed in two-piece business outfits. They watched as the women wove their way among the tables.

"Look at the casabas on the first one," Jack said out of the side of his mouth. "Yours on the second one, though, are a bit, ah, recumbent."

"Lately," A. J. replied, "I'm not that picky."

"Celibacy has its downside."

"Yeah, *down*side is the way to put it."

The two women left our view, and A. J. turned back to bearding Irickson. "Let's say Osgood's private offering works, I. mean, pulls in a bundle. Then what?"

"Then it's onward and upward! The initial public offering! The IPO!"

Jack's exuberance waned. "*That* little exercise, going public, will be a slow horse of another color. Osgood will have to hire an outside accounting firm. Commission rules."

"SEC rules?"

"Uh-huh."

"And the outside firm would catch it?" A. J. said, "the fraud."

Jack snapped his fingers. "Like that."

"So how–"

His eyes narrowed and he shook his head impatiently. "Don't soil your Fruit of the Looms A. J., if the outside firm's lead auditor ends up an officer of Edgecom. Not by name, of course."

"You mean . . . what? That Osgood would out-and-out bribe the guy?"

"It happens, A. J. What can I say?"

"Christ, Jack, you're telling me . . . plain and simple, that Osgood"–I checked to be certain that nobody was within earshot–"is a fucking crook."

"According to my little scenario he is. He was *all* bullshit when he fired me, I wouldn't put anything past him. Do you know what he stands to clear in an initial offering of Edgecom stock?"

"No, not a clue."

"Five million bucks. Minimum. That's on the stock that he can *legally* sell."

A. J. stopped long enough from shaking his head to take a long drink of his wine. When A. J. put his glass down, Jack asked him what he was working on.

"A fancy booklet about disk drives. Kind of a perq for returning to Edgecom. Un-lax time. "

Jack nodded engagingly. "Grab me one, will you?"

A. J. cranked his face into a serious look. "At twenty-five."

A. J. had downed two goblets of red wine, easily booze enough to power up the adolescent part of his imagination, and driving back to Edgecom he fantasized about an around-the-world fun cruise and other good times he could blow thousands of dollars on. His car radio was tuned to a Dallas all-news station, the frequency where he always left it. Maybe the announcer said something – God knows homicides occurred every day in Dallas – he didn't recall. In any event, suddenly A. J. could not clear his mind of the certainty that Fran did not die of an unfathomable organic injustice, that he was somehow murdered. Every day thousands of frail old men survived open-heart surgery, and Fran was a young, inexhaustible nuclear reactor of energy – with a still-healthy heart. Fran's cardiologist thought he died naturally. A. J. didn't. And the notion that Fran had been murdered became obsessively lodged in A. J.'s head, fixated there like an image in the mind of a stubborn old squatter defending his illegal but hard-won gold pit. But, murdered by whom? Only one possibility came to A. J.'s mind: Osgood. Even Irickson said he wouldn't put anything past the asshole.

# [16]

The first time A. J. irreversibly suspected that there was something fishy about the true cause of Fran's death was during his drive back to Edgecom after he and Irickson had eaten lunch together. Traffic was light. A. J. hadn't turned the radio on, and his initially vague apprehension nurtured itself undistracted.

A. J. telephoned Nick's extension and asked him to come by his office before he left for the day. At five-twenty, briefcase in one hand and an overstuffed three-ring binder in the other, Nick walked into A. J.'s office.

He laid the binder on A. J.'s desk, set his briefcase on the floor, tumbled into A. J.'s only visitor's chair, leaned back, and let his arms hang loosely at his sides.

"Now what Pop?" Nick asked, sighing as if he was irremissibly put-upon.

"I've been thinking," A. J. answered.

Nick rolled his eyes. "Again this year."

"Doesn't it strike you as odd," A. J. said, "that Fran's heart gave out? He wasn't even *my* age. And he could sure as hell run your scraggly butt off a field track."

"Nobody is your age, Pop. Jesse, maybe."

"Uh-huh. The point is, Fran could *not* have just upped and croaked. No way."

Nick's response was lifeless and impatient, "Why not?"

"I just told you, *why not*. Besides, his heart itself was sound. His doctor said so. One artery was some eighty percent clogged, but the others were clear."

As if resuscitating himself from a long time pondering an enigma, Nick took a deep breath. "So you're–"

"He was *killed*," A. J. said somberly. "Murdered."

Nick looked away. "You're positive?"

"Yes. Positive."

"You *know* that Fran was murdered?"

"I'm *damn* sure. Osgood murdered Fran so he could take Edgecom public and get filthy rich selling his stock . . . the shares he swindled Jo Ellen out of."

Nick stood up and reclaimed his briefcase and three-ring binder. "What the shit were you and Jack eating at lunch? Lotus leaves? By any chance . . . you didn't stumble across Dr. Livingstone. Did you?"

"Oh," A. J. said after a moment. "The guy nutty Stanley ran into?" He shook his head. "No, and I am not joking, Silo. So–"

"Neither am I. You're screen door doesn't latch, Pop. Get a girlfriend."

His face stern, Nick strolled from the room. "Beam me up Scotty," he yelled from the hall.

"And stay the hell out of here!" A. J. replied as loudly.

A. J. decided not to run his suspicion past Jesse, not after Nick's reaction. Jesse would have laconically told him that he was fishing a dry hole.

Neither Nick nor Jesse was a fool, but A. J. was beginning to wonder about himself. The police, he knew, would laugh him out of the station with nothing more substantial than the evidence he had on Osgood.

Strangely enough, that admission – soberly conceding to himself the weakness of his case – had a silver lining. It reminded A. J. that three days after Osgood sacked Martha he had found a large, length-wise-folded manila envelope, stamped with Martha's return address, stuffed in his mail box. Inside were four reports. A scrawled note read, "Alan, these Edgecom financial statements may become important. Martha."

A. J. should have given more thought to the note. At the time he was converting the spare bedroom in his new apartment into an office, and he indifferently set the envelope aside. The reports, a "Balance Sheet," "Operations Statement," "Statement of Equity" and "Profit for Year," were dated June 30, 1980. A. J. read all four. Nothing he read struck him as remarkable. In fact, damn little in the reports impressed him at all.

Still, he figured that Martha must have had a reason to inconvenience herself the hour it took to

Xerox and mail him the copies. He figured that she had a cache of Edgecom financial reports at home – for job protection, perhaps.

What to make of Martha's note? Obviously her motivation was not simple courtesy, her concern merely a suggestion. She had smelled a rat, whiffed a malefaction simmering putridly on a back burner at Edgecom.

A. J. finished eating a small, carry-out pizza pie around seven forty-five. At two minutes before eight o'clock, timing his call to coincide with TV station breaks, he telephoned Pat Brown's home. Pat answered his ring, and A. J. apologized for calling her at home. She seemed not to mind. The audio of a TV program faded out.

"Pat," A. J. said, "I need to get hold of Martha. I assumed you'd have her telephone number."

Pat seemed to struggle for words. "I . . . haven't heard from Martha. Nary a *peep*, Alan. I don't know what to make of it."

"So you're not even sure if she's in El Paso? Wasn't she headed there?"

"I thought so," Pat said. "It's where she's from. But I can't imagine her staying in Dallas and not calling me."

"Neither can I," A. J. mumbled. Louder he asked, "I suppose you've called her place in Addison?"

"I tried, but the phone had been disconnected."

"Darn," A. J. said sympathetically. "Her last name is Dillbeck? You said she never married?"

"Yes, sir, Dillbeck. Martha Mildred Dillbeck."

"Well," A. J. said disgustedly, "maybe I don't need to talk to Martha after all."

"Is there any way that I can help, Alan?"

Pat meant, of course, "Why do you want to talk to Martha, Alan"?

A. J. hesitated. "Oh, I only wanted to ask her about some old Edgecom financial reports."

"I guess I'll see you tomorrow then?" Pat said.

I could hear the TV audio again but at a lower volume than when Pat first answered the telephone.

"I expect so. Uh, if you don't mind, Pat, I'd rather you didn't mention this telephone call at work."

Pat promised to honor A. J.'s wish.

A. J. opened a beer. He knew in his heart that he would chase down Martha. A little booze, however, would assuage his effort.

In 1964 Allison and A. J. stayed overnight at a motel in El Paso, Texas. They were on their way to Phoenix, Arizona, to visit Allison's best friend and her husband. They had not been married a year. The second evening of their visit, Allison and her friend got into a spat while the four of them were playing cards, and A. J. and Allison returned to Dallas a day earlier than they had planned. It was the last time A. J. was in El Paso.

A. J. telephoned the El Paso police department at ten a.m. – at nine a.m. El Paso time – from his apartment. After explaining the reason for his call to two people at the station, and each time holding for long pauses, A. J. heard the name, "Detective Alvarez," spoken in a tone of weary forbearance.

A. J. had scripted what he was going to say. "Good morning, Detective. My name is Alan MacRae. I'm calling from Dallas. I have a close friend who left here in July for El Paso and I haven't heard from her since. I'm very concerned, and I'm hoping you can help me."

"Just a minute," Detective Alvarez said. After agreeing to something spoken to him by another person, he came back on the line. "Go ahead."

"Uh, you want her description?"

"Yes. What was your name again?"

A. J. repeated everything he had just told the detective.

"The missing woman is a . . . friend?"

"A close family friend."

A. J. described Martha's physical appearance and told the detective that she was sixty-five. A. J. said she was supposedly there to visit relatives, that she had been raised in El Paso. No, the only last name he had was Dillbeck. No, he did not have either her social security number or her driver's license number.

The detective asked why A. J. had waited two months to call. A. J. had anticipated his question, and he answered that he thought she had moved in with a gentleman friend in Dallas and didn't want people to know, but he had found out that that wasn't the case.

The detective said to give him a couple days and then call back on a morning. He gave A. J. his four-digit extension.

A. J. telephoned Detective Alvarez two days later. He asked A. J. for a few more days. Answering my next telephone call himself, the detective slowly repeated A. J.'s name. A. J. could hear him flicking through sheets of paper.

"Your friend . . . Dillbeck," he said, after another long pause, "left Dallas on seven ten, is that right?"

A. J. had to think a moment. "Yes, on July tenth. Possibly a day later."

"A woman meeting her description checked into the Camino Real Hotel on the tenth. The Real's our fancy hotel. Was your friend, ah, pretty well off?"

"No, not by a long shot."

After a moment, he said, "The hotel staff found a body at the Real the next morning in a three-hundred-dollar-a-night suite. It could have been your friend . . . ah, comparing your description to the coroner's report."

"A *body*?"

The detective waited a few seconds, "Yes. An overdose. If it *was* your Dillbeck . . . woman. She checked in under another name."

"Was the body autopsied," A. J. asked weakly.

"Naw," the detective said unconcerned, "autopsies cost money. We knew from the stuff she left behind . . . booze, vodka, as I recall . . . benzo pills. It had to be suicide."

"Benzo pills?"

"Downers. Tranquilizers. Besides the clothes she had on, the only other thing she left behind was her room key."

"No purse?"

"No, like I just said . . . ."

"Hold on," he said after yelling the name "Paco."

"She clearly wanted to die anonymously," Detective Alvarez said, back on the telephone.

When he didn't say anything for a second, A. J. asked, "Where's the body?"

"In a paupers' cemetery. In a press-wood casket."

The detective interrupted A. J.'s parting expression of thanks to say he had a visitor and abruptly hung up.

A. J. said to himself, "I should have made the calls at the plant on Osgood's nickel."

# [17]

As a consultant – real or in name only – A. J.
scheduled his own work hours. Occasionally Osgood
asked him to write an unimportant memo for internal
distribution. But most of the time, he kept busy
rounding "Inside Personal Computer Disk Storage
Systems" into an advertising-quality brochure. It was
the project that A. J. had suggested to Osgood the day
he flattered A. J. – by bullshit, which A. J. was too
eager and too self-importantly sure of himself to
disregard – into returning. In any event, the booklet was
a challenge. Planned as a glossy, the thirty-six pager, it
would be informative, of course, but above all a
marketing piece: solid technical information with
minimal jargon; always constituted to favor Edgecom
designs. All product pictures would somewhere show
the Edgecom logo – or at least a big part of it.

A. J. ran all his redactions of knotty technical
issues past Nick. On one of his visits, Nick was away
lunching with the IC Pacific's local sales rep, so A. J.
paid Jennerette a social visit. IC Pacific, a West Coast

manufacturer of integrated circuits, designed and produced the Doubler's main controller chip. A small, basically chemical company, it was run 24/7 by its founder. The letters IC, of course, stood for Integrated Circuit.

Jesse was sitting behind his desk staring angrily at the contents of the desk's deep file drawer. As if he had asked, A. J. told him that Nick wasn't in, that A. J. was visiting him, Jesse, not just for that good reason alone but also because of his high tolerance for the tedium of conversing with Manufacturing help.

Jesse straightened, removed his glasses, and rubbed his eyes. "I can't find my FD-400 notes," he said, shaking his head disgustedly at his file drawer.

"Aging," A. J. said, assuming a serious manner, "debilitates." You still Edgecom's head nigger of Production?"

Jesse nodded and put his glasses back on. "Have I told you lately, Bubba, how you are a big pain in the ass?"

Prompted by his bluntness, A. J. decided that he was there to pick up a floppy disk drive. "I need to take pictures of an Epson drive. For my booklet. It doesn't have to work. The drive, I mean."

Jesse's phone rang. He answered it and pointed his chin at the door. "See Sel," he mouthed.

Leaving the room, A. J. said over his shoulder, "Don't expect to see the name Jennerette anywhere in my momentous booklet 'Inside Personal Computer Disk Storage Systems'."

On his way to the prototyping lab, A. J. couldn't help but notice that half of Production's assembly tables, once monolithic hotbeds of quiet, component-soldering industry, had become handy shelves for lunch bags, clothing garments, magazines of the True Confessions genre, and weekly tabloids implying sexual intimacies between cinema stars.

Selig Hildreth, among his other trouble-shooting duties, was responsible for warranty repairs on returns, and he always had a few inoperable Epson floppy-disk drives lying around, units that had been exchanged for reworked drives. Sel, among Nick's technicians, stood out. Tall, thin, and balding in front, he was always neatly attired in pressed blue jeans and a starched, understated, short-sleeved work shirt. When A. J. sauntered into the prototyping lab, he was standing in front of his bench staring thoughtfully into a briefcase crammed with papers and absentmindedly pressing tobacco into the bowl of a white, figure-S meerschaum pipe. The name Quetsch, faded but visible, was stenciled in large block, upper-case letters inside the opened top of his briefcase. A letter, an initial A. J. guessed, printed in front of the word Quetsch was too faint to make out. Since Nick still had not returned, A. J. decided to kill time by badgering Sel.

"Where'd you filch the briefcase, Mace?" A. J. asked, stepping back as if for a better look. Sel took a moment to answer, long enough to let A. J. know he didn't like being called Mace.

The briefcase was old and scuffed, but it had to have cost a pretty penny new. It was deep, had a thick leather handle, heavy copper-plated clasps, and a substantial copper-plated key lock.

Sel closed the lid. "At a garage sale. Only 20 bucks. I.couldn't resist.

"Probably," A. J. said, nodding thoughtfully, "this Quetsch guy was a licensed exterminator who snuck dead rats out of downtown office buildings in your fancy briefcase. That's how they do it, you know."

Sel allowed that that was a possibility. "It did have a funny smell," he said, grinning.

A. J. explained the reason for his visit, and Sel pointed to a half dozen floppy-disk drives aligned face-out on a shelf under his bench. "The Bermuda Triangle of floppy drives," he explained. "Help yourself."

Backing from the lab, he told A. J. to write down the make and serial number of any drive that he carried off. "I have a luncheon date," he said, excusing his departure.

Jokingly, A. J. asked, "With a woman you know."

Grinning, Sel turned as if to answer, but he merely nodded. A. J. had not expected any answer at all, including an affirmation. Sel did not offer a name.

A. J. said to himself, "So much for engaging Sel in time-killing small talk."

A. J. found an Epson floppy-disk drive that suited his needs and left a scrap of paper with the numbers Sel wanted on the workbench.

Nick, as A. J. was leaving the prototyping lab, walked into his office, and A. J. chased after him. In only a few thousand words Nick answered A. J.'s technical question, the original reason why A. J. left for Nick's office.

"Who's Hildreth dating?" A. J. asked casually, closing his briefcase on fresh notes.

"Jo Ellen."

His answer floored A. J. "You mean . . . Fran's, Jo Ellen!"

Sometimes Nick forgot and let slip his pedantic notion that all southerners were descended from ignorant hillbillies. "No. Li'l Abner's Jo Ellen. Why not?"

"Your answer caught me off guard is all, *Silo*. Have they been dating long?"

"Since right after Fran died . . . someone said."

I changed the subject, pretended I thought that the sales' appeal of Nick's Doubler – orders were running strong – was more fleece than flank.

# [18]

Osgood strode beamingly into the room, interrupting Nick's counter argument of how it was that anyone smart enough to correctly multiply two, single-digit numbers would intuit the inherent value of the Doubler.

Osgood had a project for A. J., "One right up your alley."

After pitch-forking some laudatory horseshit Nick's way, Osgood ordered A. J. to follow him to his office. When they arrived, Pat was sitting ram-rod straight, arms-folded, in a chair facing Osgood's desk. A. J. sat down in the chair to her left.

The project that was so appositely suited to A. J.'s compositional talent was an Edgecom, capital B, capital P, business plan. Explaining that he expected a first-rate job, advertising quality all the way, Osgood demanded of an invisible but hovering spirit to proclaim who better than A. J. to produce one.

Wishing afterwards that the words had stuck in his throat the way cold catsup resists vacating a Heinz bottle, A. J. admitted to having never worked on a business plan. He didn't just crack open a door to Osgood verbosity, he blew it off its hinges.

Osgood, for an interminable ten minutes scratched out, in a block-diagram on his whiteboard, the essential elements of an "irresistibly enticing" business plan, one that was certain to convince the reader to advance a money grubstake in Edgecom.

Edgecom's business plan would open with an Executive Summary, written by Osgood himself. The history of Edgecom Data Company, A. J.'s responsibility, would follow; managers would provide input on Marketing, Engineering, and Manufacturing; Wickersham would draft an ancillary section headed Finance. Osgood would touch up all inputs and "smoothly" integrate the parts. He twice cautioned A. J. to run all financial numbers appearing in his history figment past Wickersham.

Osgood, seeing Pat's puzzled look, said to her, "Once all the sections are in, you and I will put it together. Work into the night if we have to."

Clearly, Pat was not thrilled at Osgood's conjecture, and soon he amiably asked her to leave: "And, Dear," he said, "please close the door tightly on your way out."

"You mentioned," Osgood began, as soon as his office door clicked shut, "how you'd never worked on a business plan A. J., so I want to explain something that Pat didn't need to hear."

Osgood studied his scribbling on the whiteboard and then cleanly erased the whole board. Looking at A. J., he said, "Now you know the *how* of a business plan. But do you know the *why*?"

A. J. shilly-shallied. "Why we need a business plan?"

"To sell Edgecom. To raise money. Period. That is the *only* reason the owner of a small, going business will take the time to work up a business plan. He'll *make* the time if he has to."

Osgood put the eraser back in its trough, brushed his hands together, and returned to his chair. "What penicillin is to gonorrhea, money is to a sick business. Forget that crap they teach in Business Administration 101. It may work for . . . Texas Instruments, or Arco, but–"

"I wouldn't know. I am an engineer," A. J. said, belittling his technical training.

Osgood shrugged, " No matter, you can take it to the bank, Pal. The only reason an owner of *any* small, growing business takes the time to write a business plan is because he expects his carefully tweaked projections will ultimately raise money."

"So, our business plan . . . must raise scads of money?"

"Exactly, By selling Edgecom piece by tiny piece. Bauble by bauble."

The thought of Fran busting his ass to keep Edgecom whole and to position himself as the sole owner gripped A. J.'s mind. "Bit by bit," he said softly.

"Don't misunderstand, A. J. I'm not giving up control, not selling Edgecom in that sense. That will *never* happen. Nothing will change in that respect. We do a really spot-on job and we'll generate the cash I. need to keep Edgecom afloat, steaming at sea, throttle on full-ahead. Boilers *rumbling*. Understand?"

"I think so. What kind of . . . customers are we hoping to persuade?"

"You mean, what kind of prospects? What kind of investors?"

"Whatever. Some demographics would help."

Osgood walked around his desk and sat down on the front edge. "Just convince the reader," he said finally. "I don't give a shit if its Jack Ruby . . . is he still alive? . . . or Ma and Pa Kettle. Whoever."

The office door began to open. "Later," Osgood said loudly. He looked at A. J. and rolled his eyes: the effrontery of the intruder.

"One thing," Osgood went on, "be careful not to misrepresent Edgecom's early years as a one-man show. It wasn't, you know. Fran consulted me nightly when Edgecom Data Company wasn't even a work bench in his cellar. I came up with the name Edgecom. Did you know that?"

A. J. knew better, remembered Fran boastfully telling him how the name Edgecom had suddenly, out of the blue, popped into his mind while he was still employed by Texas Instruments.

"No," A. J. answered bluntly, leveling his eyes on Osgood's face, "I didn't know."

Osgood looked away, momentarily studied a wall. "Well, it's a fact. You can ask Jo Ellen."

A. J. folded his arms and leaned back in his chair. "I was under a very different impression."

Osgood vigorously shook his head. "It just goes to show. Don't always trust your instincts, A. J. No sir, I–"

"I'm not going on instincts," A. J. said bluntly.

Osgood's was hurt: "I counseled Fran *all* the time. Daily, if the truth be known."

A. J. reached for his notebook, which he had laid on Osgood's desk and had not touched since he sat down

Raising his hand, Osgood showed A. J. its palm. "I didn't want to bring this up . . . not now. A. J. . . . I haven't quite worked everything out."

A .J. slowly retrieved his notebook.

Osgood's lips pursed, and then rolled inward; he shrugged resignedly. "I'm near to signing off on a *very, very* generous stock-option plan. It's tailored exclusively for my managers. For you, too, A. J. Herb's fine-tuning it. You're the first to know."

A. J. moved his notebook back to the front edge of Osgood's desk.

"In any event, A. J., for Christ sakes *don't* let what I'm about to tell you leave this room."

A. J. listened – wholly in doubt – and directly made up his mind that, one way or another, he would convince the police that Osgood had murdered Fran. Osgood's bullshit had become more than merely irreparable. It had over-spilled to where A. J. totally loathed the man himself.

And then Osgood offered A. J. a stake in Edgecom, a mere fragment of ownership.

The offer of proprietorship was maximally important to A. J., the signed document with the name Alan J. MacRea explicitly printed on the ownership line, was the gratuity that closed the argument. To a far lesser extent, so was the package of company stock, which, theoretically, A. J. would be able to cash-out for hundreds of thousands of dollars in Edgecom's IPO.

Consequently, A. J. did not dash from Osgood's office and race to the nearest police station anxious to finger a murderer; he had second thoughts: *"Maybe Nick was right. After all, he was a damned smart young man. Maybe I was a delusional nut case stupidly treading a path that led straight to a room where the walls were overlain with sponge rubber. Maybe Osgood truly was wholly innocent."*

# [19]

Osgood ordered all persons working on the business plan to leave a draft of their effort on his desk by eight a.m. on the Wednesday before Thanksgiving. A. J. was ready with his part the preceding Monday – until he read Herb Wickersham's four gnarly paragraphs of financial input, which A. J. was supposed to work into his section on Edgecom's early history. Wickersham's sentences, taken one at a time, were straightforward and syntactically correct. As for paragraphs explicating the marrow of a single idea, they aggregated into meaningless posturing that was beyond A. J.'s redacting skill to translate into coherent topics of understanding.

Wondering if his problem was merely unfamiliarity with the lingua franca of accounting, A. J. slowly reread Herb's first paragraph. After chewing a long minute on the content, A. J. concluded if there was a literary equivalent to the Heisenberg Uncertainty Principal he had just stumbled on to it.

A. J. scanned Herb's tabular data. The numbers were reasonable: income reflected seasonal swings and synchronously lagged production output curves. A. J., on reflection, decided the tables were *all* that made sense.

Something else bothered A. J. Was Herb's financial portrayal of Edgecom far too fanciful? Too Jackson Pollock blatant? A. J. recalled Martha Dillbeck's blunt verbal assessment of Edgecom's shaky financial condition, supported, as far as he could tell, by the reports she mailed him shortly after Osgood had Dornhoffer march her out.

It was high time, A. J. decided, to become better acquainted with Edgecom's reclusive Finance guru. He telephoned Wickersham, and Herb allowed that he could spare A. J. a minute.

Inverting the usual hierarchical business-management protocol, Herb insisted they talk in A. J.'s office, not his. Herb strolled in offering his hand. They shook. He made sure A. J.'s office door was tightly closed. Arriving empty handed, A. J. offered Herb a copy of his own financial write-up. Herb accepted it casually.

As if distraught, Herb began. "I've got to set the record straight about this Dillbeck woman and . . . that other person. What was his name?"

A. J. decided he meant Irickson. "Our former business software man? Jack Irickson?"

Wickersham nodded rapidly. "Right. That guy. Just so you know A. J., I personally had nothing to do with the canning of those two. I strongly suspect that Hummel found something that wasn't on the up and up. I'm not sure."

A. J. said that he had not given the matter much thought. In truth, both firings now and then surfaced darkly in A. J.'s mind. Neither expulsion made sense from any perspective. His mind turned back to Wickersham's underpinning of Martha's firing.

"But, A. J., please understand that I spent two long evenings pouring over Martha's work, and Hummel was spot on." He shook his head disgustedly. "We had to let her go. Both of 'em. I've been a practicing CPA for sixteen years, and" – he exhaled a long sigh – "damn steer paddies are what A. J. had to step around." The Trinity River isn't nearly as mucked up. No methodology . . . at all! None! You know what language this, ah, Irickson fellow wrote his computer programs in?"

"No, no idea."

"Basic! Imagine! A beginner's programming language!"

Uncertain of the folly of that programming madness, A. J. halfheartedly agreed that writing business accounting software in entry-level computer parlance was a misapplication.

Then, A. J. remembered that Irickson could program in demanding, machine-specific language, which is efficient but esoteric and difficult – especially compared to a student language such as Basic.

"In Basic?" A. J. replied doubtfully. "I was under the impression he" – A. J. stopped in mid-sentence and changed the sense of his remark –"Why Basic, I wonder?"

"Damn good question, A. J. Damn good. You'd have to put it to Irickson, though."

The problem, Wickersham went on, had its origin in the hobbyist mind-set prevalent at Edgecom before Osgood took over. "Karl," he finished, "had the right idea."

"Karl?" A. J. said, screwing an incredulous look on his face.

He refused the bait, did not allow A. J. the chance to belittle the notion that Karl Dornhoffer ever in his life had a "right" idea.

A. J. allowed his unbelieving expression to fade. "If Irickson's software was screwed up why'd Hummel can Martha?"

Wickersham shook his head. "I don't know about the under soil. Probably, I'm guessing now, the job overwhelmed her – the high-tech, cutting-edge business that is Edgecom? She was what? Seventy, seventy-five?"

"Fran thought highly of her."

"Yes, but there's more, A. J. That I'd . . . it's a can of worms that I'd rather not open."

"Why not? It's Edgecom business isn't it?" A. J.'s question, as he meant it to be, was a plump nightcrawler, the kind that bass and trout fight to gobble up.

Herb's eyes narrowed and his face seemed to cloud over. "I can't explain what happened," he said at last, his tone stern, "to several thousand of dollars of Edgecom revenue."

A. J. thrust his head assertively forward. "You're not suggesting that Martha Dillbeck . . . embezzled it?"

After a long pause, Herb said, "She . . . it looks like it. And I–"

"No way!" A. J. blurted out vehemently. "That is a non-starter, Herb."

Wickersham nimbly reversed his field. As A. J. learned that afternoon, Herb, with undiminished ardor, could turn one of his own arguments around on a dime, spin it a full one-hundred-eighty degrees either clockwise or counterclockwise. A fly high on caffeine could not change direction as quickly.

Herb hurriedly agreed. "Oh no! No, no, no! Not at all. Not *at all* do I think that Martha . . . that Martha . . . . I'm sure she was A-1, top-tier, hard working, all those sterling qualities. No, not for an instant am I. . . . how should I put it? Martha . . . was just plain getting old, nothing more."

"Martha," A. J. said softly, "wouldn't steal a paper clip."

"I'm sure," Herb replied, his expression thoughtful. Glancing at his write-up, he seemed surprised to find it in his hand. "Anyway, that's not why I'm here. Right?"

"I hope not" A. J. said.

Herb sighed heavily. "Where to begin? Inventory, I guess."

Edgecom's inventory records, Herb avowed, were irremediably screwed up. Inventory, therefore, was inevitably overvalued, which, "of course," negatively impacted Edgecom's bottom line. His newly installed, fully computerized, four-column accounting forms, however, would fix everything.

"And, imagine," Herb went on, "This Dillbeck woman hadn't set up a *single subsidiary ledger*! Not one! Bad-debt accounts are not merely expugnable mistakes that were easily erased by her standards of accounting. No sir, A. J. They have to be formally written off."

And so on. A. J. decided he would have learned more listening to the chatter of a magpie. At some point, as if to gather himself, Herb paused. Seizing the moment A. J. told him that he was wobble-kneed from bearing the weight of so many new ideas.

Wickersham laughed. "You're the boss."

A. J. acceded by shrugging.

"Okay then," Herb said, "let's do lunch. On me."

A. J. pleaded an appetite diminished beyond resurrection from pigging-out on Tex-Mex the evening before. They shook hands. Nodding affably, Herb backed out of A. J.'s office.

A. J. knew, beyond a shadow of a doubt, that prim and proper Martha Dillbeck would sooner parade naked at noon on a weekday amid the usual gathering of brown-baggers, eating in the shadows of monumental Thanksgiving Square in downtown Dallas, than steal a penny from anyone. By her moss-encrusted methods she had overvalued our inventory by thousands of dollars? A. J. irresolutely doubted it.

A. J. decided, finally, to accept verbatim the whole of Wickersham's herky-jerky write-up, figuring, if it came down to it, he'd let Herb defend it.

A. J. had lied to Wickersham about overeating the night before. Having bootlegged a sandwich from the lunch truck into his room, A. J. was wolfing it down when the telephone rang. It was Pat, Osgood wanted to see him right away. No, she didn't know why.

Wickersham, standing in front of Osgood's desk, his hands stuffed in his pockets, turned and greeted me politely. I'm done, he said to Osgood, who was tilted back in his desk chair, arms crossed loosely over his chest. Herb left the room, softly closing the door on his way out.

Osgood pleasantly told A. J. to have a seat. "The business plan. How's it coming?"

"Okay," A. J. answered cautiously.

"We'll hit it Friday morning," he said. "I have to . . . finish an, er, ah, agency job before coming in."

A. J. nodded, thinking that Osgood should be reminding Pat, not him, of their get-together: the day after Thanksgiving was shop-till-you-drop Black Friday, an event women are predisposed to honor religiously and even consider putting their youngest up for adoption, if necessary, for the chance to canvass every mart at a stylish shopping complex.

"Your booklet," Osgood said. "What's the title again?"

"Inside Microcomputing Disk Storage Systems."

"Inside . . . ah, how's it coming?"

"I pick up the mechanicals tomorrow."

Osgood grimaced. "You subbed the mechanicals?"

"You said top-of-the-line all the way."

"I suppose," Osgood said curtly.

Pushing back from his desk, Osgood worked a small ring of keys from a front pocket of his trousers, unlocked the shallow center drawer of his desk, and pulled it out. After briefly eyeing something inside, he closed the drawer and locked it. His eyebrows elevated delightedly. "A. J., how'd you like to become part owner of what someday will be the hottest name in personal computing?"

A. J answered that he would like that progression – enthusiastically as he recalled.

"I thought so, Pal. I have only to dot an I here and there, cross a couple of Ts, and my key-people stock-option plan is *ready!*"

A. J. leaned back, his interest aroused.

Herb, Osgood said, was smelting the ore of the plan, burning off the few impurities of a tremendously generous program. Edgecom's key people, Osgood explained, would be able to buy shares of Edgecom's Series A Preferred stock at a bargain-basement price, ensuring, thereby, that those persons who were so anointed could cash out in the IPO for tens of times their initial pop. "Naturally," Osgood finished, "that includes you, A. J."

The buzzer on his telephone sounded. Showing A. J. an annoyed look, he pressed the phone to his ear.

Osgood's testy look evaporated. "Tell Herb to come on in."

Wickersham, finding A. J. in the room, stopped abruptly. Figuring Wickersham's arrival cued the end of his visit, A. J. stood up.

Osgood shook his head. "Its okay, A. J." He turned to Wickersham: "I just went over our key-employee stock-option plan with A. J., Herb. He's the first person to know of it."

Wickersham pumped my hand vigorously. "What do you think, A. J.? If you ever come across a better plan, let me know."

"Impressive," A. J. managed to say, utterly clueless.

"I've never seen the likes," Wickersham continued, shaking his head elatedly.

The ensuing silence, planned, apparently, was meant to allow A. J. a chance to ask questions. "Uh . . .

what," he said, falteringly to Osgood, "I mean . . . when do you think we'll be going public?"

"Next year. God willin' and the Trinity River don't rise."

"Maybe I'm out of line," A. J. said in a hushed tone. "But is Jesse on your list?"

The implication of my question annoyed Osgood. "Why wouldn't he be? Of course."

"Did Pat give you my message?"

"What message?" Osgood answered querulously. "I don't think so."

"Jesse's got cancer. Dolly called me. Bone cancer. Myeloma."

Osgood fell back in his chair. He glanced at Wickersham. To me he said, "I didn't know."

A. J. said softly, "Dolly was whimpering when she told me."

Osgood shook his head slowly. "No matter what happens," he said sternly to Wickersham, "you see to it that Jesse gets taken care of. Share-wise."

Wickersham nodded grimly. "It'd be the Christian thing to do."

A. J. stood up. Herb stepped back and waved him on his way.

# [20]

A. J. removed the wax paper that tightly enveloped his sandwich and spread it on the top of his desk. The bread was mushy and dripped of relish sauce, so A. J. ate leaning over the wax paper. He finished, slouched back in his chair, and removed his eyeglasses. Furniture only yards away became blurred and ill-defined; the fuzziness of furniture and other real obstacles helped to focus his thinking on abstractions.

Two issues laid hold of A. J.'s mind. One was Wickersham's wild-assed implication that Martha had misappropriated thousands of Edgecom's dollars. A. J. knew better, knew that Martha wouldn't steal as much as a box of paperclips from Edgecom – or from anyone.

So? Wickersham was trying to . . . what? Float a trial balloon? See if A. J. would compliantly board the gondola hefted by that vast sphere of hot-air? But why the accusation at all? A cover-up? Of what? It didn't compute. Still, Martha, Miss Uprightness personified, had, after all, disappeared.

The implication became a pebble in A. J.'s shoe that he could not brush out.

And, why was Osgood offering *him* a piece of Edgecom, on the cheap, vowing that the alchemy of a public offering would transform his paper certificate of ownership into ore of gold.

In his heart, A. J. knew the offer was hush money, was a bribe to stop him from blabbing about Edgecom's true financial condition. He could never prove motive, of course, but he could prove Osgood cooked the books. If, in fact, he did. It sickened A. J. to admit it, but it was just possible that Martha herself had bent every bookkeeping rule in the book and possibly broke some. Accountants and subservient bookkeepers, A. J. knew, could skin a cat as easily forward as backward. He needed corroborating evidence . . . or whatever ambulance-chasers called back-up testimony.

A. J. struggled for hours before finally piecing together a plausible reason for Wickersham's smearing of Martha's integrity: Ingesting the slurry of a bank loan covering a shortfall of revenue ascribable to mismanagement would indeed take a long-handled spoon for investors to swallow, but downing the idea of a self-serving misappropriation by a thieving employee, would not be near the bitter swill.

In any event, A. J. chose, finally, to view Osgood's offer of Company stock as merely impounding his key to the vault holding the records of Edgecom's *true* financial situation. He could pay the impound charge –

and air the dirty linen that would unseat Osgood – any time, if it came to that.

He needed a devil's advocate.

"Too damned many things all at once," Nick grumbled, turning from his drafting table.

"Yeah," A. J. said, pretending he was pondering something. "And General Custer'd been a hero if the Indians had attacked one at a time." A. J. had read that put-down line somewhere and had been saving it.

Nick could not stifle a grin. "Up yours, Pop. Besides, I don't recall that Custer had made General yet. What is today's technical problem de jour?"

"I learned something interesting today," A. J. said plopping into Nick's desk chair. "You remember Martha Dillbeck?"

Nick nodded. "Yeah, kind of." He leaned back against his drafting table.

"Well, guess what," A. J. said. "She's a . . . master filcher."

Nick's eyes narrowed skeptically. "Martha? The old gal who ran Bookkeeping?"

"None other."

"As reported in the newspaper?"

"No! It happened while she was keeping *our* books! Fran . . . or so I was told, didn't report it."

"Martha?" Nick asked skeptically, his brow furrowed, "stole money from *Edgecom*? While Fran was here running the place?"

"That's what I was told."

"By?"

"By Wickersham."

Nick repeated Martha's name. "Hard to believe," he said, shaking his head.

"Yeah," A. J. snapped, "so goddamn hard to believe that I flat *don't* believe it."

Nick popped from his stool and closed his office door. He did not defend Wickersham, as he always had before when A. J. ripped Edgecom's first and only V.P. of Accounting. A. J. tucked that observation away.

A. J. persevered: "Martha wouldn't have stolen a blank computer punch card."

"Damn! You're even older than I had guessed, Pop. How much did she . . . supposedly make off with?"

"Over the years? Thousands."

A wide-eyed look settled for a moment on Nick's face. "Not exactly pocket change. How long did she work here?"

"She's *always* kept Edgecom's books. Even before Fran moved Edgecom into the barn in his back yard. She worked out of her home, back then."

Nick was beholden. "And Fran didn't catch it? Doesn't sound like the Francis Degeorge I knew."

"Not to me either."

Nick's telephone rang.

"Yes," he answered, "I'll get back."

He listened a second longer, repeated his words, and hung up. If Nick was not sitting at his desk, and the telephone rang, he would not answer it. A. J. doubted that Fran ever knew, but Pat sure as hell did, and more than once she threatened to render Nick incapable of fatherhood for making her walk unnecessarily from her desk to leave him a written message.

"It wasn't a girlfriend, huh?"

Nick changed the subject. "Why would Wickersham want to crap on Martha?"

"Yeah, I wondered about that myself. You remember my explanation – Irickson's, I should say – of how Osgood planned to take Edgecom public? How first he'd have to misrepresent a bank loan as sales revenue? To . . . ultimately to sucker investors?"

"Yeah. I guess so."

"I think Irickson put one in the bulls-eye."

"Meaning?"

"The Doubler is virtually the only thing we're selling. But, Sandy's doing nooners again. Connect the dots, Silo! Those two facts add up to something goddam fishy . . . sales being *way down* but income *up*."

Nick looked away. "If you say so, Sherlock."

"Anyway, I think Wickersham was floating a cover story, and he wanted to see if I bought it."

Nick slightly shook his head. "You lost me."

"Wouldn't it be easier to convince interested investors how the . . . the one-time red ink on your company's bottom line, resulted from being mugged by an employee? And not from your own shitty mismanagement?"

Nick, like most engineers, shaded his answer to any question not of a Newtonian certainty. "I guess," he answered. "If you knew the . . . person was totally honest."

A. J. fought to keep the frustration from his voice. "Hell yes, it would be easier. Even if sales declined from a market plunge."

"Yeah," Nick said finally. "Probably."

"You'd argue," A. J. continued, "how you covered out of your own pocket, that you were the only one who took a steer horn in the ass. Right?"

Nick answered wearily. "I suppose so."

"And something else, Silo, I–"

"Oh hell," Nick interrupted, "more of your grokking,"

"Goddammit, Silo! Hear me out!"

"*Okay*. I'm listening. Really."

"I admit that, for a while, I only wondered. But no more. Now I'm damn positive." A. J. poked his desk top hard several times with his index finger. "That son-of-a-bitch Osgood murdered Fran."

A. J. leaned back in the chair.

Nick stared past him; he shook his head, "You're scaring the shit out of me, MacRae. Only I don't know whether it's you personally or the . . . ramification of your cockamamie theory."

"I'm going to prove it," A. J. said, nodding persuasively.

"Maybe. But there's more than a tad of a difference between stealing money and murdering someone."

"I'll kill two birds with one stone."

"More likely," Nick said, "you'll hit some poor innocent bastard in the eye with a rock."

A. J. left Nick's office positive that he had not even scratched the armor protecting Nick's certainty of A. J.'s, stubborn wrongheadedness. Still, Nick did not fall to the floor laughing – a comportment that A. J. glommed onto.

A. J. decided, Nickerson's apathetic support notwithstanding, to present his case to the police. Figuring he had assembled adequate persuasive evidence, he would intrepidly cross the Rubicon and successfully invade any province of law enforcement that resisted his presentation – his proof of Osgood's complicity in Fran's death. Determinedly excited, A. J. was pathetically wrong.

# [21]

The walls of the one-story building, bland, static and uninviting, were courses of gray concrete blocks, fifteen counting from the grass up. An off-white corner stone, cemented neatly in place in the fifth course, was inscribed with the year 1978; the sun's rays highlighted the recessed digits. Visitors were allowed 30 minutes of parking on a side street.

Until that morning, the Friday following Thanksgiving Day of 1980 – traditionally a Christmas shoppers' frenzied "Black Friday" – A. J. had never before set foot in a police station. Already apprehensive about his mission, the duty sergeant's ill-humored greeting stoked his anxiety.

Detective Deemer led A. J. to her desk. Dressed in a Dallas Cowboys warm-up jacket, a dark-blue denim skirt that stopped four or so inches short of her knees, and western-tooled, mahogany-colored cowboy boots, her gait was a self-assured march. The denim skirt perfectly lacquered her round, trim, cantilevered buttocks. Bronzed legs began at the hem of her skirt until stopped at the tops of her cowboy boots. Her hair, coal black and cut short, gave her a youthful vintage, and A. J., on seeing her up close, added three years to the thirty that he had originally guessed was her age. Her ring finger was bare. A. J. had initially assumed she was a clerk, that she was only decorative office help. She parked him by her desk, one of four in the room.

Once over the surprise at learning that his police-station escort, a tawny, good-looking woman wearing a glossy Dallas Cowboys wind-breaker, was a City Detective, A. J. had to immediately purge his mind of thinking what a joy it would be to see if she was bronzed head to toe – so conspicuously apparent while they romped ecstatically on white percale linen. (A. J. was near the final weeks of his divorce and still without a steady woman.) Thus fantasizing, A. J. did not catch her first question.

Wryly amused at his obvious beguilement, Detective Deemer repeated her question. "You're here, Mister. . . Mik - ray? . . . to report a homicide?"

"Uh, yes."

A. J. spelled his name. "What I have is a bit thin, but, yes, ma'am, I believe I've . . . closed in on one. The victim was my boss, the founder of Edgecom Data Company. Edgecom makes–"

"Uh-huh. Where did this murder take place?"

"At Medical City Hospital. But there's more . . . ."

A. J. waited while Detective Deemer pulled out a tablet from the middle drawer of her desk.

After writing on it for a few moments, which she followed by hiding a yawn with the back of her hand, she asked, "Where exactly in the hospital? In a public restroom? The kitchen?"

"Actually . . . in a patient room. The victim was recovering from surgery. From open-heart surgery. He had the–"

"The victim was a man?"

"Yes. He was a friend, my boss. Two years younger than I am."

Deemer's left eyebrow arched slightly: "And you know for certain that . . . your boss *didn't* die of a natural cause?"

"He was poisoned, I'm . . . sure."

Deemer's eyes narrowed skeptically. She looked at where her feet were resting under the desk. "You're almost sure?" she asked, sounding a bit drained.

A detective standing midway between the two front desks talking on the telephone impatiently uttered two quick Okays, shook his head, and hung up. He glanced in our direction, concluded that I was a civilian, and did not explain the call.

Detective Deemer, scratching her cheek with the eraser end of her pencil, allowed her attention to fall back on me.

"It's possible he was strangled," A. J. said without conviction, "but I don't think so, there wasn't any evidence to–"

"What do his doctors think?"

147

"His cardiologist blew it off. Thought it was just . . . a freak, but a not too uncommon medical happening. I mean, he believed there was no *extrinsic* cause for Fran's death. "Extrinsic was the doctors word.""

Detective Deemer, as if in complete agreement, nodded rapidly. "Uh, no witnesses?"

"None. And, interestingly, Fran, I mean, Mister Degeorge, was alone when he died. Exactly as planned. I'm positive."

Deemer wrote the word "alone" on her tablet and circled it. For a second her gaze focused penetratingly on A. J.'s eyes. She asked him to spell the victim's whole name. He did, emphasizing the letter i in Francis. Deemer's slight cringe assured A. J. that she knew how the male version of that first name was spelled.

"He goes by his middle name, by Fran."

"You said he was your boss?"

"Yes. And a friend. He started Edgecom . . . founded it . . . on a shoestring."

Detective Deemer, as if trying to recall the name Edgecom, nodded slowly. "When did this homicide happen?"

"In June. On the eighteenth."

Her eyebrows shot up. "And you're only *now* reporting it?"

"Well I . . . I've been gathering evidence. And I finally–"

"Evidence? What kind of evidence?"

"It will take me a bit . . . . Still, I believe that what I *do have* will prove beyond any reasonable doubt that Fran, I mean, that Mister Degeorge absolutely was murdered. And who murdered him."

"Beyond any reasonable doubt?" Deemer's sarcasm was mildly reproving, but it was not meant, it seemed to A. J., to cut deep.

A. J. smiled wryly. "Sorry. How about, 'will convincingly show'?"

An apathetic shrug to A. J.'s rephrasing matched Deemer's initial indifference.

Writing herself a long note, and afterward, as if mentally sorting through facts, Detective Deemer leaned back in her chair. She studied A. J.'s face, wondering, he figured, how to deal with another walk-in crackpot. "At least," she said suddenly, "this won't be an every-day who-done-it since you know who the killer is."

"*Great*," A. J. said to himself, "*now she's mocking me.*"

After another second, Deemer bluntly asked, "Who do you think killed Mister Degeorge?"

"Hummel Osgood," A. J. said. "Edgecom's new owner." He spelled Osgood's name and watched as she firmly printed, "John Hummel Osgood," on her tablet.

"Hummel, is H u m *m* e l?"

"Yes, two letter m's. And I *can* prove that he boogered Edgecom's financial books." A. J. did not have the proof, but he was confident that his stretching of the truth would eventually ring out as a fact.

"You caught him red-handed mucking up the company books?"

A. J. took a second to answer. "Yes. I did, in a way. It's a long . . . bear with me."

Detective Deemer sighed. "Go ahead," she said.

"To begin, Osgood and his accountant pal are putting out financial reports that show Edgecom is making money. Damn good money. We are *not*. Hell, we're *losing* money. Every day. They are both crooks."

"Both?"

"Osgood and this guy he hired – or brought in, anyway – named Wickersham. They've apparently known each other, in one way or another . . . for a long-time."

In his rush to discomfit Detective Deemer of her skepticism, A. J. screwed up badly by elaborately discrediting Osgood and making it clear that he loathed the man. A. J. had forewarned himself against getting carried away, was afraid that negatively limning Edgecom's new president would badly undercut the strength of his charge.

Having fallen on his own sword, A. J. quickly tried to sheath it. "I'm sorry if I sound bitter, but –"

Deemer interrupted him. "Do you still work at Edgecom?"

"Yes, as a consultant. But . . . that's another long story."

She slightly shook her head. "Frankly, Mister MacRae, it's like you said up front, your evidence for the crime of *murder*. . . isn't coming together."

A. J.'s disappointment was total. "That," he mumbled, "is what I was . . . hoping you *wouldn't* say." In his full voice, he added, "But I *know* he killed Fran."

Detective Deemer stared at the word "Polo" stitched above A. J.'s shirt pocket. "Maybe," she said, shrugging and looking away. "Still, I'd need hard evidence . . . to go on."

Her eyes locked on A. J.'s. "This guy Osgood is obviously some kind of prick, but that doesn't make him a murderer."

*"Prick!"* A. J.'s jaw dropped.

Deemer smiled. "You live in Highland Park?"

Remembering that he had given the desk sergeant the address of his parent's home, the high-hat city of his privileged youth, where residents seldom used gritty epithets let alone the likes of "prick," A. J. quickly overcame his sense of embarrassment.

Deemer shrugged.

A. J. grinned, explicitly proclaiming, thereby, that Alan MacRae was not a coddled high-brow wuss. "That's an old address. I'm living in an apartment in Richardson." It seemed to A. J. like the right moment to bring up another point: "Since my divorce."

Deemer digested his answer before asking what, in particular, had caused A. J. to think that his boss had been murdered.

"To begin . . . he was an energetic, thirty-four year-old with a strong heart? It didn't – all of the sudden stop working. For another, he just *never* pooped out. He was like . . . an autistic kid."

Deemer scowled at A. J.'s use of the word "autistic," but at that moment A. J. did not assess her angry look. Her scowl faded. "So, the doctors don't believe he merely died of ordinary heart failure?"

"No. I mean, yes. They think he *did* suffer myocardial infraction. Only . . . uh, it was natural, ordinary heart failure, I mean . . . not ordinary, but *they* believe there was no outside intervention, no funny business. One of his main arteries had clogged, by something like eighty per cent, but, hell, the cardiologist told me that they caught it and . . . looped around it. Bypassed it. It couldn't have been super critical or they'd have operated sooner. He implied."

A. J. interpreted Deemer's indifferent nod as meaning that she allied herself with the doctors. A. J. gave her another moment to reflect. She did not change her mind.

"Back to your original question," A. J. said. You wanted to know what started me thinking that Fran was murdered."

"Uh-huh," Deemer answered halfheartedly.

"For one thing, like I already mentioned, I can prove that Osgood, Edgecom's new owner, is cooking the books. I'm sure he swindled Fran's widow out of her ownership in Edgecom. Then there's . . . the little things, like representing himself as the co-founder of Edgecom. Which is pure bull. Flat ridiculous. I know that for a fact. Fran–"

Deemer shook her head. "So far," she said, interrupting A. J., "you're describing crimes I'm not paid to investigate."

"I know, but . . . Osgood is doing these things so he can get the money to take Edgecom public. If he pulls it off, he'll clear five million bucks. Maybe more. An accountant friend–"

Deemer straightened. "Five million dollars is a lot of motive. For all kinds of crime."

Deemer's interest was rekindled. "Again, how specifically . . . did this Osgood person kill your boss? And when, exactly?"

A. J.'s confidence took wing. "He was poisoned by Osgood. He and Jo Ellen visited Fran in his hospital room a half-hour before he died. Jo Ellen left, leaving Osgood alone with Fran."

"Jo Ellen?"

"Fran's wife, uh, his widow. Now."

Detective Deemer, as if organizing her thoughts, stared past A. J.

"Osgood's wife is the twin sister of Fran's wife. Of Fran's widow."

Deemer nodded uncertainly. "But *how* was he killed? Has there been an autopsy?"

"No. The doctors . . . I guess in these situations doctors get together and decide if one is warranted.

Anyway, Jo Ellen . . . I doubt that Jo Ellen would allow an autopsy. If she has a say. She's . . . kind of passive. There'd have to be something obviously out of whack."

"There was no vomiting? No spasms? Nothing when the poison hit?"

"The charge nurse said there wasn't any, uh . . . screwy medical stuff. It was like . . . he had died peacefully in his sleep."

Deemer breathed a long sigh. She shook her head, "Lieutenant Hope would have me riding shotgun in a black-and-white before the day was out."

The detective who had been talking on the telephone walked rapidly from the room. "I'm downtown," he said cryptically to Deemer over his shoulder.

Deemer nodded and watched him leave.

"Well," A. J. said dejectedly when she turned back, "I guess I've just wasted your time?"

"If you turn up more evidence . . . you know, the famous *smoking gun* . . . ." Deemer's voice trailed off.

"I have a reporter friend," A. J. said, "Who–"

Detective Deemer's instant glare, A. J.'s introduction to the universal loathing of cops for the press, would have blown the tread off an attacking Army tank. A. J. clamed up instantly and tendered an apology of sorts: "May I at least buy you a cup of coffee. For wasting your time?"

"I don't drink coffee."

"Soda pop, maybe? A coke? Root beer? A *real* beer?"

Detective Deemer shook her head— unconvincingly it seemed to A. J.

A. J. glanced back on his way out of the room. Deemer, as if flustered, shifted her gaze from him to the big blackboard of notes addressing unsolved crimes.

Her image, one of a bosomy, hard-boiled, rather pretty woman, entertained A. J. on his brisk walk to the car. The radio, when he started the engine, came on, as it always did, and he turned down the volume so he could enjoy undistracted moments of vicarious sex with Detective Deemer.

# [22]

A. J. had swung by Edgecom early in the morning on that traditional Black Friday only to be tersely advised by Osgood that he and Pat would not need his help in alloying together the parts of Edgecom's vaunted, first-ever business plan. A. J. remembered thinking, *"Whatever you do Cheeks, don't apologize for inconveniencing me."*

A. J. told Pat that he would return to Edgecom after attending to personal business, and he forthwith drove to the police station where he failed to persuade Detective Deemer that his boss was murdered.

When A. J. returned to Edgecom, he found a note taped to the face of his computer screen ordering him to telephone McPherson. He did, and McPherson said, "We need to conference, A. J."

"Do *what?*" A. J. asked sarcastically.

After a pause McPherson said, "Let's get together. Say, at two o'clock in my office."

"At two o'clock I'll be home pigging-out on leftover turkey and dressing. And watching football on TV."

"Well . . . how about right now? Before things close in?"

"Before *what*?"

"Before things close in," McPherson answered vaguely. "Before . . . you know, before the usual stuff hits the fan."

"Everyone's off today. What in the hell are you're talking about, Darren."

A second or so passed. "It isn't important," he said.

A. J. thought over his reply. "As soon as I make a pit stop."

Osgood had lodged McPherson in Karl Dornhoffer's old office. He looked up from where he was sitting behind his desk and motioned at the middle of his three visitors' chairs. "A couple things," he said, as A. J. backed into the chair. "One, Hummel has given me Manufacturing."

"*Given* you?"

McPherson sighed. "Yeah. Like MaxWriter isn't enough."

"Hummel," A. J. said, "is hot to shovel dirt on Jesse's grave."

McPherson shook his head. "A. J., you misread Hummel. Like he told me, it's just–"

A. J. shook his head. "I haven't seen a prognosis yet, have you? Has Osgood?"

". . . that Hummel doesn't want to get caught shorthanded, you know, up the run without–"

"Jesse's a good man, as important to Edgecom's toughing it out as was Degeorge himself."

McPherson hastily and fulsomely agreed that Jesse was first rate, and then he abruptly changed the subject: "Mainly, I want to go over the MaxWriter project and discuss exactly where you will fit in."

"Fitting-in" was hardly what A. J. had in mind. "Your call," he said indifferently.

"My background is project management, A. J. I don't write computer programs, and I'm not a nuts-and-bolts engineer. I'm a systems man, you know, the whole schmear."

A. J. said that he had worked with systems managers at Texas Instruments. "A few," he said, "knew their ass from a hole in the ground. All of 'em were politicians."

McPherson forced a laugh. "It's a load, a lot of responsibility. I was a head project manager at Foster Systems. It's where I met Hummer."

"Met who?"

"Where I met Osgood. Those of us who know him call him Hummer."

A. J. smiled. "Oh, I get it. Like calling a big man, 'Tiny'."

Nodding uncertainly, McPherson shuffled to his whiteboard and drew boxes at each vertex of an imaginary, upright triangle. In the top box, he printed his name and underneath the words, Project Manager. In the bottom right-hand box he printed "Software Development" and in its twin box he printed "Hardware Design." He left off names.

Backing away from the board, satisfied apparently, McPherson drew a fourth box outside the three-box triangle. Inside that box he printed the letters A. J. and underneath the box the word Documentation. After another nod of self-approval, he printed MAXWRITER at the top of the diagram.

McPherson returned to his chair. "Of course, I report to Karl. What do you think?"

After a few seconds of hard concentration, A. J. rose to the occasion: "Seems clear enough," he said, squinting and nodding.

McPherson eased back into his chair. "You'll be writing the performance specs. I'm told you are the man for the job. Any questions?"

A. J. stared doggedly at McPherson's simple diagram for five seconds. "I can't think of any."

"Better get with Karl before you begin," McPherson said, nodding contentedly.

"Get with Karl? Why?"

"Karl has good ideas. MaxWriter is his baby, you know."

"Yeah. And Mutt and Jeff harnessed atomic energy. What are some of Dornhoffer's good ideas?"

McPherson ticked off A. J.'s own arguments, his points promoting the developmenting of an inexpensive micro-computing system that would be dedicated solely to the job of producing simple but well-tempered documentation. It was the line of reasoning that Dornhoffer had overheard A. J. express to Fran.

A. J. finally interrupted. "Are we beyond just *talking* about MaxWriter?"

"Indeed we are." Unrolling a blueprint lying on his desk, McPherson rotated it for A. J. to see.

A. J. stood up. Edgecom's MaxWriter would look for the entire world like a stretch version of a popular video data terminal manufactured by the Lear Seigler Company. Offered in a streamlined fiberglass enclosure, a novelty at the time, the Lear terminal was among the first work-bench video terminals that did not look like a technician's boxy kluge. Displaying twenty-four, eighty-character lines, it retailed for a reasonably low one-thousand dollars.

A. J. shook his head. "You're kidding. This will never work. Who came up with it?"

McPherson stared at the drawing a few seconds and then glared at A. J. "Why not?" he asked sharply.

"Hell," A. J. said impatiently, "there isn't *near* enough room inside. Shit, Darren, a floppy disk drive won't fit above the CRT, not like you're showing. And where's space for memory cards, a computer board, and another power supply? You jest. I'm no nuts-and-bolts engineer either, but what about all the damn heat that'll be generated? And electromagnetic interference?"

McPherson studied the drawing a good five seconds. "Of course," he said finally, "this is my first cut."

"What'd you use, a chainsaw?"

"C'mon, A. J., it's not *that* bad."

"Why would I shit you, Darren? Do you plan to bolt the power supply transformer to the ceiling of the enclosure? The center of gravity will be so damn high a MaxWriter will belly-up every time a nearby door slams shut!"

A. J. saw in his mind an office full of desk-top MaxWriters flopping onto their backs whenever someone banged shut an office door, and he couldn't stifle a grin.

"Did you talk to any of our technicians?"

McPherson again studied the drawing. "Well, MacRae, it looks like we have a difference of opinion that neither of us is fully qualified to resolve. So here's my decision. We go with this – he nodded at the drawing – until I pipe my hardware man aboard. Can you live with that? For now?"

"Do I have a choice? What's our production schedule?"

"It partly depends on you, A. J. I'm not bringing in any managers, at least not until I've approved a full set of performance specs. No later than mid-January, though. That's consonant with a schedule Wickersham's come up with."

"Wickersham! Our *financial* guy is scheduling production milestones!"

"Well . . . it squares with our plan for when we go public."

McPherson looked at his watch.

A. J. ignored the hint. "Do you have managers in mind?"

"Yes I do," McPherson said. "Good ones . . . from Foster Systems." He thought a moment. "The software programmer's a gal. Face that'd stop a tidal wave but sharp as a razor. Think you'll have a problem with that, A. J.?"

"With which? The ugly or the femininity?"

McPherson grinned. "Either? Both?"

A. J. said that he could handle the ugly, but he wasn't sure about the gender thing.

McPherson's grin faded. "Then, you're okay with the schedule?"

Mid-January was six weeks away. Figuring that he could produce a comprehensive MaxWriter performance specification in a month, A. J. nodded.

"Super," McPherson said, his contentment softening his face. "Any more questions?"

A. J. shook his head.

"Okay then, back for a second to Jennerette. Uh, while Jesse's on sick leave" – he heaved a long, overburdened-manager sigh – "I'll put one of our technicians in charge. Under me, of course. Who do you recommend?"

A. J. snorted. "None of our guys. Have you ever looked closely at Jesse's female assemblers? Half are hog bikers with hairy hands, knuckles out, tattooed on their butts. The other half's on prison work-release. It won't matter who you pick, those women will make appetizers of his nuts the first day."

McPherson drew back. "I didn't know that our Production girls were so damn tough."

"Oh hell, Darren, I'm exaggerating. Besides, it's as much a case of sugar-assed men as pepper-assed women. Our techs would lose three out of three falls to a palsy teddy bear."

That afternoon McPherson promoted a heel-digging Selig Hildreth, the oldest of Edgecom's remaining three technicians, and the only one not routinely asked to show proof of his age to buy a hard drink, to the position of Assistant Manager of Manufacturing.

As soon as A. J. heard, he telephoned McPherson. "Hildreth!" he yelled in a disgruntled tone. "It won't work."

"What?"

"A commander with a name like *Selig Hildreth*?"

"Oh, why not?"

"Everybody who hears that name will think the Hildreth sits down to pee."

"So . . . ."

"Let's call him "Mace." He likes "Mace.""

"Mace," McPherson countered, "is an insect spray. I'm pretty sure.

"No, no. A mace is a club. Invented by Macedonians. I'm positive."

"I don't know, A. J."

"Well, think about it, Darren."

# [23]

A. J. returned from McPherson's "Conference," dropped apathetically into his office chair, and fantasized that he and Detective Deemer were writhing ecstatically on the cheap mattress of his apartment bed. Someone flushed a urinal in the men's room next door, and his zesty daydream abruptly segued into his labored talk at the police station.

Deemer agreed: Osgood was a load of crap. But a murderer? Questionable – as a minimum. For his part, A. J. could not say *exactly* how Osgood killed Fran. He had all but ruled out asphyxiation. Besides taking minutes during which anyone might pop into the room, the garroting itself would leave behind the tell-tale evidence of a struggle: Fran was small but he was not puny, and though still slightly anesthetized, A. J. was certain that he'd have stubbornly fought back.

The more A. J. hashed over the possibilities in his mind, the more often that death by poisoning squirmed to the top of his list. Fran's IV had a Y-site port for injecting medicine. It obviously would work just as well for a syringe of poison. Moreover, A. J. felt certain that injecting a highly toxic liquid directly into Fran's vein would be instantaneously lethal, would immediately crater the subject's nervous system. With ready access through an IV port, there would be no needle puncture, it would only take a few seconds to administer, and in seconds the poison would reach vital organs.

Of course there was the possibility of a violent reaction, the poison causing Fran's body to begin thrashing about like a tarpon habituating itself to the deck of a fishing boat. Or maybe turn his skin cyanic. In other words, the murderer – Osgood, A. J. was certain – needed to main-line a poison that would not automatically trigger an autopsy. So, A. J. reasoned, the murderer would choose a fast-acting, symptom-less, exotic poison. A. J. was thinking that the cunning SOB would have done his research when he remembered something, a recollection catalyzed by his qualifying the deadly poison as "exotic."

A. J. telephoned Nickerson, and they met in A. J.'s office. Nick entered and closed the door, sensing, apparently, that A. J. wanted their meeting to be private.

"What now?"Nick growled bearishly, backing into the chair in front of A. J.'s desk. "You want fixed up with Sandy? I'll arrange for a weekly luncheon. On second thought, Pop, *you* getting boffed once a week? You'd go broke buying support hose."

"God forbid," A. J. replied. "And if *you* were getting any poon," he added, "your pant's fly wouldn't always precede your belly into a room."

Nickerson ignored A. J.'s abbey-of-monks assessment of his sex life. "One time," he said, pretending his mind was elsewhere, "Father backed our manure spreader into Jake Federson's hay loader, and they went to fist city over it. I separated 'em."

"I know how he did it," A. J. said, ignoring Nick's crowing.

Nick shook his head and stood up. "Christ, MacRae, not another of your Archimedes moments, I hope."

"The son-of-a-bitch poisoned Fran."

Nick crossed his arms. "This better be good."

"Do you own a pet?"

"What . . . do you mean here, in Dallas?"

"Anywhere?"

"Back home, sure."

"What kind?"

"A dog – part Lab, Nick said, pretending to carefully explore the room. "If you've charted the meaning of life, A. J., you took the wrong turn at the Y."

A. J. glanced at the ceiling and then allowed his eyes to stabilize on Nick's face.

Nick shook his head. "No. An alligator. They're easier to house-break."

A. J. pounced on his answer. "Guess what, then. You and Osgood have a kindred liking of pets. His favorite is a snake, a cobra."

Nick leaned full back into his chair. "How do you know?"

"Frankly . . . . A while back I heard Pat telling Miki, and I stopped to listen. Osgood liked to watch–"

"You were simultaneously standing next to *both* Pat and Miki."

"No. *Between* both Pat and Miki."

"And you embarrassed yourself, right? I mean, made a show of your passion?"

"Pat was impressed," A. J. answered, nodding thoughtfully. "Miki was quietly astounded."

"She's either desperately lovelorn or near-sighted."

"Whatever. Osgood enjoyed watching his snake corner and eat mice."

"So?"

"So, the guy's weird. Anyone who–"

"Hell, A. J., one time back home a neighbor kid turned a ferret loose in a calf pen with a Leghorn pullet, and we all watched it corner and kill the . . . little bird."

"Yeah, and how old were you?"

Nick shrugged. "Old enough to make damn sure we didn't get caught."

"Osgood is fifty, and he still enjoys pulling the wings off insects. I'm telling you, he's a mucking sociopath."

Nick stood up. "Maybe. But . . . see if I've got it right, Pop. Osgood keeps a snake for a pet that he likes to watch eat mice. And he may have duped Jo Ellen out of her Edgecom stock so he could sell it and get rich when we go public? And . . . ergo, he murdered Fran! Did I miss any dots?"

A. J. sighed impatiently. "No, just the picture itself."

"Maybe," Nick said. "What did your detective friend think of your poisoning theory?"

"I didn't tell her. I haven't settled on it yet."

"So, you're sailing your weird idea past me just to see if it floats?"

"It floats. I just wanted to sail it into a head wind, to see how well it beat against hot air."

Nick, after a second of digesting A. J.'s remark, allowed that Edgecom's new owner was not someone he'd want for a next-door neighbor – that if he ever married, ever became a domesticated father, and Osgood settled near, he'd sure as hell vacate the neighborhood.

"You're a hard sell," A. J. told Nick as he was leaving. Nick did not react at all. Still, A. J. knew Nick well enough to understand that his quiet departure was evidence of a mind sorting through unsavory possibilities.

# [24]

Pat was not at her desk. Her chair was pushed under it, and the top was neat as a pin, except for a notebook apparently dropped off by someone. A. J. looked at his watch. It was nine fifteen. Certain that Pat and Osgood had worked late on Saturday aggregating into a booklet the half-dozen, differently authored sections of Edgecom's fabulous business plan, A. J. decided that Osgood had given her the day off.

A. J. checked with Miki Vernon, Edgecom's switchboard operator. (As did every Edgecom male employee, A. J. never passed up an opportunity to visit Neon Niki.)

Miki had not seen Pat. While she answered an incoming call, A. J. mouthed the words "telephone number." Miki pulled out her sliding desk shelf and pointed at the name Pat Brown.

A. J. walked to his office and called Pat's home: he had a serious question about Osgood's life style, and he figured that Pat, after her struggle with Osgood, would readily tell him her impression of his after-hours activities.

Pat's husband answered. A cement contractor, he was rarely home during the day, and A. J. mentally recorded that singularity. After reminding Mr. Brown who he was, A. J. said, "If Pat's got a moment, I'd like to talk to her. It's . . . kind of important."

His next words were muffled, but A. J. could faintly hear Brown say, probably in a direction away from the mouthpiece, that it was Alan from work.

"Just a minute," Pat's husband said into the telephone.

It was several seconds before Pat picked up.

A. J. offered to call her back.

"No," Pat said purposefully. "It's okay."

A. J. again heard whispering. Something was wrong. Had he interrupted a marital spat?

Pat came back on the line and answered my pointless question regarding her absence from Edgecom; afterward, she said, measuring her words, "that suck-egg dog . . . made a pass at me."

It took me a second to understand. "Osgood? Hit on you?"

"I had to fight him off, Alan. He's a pig . . . a damn pig."

"God, Pat, I don't know what to say. I never did trust the SOB. But . . . *this*. He's debauched. Did you go to the police?"

"No. We were alone . . . he'd have just denied it. Besides, *nothing* happened."

A. J. felt hopelessly confused. "Damn, there's got to be some way–"

Pat interrupted: "Believe me, Alan, given the chance of a butt-headed cow I'd have gone straight to the police. Tom wanted me to. He was fixin' to beat the . . . you-know-what out of Osgood"

Emotionally whipped, Pat's language had regressed to the agrarian Georgia dialect of her youth.

"I'll bet," A. J. said. "What–"

"I think Tom's cooled down." Pat's voice faded: apparently she had turned to look at her husband. "Anyway, I hope so."

A. J. said, "He . . . just out of the blue?" And he immediately berated himself for asking a suggestive question about the comity of Pat's and Osgood's friendliness.

Pat did not hesitate. "I never had an inkling. Oh, he asked me out to lunch . . . twice over the past month. I *always* turned him down. *Always* put him off. He just . . . I don't know. I'll never set foot in Edgecom again. Not while that . . . so and so is still around."

"God, who could blame you? Has he . . . hit on anyone else? That you know of?"

"Not that I've heard. I'm easy pickin's. We're often alone together – unavoidably."

"Yeah," A. J. said, shading his voice sympathetically. "It  goes with the territory."

"And, Alan, I'd be *very* appreciative if you, please, please, do *not* mention . . . what happened. To anyone. I'd get phone calls, and I don't . . . want to explain."

"I promise you Pat that I won't."

A. J. repeated his pledge not to rat out Osgood – in the process, excoriated the son-of-a-bitch – and was winding down when Pat interrupted to ask why he had called. The reason, A. J. said, was unimportant.

Pat insisted that A. J. explain.

A. J. thought briefly of relating his theory of how Hummel Osgood – now a would-be rapist, at the very least – had murdered Fran, of verbally weaving the threads of his theory into a stark tapestry replete with skewed plaits and knotty snarls. It was still a moonscape, A. J. reminded himself, of murky shadows and sometimes unclear outlines. So instead he fudged it, took the angle that Osgood was obviously psychotic and should be permanently shackled to an un-flushed commode in a padded room.

"Well . . . ," A. J. answered, "remember Jo Ellen telling you how Betty got all bent out of shape over Hummel keeping a pet snake in his home? How it one time got loose?"

Pat shuddered audibly. "How could I forget? He fed it live mice."

"And probably enjoyed watching the snake dine," A. J. said. "What an ass. He's depraved, Pat."

"He's . . . something."

"Yeah. Off-hand Pat, do you remember what kind of snake it was?"

"No . . . I heard tell . . . it was big, though. I think . . . no wait, it was a cobra. You know, one of those snakes with wide heads that . . . come out of a wicker basket while some little brown man sitting cross-legged in a diaper plays a flute. In . . . India. Or, somewhere in Asia."

"A cobra!" A. J. barked. "He *is* nuts, Pat. Cobra snakes are deadly poisonous. They *can't* be legal for individuals to own. Not even in Texas."

She said, "I don't know, but I'm *sure* it was a cobra. And I'm sure you're right, Alan. Uh, do you mind? Why is it important that you know the kind of snake it was?"

A. J. did not want to go there. "Oh, I'm just . . . building a personal tickler file . . . of sorts."

Having said that, he instantly wondered what in the hell he meant. "I'm god-awful sorry to hear of your . . . experience. I'll miss you, Pat. We'll all miss you. Enormously."

"I'll miss you, too, Alan. Everyone. The whole gang." She sighed. "What am I going to tell people . . . why it was I all of the sudden up-and-quit?"

"I don't . . . know. You can bet that Osgood will make up some crap. He'll snow Jo Ellen. And bamboozle everyone, everybody but you and me. He's first-fiddle at . . . BS-ing people."

Pat sounded weary. "I'm afraid so. I love Jo Ellen, but she is not too . . . perceptive. Do you think he'll even bring it up? I doubt it."

"I'll sure press him for why in hell you upped and quit out of the blue. Like I said, he'll back away BS-ing each step that he takes. I'll . . . hold his feet to the fire."

"I'd like to hear, Alan."

"You will, I promise."

A. J. asked to speak to Tom, her husband. He came on the line, and A. J. offered to help. Pat's husband said he'd let A. J. know of any new developments. He'd best not, A. J. hinted, take matters into his own hands. Tom politely told A. J. to kiss off, and said that he had to get back to work.

A. J. spent an hour that evening in the spare bedroom of his furnished apartment, in his make-do home office, reviewing his case against Osgood. It was improving. Was it good enough to call on Detective Deemer again? A. J. thought so. Osgood had attacked a woman. Deemer would empathize.

# [25]

A. J. telephoned Nick to arrange for a time when he could visit and pick his brain about a knotty technical point that had to be covered in his booklet explaining a phase of the abstruse electronic happenings that go on inside a computer floppy disk drive. Nick did not answer, and A. J. had barely cradled the handset when his phone rang. It was Detective Deemer. A. J. thanked her for returning his call.

"I've got more on Osgood," A. J. said, "and I'm hoping you–"

"On *who*?" Deemer interrupted sharply.

"The guy who murdered the founder of Edgecom Data Company . . . at Medical City Hospital . . . he was–"

"I remember," Deemer said, adding, "*allegedly* murdered Mister . . . what's-his-name."

"Peter Francis Degeorge. I'd very much like to come by again."

She did not reply.

"I've got more evidence. And besides–"

"Just a minute," Deemer said, and after a few seconds: "Go on."

"And besides, I owe you."

"Owe me?" she said, her voice soft but clear and firm. "For what?"

A. J. explained, submitted that during his last visit he had wasted her time. "I owe you for . . . your endurance in hearing me out, if nothing else."

Deemer scoffed gustily. "I deal everyday with deadbeats!"

While A. J. was trying to think of a snappy reply, Deemer said impatiently to come by the station that afternoon. "Call first," she said.

A male sergeant, not the man of A. J.'s first visit, was working the station counter. A. J. told him his name and said that he had an appointment with Detective Deemer. He sized A. J. up, unhesitatingly decided that I was not fit for a fellowship in the brotherhood of crime-busters or of any fraternity of the rugged he-man types of which he himself was plainly a long-established member. The appraisal took the sergeant a couple of seconds; he jerked his thumb toward the door behind his post.

Detective Deemer, sitting at her desk, was dressed in a striped, purple-and-white, body-hugging, boat-neck jersey and a narrow, restrictive skirt that was two or three shades of purple deeper than the purple bands of her blouse. She was not wearing jewelry, not even earrings. A. J. noticed that bauble deficiency because twice a year, on average, he had to turn his car around half-way from home and rush Allison back for a fancy blouse pin or other decorative jewelry.

The wall-mounted blackboard was still filled to overflowing with briefs of ongoing criminal activity. To A. J., they seemed to be exactly the same ellipses as the briefs of his first visit.

Deemer nodded at the chair where A. J. had argued his case four days earlier. A. J. opened the manila folder that he had brought along, and he laid ten or so sheets of paper on Detective Deemer's desk.

"All financial reports," A. J. said, taking the chair, "of one measure or another. Osgood is messing with Edgecom's books." (A. J. didn't have the guts to say "dicking" with Edgecom's books, the word Deemer had used during his previous visit.) "They're my hole cards, but not my whole hand. I was dealt another ace. A joker, maybe."

Deemer eyed the top report and nodded.

"Those," A. J. said, gesturing at the sheets, "are indisputable facts. Osgood has misrepresented–"

"They're the *what*?" Deemer interrupted irritably.

A. J. had showed his butt again. "Okay, okay," he said hurriedly. "Let me back up. One, Francis Degeorge, the founder of Edgecom Data Company, a thirty-six-year-old human dynamo, known to have a strong heart, died unexpectedly one day after by-pass surgery."

Deemer's tone was skeptical: "He had told you that his heart was sound. I remember."

"Exactly," A. J. said. "His doctor had assured him that it–"

"Go on."

"Ah, two, Hummel Osgood, Edgecom's new *owner*, the person who killed Degeorge . . . of that I am sure, was the last person with him before he died."

"He's the man that you suspect killed Degeorge?"

"*Strongly* suspect," A. J. said, nodding vigorously.

Deemer glanced away but graciously did not roll her eyes.

"Three, I can prove that Osgood and his accounting buddy are cooking Edgecom's books"– A. J. lightly tapped the second sheet with his right index finger – "because he wants to make Edgecom appear financially robust so he can take Edgecom public and become a multi-millionaire in the offering – a lot of motive. You said so yourself."

Deemer turned up the top of the first sheet. "Where'd you get these?"

"The second set is from the woman who *used* to keep Edgecom's books . . . before Hummel Osgood canned her. She ran Bookkeeping. I knew her well, and I'm *sure* they're authentic."

Deemer seemed to be studying A. J. more than listening to his argument. "I assume," she said, her eyes firmly on his, "that the, what? Bottom lines don't square. Her's and . . . this other guy's? Anyway, I'll take your word for it."

"Yes, but–"

"Didn't we go over all this before?" She fingered my small treasure trove of reports. "You said you had new evidence?"

"Only . . . it was more like hearsay stuff then. Now it's . . . concrete, totally factual." A. J. pressed his lips into a tight, hermetic seal and nodded. "But I do have new evidence of that bastard's slimy character."

Deemer sighed, resigned to endure more of A. J.'s "evidence."

"Saturday, at work, he tried to . . . rape his secretary."

"Tried to?"

A. J.'s eyes narrowed and he reflexively nodded. "Tried to force her to . . . go down . . . you know . . . what I mean. She fought him off."

Deemer looked intensely at the other man in the room. He was obviously a fellow detective but not the same one who was present A. J.'s first visit. "Did she report it?" Her eyes remained fast on the other detective.

"No. She and Osgood were alone, working overtime. And there were no witnesses. Not when he–"

Deemer, nodding thoughtfully, called to the detective who was sitting at the desk situated catty-corner from her own. "Merle, would you mind?"

After a couple seconds, Merle sauntered toward Deemer; A. J., pulled a chair alongside her, turned it backward, and sat with his legs astraddle the chair's back rest.

"This is Mister MacRae," Deemer said.

Merle nodded slightly, and Deemer told A. J. to take it from the top.

A. J. explained how Degeorge not only loathed Osgood but also believed there was something seriously crooked in his past, which, A. J. added, Detective Deemer said she could look into. A. J. spelled out how Osgood had replaced Martha just one day after he took over Edgecom and how Herbert Wickersham, Osgood's collusive pal, had floated a cover story charging Martha with embezzlement. (A. J decided not to mention Martha's apparent suicide; it would not matter, he told himself.)

A. J. compared, side-by-side, the difference between Martha's and Wickersham's Edgecom operating statements, and he offered Irickson's theory as to how Osgood could falsely embellish sales to where Edgecom's bottom line would be written in black ink, not in an honest blood-red color.

A. J. told of getting screwed over the paternity of MaxWriter but was coaxed back for a boost in pay and an offer of Edgecom stock, which gestures, A. J. eventually came to realize, he admitted, were nothing more than bribes to shut him up about Edgecom's true financial situation.

A. J. said Osgood got off on feeding live mice to a pet cobra that he kept in a wire and glass cage in the den of his home.

A. J. said he tried to force his secretary to perform oral sex on him.

Merle nodded at each of A. J.'s accusations, but in the end, as Deemer had done earlier, he focused only on A. J.'s mention of Osgood's attack on Pat. "Did she report the attack?"

"No, she did not." A. J. added, that he was certain that Pat would confirm it "off the record."

The detective shook his head. "It's like friendly fire, when your own–"

Deemer interrupted him. "What do you think, Merle?'

"About this case? Hell, not even dicey. You might prove this Osgood guy's a fuckin' crook. Or he favors blow jobs." He shrugged. "Not our problem."

Merle returned to his desk, leaving the chair where he had moved it.

Deemer, after watching him leave, said to A. J. offhandedly, "You liked Degeorge, didn't you?"

"Very much." A. J. answered, turning away. "We were close. He was a damn good man.

"Well," Deemer said after a little while, "I don't know. I suppose you think Osgood milked his pet snake for the poison?"

"I've done a little research, A. J. said, "and . . . I think cobra venom would have worked. It's a very deadly toxin."

Detective Deemer said, more to herself than to A. J. "I might ask Osgood to come in on his own. Maybe I could get a court order, but not on what I've heard so far."

A. J. was beginning to feel better.

"Stay tuned Mister MacRae," she said after another long pause. She pushed away from her desk. "I have your telephone number."

A. J. gathered his paperwork. "If I can't buy you a Coke, how can I prove I'm not just another nut case?"

Her smile was tiny. "Wow. A whole eight ounces of soda pop?"

"Okay then," A. J. said, tilting his head back slightly, "Dinner tonight."

After a long moment, Detective Deemer said, "Not tonight. I'm at Central Booking."

"Tomorrow?"

"Make it Thursday."

"Six thirty?"

"Umm, not before."

Deemer pulled a business card from her middle desk drawer, handed it to A. J. and said to call her late in the morning on Thursday.

"Alan, but I go by A. J."

"Lennie," Lennie said, her focus back on the folder of reports.

A. J., to this day, is still unsure of the reason why Lennie agreed to date him.

Pretty young women walking past A. J. didn't exactly avert their eyes. But walking by a taller, handsomer man the same women would all but break into a hip-thrusting tango. A. J. had a paunch, growing, but not yet a basketball sphere; his hair, a tad curly and shaggy when he was a campusnik, had both thinned and receded to the balding International Date Line; and his face was so plain he could have robbed banks, unmasked, and never been picked out of a police line-up by the accosted teller. In heels, Lennie was his height, five eight. She knew A. J. was from Highland Park, hometown of the high-caste Brahmins of northern Texas, and she had likely watched him leave the precinct station in his Sedan de Ville his first visit. Regarding his insight into the thinking of women, A. J. rowed with one oar – and typically cork-screwed his way deep into the muddy bottom of that unfathomable lake of mental tides and psychic currents. "At least," he kidded himself, "she never got a chance to point and giggle."

# [26]

A. J. ate lunch with Jack Irickson the day after his
second visit to the police station, the visit where he had
again tried to talk Detective Deemer into taking up his
case against Osgood. Irickson installed and serviced all
of Edgecom's accounting needs until he was booted
from that job by Osgood. Jack and A. J. had been
meeting at the Chop House restaurant in Richardson
every other Wednesday since the week after Jack was
canned. It was A. J.'s turn to treat, so he jokingly
insisted that that obligation entitled him to draw more
heavily than usual on Irickson's accounting expertise.
Irickson glanced at his watch and pretended to write a
starting time on his napkin.

"Monday," A. J. began, his manner serious, his
eyes intently on Irickson's, "we got a visit from
Wallace Hardeman, son of the late Pop Hardeman,
Pop's only child. By any chance do you know Wallace
Hardeman?"

Irickson drew up his shoulders. "I've heard of . . .
Pop Hardeman. But no, I've never met his boy."

"Pop Hardeman," A. J. said, "got stinking rich selling supplies and services to the Texas petroleum industry. In fact, he sewed up the big East Texas find in the thirties. I met him at our home while I was still in grade school. Or, high school, maybe. Daddy was looking to raise money for the Republican Party, which was plumping a candidate for a national office."

"A noble endeavor, that," Irickson said gustily. "Go, Ronny!"

A. J. nodded affably but unenthusiastically: A. J. and his father separated, with no explicit farewells, at the political fork in the road: A. J. shambled down the leftward, liberal path; his father unrelentingly marched the ever-right-turning conservative road.

"Pop Hardeman," A. J. continued, "died in 1977 . . . I believe it was seventy seven . . . and evidently he left everything to his wife and only child. Anyway, his only child, Wallace Hardeman, visited Edgecom on Monday with his son, Pop Hardeman's grandson."

Irickson nodded. "Pop Hardeman's son and grandson paid Edgecom a visit on Monday."

"Uh-huh. They go by Roman numerals two and three."

"They're Texans?" Irickson asked grinning skeptically.

I shrugged at the implication of his question. "Wickersham escorted them into Osgood's office. Jack, I'm telling you, the office bullpen was a gymnasium of organized, non-stop activity."

190

The waitress brought their drinks and took orders for steak sandwiches, their usual choices.

"Appearances count," Irickson said after the waitress had left, referring to A. J.'s remark about Edgecom's office force simulating extreme busyness.

"No doubt," A. J. said agreeably. "Anyway, they left Osgood's office and toured the plant. Hummel was so damn airy-fairy his feet only touched the floor often enough to propel him along. Wickersham followed behind the grandkid, who had a copy of my booklet on disk drive systems rolled up in his hand. His daddy . . . ."

The waitress transferred salad plate dishes to our table from a nearby folding support stand. We thanked her, and Jack said, "Again, I'd like to see a copy of your booklet."

A. J. nodded, "I meant to get you one. I will."

"Thanks. Go on. I interrupted you."

"It doesn't matter. I was just going to say that what Osgood's senior guest found far and away most interesting was not Edgecom itself, but Miki Vernon, Neon Niki. She was perched at Pat Brown's old desk pretending to be Osgood's secretary."

"Oh, yes," Irickson said brightly. "I remember. Neon Niki. Peasant blouses and a lolly-pop ass."

"Uh, Jack, you're drooling."

"Oh? *You* can smack your lips without drooling?"

A. J. contrived a chuckle. "One of Jesse's assemblers was manning the telephone switchboard – pretending to, anyway."

Irickson shrugged.

"Hardeman and his kid came back again yesterday. So . . . what do you make of it, Jack?"

Irickson whisked a corner of his mouth with his napkin. "That's easy. Osgood needs cash to take Edgecom public; Hardeman's on the make and he obviously thinks Osgood's not tooling up to sell this year's Edsels."

Neither man heard the waitress arrive. "Okay?" she asked pleasantly, reaching to remove our empty drink glasses. A. J. and Jack each nodded and re-ordered drinks.

"So," A. J. said, "you think Hardeman wants to buy in?"

"He returned, didn't he?"

"He and his kid. Uh, how badly . . . do you think?"

"How big a wad will he ante-up for a few stacks of game chips?"

"Uh-huh."

Irickson did not hesitate. "Three hundred K."

A. J. leaned forward in his chair. "Really? Three-hundred-thousand bucks? For *what*? A dozen old worn-out banquet tables? Everything else is leased."

A. J.'s ignorance disappointed Irickson. He peered down narrowly and shook his head. "First, A. J., three hundred thousand dollars is pocket change to

Hardeman. Second, he's investing in a promise not in . . . furniture."

A. J. nodded.

"And just as important, Osgood lusts for the name *Hardeman* on the Edgecom owner list. It would suck more rich investors in. Hardeman could probably buy into Edgecom for thousands of dollars, not hundreds of thousands. If he wanted. And he very well might. Of course, the more he invests the more he expects to get back – up to a point – when Edgecom goes public."

"Really?" A. J. said. "Buy in for a *promise*? Quantified by shares of Edgecom stock?

"Exactly. That's the whole nine yards."

A. J. cut off a piece of his steak, forked it up from the plate, and gave it an admiring look. "In any case," he said, "it's a roll of the dice."

"Sure," Irickson said, "all around. Osgood's planning an IPO. Like we talked about weeks back. Hell, some IPOs are strictly crap shoots . . . most, maybe."

"Only," A. J. said, "Hardeman won't know that Osgood has loaded the dice."

"No . . . but he could find out." Jack thought for a moment. "But chances are he won't even glance at the books. Not for a mere three-hundred grand. Let me clue you in on something else, A. J., he'd rather *not* see Edgecom's books."

"How's that? I mean, why not?"

"Because knowing Edgecom's true financial state might bite him in the ass on down the road."

"But . . . Hardeman'll want to know the real financial condition of Edgecom. Won't he?"

"The *real* financial condition of Edgecom, A. J., as far as Hardeman's concerned, as far as a public offering goes, will be whatever your new vice president of finance says it is. What's his name? Wickersham? For now, let's just say Hardeman's lackadaisical when it comes to managing his investments."

"Then it's a lot Wickersham's call?" A. J. said.

"Not his call, exactly, but his . . . brisk stirring of the pot. Assuming," Jack said, nodding slowly, "the books really have been cooked. And I'll bet my pair that you're right about that."

A. J. nodded. "And they'll stay attached. When you said Hardeman was protecting his ass for down the road, you meant if it comes to it, so he can plead innocent of . . . what? Of any bookkeeping irregularities that he knew of?"

"Exactly, A. J. *He* wouldn't be complicit."

"Man, I'm getting in way over my head," A. J. said.

Irickson smiled. "Oh hell, just think of it as a fake diamond scam. Cubic zirconium wedding gems instead of worthless scraps of paper."

"Whatever," A. J. said. "How much of Edgecom does Hardeman end up owning?"

Irickson shrugged. "Fifty per cent, half the voting shares. More if he can get it. I don't think he'd take less. It depends on where he and Osgood strike a bargain. If I recall correctly . . . Edgecom's articles of incorporation allow for issuance of a hundred thousand shares of Common."

"Common being . . . .?"

"Voting shares of stock. Primarily. I'd guess that Osgood personally holds upwards of eighty-thousand shares. Of course at some point they'll split it. Ten for one – or better."

"*They* will split it?"

"Edgecom's board of directors."

"The board can do that?"

"Split the stock? Sure, it's their company. It's all procedural. Minimal SEC supervision. Remember, A. J., Edgecom's privately owned."

"Hell," A. J. said. "I doubt if Edgecom even has a board of directors."

"It does," Irickson said nodding assertively. "Edgecom is a Texas corporation, so legally there has to be one. Probably Osgood and Jo Ellen are the only ones on it. I'd bet she's president and he's secretary. Not that titles mean a damn."

A. J. returned to his point about Edgecom's dearth of assets of any measurable value. "Hardeman's buying into a dream, isn't he?"

After a few seconds of hesitation, Jack said, "Well . . . not entirely. Edgecom, after all, is a going concern . .

. wobbly, but with a first-rate technical staff and all operating structures in place. And then there's the promise of MaxWriter. By the way, what's your take on MaxWriter?"

"Hell, I tried for a year to convince Fran to tool up and make a low-end word-processing machine."

"Well," Irickson said, shrugging as if A. J.'s answer cut right to the nut-cracking issue itself, "there you go."

"Under McPherson," A. J. said, "it's a damn long shot. Of course, Hardeman wouldn't know that."

"I don't know McPherson."

"Don't go out of your way. Unless you enjoy elevator music."

"Oh, I do. Where's MaxWriter at? I mean–"

"How far along? We have a mockup, a shell. Some modeler named Egli. Did a hell of a nice job on a fake casing. There's nothing on the drawing board for its guts, for its electronics. Or for software. Osgood showed Hardeman and his kid the mockup. He had me there to field questions. The boy's sharp, but–"

"Wallace junior?"

"Roman numeral number three."

"How old is he?"

"Late twenties. He's quiet, but his father's full of himself. His father went ballistic when he found out that MaxWriter's fifteen-hundred-dollar price tag did not include a printer. Like he had a clue."

"The printer is extra?"

"Yeah. Over a thousand bucks. For a good one . . . with IBM-type letters. I mean, not dot-matrix characters. Hardeman's boy saved Osgood's ass, argued that one printer could support a half-dozen MaxWriters."

Earlier another point had bothered A. J. "Osgood can't go public and develop MaxWriter on three-hundred thousand bucks. No way. Hell, the engineering for MaxWriter alone will run that much, even stealing most of the design. Which *will* happen."

Irickson's head jerked slightly at A. J.'s mention of Edgecom's certain involvement in a practice that A. J. knew first-hand was commonplace inter-business industrial thievery.

A. J. explained: "We'll reverse-engineer a system or two, double down on the best designs of whatever competition is out there. SOP at Edgecom."

Irickson, after a pause, nodded. "You can bet your tail Wickersham's worked out the numbers, the extra thousands he'll need to cover . . . tooling and so on. Osgood will have to scam a good dozen investors. Go for, say, forty- or fifty-thousand a crack. If Hardeman signs on, he'll have it made."

"Make Hardeman his bell cow?" A. J. said.

Jack confirmed that there were no other diners near: "I think you just fucked up a metaphor, A. J., but, yeah, get Hardeman to lead the charge, to be his Pied Piper for fifing in private investors."

A. J. nodded, and for a minute both men silently surveyed the dining room evaluating the two-, three-, and four-customer tables typically set off by feminine pulchritude, which had evolved while they were chatting.

A. J. broke the silence. "Osgood could lose control. Couldn't he?"

"Of Edgecom? Naw. Only in theory. And once Hardeman buys in, they'll only offer preferred stock, and it . . . he'll make damn sure that the shares don't include voting rights."

"It's up to the owners?"

"Again, A. J., Edgecom isn't a public corporation, so—"

"So owners can do just about whatever they want?"

"Damn near. What I'd do is amend the articles, allow issuance of, oh say, three hundred thousand shares of non-voting preferred at five bucks a share. Most investors, especially the kind interested in a private offering . . . all they want is to sign in, make a fast buck, sign out, and move on. They don't give a rat's ass about future business. About immediate operations? Yes. But not long term."

"Damn, Jack, how come you know so much about this going-public gig?"

"You've heard of Clayton Foods?"

"Uh-huh. Haemer money, originally."

"I was employed by Bose, Merrick, and Young, when Clayton Foods went public; I was the BMY associate account manager."

They finished their sandwiches and drained their drinks. A. J. signaled the waitress for their bill.

"Um . . ." A. J. began hesitantly, "if I looked into reporting Osgood to the police . . . or whoever. Would you back me?"

"Me?" Jack said, scowling. "Are you nuts?"

"Your turn," A. J. said, pushing the bill his way.

# [27]

Driving back to Edgecom, his mental energy stoked by Chop House wine, A. J. mulled over Jack's explanation of the ultimate reason for Hardeman's visit to Edgecom. Essentially, by Jack's reasoning, Hardeman would chance losing what for him was pocket change before shooting a come-out roll months later in the IPO. In a nutshell, that is how Irickson assessed Hardeman's financial bet on Edgecom. As it turned out, Hardeman also liked to jiggle around a certain young, shapely Edgecom employee whom he easily slipped into his watch pocket.

Miki, as A. J. entered Edgecom, handed him two messages. Both missives, A. J. could tell from the dour look on her face, were bad news. The first instructed A. J. to call Dolly, Jesse's wife. That call was the most disheartening.

A. J. was consulting and irregularly visiting Edgecom. Jesse, since learning that he had cancer, was sporadically working half days. A. J. saw him briefly maybe three times at the plant. Jesse's attitude was positive, and he was seemingly unburdened by worry.

When A. J. called Dolly, she said the doctors could not medically treat her husband's cancer not even into remission; they had changed drugs again. She said spots were beginning to appear on his other organs.

"You know," she went on, "how Jesse thinks he's so darn tough. He should have seen a doctor weeks ago. He wouldn't listen to me. I'm . . . worried, A. J."

A. J. did not know Dolly very well, but he figured if a person's appearance counted for anything, she was as tough in her own way as was Jesse in his way. A. J. remembered thinking, *Fran and now Jesse. What the hell is going on?* Dolly, between pauses – cloaking sobs A. J. could tell – said she'd call him back.

Being a Doubting Thomas of the irreligious type, A. J. could not bring himself to tell her that Jesse would "be in his prayers," and his attempt to commiserate was pitifully inadequate: "Everyday, doctors are getting a better handle on . . . that damn disease, coming up with effective new treatments . . . . Don't give up, Dolly. Ever."

A. J. waited, but she did not reply.

The phone rang while A. J. was reading the opening line of his second message. Coincidentally, it was Allison calling. Had he received the latest correspondence from the attorney who was counseling her in their divorce proceedings? A. J. told her that indeed he had, and, furthermore, that his attorney had prepared a reply. Then, basically replaying her last phone call, Allison asked A. J. for money. Only this time she wanted a bundle: two thousand dollars. A. J. exploded, told her he was paying for every shittin' thing but her stupid telephone. He gratuitously reminded her that she was making pretty good money herself.

Allison said that he could either come up with two thousand dollars now or much more while he was celebrating grandfather-hood. It took A. J. a second to understand. Feeling every possible dark emotion but no surprise at hearing that their fifteen-year-old daughter was pregnant A. J. said snappishly, "Does she *know* who the father is?"

"She won't say."

"Won't say or doesn't know?

"What difference does–"

"Some nigger kid I suppose."

A. J. never used the word nigger, and he still does not, but Allison was a promenading, belly-to-the-rampart, bandana-wearing liberal, and A. J. was really pissed. He could imagine Allison blanching at his words. She said that a mixed coupling was thinkable, that Danielle's impregnation by a black kid was more than just minimally possible.

A. J. said he was coming by, and Allison said to stay the hell away because he'd run Danielle off. A. J. sharply reminded her that Danielle was his daughter too, the house was still as much his as hers, and he would visit whenever he damn well pleased. Allison said her scheduled student advisee had arrived, that she was through arguing, and if she did not receive the money by Tuesday, Danielle would become a mother at fifteen. A. J.'s protest fell on a dead line, and he slammed down the telephone.

Five minutes hadn't passed before Hardeman's son, dressed in tasseled loafers, dark slacks, and a front-buttoning yellow cardigan sweater, complimented by a reddish-brown shirt – ochre, A. J. supposed Allison would have called it – strolled into A. J.'s office. Still fretting over Allison's call, A. J. was offhandedly sorting through photographs that he had rounded up for a slide show, one that Osgood had assigned him to produce. It would be the entree of a buffet of tasty comestibles that Osgood was arranging for his sales pitch to Hardeman's moneyed acquaintances. A. J. was less than overjoyed at young Hardeman's interruption.

Offering his hand, Hardeman's boy said he was Wallace Hardeman the "turd." A. J. cooled down: a very rich kid who could poke fun at the decorous representation of his lineal family standing was someone he might come to like. A. J. stood, accepted his visitor's outstretched hand, and then nodded at the chair in front of his desk. Young Hardeman shook his head, said he would not be that long.

The first time A. J. saw Hardeman III, only two days earlier, he did not for a second imagine the gangly, pasty-faced lad now standing in front of him was the son of Osgood's stocky, square-jawed, thick-featured senior guest.

Hardeman III sensed A. J.'s bemusement. "I really am a Hardeman," he said, nodding good-humoredly.

A. J. pretended not to understand and sat back down. "What's on your mind? Do you go by Wallace or by Walter? Or by . . . what?"

"No. By Skip. For as long as I can remember. Umm, I never did get your name."

"Sometimes," A. J. said, shaking his head, "I forget and leave my manners at home. I'm Alan MacRae. But, I go by A. J."

"And the J stands for?"

"For nothing. It's a null initial."

"Ah. A true southern blue-blood. Been with Edgecom long?"

"All told, four years. And a few months."

"All told?"

"I was a consultant and then an employee. Now I'm consulting again."

"You're what? An engineer?"

A. J. grinned tightly. "On paper. I quit engineering eight years ago."

Skip slightly cocked his head. "Business Administration, Stephen F. Austin. I considered Engineering, but . . . ." Pointing at my computer, a hodge-podge of semi-encased, this-and-that printed-circuit cards connected together for me by Degeorge, he grimaced and said, "I have an Imsai Eighty Eighty. What in the hell is *that*?"

A. J. sniggered. "It's not fancy. But it works. Just don't breath hard on it."

"Okay," Skip said, pretending to tip back, "What, ah, then what ah, *do* you do here, A. J.?"

"Right now I'm writing the MaxWriter performance specifications . . . and working on a slide show for Osgood's dog-and-pony. He wants to rehearse a week from today. I guess you know?"

"Your background is engineering, but you're producing a slide show? Sort of a casserole of navy beans and jelly beans, isn't it?"

A. J. shrugged. "Yeah . . . but I've been in advertising seven years, almost eight. I handled industrial accounts for Brewster Simon Advertising before I signed on here. I've done all of Edgecom's magazine ads. All our fliers. And . . . so on. Fran excelled at critiquing advertising, but he hated writing it."

"Who's doing our magazine ads now?"

A. J. shrugged. "Not me."

"I'll find out," Skip said, after a moment of concern. "What's your opinion of McPherson?"

The question, abrupt and personal, threw A. J. "How do you mean?" he replied cautiously.

"As an engineer." Skip said. "As our MaxWriter project manager."

"I hardly know him. I've never seen him slugging it out over cosines and algorithms. Osgood, though, would have you believe he's the reincarnation of Isaac Newton."

Skip's face continued to register concern. "Did you say the second coming of Wayne Newton?"

A. J. could not hold back a grin. "No. You said Wayne, I said Isaac."

Inferring, apparently, that he and A. J. had synched regarding Darren McPherson's shortfall of inborn ability, Skip sallied forth again. "Osgood's a gas bag, isn't he?"

Buoyed by his put-down of McPherson, A. J. did not hesitate. "Mostly."

Skip smiled. "Who's writing MaxWriter's software?"

"McPherson has an outside person in mind. Some gal from Foster Systems."

Hearing that Edgecom's as-yet un-hired MaxWriter programmer would be a female, Skip's worried look faded. Offering his hand, he said he'd be seeing A. J.

Skip did not visit for long on that first day of acquainting himself to A. J., noticing, A. J. had hoped, that he, A. J., wanted to work on the dog-and-pony show, his new top-priority assignment. Moreover, anxious to begin, A. J. was not interested in hearing more of Skip's bio – or for that matter of his life *style* – particularly after he told A. J. that he had asked Sel to drill a peephole in the back wall of the women's restroom.

He had truly wanted a hole drilled, Sel told A. J. later that day: "Skip," he added, shrugging at A. J.'s unease, "didn't seem to be kidding."

# [28]

Lennie's apartment was situated a scant three blocks from Edgecom's former retail site on Proctor Street in Garland, Texas. A corner, three-room unit, it was not rooted in a better part of Garland, a city far different in every way from a Mediterranean principality.

A. J. all but crapped at seeing her outfit: a jacket-like, gabardine blouse was loose-fitting and at least a size too large; a skirt, that, on the other hand, was skin tight. A. J. greeted her pleasantly, while thinking, *"We'll eat at a fast-food joint, watch a movie, and then I'll take her straight home."*

She said her favorite evening repast was Tex-Mex food. The possibility of dining at a Taco Bell flashed through A. J.'s mind, accompanied, at once, by the notion that they could eat their food orders in his car.

Tex-Mex was also A. J.'s favorite once-a-week cuisine. In Dallas, there used to be (and I presume there still are) nearly as many Mexican restaurants as there were corner gas stations. A. J.'s favorite, La Cabana, served huge, fluffy chili rellenos – to A. J.'s way of thinking the preeminent Mexican dinner entree – and La Cabana's tequila-loaded margaritas were served in goblets so big that a woman had to use both hands to heft one to her lips. Abstinence had nuclear powered A. J.'s sex drive, and his thinking went: after a couple margaritas, we'd both be half snockered and either grappling naked in his apartment bedroom or her's. And the hell with her attire.

They arrived at seven o'clock at the La Cabana restaurant. The traffic had thinned, and their drive only took ten minutes. After a margarita apiece and full meals, A. J. drove a mile to a Harvey Motel, a popular Dallas watering hole with a small dance floor and a four-piece, part-time house band that played western swing music.

On this evening, printed on a placard taped to a tripod standing left of the center of a make-do stage, were the words: SIXTIES REDUX!

By ten o'clock, further primed with the motel's Harvey Wallbangers, they were dancing – she was dancing, A. J. was flopping around – to popular sixty's era music. In particular, A. J. remember the song *"Do you want to dance?"* because, after the first few notes, Lennie murmured, "The Beach Boys."

"Your favorite version?" A. J. asked, hoping that his remark, if nothing else, made sense.

Lennie shrugged. "That and a . . . slower one by Bette Midler."

Deciding to leave well-enough alone, A. J. hurriedly changed the subject.

Still, while they were dancing, A. J. learned, two things: one, that Lennie's firm, well-turned legs were not formed of muscle sculpted from water skiing: they were finely turned by hips swinging left and right and in and out to fast, pulsing music, and, two, that her loose blouse camouflaged a small revolver, a weapon that she was enjoined by a City of Dallas Police directive to carry at all times while meandering around Dallas County.

The band broke for "ten." They returned to their table, finished their drinks, and A. J. ordered another round.

"Why not?" A. J. asked, looking at Lennie helplessly, '*Come on baby, light my fire,*' at least I could have kept up."

"I'll bet," she said. "And maybe even jived with a high-school band's performance of *God Bless America.*" Lennie's smirk leavened into a good-natured smile.

A. J. asked Lennie if she worked out. She nodded functionally, and, A. J. told her that he used to, which was kind of true. They had all but finished their drinks when the band returned, and they began dancing to another upbeat 1960s song. Lennie slipped her hand inside A. J.'s unbuttoned blazer, worked it into a rear pocket of his pants, and pushed his buttock hard against her groin. Leaning back, which pulled them even tighter together, she looked A. J. in the eyes and smiled.

"Damn it, Dear," A. J. murmured, "you're killing me. Let's get a room."

Lennie dissented. "How far is your place from here?"

"Not that far," A. J. said. "I'll show you my macramés."

There were no awkward moments at his apartment: A. J. wasn't drunk but still he was too bagged to feel selfconscious about their first sex. No matter its choreography, Lennie was not the least bit selfconscious about undressing and making love. A. J. did not open the bed, that is, he did not throw back the overspread.

After the briefest of foreplay, A. J. leaned away from the bed and opened the drawer of his nightstand. "Don't bother," Lennie said dryly. "It won't happen."

A. J. fell back, rolled up, and shortly Lennie was guiding him into her. It came to A. J.'s mind that his Ex – or soon to be Ex – would as likely wrap her fingers around the shank of a fresh dog turd as curl her digits around his member. The thought didn't last.

"Move off!" Lennie ordered, poking A. J.'s side.

A. J rolled away. Lennie found his hand and placed it on the cleavage of her vagina. Whispering as if silence had suddenly become important, she said, "Middle finger, A. J.

"My clit."

"Up."

The word clit meant nothing to A. J., but long-delayed enthusiasm, unintentional or not, helped to camouflage his ignorance.

Pushing A. J. back, Lennie curled her hand around his penis and began rapidly stroking. "Okay?" she murmured – approximately.

"Uh-huh," A. J. said, "but . . . it's . . . been months . . . ."

She did not stop. "Never mind, Dear. Come hell or high water, we're *both* going to enjoy a little safe sex tonight."

And they did – masturbated each other. A. J. ejaculated in her hand – and elsewhere. All Lennie did was to say, "Where's the Kleenex?"

A. J., after ten or so minutes, recovered, and eventually, with Lennie's help, was able to assume the usual horizontal coupling of missionary sex. Then A. J. all but ran out of steam before she orgasmed – anyway A. J. thought she got off.

Eventually, A. J. came to understand that women were experts at faking that intense sensation of pleasure; he knew damned well that his Ex never truly climaxed.

They moved away from the damp spot A. J. had gushed on the blanket when he ejaculated into her hand.

"It's cigarette time," A. J. said.

"Huh?" Lennie said. "I didn't know you smoked."

A. J. said, "I don't," and Lennie poked him hard in the ribs.

A. J. worked his arm under Lennie's shoulders and pulled her onto him. After a long French kiss of robustly exchanging tongues, she pulled away and exactly confronted A. J. with her eyes. "I could go for a clit, too," she said intently.

"Do what now?" A. J. said.

"Uh, later," she answered, adding, after a couple seconds, "let's shower."

We dried – each other somewhat – left the bathroom, and A. J. clambered back into bed. Lennie, an interminably long ten minutes later, stopped next to the side of the bed where A. J. had crashed. Lennie was shoeless, but otherwise dressed.

A. J. forced a smile. "You're sure decked-out funny for bed," he said, sweeping his eyes up and down her frame.

"Another time, A. J. I may have to testify in the morning. I had a hell of a night."

A. J. remembered wondering whether he should believe her or not. One thing he could tell, she was no longer unvaryingly tipsy.

A. J. rolled from the bed. "Mind," he said, sitting naked on the edge, "if I don't see you to the door?"

Lennie said, "Damn right I mind. But . . . if you do drive me home, I'll have to cite you for public nudity."

"I wasn't thinking . . . ." A. J. said dumbly.

Shutting up confusedly, A. J. began dressing. Lennie slipped on her shoes, sat down on the side of the bed, and waited.

At her apartment door Lennie kissed A. J. lightly on the cheek, Detective Deemer again, and let herself in.

"I'll telephone you," A. J. said.

She shook her head. "I'll call *you*."

A. J.'s spirits plunged faster than the Dallas temperature when a "Blue Norther" blows through.

"At least," A. J. consoled himself driving home, "the evening ended better than it began."

A. J. was standing bare-chested in his apartment staring at the bathroom mirror when he remembered the postcard from his mother. Since she and his father had been late in leaving Dallas, they'd be staying in Hawaii straight through winter and would not return until March. They would mail Christmas presents for Danielle and for A. J. but not for Allison, whom A. J.'s mother explicitly despised. A. J. fell asleep after wondering for a good spell what she'd think of Lennie – if she ever got to meet her.

A. J.'s mother was a pretty woman but a consummate prig. Their marriage – her's and his father's – was an accommodation, a territorial armistice not a certifiable wedlock. A. J.'s mother raised him. His father did not care much one way the other about either the pace or quality of A. J.'s maturation. An indefatigable rounder, A. J. knew damn well his father would hit on Lennie the first chance he got.

Unlike A. J., his father, "Daddy, as A, J, had called him since he could pronounce a name ," was lanky, ornamented with semi-rugged features, and whether it was winter or summer he sported a fabricated bronze complexion. Almost totally bald, but outgoing – brazenly it seemed to A. J. – women just flat found him sexy. When A. J. was twelve or so, his father caught the clap; A. J. did not know about it until years later. A. J. remember wondering, when he first heard the story, if he passed it on to Mother. Probably not, A. J. decided, since it was usually spread through one or another form of intimate sexual coupling.

# [29]

A. J. waited, hoping that Miki would intercept the telephone call. She did not, and after four rings he answered himself. Focused on trying to decide if a memory-hogging MaxWriter setup function was of more than marginal utility, A. J. was brusque.

"Yes!"

It was Lennie. "Yes, your ass," she replied sharply. "I'm dying for some Tex-Mex. It's been a long week."

"Lennie! A. J. blurted. I was beginning to think–"

"I called your apartment."

"Yeah, I'm here most of the time, writing the specs for a low-end word-processing machine that we're going to produce. Any trouble reaching me?"

"Naw," she scoffed. "I told whoever answered that I was a police detective with a bench warrant for an Alan J. MacRae."

"Laugh," A. J. said. "Please laugh."

"Ha, ha," Lennie said flatly.

"Yeah, ha, ha," A. J. repeated. "I was beginning to think I'd tuckered you out last Thursday."

"Thought you'd done *what*?"

"Tuckered you out. *Tuckered!* What'd you think I said?"

"Wait," she said. Shortly, she was back on the line: "Just what you thought that I thought. What else?"

"I gather you're at work?" A. J. said.

"I just got in. Real police work last night. I had to make an arrest."

"Not by yourself, I hope?"

"No. Merle was with me. A mama coke dealer. On Greenville Avenue. Lower Greenville's a shit-hole."

"She come peacefully?"

"Umm, after a fashion. Merle grabbed her by the crotch and said he'd rip off her twat if she didn't settle down."

"He gets away with that stuff?"

"Doesn't leave finger prints. She all but cuffed herself."

A urinal in the men's room began flushing. "Listen to this," A. J. said, moving the telephone handset closer to the wall that was seeping sounds of rushing water.

The sound faded, and A. J. said, "Know what that was? Next to my office?"

"I know what it wasn't," Lennie answered. "It sure as hell wasn't you voiding your bladder."

"You wish," A. J. said, after overcoming the slam. "How about I pick you up at seven tonight? We'll swing by a Taco Bell."

"And go Dutch again I suppose. Make it six-thirty. We need to talk. Before you get bagged on margaritas."

"Exactly," A. J. replied sarcastically.

Lennie was attired in the same misfitting, ho-hum, outfit that she wore on their first date, except her blouse was light gray not off-blue.

"It's in your court, I say cleverly," A. J. said mockingly as he backed from the parking lot of her apartment building. They had scarcely left the exit when Lennie said, "Bad news. Osgood's clean."

"Damn. Is that it? I mean . . . is that *it*?"

"It could be he was never booked. Maybe . . . some clerk–"

"The bastard," A. J. said, interrupting her. "He'd bribe his way out of a . . . damn parking ticket."

"Maybe somewhere a vaunted police clerk fuggled the record keeping. I talked to Lieutenant Hope, and he said to–"

"Lieutenant who?"

"My boss," Lennie said. "Lieutenant Brandon Hope. Abandon Hope, we call him. He told me to go ahead and see if I could persuade Osgood to stop by for a *friendly* chat."

A. J. said, "That'd work wouldn't it?"

"If he can be persuaded," Lennie said, adding after a moment. "What I won't do for a little nooky."

A. J. felt his brow furrow. "Do what now?" he said.

"Won't do for *you*, I mean! Damn it, A. J.!"

"I *knew* who you meant! A. J. said heavily. Only he did not, and he was relieved by her angry rebuff.

"Tomorrow," Lennie said, "I'm telephoning Osgood. You have anything new? Anything that might help me convince him to get his ass in here?"

"No. Only . . . this is way out. The woman who kept Edgecom's books for Fran?"

"Who?"

"The old gal Osgood canned his second day at Edgecom, Martha Dillbeck? She's disappeared. Those financial reports I showed you? The ones that were prepared by Osgood's hand-picked accounting dork? That I knew damned well were a sham? Martha, I was sure, could explain the difference between her numbers and his."

"What's Martha's last name again?"

"Dillbeck. Two Ls."

A. J could tell from Lennie's brief silence that she was scribbling the name in her notebook.

"Any chance," she said, "that the Pat Brown woman might change her mind . . . I mean, report her forced oral sex?"

"She told me the sex never happened," A. J. answered bleakly. "I seriously doubt that Pat would reconsider. But, I haven't kept in touch."

Giving A. J. a sidewise glance, Lennie said, "Check it out and let me know. I won't goose Osgood until I hear from you."

That evening was virtually a repeat of our first date, only Lennie spent the night at A. J.'s place. Again, Lennie would not initially accede to having missionary sex. "Meanwhile," she said, putting me off, "keep your signaling finger cocked."

"As always," I said. "I mean, you bay-ut!"

Pat Brown, when A. J. called her the next day, told me she had found a new job. She adamantly refused to report Osgood's assault to the police.

# [30]

One of A. J.'s lesser vices, which always pissed-off Allison, was pigging-out on pizza and beer on Saturday afternoons in the Fall and Winter while he watched a Southwest Conference athletic contest on TV. When the telephone rang, A. J. was washing a bite of pizza down with a swallow of beer and waiting for the start of what he knew would be a rough, hard-played basketball game between the University of Texas and Texas A&M University.

A. J. cleared his throat and answered the call.

It was Lennie. She did not explicitly greet him. "Any plans?"

"None," A. J. replied emphatically after a moment of uncertainty.

"I'll be another hour," Lennie said.

An hour passed and then a second hour dragged by. A. J. finished another long-neck, and was getting a little tense when his tinny doorbell chimes rang.

Wearing a snug T-shirt, cut-off shorts, and moccasins, but sockless, Lennie bussed A. J. lightly on the cheek. Slipping off her handbag, she sat it down carefully on the end-table by the sofa. A. J. heard a slight clunking sound and was reminded of how Lennie hated the regulation requiring her to carry a handgun. Like her fellow detectives, most of the time she ignored it.

Holding A. J. off with her hands, Lennie leaned forward and planted another quick, make-do kiss on his cheek.

"Damn, Lennie," A. J. said, trying to embrace her. "I'm only *human*."

"Damn, A. J.," Lennie said, mocking his whiney tone, "I'm only a woman . . . a *woman*, get it?"

A. J. sagged theatrically. "You enjoy seeing me twist in the wind, don't you? Scowling as if angry, he added, "Exactly how much longer before you finally become menopausal?"

Lennie sprouted an offended look. "You wouldn't like that, Dear. Trust me."

"No?"

She made a shishing sound. "You'd throw a piston . . . or . . . something just backing out of the garage." She saw A. J.'s dubious look, and added, "Or, so I've been told."

A. J. stared at her dumbly; Lennie shifted her position. "What's on the tube?"

After a couple seconds of wondering precisely what she meant, A. J. quit trying and answered her question. "Round ball. Texas versus Texas A. and M. You ever watch?"

"I *went* to a game at College Station," Lennie said. "What quarter is it?"

"Quarter?" A. J. said. "College basketball games are divided into halves. It's nearly the end of the first half."

"I forgot, Lennie said." She pulled A. J. toward the sofa by his hand. He broke away, opened a beer, and handed her the bottle. Lennie patted the sofa pillow next to where she was sitting. A. J. sat down, kicked off his slippers, and rested his feet on the coffee table.

Chucking her moccasins, Lennie laid her legs on top of A. J.'s "Who's winning?"

"I don't know," A. J. said. "You have beautiful legs . . . or I'd know." He studied the screen. "Texas is ahead . . . by eleven."

"Oh crap," Lennie said instantly. After finishing a pull of her beer, she added, "I'm an Aggie fan."

"Figures," A. J. said, sniffing hard.

Generally perceived as a conservative, blue-collar university, the students of Texas A&M were frequently the butt of crude "Aggie Jokes" – in Texas, the Dumb-Pollock jokes of the fifties and sixties.

Lennie ignored A. J.'s mockery. "How come you're an Aggie fan?" A. J. said.

"I had aspirations." She did not elaborate.

"I went to SMU," A. J. said.

"You told me."

225

A. J. might have told her, but he didn't think so; he figured she had found out by doing a computer search at work.

An Aggie forward intercepted a Longhorn pass, scored a break-away dunk, and Lennie showed the TV a double thumbs-up. Texas called a time-out. The TV station immediately began broadcasting a commercial, and A. J. muted the audio.

Lennie set her beer on the end table. "I finally got a call through to Osgood," she said. "Late yesterday. I had to pull rank, though."

"You told Miki it was the police calling?"

"I told somebody."

"How did he . . . what'd he say? Is he coming in?"

"Shhhiiit no. He flat-assed refused. You're right, he's slick. He knew damn well–"

"I told you," A. J. interrupted, nodding presumptively.

". . . that I was just whacking him off. I told him it was only routine, the usual bull. He's no virgin, that's for sure. The son-of-a-bitch said he was busy and told me to call him back. I hinted that I might get a warrant. That just scared the shit out of him. He said he'd have my badge for spreading false rumors about him. I sweetly told him that our conversation was being recorded. That puckered his ass a little."

A. J. said, "You made history if it did . . . if you muzzled Hummel, I mean."

Lennie turned back to the TV.

"Damn," A. J. said. "I *know* that son-of-a-bitch killed Fran."

"I wish I was as certain, Hon."

"So now what?" A. J. said. Lennie nodded and A. J. turned off the TV.

Tired sounding, Lennie said, "I'll talk to Hope about getting a warrant. It'll be a long shot, but he may be able to convince Bob Hoover to talk to a judge . . . to the *right* judge."

Lennie waited for A. J.'s reaction. It was the first time A. J. had heard her mention the name Bob Hoover, and his nod was ambiguous.

Lennie understood: "Robert E. Lee Hoover is an Assistant District Attorney, an ADA. Most Assistant District Attorneys," Lennie added, "are nitpicking jerks who think they're the ultimate white-collar studs. Bob's okay, though. Actually, he kind of likes me. How badly do you want to go through with this?"

"Not that badly," A. J. mumbled.

"God damn, A. J.," Lennie said, grinning. "You are so easy. I could pick your pocket wearing welders gloves."

Her smile faded when she saw A. J. was not totally appeased. "Let's get one thing straight, *Mister MacRae*, I only date *one* man at a time."

Evidently A. J.'s relief showed because the next moment Lennie demanded to know why A. J. had let her run out of beer, insisted that I explain my de-volution into a half-assed host now that we were a bit closer. A. J. fetched another beer. Lennie took a long swig, snuggled against A. J., and quickly fell asleep.

We ate a late supper at a Spaghetti Warehouse restaurant situated in a renovated area of downtown Dallas.  Lennie spent the night with A. J., and in the morning A. J. complained that he couldn't sleep because he had to lay on a broom handle all night. Lennie straight-facedly replied that she did not even know that he owned a whisk broom.

# [31]

A. J.'s telephone rang while he was admiring the perfectly rectilinear layout of Edgecom's first, preeminent commercial product, a plug-in printed-circuit board that connected an audio cassette player to a microcomputer – as personal computers were first called – for storing large quantities of digitized data. Designed by Fran some four years ago – and Edgecom's maiden market offering – A. J. had selected it for the opening slide of what was to be Osgood's dog-and-pony show – the revue that would enrapture potential Edgecom investors.

Lennie did not return A. J.'s "hello," which was how she often opened a telephone conversation. "I've only got a moment," she said. "Bob Hoover flat turned us down. Said that every judge in Dallas would disbar his ass if he went before him or her with all we have on Osgood. That's the bad–"

"Balls," A. J. interrupted wearily.

". . . the bad news," Lennie continued. "The good news is that Bob said we just may have enough circumstantial evidence to get Degeorge's body exhumed."

"Damn, Lennie!" A. J. said, his energy regenerated. "Exhumation is even better. When will you know?"

"Bob'll have to see a judge . . . the right one, but hopefully this week. If the judge agrees, we'll have a court order in a couple of days. Please understand, Dear, that my 'if' is spelled with a capital I."

"I know, A. J. said. "If all goes okay, who will do it?"

"The exhumation itself? We'll be in charge. Me, probably."

"Perfect. When? Roughly?"

A. J. could hear men arguing heatedly in the background.

"Morons," Lennie whispered. The argument ended. "Bob will have to shop for a judge. It could take days."

"Ball park?"

"I have to run."

"Quickly," A. J. said, "one more thing. We've got a mole right here at Edgecom."

"A mole?"

"A spy. For our side. Our new owner's son."

"Don't chance it, A. J. He might tip our hand. Keep him in mind, though. I've got other fish to fry. I'll stay on Hoover's ass."

"We still on for tonight?" A. J. asked.

"If I don't call."

"I'll take the phone off the hook," A. J. said, but all he heard was the click of her telephone handset being reseated.

A. J resumed examining the circuit board designed by Fran. Now indifferent to its squared-up layout, he began wondering if recording the digitized output of a computer on an audio cassette was a clever engineering adaptation or an amenable collaboration between two different electronic utilizations. A. J. decided there had to be some "housekeeping" going on, as engineers call the task that circuitry performs managing important data massaging and routing chores.

# [32]

Skip, carrying a rolled-up magazine in one hand and an unopened Dr. Pepper can in the other, dropped into the chair next to A. J.'s. Someone, probably one of Dornhoffer's order-takers, had placed four plastic folding chairs side-by-side against the back wall of the conference room, which is where A. J. had settled in.

Skip opened his can of pop. "I insisted," he whispered, "that you be allowed to attend,"

Nodding, A. J. said, "I wondered."

Osgood, standing behind our boxy wooden lectern, which was pushed tight against the far end of the conference-room table, was slowly turning the pages of a copy of the script for the Edgecom dog-and-pony show. A play in three acts, the production was meant to persuade Wallace Hardeman's wealthy acquaintances to invest thousands of dollars on a chance to hit the jackpot when Edgecom went public. Today's dry run was a crucial rehearsal.

Copies of the business plan and A. J.'s booklet, "Inside Microcomputer Disk Storage Systems," were paired and neatly stacked on the table in front of empty chairs lining the table's sides and the end opposite the lectern. Wickersham, Dornhoffer, and McPherson, were wandering aimlessly near the front of the room. Wickersham's face hung boredly.

Osgood, after glancing at his watch for the nth time, beseeched the ceiling for an explanation of what in the hell it was that could have *possibly* delayed "Walt." Suddenly glimpsing Skip sitting in the back of the room, he contrived a smile.

Ten minutes passed. A muffled buzz, the fast chattering of the relay controlling the latch on Edgecom's main front egress door, filtered through the wall separating the conference room and the lobby. Wickersham, Dornhoffer, and McPherson hurried to chairs that had been placed in a line to the side of the podium.

Osgood cheerily greeted his visitor. Wearing cowboy boots and a tawny, wide-brimmed, high-crowned cowboy hat, Hardeman grunted and asked where he should sit. A. J. had never seen him when he was not wearing a cowboy hat, and A. J. would not have been surprised to hear that it stayed on while he was making love.

Osgood, as graciously obsequious as a glad-hander at a fine restaurant, waved at a chair that had been pulled slightly back from the head of the table. Offering Hardeman a copy of his speech, he stepped up to the podium; gripping the top side edges, he greeted the empty table: "Good afternoon. Welcome to Edgecom Data Company. I'm Hummel Osgood. I founded Edgecom."

After allowing his words a moment to register, he nodded at Hardeman: "Y'all know Walt I'm sure."

Turning back to squarely face the table, he continued: "Edgecom manufactures add-in electronics for personal computers . . . encapsulated electronic modules and printed-circuit boards that plug right into a personal-computer mainframe. These electronically sophisticated circuits significantly enhance the performance of a personal computer – make one run faster and cooler."

"Please note my use of the term *personal computer*. Originally called microcomputers and then home computers, these small, desk-top, extremely powerful machines, now called personal computers, are fast coming into their own. Sales are increasing exponentially; one expert has compared the explosion of sales to the *Big Bang* theory of the beginning of the Universe."

Osgood loosened his grip on the podium. "We've been in the business of making these circuits for four years, for fifty months – give or take a week – going back to when the very first personal computer reached the market. Sales of add-in and add-on parts chart out almost vertically.

"We're a pioneer, one of a handful of start-up companies that have prevailed . . . and succeeded. We know how to *make* personal computers. From the foundation up. And we know how to *sell* personal computers."

He paused.

"Today, Edgecom is privately owned. But, we intend, one way or another, to go public . . . soon. Unfailingly, by the middle of next year."

A tsunami of Osgood verbosity followed. Most of it was blatant fabrications supporting a claim of his "ground-floor" engagement in Edgecom's start-up.

After a good five minutes, he stopped articulating his sham involvement in Edgecom's founding and peered at Skip. "Here, I thought I'd introduce you Skip, but, ah, I guess that's an option?"

Engrossed in reading his magazine, Skip did not know he had been asked a question.

His father's bellow was un-attenuated. "Skip! For Jesus H. Christ! Do you want to be a part of this wing-ding or *not*?"

It took Skip a moment to assimilate the question. "To what purpose?" he finally asked glaring peevishly at his father.

Hardeman shrugged indifferently. Skip's gaze returned to his magazine, and he casually turned a page. Osgood's attention fell on his trio of managers. He was fattening Herb Wickersham's résumé when Hardeman interrupted him: "Hummel! You tryin' to aggravate everyone I'm inviting? For God's sake, boy, *don't* mention Herb's graduation from that Horton school in Pennsylvania. This is Dallas, not . . . Pittsburgh."

Osgood nodded apologetically. "Good point, Walt. That's one of the reasons for this dry run: to make sure I don't offend by stepping on any toes."

"Also," Hardeman said, nodding in agreement, "here's a suggestion. Shouldn't I say a word or two? I'll know everyone."

Osgood, all but shaking his head, turned from Hardeman toward his triad of hand-picked stooges. "What do you think, guys?"

Every "guy" fulsomely agreed with Hardeman.

"Make that unanimous," Osgood said, nodding as if pleased.

His judgment validated, Hardeman's head bobbed approvingly. "Work me in," he said to Osgood.

"Great," Osgood said. "At the best possible time, A. J."

After verbosely covering the experience, intelligence, and doggedness of Wickersham, Dornhoffer, and McPherson, Osgood turned over a page of his speech and peered imploringly at Hardeman.

Startled at suddenly being the focus of Osgood's attention, frown lines decorated Hardeman's face.

Skip tittered. "Daddy wasn't listening."

"Okay so far," Hardeman said after a few seconds had passed.

Osgood smiled and said he thought, at this point, that a few well-chosen words about the personal computing industry's early years were appropriate. "Here's where I thought you'd step in, Skip."

"Me?" Skip asked sourly. "I hate history."

"Just a thought," Osgood mumbled.

"Damn," Skip said from the side of his mouth, his voice low, "we'll be here forever. Hummel would take ten minutes announcing that his gonads were melting."

A. J. whispered the often satirized first line of a long, dowdy Victorian novel: "It was a dark and stormy night . . . ."

Osgood turned to pitching MaxWriter, the icing on his marble cake of deception. Twice, nodding respectfully at A. J. he implied that he was no less a maven of the craft of computerized word manipulation than himself. Wrapping up his laudatory summary of MaxWriter, he turned to Dornhoffer. "Karl, at this point I'll ask our visitors for questions. And right away you unveil MaxWriter." He gestured. "It'll be sitting right there."

Dornhoffer pointed at an imaginary table and nodded enthusiastically.

Osgood addressed McPherson: "Darren, you are *always* ready to zealously field any and all technical questions. Some of our guests won't know didly shit about word processing. Don't wait for me to call on you!"

McPherson, being no less a loyal team player than Dornhoffer, was stirred to nod excitedly. Wickersham busied himself retying his shoe.

It was time, his long, chimerical overture finished, for Osgood to beseech his guests for money. One moment he was proud as a peacock, the next as meek as a tit mouse, and somehow, sometimes, A. J. swore to God he managed to be both vain and docile simultaneously. Here, without attribution – every remark is Osgood's – is the gist of his pitch:

"Edgecom can design the hardware and we can write the software. We can manufacture, distribute, service, and market. What Edgecom cannot do, on its own, is generate enough hands-on capital to finance the development of MaxWriter. *And* concurrently go public. Not in the time frame that I have in mind. Timing in our business is critical: if you're behind, you're dead. Electronics is a *very* fast moving, faster even than medicine or plastics. We don't extrude aluminum here."

Osgood pretended to pause for a drink of water. "We are currently running four product lines, as you will see when we tour Manufacturing. Those lines, even if we don't introduce a single new product, will write Edgecom's bottom line in black ink well into nineteen eighty two.

Looking ahead? In this business, one should consult an astrologer. In fact, I might. Heh, heh.

IBM is about to introduce its own microcomputer, calling it a personal microcomputer, a PC, a generic *personal* computer. Anyway, that's what my spies tell me. So are Hewlett-Packard and Western Electric. Those guys are super heavyweights. They'll set up their own retail outlets, and independents will die on the vine once those gorillas leave the underbrush."

Osgood paused, and Skip whispered, "His spies my ass. He read that stuff in *Byte* magazine."

"The bottom line?" Osgood was saying, "A very different market is evolving. There will always be a market niche for specialty home computer products, and an after-market for independent second-sourcing firms like Edgecom. And we will be there, too. At least in the short run. Our goal, however, is to move up a weight class. All our people are veterans of micro-computing infighting. They can take a punch, and they can counterpunch."

"But . . . hauling on your own bootstraps can only lift a company so high. By bulking up financially, Edgecom can take on anybody. We know all the moves, when to duck, when to throw a haymaker. It's time now for Edgecom to move up a weight class. The personal computer business is a hundred-yard dash, not a marathon."

Osgood, obviously pleased with himself, looked smugly at Hardeman. "I'll stop here for questions. For audience participation. Then I'll wing it." He smiled at his managers. "With beaucoup help, of course."

Dornhoffer and McPherson nodded. Wickersham stolidly peered straight ahead.

I whispered to Skip. "Why's Herb got a broom handle up his ass?"

Skip shrugged: "He and Osgood are fighting. Who knows?"

"Afterwards," Osgood was saying, "I'll hold up the stock purchase agreement, mention that our goal is to raise a million dollars. Then I'll go into the slide show."

He looked at Hardeman, and Hardeman stared back, his eyes as blank as the surface of a glass of milk.

Osgood nodded. "I could do the slide show first, and then I could give my presentation. After which, we tour the factory. How does that strike you, Walt?"

"Move the slide show up. But I'm flexible."

"My thinking, too," Osgood said nodding thoughtfully. "I'll open with it."

Osgood looked at me. "A. J., I'll need a curtain-raiser . . . and then the AC-50 slide, okay?" He looked to his left. "Guys?"

The middle guy, Karl Dornhoffer, hurried to his feet. "Hummer," he said. "You could sell sand to an A-rab. I'm inclined to think, though, same as Walt, that opening with the slide show would be the best way."

McPherson, nodding non-stop, stood, and in a long, cluttered discourse said that he, too, was impressed. Wickersham, stood, gave a little shrug, pushed his chair toward the table, and leisurely left the room. A. J.

nudged Skip, who was still intensely reading his magazine. "I'm leaving," he said.

A. J. fell-in behind Wickersham; Skip followed A. J. out.

# [33]

Sounds of male and female whoops and laughter, coming from the office bullpen, wafted into A. J.'s provisional office, the room next to the men's latrine. The merrymakers were heading his way.

A. J. was working on specifications for MaxWriter. It was the Wednesday of Christmas week; two days after Osgood had rehearsed his dog-and-pony show, the production crafted expressly to unzip the bulging wallets of the acquaintances of Walt Hardeman. It was Osgood's first show, and he was taking his guests on a factory tour. Expecting a few sidelong glances as the group passed his office doorway, A. J. began concentrating fiercely on a page of handwritten notes.

Led by Hardeman, with Osgood fast on his heels, eleven visitors, seven men and four women, filed past. One man, clearly the oldest – thinning milk-white hair, ruddy, mottled face – was wearing a lanyard of woven leather weighted in the front by a turquoise trinket only a little  smaller than a kitchen skillet. Coatless, his shirt was a solid blue pullover open at the neck. The six other men, all fiftyish, all wearing slacks that broke perfectly at their insteps, and all attired in sportcoats garnished with brassy sleeve buttons, were indistinguishable in grooming from one another. The women were fitted out in smart, wool slack suits with silky neck scarves tucked inside jackets. Skip brought up the rear.

Trembling, his hand over his mouth, his eyes on the floor, Skip slowed in front of A. J.'s doorway and marked time while the others pulled away. After falling a yard or so behind the others, Skip darted into A. J.'s office, tumbled into the guest chair, and noisily expelled a full lung of air.

"I'll bite," A. J. said when Skip stopped snickering. "What in hell's going on?"

"You should have been there," Skip said, desperately trying to unite words orphaned by his laughing.

"Oh? Clue me."

Skip was so agog with the humor of the situation that he had trouble answering. "Because . . . because . . . somehow Norman's Cannon got wheeled out of mothballs . . . nine rounds were fired! and then it . . . hauled ass!"

A. J. understood: Norman Israel had written most of the software for Edgesales, the system used by marketing personnel to capture and process sales data and print invoices, and one module of Israel's program consisted of the code that generated the opening screen, an all-caps banner-graphic of the name Edgesales. As a prank, he had coded a second opening, one enhancing his original version with animation. Comprised of many more program lines, but readily hooked into the host program in place of the original software module, the bootleg version came up with a cannon resting at the bottom of the screen. Clearly a weapon of Revolutionary War vintage, it posted, in nine separate bursts of phosphorescent buckshot, the word E D G E S A L E S along the top of the screen. Neat. Except, Norman's Cannon looked more like a simple line-drawing of male genitalia than an artillery piece. Its wheels, balloon-looking to begin with, were too far aft to suggest any semblance of balanced firepower. Its barrel, initially aimed sharply upward, shrank lengthwise, degree by reluctant degree, after each letter was posted. And after firing the last letter S the whole "cannon" rolled bumpily off the computer screen dragging its exhausted barrel along behind.

Someone, most likely Selig Hildreth – and no doubt at Skip's behest – had re-installed the Edgesales programming code that was Norman Israel's legacy to animated business programming. Edgecom's visitors, Osgood's first group of potential investors invited in for a private offering, had been an unwitting audience to Israel's banner-screen peep show.

"Oh no!" A. J. said, as if aghast at what he was hearing.

Skip nodded energetically.

"What happened?" A. J. said. "How'd–"

"You should've seen Osgood. He didn't know whether to laugh or cry."

"Among other things, he lost his power of speech . . . if you can imagine that."

A. J.'s shoulders drooped. "Just my luck not to be there. You hope he lost it. Who ran the demo?"

"Jonesy."

"Too bad that it wasn't . . . ."

A. J. warned Skip with his eyes: Dornhoffer had backtracked and was peering into the office.

A. J. leaned sideways, looked past Skip, and shook his head. "Nothing!" he yelled.

Dornhoffer, taking his time, finally left.

A. J. nodded at Skip. Skip glanced backwards, bounced up, and closed the door.

"You can't win 'em all," A. J. said after Skip had settled back into the visitor's chair.

"Right!" Skip said. *Meaning?*"

"If it had been Peggy, instead of Jonsey, she'd have asphyxiated the whole damn office bay."

Skip, between giggles, said he neither knew Peggy nor understood why she would have been uniquely stimulated to odiously aerate the room through her underpants.

Peggy Swaney, A. J. explained, was handpicked by Dornhoffer to be Edgecom's lead telephone order-taker. "You couldn't pry an off-color word from her mouth with a crowbar. She was the person most egregiously offended when Israel debuted his Cannon for the entertainment of selected employees, including A. J. At the time Fran still personally oversaw the efforts of Peggy and her coworkers. He watched as Israel's peculiar looking artillery piece did its thing, and he nearly busted a gut laughing. Peggy watched and did a lot of heavy sniffing."

"How about the rest?" A. J. said to Skip. "Our other very well-heeled guests?"

"One woman acted highly put-off, but another couldn't stop sniggering. I didn't know either one. I thought Lars Petersen was going to croak from laughing so hard."

"Was he wearing a western string tie?"

"Yeah, with a boulder hanging from it. Bent over like he suffered from osteo."

Petersen, Skip explained, was an old friend of his late grandfather. "He started Lone Star Employers Casualty. Ever hear of 'em?"

"I don't know," A. J. said. "Who can remember one insurance company from another?"

"Petersen is *really* loaded."

"*Speaking of loaded*, ah, How'd your Daddy react?"

Skip looked around helplessly. "Daddy isn't much into humor."

"Overall," A. J. said, "how'd it go? Hummel's sales pitch, I mean."

"Not bad. Your slide show was a moon landing. Hell, A. J., they're all friends of Daddy. Up to their ass in money. I'd be surprised if even *one* of them doesn't pony up a big wad. Petersen told Daddy to count on him for fifty grand. I heard him. Everyone did."

"Times ten guests . . . that's a half million dollars."

Skip nodded. "Yep. How many shows does Osgood have in mind?"

"I don't know. A half dozen, maybe."

In fact, Osgood invited investors to four dog-and-pony shows. Irickson figured that he would try sluicing a million dollars from the near bottomless assets of Hardemen's friends. A. J. presumed Osgood reached his goal – may have topped it – because a week after the last show he jacked up the wages of every employee – if a light shower after a long drought amounts to a true rainfall. I'd have been surprised, hell, stunned senseless, if it turned out that Osgood had not prodigiously raised his own salary, and maybe Wickersham's too, although lately the two men rarely spoke to one another. Osgood's bigheartedness did not extend to consultants.

# [34]

Miki, as A. J. cruised through Edgecom's lobby, beckoned to him from her post at the switchboard. "Call *Lennie* at work," she said. She eyed A. J. slyly; her overt curiosity lightened his step.

A. J. had returned from visiting the shop that printed his booklet on the inside poop of floppy disk drives. Edgecom was almost out of copies, and A. J. wanted to make two small redactions before another press run. He remembered thinking on his way that if Fran was still running Edgecom, he would never have considered making the non-essential corrections because of the cost: several hundred dollars for updated mechanicals and at least one new offset printing plate.

Lennie kidded about misrepresenting A. J. as police quarry to whoever answered the telephone at Edgecom. She did not, of course, explicitly advance that fabrication, but she doubtlessly would have if it wasn't for the possibility of seeding co-workers' minds with inferential rumors about her investigation.

"We got it," were Lennie's first words. She did not have to explain: "It," A. J. knew, was the court paper allowing the disinterment of the remains of Peter Francis Degeorge.

"You are," A. J. said, "by far my favorite detective."

"Detective!" she exclaimed. "Is that it?

"My favorite *girl?*"

"Girl!"

"My favorite adult female person. "

"I might as well be a mannikin."

"My beloved femme fatale. Only . . . you're so damn arthritic."

"If I was any more limber A. J., you'd either be dead or hospitalized for life with chronic lower-back arthritis."

"What a way to go!" A. J. replied excitedly.

It was eight days after she heard Bob Hoover's arguments and reviewed his support affidavit before the Honorable Eustace Washington issued her order. Judge Washington had allowed time for those persons who might object to the exhumation, if any, to come forward. Standard procedure, Lennie told A. J.

Once it was clear that a court order would be forthcoming, Lennie visited Jo Ellen at her home in Frisco to present Judge Washington's decision. Jo Ellen, when she heard, turned pasty white. It was a reaction, Lennie said, that was not unusual, not for a spouse who heard out-of-the-blue of that impendence.

In any case, it wasn't long, Lennie said, before Jo Ellen got her sea legs back and began listening thoughtfully.

Jo Ellen had company while Lennie visited: "Some nerdish character named Hildreth. He didn't once open his mouth. Just sat there deaf and virtually rigid, eyes on the floor."

A. J. verbally sketched Selig Hildreth, told Lennie that he was an Edgecom technician who had been laying Jo Ellen even while Fran was alive. Lennie immediately wanted to know more about Hildreth. A. J. told her that he was a good technician but standoffish, which was about as much as he knew about Hildreth. A. J. figured her interest was incidental. He was wrong: Lennie was back on the clock.

Lennie left the Degeorge residence with Jo Ellen's verbal consent – belated and nugatory anyway – to proceed with the exhumation. Osgood, A. J. had explained to Lennie, was married to Jo Ellen's twin sister, Betty, adding that like most identical twins they were as close as snakes' testicles, and that Osgood would hear within hours of Lennie's visit.

A. J. said he'd watch Osgood for signs that he was feeling the heat. He suspected that Lennie internalized a roll of her eyes. Anyway, he again suggested using Skip Hardeman as a mole, figuring Skip would be around Osgood more than he would, and that he might overhear Osgood mention a fact important to their case. Lennie again told A. J. to deep-six that plan – or risk Osgood catching a rocket to Mars.

Screwing up his eyes skeptically, A. J. said, "You think so?"

"Yes," she answered, "Jet one way to God only knows where."

A. J. continued plugging away at the documentation that would describe in detail how to run MaxWriter. He and Lennie had begun seeing each other nightly – sometimes, depending on her assignment, only for supper, other times for supper and a stay-over at A. J.'s place. As a detective, Lennie's hours, were pretty much her own choice. The only time they could not rendezvous, at least to eat, were those days when the queue of lawbreakers at Central Booking was long or when a District Attorney asked her to stick around to discuss the facts of a crime that she had investigated.

Initially, A. J. was infatuated with Lennie. Pure and simple, he was hot for her lithe, supple, youthfully breasted body. After a half-dozen dates, however, he got a fix on her personality, came to understand that she was innately good-hearted – albeit anything but soft-hearted.

Yes, Lennie could be as sewer-mouthed as a Marine boot sergeant, a tendency A. J. blamed on her job, which began with her rookie days working the tough neighborhoods of Dallas. She sometimes shot from the hip, and she wasn't above discomposing a pestering stranger by calling a spade "a fucking shovel" – a phrase that she had used on A. J. his first visit to the police station. Lennie picked her spots, however. Her direct, explicit mention of four-letter words, she once told me, was a tactic of sorts, a way to separate female kooks, especially, the ones bearing false witness from real citizens offering useful facts. Male kooks, she said, were turned on, and then they forgot their original objective. The longer they dated the more polite her language became, her communications with A. J., anyway.

Lennie was disinclined to talk about her upbringing – somewhat, A. J. thought, because of his own silver-spoon rearing. Over time, however, he learned that her father was in law enforcement; that her hometown was Tyler, Texas; that she had been busted in high school for smoking pot; and that she had earned an associate degree in criminology at the local Tyler community college. A male sibling – her only sibling – who was six years her senior still lived in Tyler.

Lennie was all but formally engaged at seventeen to a star running back of the perennially tough, Tyler High School football team, where a fellow student, NFL Hall of Famer Earl Campbell, would one day bust through high-school defensive lines at will. A two-years-older classmate – apparently not the star running back – fathered her child, a blue-baby that soon died. A. J. guessed she and the father just drifted apart; she did not elaborate, and A. J. wasn't dying to know. Lennie *had* to tell me that she had born a kid. It was a virtuous part of her nature.

A. J.'s apartment telephone bill included a weekly call, on average, to the city of Tyler. Lennie insisted on paying the charges. They argued and A. J. lost the haggle; that is, an open cache of dollar bills slowly accumulated on the stand holding the telephone.

Lennie opened up about her teen years after one of their frequent disagreements over who should pay for the telephone calls to Tyler. Between her twelfth and thirteenth birthdays her father, a Smith County deputy sheriff, shot and killed her mother by brutally jamming the gun into her mother's mouth and blowing her brains out. Afterward, he showered his own brains against a bathroom wall.

Lennie knew her mother was unfaithful: One afternoon she came home an hour early from school and heard her mother having intercourse in her bed, that is, in Lennie's bed. Later she learned her mother's boyfriend was her father's fishing buddy, also a sheriff. She came to realize it wasn't their first rendezvous at her home, remembering having a few times found her bedroom mysteriously different in a minor way from how she'd left it, not unkempt, but her pillow cocked funny or something amiss. She attributed her mother's stealthy co-opting of her bedroom to the unwritten rule disbarring her father from entering the room.

Her father often took her and her brother fishing, to auto races, and to other predominantly male entertainments, and it seemed to A. J. that his death hurt Lennie more than the death of her mother. She and her brother were quickly provided room and board by an uncle, their father's brother, one of Tyler's prominent rose farmers. All her telephone calls to Tyler were to her aunt's and uncle's home.

Once, A. J. arrived twenty-five minutes late for one of their dates. If Lennie was angry, her indifference was an Oscar-winning performance. Allison, on the other hand, wanted A. J.'s pecker shellacked and mounted trophy-style on her jewelry cabinet if he kept her waiting five minutes for anything.

Out of the blue, Lennie surprised A. J. with the gift of an eighty-dollar, Texas Instruments, constant-memory pocket calculator. A. J. had to drag her to Tiches Department Store so he could respond in kind. She allowed him the final say (he thinks) on a coordinated skirt, blouse, and jacket set. A. J. hustled her past Jewelry and Perfumes, Allison's favorite candy stores, to the department where his Ex picked out her working dresses. It was bad enough that his new sweetheart had no choice but to deceive with baggy clothes, at least, A. J. told himself, she did not have to clad her luscious body in garb apparently purchased from a K-mart sidewalk sale.

Oddly, for a woman – at least, as A. J. judged those things – Lennie sometimes could not smoothly express herself. Engineers also tended to be choppy verbal communicators, something A. J. had seen often enough in the elliptical mutterings of his fellow engineers at Texas Instruments – not to mention the techs at

Edgecom – so A. J. was used to seeing a person trip over his or her tongue attempting to verbalize a thought. Moreover, A. J. figured the small impediment made Lennie a better investigative officer, made her more analytical: A. J. was of the opinion, and still is, that first-rate verbal and analytical aptitudes rarely cohabitated in the same cranium.

It was another matter, however, when Lennie blew hot. Then, one of her salvos of four-letter words, besides crystallizing her point, would shrink the pecker of an NBA center.

Lennie was good at repartee, an expert at quick digs, and she often bested A. J. (And he always thought that he was pretty quick with a snappy barb.) Once A. J. whimsically proposed that "cutting me off" – abstinence A. J. had in mind – was fit punishment for one of his careless breaches of mating-game etiquette, and she shot back that cutting him off was not an option as he apparently had already suffered that method of redress. A. J. laughed politely. Later, when it dawned on him that she was talking dimensions, not deprivation, he was less amused.

When A. J. told her she'd have to help him pick out a Christmas present for his daughter Danielle she replied, "Not a chance. I hate to shop."

A. J. composed an astonished look.

"Some men," Lennie countered, "*real* men, like to crochet. What was the name of the professional football player who–"

A. J. cut her off. He knew who she meant: Roosevelt Grier, a huge NFL lineman, one of the Los Angeles Rams' so-called "Fearsome Foursome," who chilled out by embroidering.

"Likewise," A. J. said, "some men arrange posies, decorate store windows . . . sit down to pee."

Lennie had to work every day of Christmas week, 1980, and she and A. J. did little celebrating. She never once uttered the word "Mass," and A. J. took it – her Irish surname not withstanding – that she was not a Catholic. She putatively was, however.

For Christmas, A. J. gave her two pants suits from Tiches and accessories selected by the clerk. (Yes, in public her loose-fitting garments embarrassed A. J.) Lennie insisted that A. J. recommend a Christmas present for himself, one from her. She became impatient and then snippy when A. J.'s third suggestion was a pick and shovel. He finally suggested a gift certificate, and Lennie gave him a hundred-dollar gift certificate from a big hardware store in Plano, Texas. (You can't win 'em all.)

Lennie decorated our apartment with a plastic, table-top, three-foot-high Christmas tree sporting a rainbow of decorative lights that flashed on and off. She sent a package to her Aunt and Uncle in Tyler, and a card – probably with a check inside – to her brother.

A. J. gave Danielle her Christmas present that Wednesday afternoon (the twenty-fourth), two one-third carat, diamond earring studs. Danielle gave her father a necktie. A. J. knew Allison was behind her niggardliness, but it still hurt.

# [35]

The second gathering of Hardeman's well-off friends marched Indian-file past A. J.'s office door. As before, Hardeman led the way and Osgood obsequiously followed. Skip was not with them. Evidently Israel's Cannon had been re-mothballed because there was no preceding laughter or giggling. A. J. was again whittling down his list of MaxWriter function possibilities when Nick ambled into his office.

A. J. leaned back and waited until Nick finally gave him his undivided attention. "Should I specify a default option for MaxWriter?"

The sudden gleam in Nick's eyes signaled A. J. that he should not have asked. "A *what*?"

"Say, a user tries to retrieve a particular text file and enters the wrong command. Or a non-existent one? Or, say, enters wx4dullar-signz or something else screwy?"

"Sure, Pop. Have MaxWriter default and flash a message on the scope, 'No such command, Bonehead.'

Hell, won't it automatically tab left or somehow lock-up?"

"Yes, bad example. What if–"

"Or . . . the default option might flash, "Dumb Bastard, exclamation mark."

"Funny, Silo. But my turn's coming. S*omeone,* for whatever reason, murdered Fran. Lunch for a *week.* Put your money where your mouth is."

Nick shook his head. "If you got lucky and turned out to be right you'd pig out every damn meal."

A. J. sighed and faked weariness. "How much RAM memory would a Save/Get function suck up?"

"Too much," Nick answered promptly. "You get overly fancy playing with text and MaxWriter will barely have enough RAM left to accommodate a memo . . . not one of Osgood's anyway."

A. J. threw his pen down in mock disgust.

"Of course," Nick said. "You could include a Save/Get and name our word processor *Min*Writer. Think Brasshead would go for it?"

A. J. nodded disgustedly. "Why," A. J. said, raising his voice, "are you bothering me, Silo?"

Nick twirled A. J.'s visitor's chair on a rear leg to where it was facing A. J.'s desk and sat down. "I'm desperate for male companionship, even if my choice of gender is marginal. What's the word on the street?"

"On the street," A. J. replied slowly. "Well . . . Skip thinks that our first invitees pledged a half million bucks. Promised by Osgood, no doubt, that someday Edgecom will topple mighty IBM."

"A half million?" Nick said smiling sardonically. "I'm not surprised. Did you see their cars?"

A, J, shook his head.

"One piker arrived in a Lincoln. The rest were driving Jags and Mercedes. Except one cat, who wheeled up in a V12 Aston Martin." He mimicked the imperturbable voice of Sean Connery's James Bond character: "Martin. Aston Martin."

"Give me a minute," A. J. said, "and I'll figure it out."

"I imagine you're tight with the first group of Hardeman's pals?"

"Only the females. Except, I fish Lake Tawakani on weekends with the old codger who was wearing the rock around his neck. Actually, he *owns* Lake Tawakani. He was with the first group."

"The first group was bigger," Nick said.

A. J. disagreed: "Seven men both times."

A. J.'s telephone rang, and Nick stood up. A. J. figured it was McPherson calling: he had already bugged A. J. twice on trivial matters. A. J. nodded toward his office door, suggesting to Nick that he should leave; Nick dropped back into the chair.

A. J. gave him a mean look and said to his caller, "Talk."

"It's me," Lennie said. "Bad hair day?"

"No, Dear, I expected it was a pecker-head who'd already called me twice this morning."

"The body's at the morgue."

A. J. waved goodbye to Nick. He grinned but did not move. A. J. gave him another mean look. He distended his grin.

"Great," A. J. said to Lennie. "That's . . . great."

Now that the moment of truth had arrived, A. J. was suddenly gripped with a mild case of the yipes. Evidently it showed in his voice.

"Christ, don't break into a dance," Lennie said, with more than a shade of annoyance.

"It's not that. It's . . . I'm being accosted by a dumb engineer."

"Nickerson?"

"Yes, Silo. The ugly Iowan."

Nick rose again and backed toward the door.

"The dumb shit's has finally taken my hint." A. J. paused until Nick had cleared the doorway. "I'm ecstatic, Sweetheart," A. J. said with concocted enthusiasm. "When will we know something?"

"I'm waiting to hear. At this moment, there's only one other body is in the holding queue."

A. J.'s apprehension returned. "Jesus, Lennie, what if Fran really did croak of natural causes, how–"

"Jesus, *Alan*," she interrupted, mocking his whiny tone of voice. "It'll be my ass, not yours."

"You know damn well, Dear, that I'll be sick to death over it, over *you*, if I'm wrong."

"I know, Hon," Lennie said, adding, after a moment, "It wouldn't be a big deal."

"What? My getting sick to death?"

"Well . . . that. And me getting my ass reamed by Hope."

A. J. did not buy into her brushing-aside the punishment but decided to let that dog sleep.

"I'm driving downtown tomorrow," Lennie said. "Care to see a body opened?"

"I . . . yes. Hell yes, I would. I'd be allowed to watch?"

"I think so. If Dot . . . if Doctor Gisewight does the examination. You're positive you want to watch?"

A. J. chuckled weakly. "No, I'm not *positive*. But I'm . . . game."

"You and that . . . cutesy girl prancing around naked in the woods. You know what happened to her."

"Yeah, yeah," A. J. answered vaguely. "She told a hunter that she was game, and he shot her. I'll be there!"

"I'll set it up and call you back."

In ten minutes Lennie was on the telephone again. "We're in. Gisewight got the job. You know how to get there? Get to the morgue? If I can't drive?"

A. J. said that he only knew that the morgue was located near downtown Dallas, and Lemmie gave him directions, including exactly where to park.

# [36]

A. J. and Lennie donned paper smocks in a small anteroom. The wall opposite the room's entrance was lined with shiny steel clothes lockers; A. J. hung up his sport coat in one. It was the only locker they used.

A. J. sniffed hard twice.

"Formaldehyde," Lennie said softly.

Dr. Gisewight, from inside the examination room, glanced at a big wall clock and nodded at Lennie. The examination room, thirty-foot by thirty-foot, A. J. judged, was disagreeably cool in both aura and temperature. Four super-illuminated tables, paired and aligned but widely separated, consumed a large square of space in the middle of the room. A body, covered completely except for a motley looking foot with a tag fastened to its big toe, was lying on the table catty-cornered from Degeorge's sideboard.

Lennie introduced A. J. to Dr. Gisewight. Wearing scrubs, her mouth and nose covered by a white paper mask, she nodded as warmly as if Lennie had wheeled up a table of decomposing road kill. A tall, angular woman, she struck A. J. as four or five years too young to be referred to as middle-aged. She remained grim faced. Pulling on a prophylactic glove, she stared intently at Degeorge's shroud-covered body.

"Ready?" Dr. Gisewight asked Lennie.

Lennie looked at A. J. He didn't react at all; Lennie nodded at Dr. Gisewight.

Dr. Gisewight effortlessly whipped the heavy white-duck wrap off Fran's body and allowed it to fall in a disorderly pile at the foot of the table. A. J. was not shocked, as Dr. Gisewight seemed to expect he would be. He was briefly immobilized, however, at the sight of the determined look on the seemingly molded likeness of Fran's face. Lennie, her focus elsewhere, let out a long, low wolf whistle.

A. J. was surprised at how little the body had decomposed, and he said so.

Dr. Gisewight concisely offered that a sealed container protecting an embalmed body synergized to many months of preservation.

"One hears stories," A. J. said apologetically.

Dr. Gisewight bit his head off: "One watches TV."

"Sorry I mentioned it," A. J. mumbled.

Lennie stirred slightly. If Dr. Gisewight heard A. J.'s sarcastic apology she did not let on. It was likely, A. J. decided, that his remarks meant nothing to her.

Dr. Gisewight's eyes swept Degeorge's body. "So far, all I see is a case of natural mortality. You think he was poisoned?" she said to Lennie.

"I do," Lennie said, nodding.

A woman, younger and stockier than Dr. Gisewight and similarly outfitted, but carrying a clipboard, walked rapidly into the room, and stopped alongside Dr. Gisewight.

"Alice is interning," Dr. Gisewight said absentmindedly, her gaze slowly scanning Fran's body. "She'll be taking notes."

Alice nodded diffidently.

Lennie described the method by which A. J., and by now, Lennie herself presumed – more or less – that Degeorge had been poisoned.

Dr. Gisewight nodded, drew a deep breath, and slowly exhaled. She addressed the intern. "Okay?"

Alice nodded affirmatively. Dr. Gisewight pulled a ceiling-suspended microphone down and began: "External examination. The body is that of a thirty-four-year-old, well-nourished, moderately well-muscled male" – she pulled a scrap of paper from a pocket of her jacket – "weighing 152 pounds and measuring sixty-four and one-half inches in height. The scalp is thinly covered with close-trimmed, wiry, naturally black hair. The face is clean shaven."

Dr. Gisewight waited for Alice to finish writing on her clipboard and then continued describing Fran's physiognomy, as well as pinpointing the locations of the immature chest scar of his heart surgery, several aged scars, and a now-immortal bruise.

"The investigating detective," Dr. Gisewight mused, her attention still fixed on Fran's body, "thinks the subject was . . . efficiently murdered, that poison was injected into his vein through an IV valve. So at this time I will not examine the remains for needle marks." In an aside to Alice, she added, "Ordinarily I'd go over every square centimeter with a magnifying glass."

As if doubtful, Alice's eyes slightly narrowed.

"Yes," Dr. Gisewight said to Alice. "*Every* square centimeter. Between his toes, under his testicles . . . pluck some of his pubic hair. Everywhere."

"So much for the external," she went on. "I'm ready to open." She looked at Alice and then said to Lennie, "Grab your bottom, Detective."

Lennie looked at A. J., "Both hands, Dear."

A. J. nodded and watched as Dr. Gisewight pulled a small, electrical, hand-held saw with a rotating blade, which A. J. later learned was called a Stryker saw, from a deep drawer of her tool cabinet – and that is the last thing he remembered about the autopsying of the body of his friend Peter Francis Degeorge.

The room looked unfamiliar. A. J. heard a rustling sound to his right and glimpsed a nurse – or who A. J. assumed was a nurse – standing at the foot of a cot next to the one he was lying on. He stared straight ahead for a few seconds. Lennie, her eyes narrow and face purposeful, walked slowly toward him.

"Hi." Her smile was weak and obviously forced.

A. J. tried to sit up.

"Better not," Lennie said, moving quickly to A. J.'s side and lightly pushing him back down.

A. J.'s senses gradually returned. "We're at the morgue?"

Lennie smiled. "I am. I'm not sure where you are."

A. J. rubbed the back of his head fingering the place where the throbbing was greatest. There was swelling but no cut. He hazily figured out what had happened.

Lennie, seeing that A. J. had come around, said, "You hoity-toity weenie," "you scared me to death."

A. J. smiled tepidly. "Serves you right."

"Men," Lennie said scornfully. "I should have known."

Lennie helped A. J. sit up to where he could put his feet on the floor at the side of the cot. He sat there a few seconds and then stood up. Lennie steadied him. The woman whom A. J. at first mistook for a nurse helped her.

"I'm fine," A. J. said after a few seconds passed. He could not stop shaking his head slowly in self-disgust. "Anyway, I saw beautiful sunflowers. . . by Van Gogh."

Lennie, after a second, nodded. "Not a naked woman?"

Lennie walked A. J. to his car. "What happened after I conked out?" A. J. said, reaching for a door handle.

Lennie shrugged. "I'll have to call Dot. I've watched her before and I can guess."

"Please do," A. J. said. "Only don't explain things too graphically."

"Most likely she snipped off some tissue samples . . . inspected his organs . . . stirred around in his stomach and–"

"I noticed how you also felt duty-bound to inspect his, ah, organs."

". . . looked at other places for discoloration. And so on." Lennie nodded innocently. "It's a perk of my job, Hon."

A. J. said, "You probably hang out here."

Lennie said, "Many things hang out here. The place swings. Dot might send some of his parts to another forensic lab."

"To another lab?"

"One with expertise in poisons. Maybe she won't have to."

"That will take what? Another week? When do you think we'll know?"

"It depends," Lennie said, sighing. "Were in the middle of Christmas holidays, and . . . you know the drill. People take off, visit relatives, et cetera, et cetera. I'd guess two weeks. Does it matter?"

"I won't sleep well until we hear, and you know me when I can't sleep at night, my lovely."

"And you know *me* when you can't sleep at night, lover boy."

"That's cold," A. J. said.

Lennie several times changed the subject. When A. J. tried to open the car door, she held it closed with her knee – for much longer than A. J. thought necessary. Had A. J. been the age I am now, he likely would have stifled a tear at her concern.

# [37]

Lennie was waiting for A. J. at his apartment. A. J. had given her a new key, but on that day in mid-January, 1981, it was the first time she had used it – or had to as A. J. was always home by mid-afternoon. Dr. Giscwight had called her at work. The floor of the upstairs apartment entranceway amplified the clatter of A. J.'s footsteps.

We embraced, but Lennie quickly pulled away. Why, she demanded to know, was he a good hour late.

"Skip wanted to talk," A. J. said. "And that boy *do* get carried away."

She hooked her arm inside A. J.'s, walked him to the sofa, and gently pushed him onto it. Her voice was tired sounding. "You want a beer?"

"I don't know," A. J. answered uneasily. "Do I?"

The corners of her lips began slowly edging out and up, the beginning of one of her foxy grins.

"He *was* poisoned!" A. J. cried.

"No ifs, ands, or buts!" Lennie pretended to wipe sweat from her forehead. "Gisewight has the proof.

Something about . . . tissue stains. She lost me, but there's not a shadow of a doubt."

A. J. jumped up and hugged Lennie. They improvised a dance, and tumbled onto the sofa giggling.

"I knew the son-of-a-bitch killed him," A. J. said. "The hell with beer! Champagne, all around!"

Lennie's grin faded: it was miserable outside, one of Dallas' infrequent, bitterly cold winter nights. "Or," A. J. said, noticing her sudden long face, "I could order Chinese food delivered to us."

She shook her head. "There's a glitch, Dear."

"Oh balls! There's always something. What? How big?"

"Not, ah . . . . It depends."

"Depends? Depends on what?"

"Your boss was poisoned allright. Definitely murdered. Only it wasn't snake venom."

"You're sure?" A. J. asked crossly.

Her look was flint hard. "Hell yes, I'm sure. The poison was a chemical called potassium permanganate."

"I knew you were sure, Hon," A. J. said apologetically. "Hold on a minute, I took a year of chemistry at SMU."

Returning from the bedroom that he had morphed into a makeshift office, A. J. began reading aloud from his college chemistry text book: "Manganese is of great industrial importance blah, blah, blah. Oxidation states of plus two, plus three, blah, blah, blah. The most familiar, permanganate, blah, blah . . . ."

A. J. skimmed several paragraphs, the usual no-fat lines written by chemistry wonks. Poking at a page, he pronounced the letters of permanganate's chemical shorthand: "M, little N, O sub four."

A. J. skimmed another paragraph. "Strongly acidic. Purple colored."

He read another few seconds to himself and looked up. "That's about it. As much as I can understand."

Lennie was nodding impatiently, and A. J. snapped the book shut.

"Yes," she said, "Gisewight told me that potassium . . . whatever has lots of uses. As a diluter, a tablespoon in a couple gallons of water. At full strength it had to be instantly deadly."

"It's a silver bullet, eh."

"Yes. But hell, Dear, don't you see what this means?"

On cloud nine at hearing the autopsying of Fran's body was not in vain, A. J. totally overlooked the implication of the fact that the deadly poison wasn't snake venom. Lennie's unwavering look demanded that A. J. answer her question.

"Damn it," A. J. said, the veil finally lifting from his eyes, "*anyone* could have murdered Fran."

Lennie nodded. "Not anyone. But I'll sure have to re-visit big O . . . reconsider who all had opportunity. Like . . . who all visited him that night."

"Shit. Even I was there."

The gotcha version of her grin returned.

"Exactly as I thought," A. J. said grudgingly. "You hate men."

"Most," Lennie agreed.

"Never mind," A. J. said, cocking his head disdainfully.

"Up yours," Lennie mumbled – A. J. guessed that is what she said.

"That's another motive," Lennie said exhaling heavily, "another aspect I'll have to revisit."

A. J. nodded agreeably. "Good. I'll be completely exonerated."

Lennie shrugged. "The truth will out."

A. J. said, "Up *yours*, detective."

They stared sappily at each other.

A. J. said, finally, "Potassium permanganate? I'm surprised Fran didn't turn the hospital room into a car wash when that stuff hit his gut."

. . . Lennie shook her head. "His death was instantaneous. Gisewight said the fatal injection was a load, a heroin and poison cocktail. Keep in mind, your boss was already loopy on Demerol. Gisewight said he never knew what hit him."

"Well," A. J. said, "that is a blessing anyway."

"I interviewed the swing-shift nurse," Lennie said. "And I also talked to an aide who worked third shift that evening. She said that–"

"When? When did you talk to them? You never told me."

"No, maybe I should have, but who the hell were *you* back then? We'd hardly met. Anyway, Gisewight said if your boss had *ingested* the poison there'd of been stains on his lips, in his mouth . . . down his food pipe. There wasn't. She went all over his body for needle marks. It had to have been shot into his vein through that . . ."

A. J. completed her sentence: "Through the Y-site IV valve."

"Yes. Dot went technical on me, but basically she said there was staining of some of his . . . body tissue. That was the key. She had obviously read up on potassium . . . whatever. Absorption of it destroys cells . . . of the central nervous system. I think I got that right. It used to be–"

"You know," A. J. interrupted, "if you think about it, Osgood's not so damn dumb as to have used venom from his own pet snake."

Lennie's expression was rapt. "You think? He sure as hell didn't expect there'd be an autopsy. Besides, some poisons are virtually undetectable. I don't know about cobra venom."

"Fooled everyone," A. J. said not too pleasantly. "Even the doctors. Especially the doctors."

Lennie tilted her head apologetically. "I didn't say it Hon, but I was never comfortable with your . . . idea that the poison was snake venom."

Someone entered the next-door apartment, and out of habit they stopped and listened. "Her boyfriend is with her," A. J. said grinning. "One of 'em, anyway. It depends on the day of the week . . . the time of the day . . . the alignment of the planets . . . ."

Lennie shrugged. "Gisewight said you can buy a box of that poison, diluted, for twenty bucks at any pet shop that sells pond fish, it's–"

"Really," A. J. said. "Over the counter? You're not surprised?"

Lennie shook her head. "No. Lots of household products are mildly toxic. Gisewight and I had a long talk. There have been cases where children died from eating potassium . . . whatever. It looks like tiny purple beads, like the decoration sprinkled on cakes. Catfish farmers use it to rid their ponds of parasites. Years ago, and it may still happen some places, women used it to encourage the discharge of a fetus."

A step toward returning his chemistry textbook, A. J. stopped in his tracks. "Oh? How?"

"You don't want to know."

"Yes I do."

"By douching."

"Ouch."

# [38]

They could hear rhythmic sounds coming from the other apartment. "Quiet, woman," A. J. said suavely to Lennie. "They've coupled."

Lennie grinned. "They didn't make it past the living room."

We both listened. After a moment, Lennie said, "Turns out my boyfriend's a damn voyeur."

A. J. pressed a finger to his lips, "Shhh. You want to break the connection?"

"You should go and take notes," Lennie said, shaking her head censoriously.

"Damn. I lay a serious murder right in your lap and you thank me by maligning my innate morality."

"Some murders," Lennie said, *are not* serious?" The look on her face buttressed the sarcasm of her words.

"You know what I mean."

"Were you blowing smoke up my skirt, or are we going out for champagne?"

"Only because you screw like a mink in estrus. And I've been at sea for a year. Grab your coat, Beaverette."

Lennie pulled her jacket from the coat closet and A. J. slipped into his, which he had tossed on the sofa.

"Let's try that new Ruth's Chris restaurant," A. J. said, backing the car from their assigned parking stall.

"I don't feel like a . . . big steak, Hon. How about we eat at Tractor Tom's?"

A. J. recognized her wifespeak for the command that it was. "Okay," he said. "Where's it at? I never heard of Tractor Tom's."

"On Skillman, a couple blocks south of the station house. The owner's hung up on old farm tractors. The table-lamp bases are . . . Farm alls?"

"International Harvester Farmalls? Yeah. Probably. Red tractors with big rear wheels?"

"Uh-huh. It's a cop hang-out, more a bar and gril really. Never been held up. Surprise! Bob Hoover and Brandon Hope will be there . . . most likely half soused. It's a merit badge for Hope, too."

Lennie, seconds after we arrived at Tractor Tom's, was the center of attention, the toastee of Hoover, Hope, and six or seven other slightly looped cops, including the sergeant working the station's public desk the first time A. J. visited Lennie.

Lennie steered me to where Hoover and Hope were sitting together at one end of the bar. She introduced Hoover by his full name, Robert E. Lee Hoover; Hope she introduced as Lieutenant Hope. They were the only celebrators wearing suits. Both men had fully loosened their neckties and the knots of both ties hung a good six inches below their respective necklines.

Bald, his eyes dark and sunken, Hoover stood and offered his hand. Hope nodded. Even sitting, Hope was almost Hoover's height. A. J. remember thinking that Hope, when he was a patrolman, likely never had to call for a backup. His ruddy complexion looked out-of-place in a business suit.

Lennie excessively insisted that A. J. receive ample credit for her collar, and Hoover, obviously feeling the booze, turned and shouted, "Let's hear it for A. J."

Glasses were raised, and A. J. was fulsomely toasted. After the hooraying, judging from all further attention directed his way, A. J. had morphed into a bucket of rocks – or maybe into a newspaper reporter.

Lennie had warned me on our way to Tractor Tom's that most cops were implacably randy, especially after a drink. Some, she said, would grab her ass. She said A. J. should let everything he heard go in one ear and fly right out the other.

She was right about her fellow officers. In another setting, among any other group of men, A. J. would have cut loose after three drinks – or sooner. And likely, got his clock wound.

Once, however, A. J. did totally lose it. Returning from the can, Merle, the detective who sat-in when A. J. informed Lennie that he knew Fran was murdered, had

Lennie by the wrist and was loudly demanding a lap dance. A. J. took two steps toward where Lennie was sitting. Another cop blocked his way. He kept his back to A. J., but could sense his movements. When he finally let A. J. slip past, Lennie had broken away from Merle. When Merle followed her, she turned and kicked him square in the crotch. He froze for a second, hobbled to the bar, and bent over to where he was resting his forehead on folded arms leveled on its top. Lennie strolled leisurely to our table, turned, and showily toasted Merle with her drink. From the outpouring of laughter, A. J. guessed that he was the only one who failed to see the humor in her mock salute.

Lenny that night became aroused to tumescence, the first time since she and A. J. had met. A. J. knew it was not him who had pushed her hot button, but he figured what the hell, even a blind pig gropingly stumbles onto an acorn now then.

# [39]

Lennie left for work late in the morning of the day after our evening at Tractor Tom's celebrating the true cause of Fran's death. She and Lieutenant Hope arrived at the station simultaneously. They spent the next hour in Hope's office winnowing the list of persons who had both motive and opportunity to kill Fran. Eventually, they sifted out two people: Hummel Osgood and Fran's widow, Jo Ellen.

That night A. J. told Lennie that her investigating Jo Ellen would be like panning the Trinity River – the stream that in the summer slowly crawled through Dallas – for gold. "You won't find any," A. J. assured her. "Either gold. *Or* a smoking gun."

Lennie backed me out of the batter's box with a high, hard one. "You know people," she said, "like I know electronics."

"What," A. J. demanded, "could Jo Ellen possibly have for a motive?"

Lennie shook her head disgustedly. "Insurance money, Mister smart engineer. Maybe the only thing your boss *really* loved was electronics."

"Meaning their marriage was all show? I'd sooner suspect the Pope of vandalism."

After a long second of quiet weariness Lennie said, "I'm hungry. Let's go eat."

We dined that night at Foister's Smoke House, a weathered, red-neck, ribs-and-brisket restaurant in the long-settled, downtown section of Plano. It was a part of the town that was either avoided by or unknown to the damnyankee carpetbaggers of Jesse's loathing. It was A. J.'s first visit to Foister's.

Lennie ate slowly, worked each bite of her brisket slices into digestible beef. "We'll get a search warrant," she said suddenly, interrupting my whining over the decline of the once-mighty Dallas Cowboys football team. "We could get lucky."

Seeing the blank look on my face, she back tracked, explained that they would bring Jo Ellen in first, clear her as a suspect, and then take off the gloves and go after Osgood. "I'm betting Jo Ellen will report voluntarily. I won't search her place, unless she acts funny. Which you promised me, *Abner*, ain't gonna happen."

"I didn't *promise*. What I said was I'd sooner suspect . . . anyone else. You're sure Osgood won't take off?"

"Of course, I'm not *sure*. He'd be abandoning . . . you said, five million bucks? Would you skip if you thought you could beat it?"

"I don't know. It might depend on whether or not I was actually guilty."

"So, if he hangs around he's innocent?"

"I didn't say that. You're the people person, Detective. I's ah thik enginuer."

We concentrated on eating. Quietly, in disconnected mutterings, Lennie fretted over how to prove that Osgood injected the poison.

"That," she said, after a long deep breath, "will be the rusty nut on the chastity belt."

A funny thought crossed A. J.'s mind: "Apparently you don't know that the nuts on chastity belts are wing nuts?"

Lennie did not know, nor did she care to learn that wing nuts were designed for easy loosening by fingers alone.

Nodding absentmindedly, Lennie said, "Maybe, something will come from the search. You were whining about the ineptitude of the Dallas Cowboys?"

Lennie reckoned correctly: Jo Ellen willingly reported to the police station for questioning. Only routine, Lennie assured her. We tell them, Lennie explained to me, that in homicide investigations everyone with a pulse who knew the victim gets interviewed.

"By the book, huh?"

"Chapter one."

"How'd it go?" A. J. asked Lennie at home the evening of the day that she interrogated Jo Ellen.

"We'll talk," she answered, hurrying past A. J. "I have to pee."

"She was clean, wasn't she?" A. J. yelled after her.

"For Christ sakes!" Lennie yelled back,"would you hold *your* water."

A. J. opened two beers, pulled a chair away from the kitchen table, sat down, and kicked a chair out for Lennie. She joined him and took a swig of her beer. "Your ex-boss's widow," she said, "is not as dumb as you seem to think."

A. J. shrugged. "It's how she always struck me."

"She saw through my bullshit about our talk only being routine. Goddamn Merle laid it on too thick. I hate to work with that dumb ass. He's so–"

"Yeah," A. J. interrupted, "I remember him from the party at Tractor Tom's."

Lennie relaxed a little. "If it makes you feel any better, I doubt she killed him."

"Some," A. J. said nodding once quickly.

"However"–for a second, her word "However" was homeless – "there's a complication."

"Damn it, detective," A. J. said. "You always muddy the water. What now?"

"Tell me again," Lennie said, "who was at . . . who all visited Degeorge in the hospital the night he was murdered. That you are *sure* of."

A. J. removed his glasses. "When I arrived, Jo Ellen and Betty, Jo Ellen's twin sister, were there." A. J. paused. "So was Osgood. Then I left. I passed Selig Hildreth coming up the steps heading, I presumed, for Fran's room. After that . . . I don't know."

A. J. balled his hands into fists, rubbed both eyes, and put his glasses back on.

"So," Lennie said, "you can vouch for Jo Ellen, Hummel and his wife, and this dorky Hildreth guy?"

"That I personally saw at the hospital? Yes. Incidentally, sometimes Hildreth is jokingly called *Mace* at Edgecom."

"Okay, then," Lennie said, after a silent moment, "according to Jo Ellen, she walked her sister and her sister's husband . . . the Osgoods, to their car. And when she returned, Hildreth had left. She had passed him as he was leaving. And her husband was dead. Your boss by then had given up the ghost."

Lennie waited a second for A. J. to comment. When he did not, she said, "In other words, Hildreth was alone with Degeorge for some twenty minutes, for however long Jo Ellen spent visiting with her sister and her husband . . . Hummel."

"Making Hildreth a suspect?"

"Yes, if Jo Ellen was straight with me."

"But why," A. J. coaxed, "would Selig Hildreth want to kill Fran?"

Lennie shook her head. "Here we go again." she said, adding that A. J. saw through people like she saw through brick walls. "You knew he had been regularly laying Jo Ellen even before your boss was killed . . . before he was murdered?"

"I'm not sure I *knew* that. They'd been seen together and . . . anyway, I thought it was *after* Fran died."

"Hun-uh," Lennie said, shaking her head. "Jo Ellen didn't try to fudge it, probably figured I'd done my homework. And that's another reason I don't believe she's the air-head you seem to think. Hildreth had been humping her for a year. She admitted it. But in the same breath she said, tit for tat, that her husband was screwing his secretary. Did you know that?"

"Fran boffing Pat? Not for sure. But I'm not surprised."

"Off the top, Hon, there's a damn good reason why Hildreth might have wanted to kill Degeorge. Insurance money. Again."

"Insurance money? You mean . . . how? He'd marry Jo Ellen?"

Lennie nodded. "He's been in her pantys for a year. Plus, he'd probably like to take over Edgecom. Who knows? Maybe all along *he* had in mind the idea of taking Edgecom public."

"Hildreth," A. J. said musingly, "could never run Edgecom let alone take it public."

Lennie shrugged. "In any event, it didn't work out that way. But, who knew?"

A. J. let on he was miffed. "You know something Detective. This constant undercutting of my case against Osgood? You're starting to curdle my urine, bit time."

"If," Lennie said, ignoring my sham complaint, "Jo Ellen's clear on the sequence of visitors, Osgood was never alone with Degeorge."

"Yeah," A. J. said dismissively. "*If* Jo Ellen's not . . . all screwed up."

A. J. finished his beer, stood up, and stretched. "Ready for another?"

Lennie shook her head; A. J. opened a beer and returned to his chair. "I have to admit something, though."

"*What*?" Lennie asked sharply after a few seconds, clearly unhappy that A. J. had broken her concentration.

"I know for a fact that Fran had a million-dollar life insurance policy on himself. He told me so. And knowing Fran, I'd bet he told most of Edgecom."

Lennie nodded, "Probably Edgecom paid the premiums."

"Legally?" A. J. said.

"One way or another," Lennie mumbled. "I'm going to dig a little tomorrow, see if the name Selig Hildreth turns up in one of our felony databases."

"The police categorize crimes that way? What? For fast access?"

"I don't know," she answered, "Does it matter?"

Rebuffed, A. J. said, "Anyway, Osgood's still a turd of dog shit."

Lennie stared at A. J. for a long second. "Jesus, Hon, the man has you by the gonads." After another long second, she added, "How come you didn't fetch me a beer?"

# [40]

Edgecom's technicians, respecting their bounden duty to assign new employees befitting nicknames, soon pegged Albert Steen with the handle "Albert *Ein*steen" and Harriet Muckinhaupt with the nickname "Cozy-Legs Lou."

Steen was smart. He came by his nickname, however, because he wore his hair long, and he constantly tilted with furniture: chairs, especially, found sundry ways to corral him. Harriet's nickname was a reflection on her negligent manner in keeping her legs shaved. Two technicians, exchanging observations, came up with the nickname Cozy Legs Lou. How did Cozy Legs Lou win out over Harry Legs Harriet? A. J. didn't even try to guess.

Both Steen and Muckinhaupt reported to Edgecom on the second Monday of January, 1981. Commissioned to jointly manage the development of MaxWriter, Steen was a degreed electronics engineer and Muckinhaupt a degreed software programmer. Both had been recruited from Foster Systems. Steen, A. J.

guessed, could look back on forty. A. J. estimated that Muckinhaupt, by a year at most, looked ahead to thirty.

Apparently money was gushing in from Hardeman's wealthy friends because employing Steen and Muckinhaupt was only the beginning. By mid-February, the previously underused office bay had become a labyrinth of one-man cubicles formed of mobile, cloth-upholstered room dividers. And before many more weeks, all regular office rooms and most of the permanent cubicles were occupied by serious, business-suited young men who Kabuki danced to Osgood's formalized blather. Rare, in fact, was the hour when Osgood was not ensconced at the head of the conference-room table chairing a meeting. As rare was the upshot of one of his meetings any more than an impossible production schedule, which was forthwith ignored, utterly, even by the intensely conscientious white-collar new-hires.

Edicts were posted. One forbade factory workers from entering the office bay, except on "Official Business." A red-bordered copy of the directive was pinned dead-center on the main bulletin board serving Manufacturing. Someone – cognizant of the fact that both the men's and women's latrines were in the office third of the building – printed over the directive in heavy El Marko ink, IS PISSING and SHITTING OFFICIAL BUSINESS? And someone, in a different hand, added, HARDLY! RELIEVE YOURSELF IN THE PARKING LOT, SNOOTY. The demeaning notations circulated, and Dornhoffer became Edgecom's Captain Queeg, the ball-bearing-clicking, schizophrenic Naval officer of Herman Wouk's *The Caine Mutiny*. The fictional Queeg, verifiably delusional, was obsessed with imprisoning the men that he imagined were dangerously subversive."

Selig Hildreth was again assigned the job of managing the technicians, and Herman Cronk was hired to take over Manufacturing. Reassigned, Hildreth loyally explained to his men that the intra-plant travel constraint had nothing to do with social or vocational class differences, but was entirely a matter of secrecy essential to the maturing progress of MaxWriter. The next day, Dwayne the Draftsman, as everybody called him, gave notice, claiming he had not seen so much chicken shit since his student days cleaning poultry cages at a Texas A & M University research farm.

Homer Cronk was also recruited from Foster Systems. McPherson, according to Nick, convinced Osgood that wearing but one hat, specifically a headdress – no different in importance from the feathered bonnet worn by chief Crazy Horse – was the only sure way he could bring MaxWriter in on time. Osgood went along with McPherson and approved an offer to Cronk.

Cronk, a slender, fussy, born-again Christian, his butch haircut true as a carpenter's square, set himself up in one of the carpeted Engineering offices. Jesse's office, the middle of the three offices looking out on the production bay, where he should have quartered himself, went begging, and it remained unused except as a cloistered site for lunchtime brown-baggers. (As if Jesse's room was hallowed, the diners, when they finished eating, always picked up and restored the room to exactly the way Jesse had left it his last day at Edgecom, going so far as to spread the schematic that he had mindlessly walked away from, back on the top of his desk.)

Amazingly, Osgood approved Cronk's hiring of a production expediter. Nick, who, while still an Iowa farm kid had become vicariously interested in sailing, compared Cronk's delegation to the mounting of a bowsprit on a raft formed of railroad cross ties.

Cronk engineered another major personnel change: he fired Sandra Welcheck, Edgecom's long-time buyer and reigning queen of complimentary nooners. Once a hierarchical peer of Jennerette, Nickerson, and Dornhoffer, she had been demoted and was reporting to the head of Manufacturing – briefly, in Jesse's absence, to Hildreth, and then to Cronk himself.

Cronk had his reasons for firing Sandy: she was a philanderer, a drunk, and, covertly, a heathen. Besides, she treated him like an autocratic little weasel, which was too close to calling a spade a spade.

A. J. witnessed Sandy's revenge. It took place in the men's restroom mid-afternoon of the day after Cronk sacked her. Cronk was relieving himself at a urinal, Sandy, bagged, burst into the john and began loudly ascribing Cronk's ancestry to one or another of large four-legged farm animals, punctuating her abuse with well-aimed kicks to his butt. Thus distracted, Cronk emptied his bladder everywhere but in or near the urinal, to which – after Sandy's first energetic boot – he had attached himself with both hands to the plumbing at the top. A. J. rescued him, more or less, and was unavoidably vomited upon by Sandy.

Cronk replaced Sandy with someone named Huey Remey. Remey was lodged, not in Sandy's spacious old office, but in one of the new ersatz offices formed of upholstered partitions.

Also, sometime late in 1980, or perhaps early in 1981, Edgecom Data Company, Inc. was re-christened Edgecom Data Corporation.

Thus, chaos and confusion were the conditions at Edgecom on the day the police arrested Selig Hildreth. Lennie, accompanied by a male detective, made the collar, walked him out in handcuffs. A. J. was at home when it happened. Nick telephoned him – likely before the police cruiser had left the Edgecom parking lot.

# [41]

Selig Hildreth became a suspect in Fran's sudden, unexpected death the moment Lennie heard he was bedding Fran's wife. A. J. provided Lennie with his Social Security number. Staunchly doubting Hildreth's complicity, and therefore dubious about that nine-digit number's importance, A. J. had no qualms about passing the number on. Still, he was careful to prevent Hildreth from finding out that he had involved himself in the stealth transmission of it to Lennie.

In 1980, computer databases were not structured with the design eloquence of later years, and data access pathways were sometimes rife with detours that measurably slowed data processing – the inputting of data coded on a stack of manually formatted IBM punch cards, for example. Anyway, computers were premium assets limited in availability. It was often hours, sometimes a day, not mere seconds, before a data search could be executed.

Sometime early in January, Lennie telephoned A. J. at Edgecom, made certain that he was alone, and then disappointedly explained that after a long attempt she had bombed again, had failed to get a computer hit on Hildreth's Social Security number.

Still tenaciously convinced that Osgood killed Fran, A. J. all but yawned. "So . . . back to square one?" he asked placidly.

"Afraid so," Lennie replied.

Certain that Osgood was guilty, A. J. was not disappointed at hearing that the target blip on Lennie's oscilloscopic radar screen – if such a blip even existed – was buried in the scope's mud, in the numberless sporadic and transient pinpoints of electronic noise.

"It's possible," Lennie said after a pause, "that Jo Ellen is confused over 'the who' and 'the when' of her husband's hospital visitors that evening."

A. J. agreed, but kept his low opinion of the balmy power of Jo Ellen's lubricant-starved cerebral mechanimism to himself. "It's also possible," he said, "that she and Betty had left Hummel alone in Fran's room to gossip in private, isn't it?"

Lennie did not answer A. J. 's question, so he teased her: "You know how women are."

"I'll see you tonight," Lennie replied abruptly.

A. J. assumed Lieutenant Hope was headed her way.

A. J. watched Lennie park her car from the living-room window of their apartment and then cracked the apartment door. Lennie walked in hesitantly, her mind elsewhere. They embraced, but Lennie quickly backed away.

"It's that bad?" A. J. said, leaning back.

"No," Lennie answered after a long sigh. "It's just that . . . Lieutenant Hope told me to bring Osgood in, that Hoover will argue the arrest warrant."

"That's so terrible?"

"For a couple reasons. For one, Osgood doesn't have a rap sheet. For another, I personally don't think he's our boy. Sorry Hon. He may be crooked as a dog's hind leg, but a murderer? I haven't bought into that possibility, yet."

"Womens' intuition?"

"Partly. When I asked him to voluntarily meet me at the station, he all but blew me off the phone laughing. Remember? I got pissed and implied that I'd get a warrant."

"Yeah," A. J. said nodding. "He didn't exactly dirty his Fruit of the Looms at hearing that."

"Besides," Lennie said, "there's the question of opportunity. He *had* to have been alone with Degeorge to inject the poison. Jo Ellen said, in so many words, that he never was."

"According to Jo Ellen," A. J. muttered.

"So far . . . ." Lennie left her thought unfinished.

"When will you pick him up?"

"Depends. After they cut the papers. What time does he usually arrive at Edgecom?"

"Lately . . . not before eight-thirty. At least not on the days I've been there in the morning."

A. J. arrived at the plant at eight o'clock on the day of Osgood's arrest. A. J. had resolved to stay as long as necessary to see that the man whom he absolutely knew had killed Fran was securely cuffed and ignominiously marched into a waiting police cruiser.

Sometime before mid-morning, obviously excited over something, Nickerson and Selig Hildreth marched into A. J.'s office. Nick was auspiciously wearing a dress shirt. Stuffed into its breast pocket was his only necktie, likely a hurried and indifferent purchase. The police detailed to arrest Osgood had not yet arrived.

Eyeing his shirt, A. J. asked, "Running with the big dogs now?"

Nick spit out the word "no." Sel, garbed in his usual neatly laundered work clothes, sniggered.

A. J. did not remember what the two men were turned-on about – a circuit-design serendipity, likely. What A. J. did vividly recall, however, was the picture that shortly formed in his mind, the image of two block-letter words – a person's first and last names – stamped on a cloth medium. The image popped into A. J.'s head when the usually somber Hildreth cackled at something Nick had said. Although the image was unclear – like watching a high-flying monoplane with cheap binoculars – A. J. could not purge it from his mind. Nick's non-stop chatter did not help.

Eventually the two men, their excitement allayed, left the room. A. J. waited a few seconds, closed the door, returned to his desk, and removed his glasses.

The letter Q came to mind first, and then the word Quest and then Quench. And, finally, Quetsch. *Ronald Quetsch*!

A. J. printed the name on the back of a tablet and telephoned Lennie. "I've got something else," he said, fired up.

Her eyes, A. J. knew, had to be slits of skepticism. "*Something* else?"

A. J. described how he had accidentally spotted the name Ronald Quetsch printed inside the top of Sel's briefcase. "Sel," A. J. said, "claimed he purchased the briefcase at a garage sale."

Silence.

"Sel," A. J. went on, "never shopped at a garage sale in his whole freaking life, Dear. He's not the type. He drives a Porche. Wouldn't be caught in public wearing a T-shirt. We're not bosom buddies, but I know him *that* well."

Lennie still said nothing, and A. J. reminded her that only a few days earlier he was a credible suspect centered in her investigatory cross hairs. "Opportunity and Jo Ellen's million-buck insurance policy," A. J. added. "You convinced me of his possible culpability."

"Christ," Lennie said after a few more wordless seconds, "Hope will make me wear a fishing license."

Keyed up, A. J. for a moment confused the name "Hope" with the noun hope. "Oh," A. J. said, "You mean Lieutenant Hope?"

"Uh-huh," Lennie answered off-handedly. "Tell you what Hon, I'll see if I can . . . spell the name for me."

A. J. spelled the name Quetsch and spoke the name Ronald. Lennie confirmed the spelling of Quetsch and then said she'd see me at home, but not to worry if she was late because she had a busy afternoon ahead. "Busy" was Lennie's way of shading the fact that she'd be helping to serve an arrest warrant.

While A. J. was on the telephone, Osgood was escorted by two police officers to a black-and- white sedan.

A. J. was about to doze off when he heard a key being pushed into the locked apartment door. He had napped after supper and was fighting the urge to catch another nap. Lennie, before A. J. reached the door, stepped into the apartment. Strands of her always perfectly well-behaved hair clung to her forehead. Her hand covered a place where a button hung by a thread from her blouse. Her lipstick was smeared, and her rouge was unevenly applied.

"Umm," A. J. said, his embrace dissolving into underplayed concern, "do I want to know?"

Lennie pursed her lips and shrugged. "No big deal," she said. "I was patting this piece of shit down and he turned on me. Merle damn near killed him."

I was surprised, and a tad uneasy at hearing her utter the word "him" in reference to their quarry. Usually, to Lennie's unflagging disgust, she only helped apprehend females. Relieved that she was not badly injured, but at the same time mildly unhappy that he was not the Sir Galahad who had smote her attacker, A. J. was a second deciding how to reply.

"When you say, 'turned on me'," A. J. said, separately enunciating each word, "what . . . exactly do you mean, Hon?"

Lennie pulled her blouse away from her shoulder. An inch-wide, six-inch long pinkish abrasion reached part way around her neck.

"The shit-ass tried bulldogging me. Marilyn smeared something on it at the station. It's nothing."

"Nothing my ass," A. J. snapped.

Lennie shook her head and gave A. J. a settled look meant to devalue the scrape on her neck.

After a few seconds, A. J. said, "Feel like a drink? One of my famously super-dry waterballs?"

Lennie again shook her head. "No, Dear. What I'd really like is a cup of hot chocolate."

A. J. chuckled. "Hot chocolate. From *our* kitchen?"

"I know," she said wearily. "I'll settle for an aspirin."

A. J. dug a tin of aspirins from her purse and drew a glass of water from the spigot in their kitchen.

Lennie downed three aspirins with one gulp of the water. She handed me the glass. "Oh," she said, "as we were leaving the apartment, I asked Downtown to search Felonies for a 'Ronald Quetsch.'"

A. J. nodded appreciatively.

"We might even have an answer tomorrow. Out of curiosity, I counted the number of Quetschs listed in the main Dallas white pages. There's only three."

# [42]

Lennie left for work a half-hour early. A. J. walked her to his car – she enjoyed being seen driving a Cadillac – and kissed her on the cheek through the open driver's-side window. "Be careful, he said." She shrugged a *que sera sera* and rolled the window up. A. J. returned to the apartment, showered, shaved, and dressed for a day of what he expected would come down to boredly twiddling his thumbs while at Edgecom.

A. J. had just taken a sip from his second cup of coffee when the telephone rang. It was Nick. In sentences comprised of mostly four-letter words – each one negatively qualifying the word "cop," and sometimes the word "pig" – he said that Selig Hildreth had just been arrested and unceremoniously driven away in a police cruiser. "Did I know," Nick demanded, "what in hell was going on."

"They arrested Hildreth?" A. J. answered vaguely.

His unfeeling reply angered Nick. "Yes!" he snapped. "Just now! Someone said they read him his rights! The whole damn TV crap! You knew about this?"

"I did know," A. J. said blandly. "The man they arrested wasn't Selig Hildreth. Your lead technician's real name is Ronald Quetsch, and he–"

Nick all but bit A. J.'s head off: "What the hell are you jabbering about?"

A. J. finished his sentence. ". . . murdered Fran."

"Not Sel! No fucking way!"

"Yes, Sel. He *fucking* well did. Do you know where I live?"

Nick's voice trailed off. "Why . . . you're not coming in?"

"Later. Anyway, Edgecom's the wrong place to discuss what just happened."

"Where do you live?"

Nick was at A. J.'s apartment door a good five minutes sooner than A. J. himself could have driven the four miles from Edgecom while encircled by heavy traffic. A. J. gestured at the apartment's one overstuffed chair and backed onto the sofa. When he suggested coffee, Nick opted for a Dr. Pepper.

"You knew, of course," A. J. said, "how I thought all along that Osgood murdered Fran?"

"Yes. So?"

"So, I blew it."

"You, blew it?"

"Me and a detective named Deemer. It's her case."

"*Her* case?"

"Lenore Deemer. Lennie. I've been seeing her."

"You mean, dating her?"

"Yes. We're living here."

Nick's eyes swept the room. "So you blew it?"

"Like I kept telling you, Fran really *was* murdered. Only, not by shithead."

"Not by Osgood?"

"No, but he *was* poisoned. I told you how."

A. J. waited for a nod of understanding; it was moments wasted.

"Lennie ruled out Osgood's involvement, totally. She said he couldn't have been the one who injected the poison."

"Lennie?"

"Detective Deemer."

"But Osgood *was* there that night. Wasn't he? Visiting?"

"Yes. But he was never alone with Fran. And there's other gaps in–"

"*Never* alone? How do you know?"

"From Jo Ellen."

Nick rolled his eyes and looked away.

"As it turns out, it doesn't matter whether or not Jo Ellen got it right."

"It doesn't matter?" Nick said, his look insinuating that A. J. had to be wrong.

"Nope."

Nick fell into a petulant silence. A. J. poured himself another cup of coffee and returned to the sofa.

"You remember seeing the name Ronald Quetsch printed inside Hildreth's briefcase?"

"I don't know. I guess so. He bought it used."

"In 1975, in San Angelo, Texas, a Mister Ronald Quetsch's girlfriend disappeared." A. J. paused. "And three days later parts of her body . . . stuffed inside black plastic garbage bags turned up in a dumpster at a truck stop on Interstate 10 . . . including one bag containing her head by itself."

A. J. paused again; Nick stared at him intensely.

"The murder is still not A-to-Z solved," A. J. said, "but Quetsch, or Hildreth, or whatever his name, is still the top and only suspect on the police list."

A. J.waited for a third time, even longer, but Nick remained tight lipped.

"A grand jury no-billed him."

Nick shook his head. After several seconds he gave a "so what" heave to his shoulders. "I thought if a grand jury doesn't indict, the accused is damn near certain to be innocent?"

"Not if the prosecution blows it," A. J. said. "At any rate, the San Angelo police are absolutely convinced that Quetsch killed his girlfriend and chopped her into . . . pieces."

Nick kneaded the back of his neck. His gaze downward, he insisted that his soft-spoken lead technician could not possibly have killed anyone, let alone hacked a person's body into conveniently transportable parts.

"The fucking police!" Nick said, with intense disgust. Looking up, he raised his voice. "What could Sel gain by killing Fran?"

"For starters," A. J. said, "dibs on the proceeds of a million-dollar life insurance policy."

Nick, his nimble mind typically on fast-forward, instantly understood. "They *are* shacking," he mumbled, alluding to the affair between Hildreth and Jo Ellen, Fran's wife.

"For a year. Maybe longer. Who knows?"

"I still don't buy it. You mean there's no question but what Sel at some point was alone with Fran that night at the hospital?"

"For as long as it took Jo Ellen to walk her sister and Hummel, her brother-in-law, to their car and then return to Fran's room."

"Which doesn't prove anything, maybe–"

"Silo!" A. J. said sharply. "It's a no-brainer. All the pieces fit. Lennie says he'll fry."

A. J. was impatient with Nick's bullheadedness, or he never would have repeated Lennie's callous remark. He wanted to bite his tongue off.

"Fucking *cops*," Nick repeated angrily.

"You don't know the whole story," A. J. said.

Nick finished his Dr. Pepper and crushed the can. Neither he nor A. J. spoke for several seconds.

A. J. said quietly, "He'll be arraigned and then hauled back to jail. Lennie says there's no chance he'll bail. If a judge does grant him bail, it'll be, like, for a million bucks, cash."

"Then what?" Nick asked pensively. "A grand jury hearing I suppose?"

"No," A. J. said. "You've got it bassackwards. Like I mentioned, a grand jury indicts. Then he'll be arraigned, and then he'll stand trial."

"So? What in hell difference does it make?" Nick fell hard back into the chair. "This is Dallas, Texas."

Nick's allusion was to the likelihood of Hildreth's complicity in Fran's death being decided by twelve people chosen from a pool of irremediably hard-shelled Dallas Christians.

"The cops," Nick said, "have compared finger prints I. suppose?"

A. J. nodded.

Nick understood instantly, comprehended that A. J. had betrayed both Hildreth and him personally. His disapproval was optimal.

"Get off it, Nickerson," A. J. said stiffly. "Hildreth already killed a woman . . . that we know of . . . and now Fran. And I'm supposed to look the other way? I loaned a floppy drive to the police, one Hildreth had worked on. Given what I knew, what would you have done?"

Nick shrugged. "How has he been passing himself off as Selig Hildreth?"

A. J. had asked Lennie the same question. "Easy, Lenie said. One way is, you roll a street drunk, steal his social security number and then apply for a new card using his name. You tell the Agency that someone stole your wallet – give 'em your new address, and so on."

"It wouldn't be that easy to get a new social security card."

"Oh?" A. J. said disparagingly. "You ever try? Mostly, you just show up at a Social Security office."

"There has to be more to it."

"Barely. You might be asked your mother's maiden name."

"Rolling a drunk for his social security number is your detective girlfriend's theory?"

A. J. nodded. "She said that winos have been murdered for their ID's."

"And exactly how," Nick wanted to know, "would one go about getting the maiden name of the drunk's mother?"

"Oh hell, Silo," A. J. answered impatiently. "You'd sweet talk the wino. Start a conversation about his ancestry. You know, 'Where you from, Ol' Buddy?' Go from there."

Nick breathed a long sigh. When he did not stir for several seconds A. J. said, "Dead winos end up as numbers in paupers' graves."

Nick stood up. "I won't say anything. No one knows I'm here."

"It's up to you. It'll all come out eventually. Including my part. If it matters, Lennie doesn't even know your name. Anyway, not in connection with this god-awful mess."

"Shit," Nick said contemptuously, "the prosecution would have to declare me a hostile witness."

A. J. stood up. "You know, "he said, "it's even possible Hildreth is innocent."

Nick shrugged. "By then . . . who knows. Edgecom won't be around. I *do* know that. I haven't lifted a finger productively since Osgood took over. All those morons in business suits running around the office recording their hiked-up accomplishments in company diaries issued by Brasshead. The idiots couldn't collectively invent a push broom."

"They're just decoration on the box the cake came in. It fools visitors – investors. That's all Osgood cares about."

Nick walked to the apartment door. "I'm giving notice. I should have months ago."

A. J. decided to force his hand: "You a part owner yet?"

"Nope," he answered harshly.

By the time of Hildreth's arrest, Nick knew unequivocally that Hummel Osgood was a definitive sleaze and, if he believed A. J., no less than an out-and-out crook. The opportunity to cash-out for several hundred thousand dollars in Edgecom's IPO tethered Nickerson to Edgecom, as it would most men, let alone a twenty-six-year-old raised on a slim-pickings hog farm in Iowa.

"Don't hold your breath," A. J. said. "You know how you'll get to own a piece of Edgecom? Same as me. Buy shares on the open market after we go public. *If* we go public."

A. J. followed Nick to the door. He let himself out, and A. J. watched until he disappeared around a corner. Nick did not look back.

If Osgood had shown anything but utter indifference to the arrest and incarceration of Selig Hildreth, Nick may not have quit Edgecom, insisting unshakably that Hildreth couldn't abide anyone not committed to the same sentiment as himself, least of all to the man he worked for. Not that Osgood would have cared; in fact, the bastard was just cunning enough to have planned it that way.

Selig Hildreth did not confess to murdering Francis Degeorge, so Bob Hoover, early in February of 1981, filed a bill of indictment with the administrative office of the Dallas County Criminal District Court System. Later in the month, Hildreth/Quetsch was indicted by a grand jury and arraigned two weeks afterwards. Charged with first degree murder, the judge denied bail. He set the trial date for September 14, 1981, a Monday – balancing, Lennie posited, the defense's plea for as much time as possible and the prosecution's demand for a quick trial.

# [43]

Lennie's apartment lease expired on February 14$^{th}$ of 1981, and she moved in with A. J. the last Tuesday of January. Her apartment was furnished, and she and A. J. hauled everything she owned in his car in one trip: clothing, including eight pairs of shoes, miscellaneous bathroom stuff, a few keepsakes, a limited cast-iron dumbbell set, and four books. Lennie did not own a cooking pan or a single piece of authentic table china; the kitchen flatware drawer held tools: two screwdrivers, a utility knife, a tack hammer, and pliers.

Most evenings she and A. J. lazed away the hours by themselves: Lennie would have been uneasy in the company of A. J.'s friends, and the first time one of his fraternity chums put on the Ritz she'd have de-nutted him with a salvo of four-letter words. Nor was Lennie dying to introduce A. J. to her girlfriends, all cops, and all of whom, A. J. suspected, were as pungent as a mustard condiment and as hard as tungsten metal.

Except for the night of their first date, Lennie would not let A. J. take her café-hopping in either

Dallas or Fort Worth. A. J. assumed she was leery of being recognized, but she never said so. They dallied away two weekends at Salado, Texas, a village some thirty miles south of Waco, Texas, that had developed into a dozen chic, arty, highbrow marts and perhaps five- or six-dozen upscale homes. Their first relaxing, mostly corporeal weekend sojourn, took place a month after they began cohabitating.

A. J. also distinctly remembered Lennie reading his copy of *Honor Thy Father*, Gay Talese's acclaimed non-fiction book about the adversities of a New York City, Mafia-connected family, and together they watched a re-run of the first *The Godfather* movie.

They always ate their evening meal out together, usually supping in a rear corner booth at Foister's. Lennie absolutely would not sit with her back to a restaurant entrance. A. J. also liked to face the entrance of any closed room, but Lennie was unyielding, so they always waited, if necessasary, for a front-facing booth or table to open.

A. J.'s folks returned from Hawaii the end of the first week in March. A. J. 's mother finally telephoned him on the following Wednesday. A. J. was in the bathroom, and Lennie answered the ring. The doors and walls of their apartment only slightly attenuated sound, and A. J. heard Lennie's every word:

"MacRae's."

Pause.

"Yes, you dialed the right number."

Pause.

"He's taking a shit."

Very long pause.

Softly: "Yes, ma'am, I'll tell him."

"Who was it?" A. J. yelled, washing his hands. Lennie did not answer. When he reached the kitchen, Lennie was sitting at the kitchen bar with her face cradled in her hands.

"My God, Hon," she said into her hands. "It was your mother. I thought it was Allison."

A. J. did not croak from laughing, but a minute later he was still giggling.

"What'd she say?" A. J. finally managed to ask.

"Nothing," Lennie said, looking up, but not at A. J. "Not for a long time."

"Damn, and I was just getting to like you."

"It's not funny, A. J. She wants you to call her."

"I thought it was hilarious," A. J. said, putting his arms around Lennie' shoulders. "Forget it Hon."

Lennie, her face suken from self-reproach, ambled to the sofa. On the way she fetched one of her trade magazines from the coffee table and began studying the back page. It may have been upside down, for all she knew.

A. J. telephoned his folk's home, and his Daddy answered.

"Welcome back," A. J. said, spiritedly.

"Who is this?" his father replied, impatiently.

"Your favorite son." (As an only child, A. J. was also – and more accurately – his least favorite son.)

"Here's your mother."

"Who *was* that hussy?" were his mother's first words.

"A swinging little doxy I picked up at a bar."

"Don't be that way, Alan. Who was she?"

"A special woman," A. J. said, earnestly.

His mother thought A. J.'s answer over. "What does she do?"

"Arrests bad people."

"Are you drinking?" A. J.'s mother was not being funny; she did not know how to be funny.

A. J. snickered. "She really does arrest people. Usually they're bad. Usually."

Lennie looked up from pretending to read, turned her face away from A. J., and weakly shook her head.

"How's Danielle?" A. J.'s mother asked after another pause.

The surgical discontinuance of Danielle's pregnancy flashed through A. J.'s mind, and he inadvertently hesitated before answering. "Your favorite granddaughter is fine," he said, after a second.

A. J.'s mother sensed his hesitation: "Are you sure?"

"Positive. She loved her Christmas presents. Did you get a thank-you card?"

"No," his mother snapped. "That's not Danielle's fault. It's her mother's."

A. J. thanked his mother for his Christmas gift, a pair of rich-looking, hand-made leather sandals that he truly liked and that actually fit. A. J. told his Mother that Santa Claus had left Christmas gifts for her and Daddy, and that he would bring them over the first chance he got. After exchanging stereotypical health banalities, they hung up.

I sat down by Lennie. "We'll have to go there sometime."

Her eyes did not leave the magazine. "Yeah. Sometime."

# [44]

By the end of the summer, Lennie was spending most of her working hours bolstering her case against Quetsch, nourishing the monkey that had unsuspectingly pounced squarely on his back – on the day his girlfriend's body parts began showing up in dumpsters at truck stops located on the outskirts of San Angelo. Lennie wanted to turn that clinging simian into a silver-back gorilla for all to see.

Entertaining A. J. with inside police stuff, she apprised him of her progress every few nights, sometimes digressing into topics like how, before fellatio, some prostitutes, those who gagged on a payload of come – of "jism," she called it – lined their mouths with condoms; how half the black males she arrested offered her cunnilingus to orgasm for a promised favor – or for no restitution at all; how in two-party cruiser patrols some female cops craved her ass as much as the men; and how it was that males and females paired for black-and-white patrol, invariably fought or fornicated, often barely taking a breath between entwining in those two generally disparate activities.

Woman cops, she insisted, itched for sex as much as male officers – were as horny as men, is the way she put it. A. J. was skeptical at her telling him that when she illuminated the back seat of a car parked on a dark street, often as not, a female perched with a foot on the floor and a knee on the seat, was performing oral sex on a sap-eyed male aslant in the seat's corner. A. J. may have looked surprised. Anyway, she shrugged, said she just "let it go," meaning she overlooked their "horizontal recreation," as she called it. Lennie, at the time, was a beat officer.

One evening they were huddled on the sofa watching a Texas Rangers baseball game – at any rate, A. J. was watching the game – when out of nowhere Lennie said, "There are times when I could strangle that damn Hoover!"

Her sudden flare-up surprised A. J.: "Bob Hoover?"

Attorney Bob Hoover was the only Hoover A. J. knew, but for a second he could not uproot the name from deep in his memory.

"Damn district attorneys," Lennie said. "They're all alike. They never get hot for a case until a week before the trial. Then they blow steam out of their . . . butt."

A. J. muted the TV. "What's bugging Hoover? The trial's still a month away."

"Oh hell, he can't get it up worrying over Jo Ellen's testimony."

"I take it," A. J. said, "he's met Jo Ellen?"

"Accidently. The day I interviewed her."

"No wonder he's anxious. I mean, it's no wonder–"

"It's not her personality, Hon. He's hung up on the idea that *her* testimony has got to be the stake through Quetsch's heart."

"A Lone Ranger's bullet."

"Uh-huh. Hoover's afraid he'll learn first-hand that Quetsch has a gun-slinger's quickness for flipping a bird."

"So? What about all the other–"

"Hoover thinks the motive is weak. He wants me to check Quetsch's apartment again. We already scoured the shit out of it. He's getting another damn search warrant."

"What's he think was missed?"

"Oh hell. A video tape of Quetsch hacking apart his wife. Every ADA wants an eight-by-ten glossy of the perp pulling a smoking gun away from the victim's head."

"I suppose the defense has searched his apartment?"

"No. We'd want an officer there. And I'd know about it."

"Don't you guys search a place as soon as possible . . . to preserve the evidence?"

"Always. But his apartment is secure. I don't have a problem with that. It'll be a waste of my time, is all."

The Rangers had fallen eight runs behind by the seventh inning, so A. J. switched to a local TV station that was broadcasting the early Late News. A. J. finished his third bottle of beer and fetched another from the refrigerator. Lennie still had beer left in her first bottle, but she nodded when A. J. offered to bring her another.

Not that it especially mattered, not on that particular evening, but sometimes a couple of beers set Lennie's tongue to wagging. This was one of those times.

A. J. muted the TV on his way back to the living room. "How good is Bob in the court room?" He left Lennie's beer on the coffee table, and flopped into the over-stuffed, living-room chair.

"He's one of Wade's better persons," Lennie answered. Only, he can be dull as a puddle of mud. Sometimes he sounds like he's reading from an algebra text book."

The name "Wade" was Lennie's verbal shorthand for Henry Wade, Dallas County's long-time District Attorney, the Wade of Roe v. Wade and the successful prosecutor of Jack Ruby. Wade was another of the men whom A. J. had met at one of his father's Republican fund-raising parties. As A. J. recalled, his daddy was bent on converting Wade politically.

"I gather that algebra wasn't your favorite high-school subject."

"Who in the hell," Lennie said, looking about helplessly, "cares how long or where two trains leaving at the same time from different cities . . . yakkety, yakkety, yak. Give me a break."

"The passengers," A. J. said grinning.

"Right," Lennie replied. "Anyway, Hoover can close okay. Honest-to-God, some DA's couldn't zip up their pants without pulling out a swatch of gonad hair."

"So, are you're going back to Quetsch's apartment?"

"I'll have to, once another search warrant clears. I'm taking Sharon this time. Sharon Rosenberg. She's a lab rat."

Rosenberg, it took A. J. a second to understand, was a police laboratory technician.

"What about Quetsch's criminal past?" A. J. asked. "How the hell much evidence does Hoover need?"

"No, Hon. Quetsch is *not* a criminal. He was no-billed, remember. Anyway, it'll come down to what the judge allows. Probably zip about his hacked up girlfriend."

"Who's the trial judge? Have you heard?"

"Yes, from the indictment. Philip Stanley Wiggins. P.S. Wiggins. Merle says he's okay. Sanctimonious. Like some judges aren't. At least he's not an ACLU jerk-off. I've never testified when he was working."

A. J. said, "You wanted Wilbur Cantu?"

Judge Cantu, Lennie had once told A. J., would jail his grandmother for spitting. A. J. was not great at remembering names, but even he could not forget a name as oxymoronic as Wilbur Cantu.

Lennie shrugged. "Luck of the draw."

"Who goes first in a criminal trial?" A. J. asked. "I've never seen one . . . TV versions."

"The prosecution. Hell, Hon, you can't defend someone before he's charged – before he or she's accused."

"Yeah," A. J. said. "Stupid question."

"Judge Wiggins will look at Bob Hoover and say, 'Mister Hoover?' And Bob will say, 'Thank you, your Honor.' Then Bob'll step up to the podium, begin with, 'May it please the court' – they always say that – and then, addressing the jury, he'll say, in so many words, that the evidence convincingly shows that Quetsch killed your man, Francis Degeorge."

Lennie finished the ounce or so of beer remaining in her first bottle and took a courtesy sip from her second bottle.

"Hoover may try to bring up greed as a motive," she went on, "which the prosecution will object to, and then he'll–"

"Object to? Because?"

"Because it's an inference. And in-tangential. Motive's a tough nut. Hoover can set it up, but he can't explicitly argue greed. Theoretically he can't. Not in his opening statement."

A. J. nodded. "In his closing, but not in his opening?"

Lennie was enjoying her role as a pedagogue, and A. J. was gleaning answers from someone who had walked the walk. The fact that he would have to testify piqued A. J.'s curiosity.

"How do you know all these things, Detective?"

"I took Police and Archangels 101 at Tyler CC, remember, Dear? And, I've been there, done that."

A. J.'s eyes enlarged: an ignorant but eager pupil. "Then what?"

"After Hoover finishes, Wiggins will invite the defense to begin. Then Quetsch's lawyer will tell the jury how our . . . that the prosecution's evidence is all circumstantial. Like somehow it being circumstantial taints it. And then he'll sprinkle holy water on the sanctity of reasonable doubt. Those are givens. Beyond that, who can say?"

"When do you suppose I'll testify? Assuming I do."

"Early. Maybe the first day even. I'd guess you'll be the . . . third witness. Bob will–"

A. J. interrupted, "The third batter in baseball is always a good hitter."

"If you say so. Bob will work up an Order of Proof, the sequence in which he'll call his witnesses. And he'll go from there. Every time I've had to testify, I was the prosecution's first or second witness. Usually to describe the crime scene. Most were trials of . . . violent felonies, sometimes bloody murders." Lennie slightly shuddered.

Lennie interviewed every witness scheduled to testify at Quetsch's trial, and she always concisely related the results to A. J. in the evening. She said that Jo Ellen was the only real pain in the ass. "Not counting," she added disgustedly, "your pal Nick." A. J.'s smile was more lopsided than cunning, the cagy look he had tried for.

"Jo Ellen put me off twice. And she seemed confused over the sequence of visitors on the night her husband bought it."

"That surprises me," A. J. observed sarcastically.

Lennie shrugged. "If she dances at the trial . . . . She's got to testify that she walked the Osgoods to their car . . . and left Quetsch alone with her husband. Like she said."

"I told you she's an airhead. What if she screws up?"

Lennie became introspective. "Hoover," she said, finally, "will have to suck it out of her."

"It'll take a shop vac," A. J. said.

"I take back every bad thing I ever said about Bob Hoover." Approximately, those were Lennie's first words when she returned home from work on the day she re-visited Quetsch's apartment. Rosenberg, her "lab rat," had scratched up a quarter teaspoon of potassium permanganate granules from the kitchen floor in a small opening between the sink stand and a pots-and-pans cabinet. Lennie could not have been happier had she turned up a purple-stained hypodermic syringe engraved with Quetsch's initials.

# [45]

Work breaks at Edgecom were now beginning with one of Jesse's assemblers editorializing on the spectacle of Selig Hildreth's escorted march to a waiting police car. The innately tranquil Hildreth a dastardly criminal? Impossible. Still, the rumors flew around Edgecom like boll weevils feasting on a field of cotton buds.

Collectively, that was the belief, embodied, if perversely, in a remark by Juanita Grubb, Jessie's favorite lead assembler, who was alleged to have said that she'd have been no less shocked to learn that her husband had been arrested for fidelity. According to Nick, Juanita truly came up with that quip. In any event, A. J. knew this: Juanita's husband – reputed to eagerly sample the favors of any tepidly willing female – at one company picnic enjoyed a vertical copulatory romp, with one of Juanita's subordinate assemblers, behind the park's remote, cement-block rest room. A witness had urged a fellow male picnicker to snap a picture. If he did, the print was never circulated: Pat Brown would have boot-legged A. J. a peek.

By early April, Selig Hildreth was enduring a monk's dull existence alone in a cell at the Dallas County Prison, and the drama of his arrest was now seldom mentioned by the workers at Edgecom. Meanwhile, Dornhoffer and Skip had begun demonstrating a prototype MaxWriter to regional office equipment dealers. Skip, along for technical support, told me that MaxWriter sold itself.

Measured against the boxy, home-brewed, unbundled word processors of the time, MaxWriter was a sleek, fine-looking machine, a turnkey system with nothing that had to be plugged in or hooked on, except a printer. Moreover, the commercial market was virginal, un-penetrated by competition. There was, however, a problem – with MaxWriter itself.

Steen, MaxWriter's lead architect, induced by a hefty raise in pay to leave Foster Systems where he designed energy-transforming electronics for NASA satellites, was a top-flight hardware man. In fact, he was *too* good from the standpoint of designing quality into a product: his MaxWriter would have survived a crunching high-G rocket launch and then circled the earth forever unfazed by the unforgiving zero cold of outer space.

Because structural integrity, to Steen's way of thinking, was such a venerable part of design, Edgecom's first one hundred MaxWriters projected to cost a whopping twenty-eight hundred dollars each, and to retail, therefore, for around four thousand dollars, not including the cost of a printer. Every prospective dealer balked out-of-hand at the cost, and none placed an order.

Consequently, the world's first microcomputer-based system dedicated exclusively to word processing, a machine which, Osgood boasted to Hardeman's wealthy friends, would do for written communications what freight trains did for shipping cargo, floundered while still in dry dock and went adrift when it was skidded into water.

When MaxWriter perished, virtually on the day it was christened, Steen, now with nothing to keep him busy, spent a week sizing up the situation and concluded that Edgecom should abandon MaxWriter at once and commit the company's technical resources, that is, himself, Harriet Muckinhaupt, and two new technicians to the development of a LAN, a novel, so-called, Local Area Network system; Nickerson, accompanied by Edgecom's sole remaining veteran technician, had quit Edgecom in February for jobs in Austin.

A local area network allows several ordinarily self-sufficient computers to directly exchange data and share in the use of expensive peripherals – typically a printer and a high-capacity mass data storage device. Steen persuaded Osgood that Edgecom, with its core expertise in both data storage and word processing, was ideally positioned to develop a short-range LAN, to get in on the ground floor of that industry and hack out its own niche in what he guaranteed would one day be a run-away office business. "Think Xerox copying machine sales," Steen unblushingly advised Osgood.

With Steen in tow, Osgood presented his case to Hardeman. By virtue of his large stock holding, Hardeman had become Edgecom's de jour four-star general. Osgood, however, with Hardeman's blessing, continued as Edgecom's nominal chief executive. A day after consulting with his son, Hardeman gave Osgood permission for Edgecom to cast off and steam "full ahead" into that stormy but still uncongested sea of Ahab-helmed Pequods that were bent on harpooning a large haul of the LAN business.

Thus, for the second time within a year of Degeorge's death, Edgecom set sail on a virtually uncharted sea. MaxWriter was richly financed by the speculative thousands put up by Wallace Hardeman and his wealthy friends, funds that were enough to get ELAN – the name Steen proposed for Edgecom's local area network (only to learn months later that the name had already been taken by a start-up LAN company in Palo Alto, California) to the drawing-board stage.

Steen, on the day he received permission from Osgood to begin developing ELAN, promised he could deliver solid, tangible evidence of his brain-child early in the Fall. And in October he surrendered to Hardeman's examination a 20-page book of design specifications, a binder of logic block diagrams, a dozen engineering sketches, and a half-inch stack of programming flow charts – an aggregation of paper that would have choked a hippopotamus but at the same time done any Department of Defense contractor proud.

Hardeman took one look at Steen's offering of specs, flow charts, and so on, and blew his top. Glaring at Osgood – a man suddenly obsessed with studying Steen's easel of flow charts – he said he wanted to see a real, working system, and he wanted to see it in one month. Or else!

After a minute of his usual, placid rumination, Steen said he'd have ELAN half ready by four weeks – right on schedule. Thereafter, he calmly assured Edgecom's blustery commander-in-chief, that the development of ELAN would move ahead at a much faster clip.

Silence prevailed while Hardeman, glowering at Harriet Muckinhaupt's stack of fan-folded program sheets, considered Steen's plan. After sneaking a glance at Skip, he pounded the table with his fist and commanded Steen to get on with it. Steen allowed that he was pleased with that decision and suggested they move on for a look at ELAN's hardware.

Introduced to Hardeman as one of his "electronics guys," Dick Sickles held up a printed-circuit board and explained that it would connect any make of printer to ELAN. Ted Barrickman, introduced to Hardeman by Steen as his "other electronics guy," explained that his circuit would connect any make of hard-disk storage system to ELAN. Hardeman asked to see the circuits in operation. As one, the two technicians, both long-haired, scraggly bearded young men, blithely explained that their circuits were still in the debugging stage.

His glare rekindled, Hardeman again demanded to see something concrete in one month, Or else!

Steen arranged to demonstrate his prototype ELAN on the seventh of July, the Tuesday after the four-day Fourth of July work break. Everyone still working at Edgecom was invited to the office bay to watch the show, where, beforehand, Steen and his two technicians had positioned an expensive selectable-font printer and a brand new high-capacity hard-disk drive on one side of the big room and two stock computer terminals on the other side. Data was exchanged through a coaxial cable attached in parallel to the hard drive and to the printer through two small aluminum boxes the size of folded men's wallets. Each box contained a circuit that was designed either by Sickles or Barrickman.

The room became deadly quiet.

Osgood said to Steen, "Fire when ready, Gridly!"

Steen, after a moment of uncertainty – likely trying to figure out what or who in the hell was "Gridly" – nodded at Harriet Muckinhaupt. Muckinhaupt, sitting stiffly alert at one of the two computer terminals, briskly struck a few keys. A light on the hard-disk drive flickered; the drive hummed briefly and stopped.

Harriet studied her computer screen a second and again entered a short word. As before, the drive responded briefly and died. After glancing nervously at

Steen, she moved to the other computer terminal and tried a third time. Once more the drive failed to remain awake.

What happened next, Steen and his people emulating Keystone Kops practicing a Chinese fire drill, lasted a long minute. When calm returned, Harriet tried a fourth time. The problem persisted.

Steen, his face, conscripting the color of a gray Marks-A-Lot, said he could not explain why ELAN wasn't working, that it had operated perfectly an hour earlier.

Hardeman asked Steen how long he needed to fix the problem, and when Steen said to give him ten minutes, Hardeman told Osgood that he was going to lunch. He said loudly that he had reached the end of his rope.

At one-thirty the hard drive worked perfectly. But, now the printer, when commanded by Muckinhaupt to print a document that she had retrieved from her computer's RAM memory, clicked once and went dumb. It took Sickles only a second to realize what was wrong and only a little longer to re-toggle a micro-switch mounted inside the lidded aluminum box housing his printer interface circuit. By then, however, it was too late: Hardeman had stormed out.

No one dared buck Hardeman, and for several long seconds the office bay was a becalmed sea, a quiet, scum-covered pond of inactivity. Then, with a sad-sack flourish, Harriet poked her keyboard the few times it took to command the remote printer into operation. Immediately it began chattering, and soon paper began stuttering out. The printed message, announced by the title in boldface, began, "Greetings to the Officers of Edgecom Data Corporation!" It continued, in a regular type face, after advancing the paper two blank lines: "You have just witnessed ELAN in action!" A bulleted list of ELAN's features followed.

Skip promised Steen he'd change his father's mind, that he would move mountains if necessary to convince him to keep ELAN alive.

Skip's optimism was short-lived: he could not keep his promise. When his Daddy set his mind – Skip later admitted to A. J. – he didn't only become pig-headed, his skull became bullet-proof to any and all persuasive missiles, including the incendiary-tipped arguments of his own son.

# [46]

While two MaxWriter machines were aggregating component by component into expensive consoles of handsomely primped icons, and Steen was fathering ELAN, Osgood was thickening the icing on his marble cake of deception, a business that was once a recumbent but otherwise principled enterprise. The time had come, Osgood finally decided, to change Edgecom's tawny hide into tiger stripes, to transform his wobbly, over-financed, unambiguously mismanaged enterprise into a publically owned corporation.

Going public is expensive and complicated. And Osgood immersed himself totally in assembling what he had hoped would be a troika of winners: an outside accounting firm for independently auditing Edgecom's books; a legal counsel steeped in the ways of the Security and Exchange Commission; and a company with deep-pocket connections that was willing to promote underwriting the multi-million dollar venture.

Edgecom's reservoir of private funding was steadily dwindling. Sales revenue had fallen from a slow trickle to a quenched flow not unlike the drift of the Trinity River, bisecting Dallas, that flowed modestly in winter but crawled feebly along during hot summers. In actuality, proceeds of the successful private offering not only paid the salaries of the new recruits but also covered the lion's share of all other operating costs. Edgecom's reservoir of cash, however, smacked of a water tank with a rusty, perforated outlet spigot and an input pump grinding to a halt. It became imperative, therefore, that nothing impede Edgecom's timely public debut, including, foremost, the chance of asphyxia caused by the morbidly diseased Receivables account that Wickersham's after-hours Heimlich maneuver resuscitated periodically.

Lee Appleby of Cohn Warren & Associates headed the two-man team hired by Osgood to audit Edgecom's financial books. Recommended by Wickersham, Cohn Warren & Associates was an independent, Arlington, Texas-based accounting firm. Skip told A. J. he was surprised that his daddy, who for years had hacked around a private Dallas golf course with two senior partners from the Coopers & Lybrand branch office in Dallas, went along with Wickersham's choice.

Appleby, fiftyish, was tall, prissy, and, according to Skip, a consummate stuffed shirt. He brushed his black-dyed hair straight back, and he wore weighty Cary Grant-style, horned-rim eye glasses. His suits were English cut. He could pass for an aloof British diplomat – except, betrayed by his Texas accent, he was a handsome paradigm of the time-worn saying of the inextricability of a rural upbringing.

Before long, Appleby and his associate found a blatant impropriety in Edgecom's financial records: namely, they uncovered the fact that dozens of Edgecom's archived bank deposit slips did not square with duplicates held by the bank. In no time they unearthed the basis of Wickersham's padded sales figures, the opaque parcels of legal tender passed through the J. Hummel Osgood Advertising Agency and smoothly slipped into Edgecom's Receivables account.

I asked Skip how his daddy reacted to the obvious boogering of Edgecom's books. Osgood, he answered, befuddled his daddy, took him in, claimed a onetime employee, Degeorge's supervisor of bookkeeping, had embezzled thousands of dollars, but he, Osgood, had covertly smoothed over her pilferage with funds drawn from his own hard-earned savings account.

The "onetime employee," Martha Dillbeck, A. J. explained to Skip, was Edgecom's veteran lead bookkeeper, whom Degeorge, among others, inevitably praised. A. J. explained, additionally, that she was inscrutably sacked by Osgood on his second day of running Edgecom.

Skip said that Osgood assured Lee Appleby and his daddy, Hardeman II, that it was absolutely his very last wish to misrepresent the financial situation of the company that he had built brick by brick with his own scarred and tattered hands. Edgecom's books, he wincingly pleaded (Skip's words) might be a bit skewed in the eyes of the law but what he did was neither immoral nor unethical, as God himself would surely attest to.

Of course, the "hard-earned savings" of Osgood's sympathy-arousing sob story, in truth was the money loaned to his advertising agency (a loan probably co-signed by Osgood's wife). Irickson, God bless him, had theorized that the proceeds of a bank loan would be stitched together in a way to obscure the true source of the money.

Apparently Hardeman did not catch the huge difference in funds between what Martha could possibly have stolen and the amount of money it took to resuscitate Edgecom's asphyxiated bottom line. To this day, A. J. is unsure of Skip's complicity, of whether or not he knew his father was, in fact, aware of the impossibly huge disparity between the two sums.

Osgood, A. J. said to Skip, could out-mutate a Dorian Gray painting. He did not understand, so A. J. said that he could out Checkers Nixon. He still did not get it, so A. J. teased him about the academic quality of Stephen F. Austin University, his alma mater. Skip indifferently replied that his father "bonded" Stephen F. Austin – SFA as he called it. In other words, Skip's selection of a school was the upshot of his father's underwriting of a loan to that big public Texas University.

"Besides," he added grinning wryly, "I figured the name Hardeman should at least be worth a letter-grade per semester per academic subject."

Skip said his father seemed to believe Osgood's story of Martha's business deceit. He said he was inclined himself to believe it. A. J. thought, at the time, had Skip known Martha Dillbeck he'd have puked his guts out at Osgood's version of what was behind Edgecom's financial paucity. Moreover, to this day A. J. is reasonably certain that Skip was abjectly ignorant of the amount of cover-up money involved.

A. J. said to Skip, "Suppose Martha's innocent?"

Skip shrugged and turned away. "Suppose she's guilty."

Later, Osgood, alone with Hardeman and Skip, intimated that Appleby could be had – could be laid, is the way he put it. A. J. asked Skip how his daddy reacted to the reality of that communion of soiled minds. Skip cut the air over his head with a wave of his hand.

"Went by him like a Nolan Ryan fast ball, huh?"

"Exactly," Skip said after a moment of indecision – or perhaps after a second of stonewalling. A. J. wasn't sure.

A. J. pressed Skip for more on Osgood's hush-hush remark addressing Appleby's supposed affinity for payola, but he stiffed A. J., said he never bothered himself with the politics of his daddy's businesses. A. J. did not ask Skip if he ever bothered himself with the morality of his daddy's businesses. He should have, but he wanted Skip to spy for him.

A. J. recalled how Irickson, at one of their lunches, told him that Hardeman likely as not would overlook any miscreant behavior by Osgood, adding, cryptically, that A. J. should "think about it."

A. J. did think about it, until it dawned on him that it would be grossly stupid, suicidal from a money-making standpoint, for Hardeman to turn whistle-blower and upset a cart loaded with ripening bananas harvested from his own orchard – that was thundering wildly toward a zoo of starving chimps.

A few days after Osgood's sorrowful confession of the "real" reason behind the cooking of Edgecom's books, Skip said he passed Appleby in the hall marching briskly away from Osgood's office. "I doubt," he confided to A. J., in so many words, "that Appleby owed the dreamy look in his eyes to a toot of coke."

A. J. glanced around quickly. "In other words–"

Skip interrupted A. J. contemptuously. "In other words, Appleby was enumerating the many perquisites owed a high-level executive of a high-tech, leading-edge corporation." Skip shrugged. "Or maybe he was only considering strategies for minimizing his 1981 personal income tax."

"You're pretty sure?"

"No, I am damned sure," Skip replied.

"The other guy from Cohn Warren?" A. J. said. "Where was he at?"

Skip shrugged. "Don't know. I haven't seen him around lately."

That night A. J. called Irickson. He told him he had perfectly crystal-balled Osgood's plan, and that he should be betting on derby ponies. When A. J. got around to the question of Appleby's associate, he said that most likely Appleby convinced him to look the other way, that Osgood's bookkeeping fan dance was a no-harm, no-foul, skirting of SEC rules. A. J. guessed that he unwittingly looked skeptical, because, Jack went on to say, that auditors sometimes did those things: ignored minor improprieties if the owner was not clearly a crooked, run-of-the-mill schmuck. Irickson said he might have let it slip by himself if he was sure he was not being crapped on. "Maybe," he added, "a few bucks changed hands."

"But," A. J. objected, "wouldn't the guy eventually see he'd been had?"

"Not for months," Jack said. "Maybe Appleby promised him . . . five per cent. Life goes on."

"Jesus Christ, Jack," A. J. said, "are *all* businessmen on the take?'

"I'm not," Irickson said.

Skip told me a week later that the name Ronald W. Wizorak had been added to Edgecom's stock registry book. A. J. had no idea, he replied, when Skip asked him, who Wizorak was, so Skip said he'd look into it.

Ronald Wizorak, it turned out, was the ninety-two-year-old, widowed father of Lee Appleby's wife.

Enfeebled and bed-quarantined, he was sharing a room in a nursing home with another aged male resident.

"Who do you suppose," Skip asked me, tongue-in-cheek, "holds Mr. Wizorak's power of attorney?"

# [47]

It was mid-morning when Dolores Berkbile, Osgood's new secretary, telephoned A. J. and asked him to report to Osgood's office at one o'clock for an assignment. For a week – over and above obsessing with the conviction that he had murdered Fran – A. J. had doggedly tried to meet with Osgood; chiefly, he wanted to study Osgood's deportment of late. Also, bored crazy, he was ready to tackle any job. Hummel, however, was always too busy to see him.

A. J. knew he should have given notice weeks ago and quit on the spot. He rationalized, however, that the work was easy and the pay adequate. In truth, A. J. vainly clung to the hope that Osgood would cut him in on Edgecom's IPO – for the cachet of ownership, not for the money that selling his tad of Edgecom stock would bring. Yes, vanity was (and still is) one of A. J.'s several frailties.

Twenty minutes later the phone rang again. Dolores apprised A. J. that something had come up, but that Mister Osgood would see him in his office at five-thirty sharp. A. J. arrived at the plant at five-fifteen. The only cars still on the parking lot belonged to Osgood and Dornhoffer.

The "Light Brigade" of British cavalry charged innocently – and mindlessly – into a sweep of blazing Russian guns. A. J. marched childlike into Osgood's office, suspecting nothing until he saw Dornhoffer sitting in full smirk on the sofa at the back of the room. Dornhoffer's coat and vest were lying on the sofa beside him, his necktie was loosened, and his shirt cuffs were rolled back. Osgood pointed at a lone chair positioned some three feet in front of his desk. Dornhoffer closed the office door and returned to his seat. A. J. remained standing in the middle of the room where he had stopped abruptly.

"Sit down, MacRae," Dornhoffer ordered.

A. J. did not turn from facing Osgood. "Fuck you, Brasshead."

"Then, you know why you're here," Osgood said, leaning slightly to look past A. J. at his vice president.

A. J. was about to be drummed out of the service of Edgecom Data Corporation, that was obvious. But why should his long-pending dismissal take two people? Because, Lennie explained to him that night, Osgood was a rapist – to the core, a man who thrived on subjugating others. He wanted to dominate you, trample you underfoot. And Dornhoffer was there in case you forcibly resisted.

"I did resist," A. J. told Lennie, "and I got knocked on my ass."

"Yeah, I know why I'm here," A. J. assured Osgood brusquely. "But I'd like to hear it from your own goddamn sausage lips. Brasshead is here to hold your coat?"

Dornhoffer, in the same low menacing voice as before, told A. J. to shackle his tongue.

As if shooing a fly, Osgood flicked his fingers. "Ignore the simple bastard," he said to Dornhoffer.

Osgood offered why it was that A. J. was no longer fit to work for Edgecom Data Corporation: besides being a lazy, two-faced prick, A. J. was provably incompetent. Osgood crimped his lips and shook his head disgustedly. McPherson, he told Dornhoffer, would have to massively rewrite A. J.'s MaxWriter specifications.

A. J. said to Osgood that McPherson and Dornhoffer together knew less about word processing than Miki Vernon knew about the parceling and routing of incoming phone calls.

Dornhoffer grunted – sounded to A. J. as if he was rising – and Osgood, his eyes still on A. J., vigorously shook his head.

Apparently Dornhoffer again settled back into the sofa because Osgood continued. Furthermore, Osgood said, A. J. had some explaining to do in the matter of Pat Brown precipitously quitting Edgecom. To that point, A. J. had listened indifferently to Osgood's rot, intentionally refused to give either him or Dornhoffer the opportunity to rebut and scale up a disengenuous offense.

"Meaning *what*?" A. J. broke in sharply.

Osgood looked at Dornhoffer. "The Saturday that Pat and I worked on the business plan? She was fine when I left. Now I–"

A. J. exploded. "You son-of-a-bitch! I left before you!"

The smoldering fuse had reached the powder. A. J. rushed at Osgood, and before Dornhoffer could stop him landed his right fist hard on Osgood's face. His left fist glanced off Osgood's head, off his football helmet of sculpted hair. A. J.'s second right missed altogether.

Dornhoffer's thick arms encircled A. J. from behind, and he whirled him in the direction of the door. A. J. stumbled and fell, and Dornhoffer half dragged and half threw him from the room. A. J. had enough sense not to jump up and start swinging at Dornhoffer, who, he knew, would have welcomed the opportunity to beat him, senseless. Besides, A. J. was slightly consoled at seeing Osgood holding a handkerchief to his face and pawing through one of his desk drawers.

Dornhoffer followed A. J. to his office, shoving him hard in the back every few steps. He watched A. J.'s every move from a yard inside the doorway of A. J.'s office.

A. J.'s floppy disk drives had been emptied of their diskettes, his briefcase had been rifled; his computer had been unplugged, and two of his computer's memory cards had been removed. The disembowelment was competent, exhaustive, and so down-to-the-last-detail-finality that A. J. knew it had to have been carried out by one of Edgecom's new technicians. He was still pissed at the unmitigated thoroughness, even though he knew the purging was done at Osgood's bidding. When A. J. slipped into his blazer, he found every pocket hanging inside out. On his third and last trip to his car, Dornhoffer watched his every step, arms folded across his chest, same as he did A. J.'s first two treks from the side-door stoop to his car. Dornhoffer was still watching, arms still across his chest, when A. J. pulled from the parking lot.

A. J. was wearing a T-shirt and denim shorts when the call came in. He and Lennie had talked late into the night. She was still in bed and A. J. doubted she heard the telephone's bell.

Obviously upset, it was Skip Hardeman. "A. J.!" he blurted, his greeting a barely tempered shriek. "I just heard. *What* . . . happened?"

"Wel-l-l," A. J. said, drawing the word out facetiously, "I'm no longer in the employ of Edgecom Data Corporation."

"I know *that*," Skip said agitatedly, "why?"

"It seems I'm a mouthy pain in the ass, among my several personality shortcomings. Furthermore, I don't know shit from Shinola about word-processing."

A. J. had grown to like Skip, and Skip had inexplicably taken to A. J. Skip reminded A. J., not in any physical way, of Nickerson – his youth and quick mind, A. J. supposed.

Their telephone conversation lasted a good quarter hour. Skip did most of the talking. He angrily challenged the reasons for A. J.'s canning and bitterly scored the personalities of Osgood and Dornhoffer. After conventionally praising Wickersham, he was briefly silent, probably disappointed because A. J. did not buttress his veneration of Edgecom's nominal CFO.

"You mean Hysteresis?" Skip said, when for some reason A. J. brought up McPherson's name.

A. J. laughed. "I never did hear who came up with his nickname."

"I'm not sure either. A technician is all I know."

Skip homed in again on Osgood, said his string of four-letter-words belittling Edgecom's putative CEO was a three-pointer launched and sunk from mid-court. He asked point-blank if Osgood truly co-founded Edgecom. "Hell, no," A. J. snapped.

In the middle of another of his expletive-laced replies, however, A. J, remembered how his own words in the business plan modestly perpetuated that canard; he backed off, regrouped, and turned to flailing Dornhoffer for stealing his MaxWriter game plan.

How much of A. J.'s tirade Skip bought into was problematic, but A. J. was too pissed to care. Skip said not to burn any bridges, asked where A. J. lived, and said he'd like to stop by. Anytime, A. J. told him.

Skip and A. J. kept in touch. Skip had it in his head that someday A. J. would be back working at Edgecom. A. J. fancied – to himself he said, "Excuse my ego." – that Skip wanted him to run Edgecom, something Skip could have easily arranged through his father.

Anyway, their friendship flourished, as did his relationship with Harriet Muckinhaupt – to where he was no longer perpetually chin-drooling horny – and he and A. J. not only talked often on the telephone, but one evening Skip and Harriet and A. J. and Lennie dined together at the Old Warsaw, a snooty Dallas restaurant. Afterwards they drove across town to watch the new Mavericks basketball franchise play the Los Angeles Lakers at Reunion Arena. Their court-side tickets were courtesy of Skip's connections. Both raucous Maverick fans, it was soon obvious, however, that neither Skip nor Harriet knew a basketball screen from a house screen door. The two women, implacably different in every way imaginable, hit it off like two ever-appalled snoots at a fancy soiree. It was their first and last double date.

Skip thus became A. J.'s "mole" at Edgecom – not exactly the staunch turncoat spy A. J. had hoped to recruit when he first mentioned that possibility to Lennie – but his all-seeing, multi-lens fly on the ceiling at many important happenings, both within and without the cement-block walls of Edgecom.

# [48]

All the applicable want-ads listed in the *Dallas Morning News* were for low-salary, entry-level positions, and it was two months before A. J. found a job. He took up golfing again, playing on the days when he was neither interviewing companies that were hiring, nor helping Lennie work-up her crime reports.

A. J.'s father was a golfing zealot. When he was fifty-nine, he had a heart attack while hoofing it from a green to a tee at the Dallas Country Club, a popular playground for the well-heeled of Dallas. He recovered, retired, and played every chance he got, winter and summer, until he was killed some eleven years later on the day he ran a stop sign driving home – half looped – from a match, and was broadsided by a Dallas County dump truck. Relatives and friends – mostly golfing buddies – paid their respect to a closed casket. "Daddy," as A. J. had called his father ever since he could talk, was not so much a golfing nut as he was a nineteenth-hole drinking nut, something A. J. eventually came to understand.

Daddy had tried to interest A. J. in golf when he was twelve or so, and A. J. played perhaps ten rounds with friends from Texas Instruments when he was in his late twenties. Like other duffers, he could neither hit the damn ball straight nor read a green any more than he could read Urdu images.

Hoping to rekindle his interest, A. J. completed two sessions of instructions at a driving range. After the second practice he telephoned Daddy, who charitably agreed – charitable for him, anyway – to meet A. J. for nine holes at a public Greens that straddled the Garland-Richardson border.

Right off Daddy asked A. J. about Lennie; he and A. J. were waiting at a patio table for their turn to tee off. A. J. told him her name, said that she was a police detective, and the inquisition began.

"You two shacking?" his father asked.

"None of your business."

"How long have you been seeing her?"

"Years. Why?"

His reply, which A. J. had not anticipated, surprised A. J.

"You were still married to Allison? At the beginning?"

"Yeah. Legally." A. J. shot his father a warning look, a reminder, he hoped, that, regarding the subject of philandering, his father lived in a glass house.

After a long second his father said, "How old is . . . Lennie?"

A. J. sighed noisily. "Jesus Christ, Daddy. She's thirty-three. And before you ask, she's unattached and unencumbered."

"She's never been married?"

"I don't know.  And frankly I don't give a shit."

"Good looking?"

"Above average." A. J. turned to watch a player in the foursome ahead of them tee off.

His father focused on the man's drive: "Over two hundred yards. Damn straight, too. Her face doesn't make a damn. How about her ass?"

A. J. stood up and began walking toward the tee.

"When are you going to bring her by?" his father asked from a yard behind A. J.

"Sometime when you're not home," A. J. answered over his shoulder.

That night, at the apartment, after they both had a beer, A. J. said to Lennie. "When do you want to meet my folks?"

"Never," Lennie answered instantly.

A. J. nodded. "I can't honestly say that I know the feeling, Dear. Allison and I were neighbors, and I met her parents when we were still kids. Look, why not get it over with?"

"Because," Lennie bluntly answered, "your mother hates me."

"She doesn't *know* you," A. J. said. "But she will in time. Hate you, I mean. That's my mother. Piss on her. What do you care?"

Lennie stared at me. "It's not working," she said sullenly.

"Damn," Lennie," A. J. said. "I'm serious. We are *not* a close family."

Lennie looked at A. J. and shook her head insanely back and forth. "Tomorrow evening. Whenever."

A. J. watched the news on TV while he was waiting. Lennie had hardly spoken two words since arriving home from work. His mother was expecting them at seven o'clock for dinner. A. J. could not talk his mother into eating at a restaurant. Truthfully, his mother was a good cook, so it was little matter to A. J. Lennie, when A. J. told her they would be eating at his folk's house, all but fled the apartment.

"What do you think?" Lennie said. Her head was turned, and she was fiddling with an earring attached to her ear, the one turned away from A. J.

A. J.'s attention was on the TV – on a sports program – and he hadn't noticed Lennie enter the room. She was wearing the same baggy outfit she wore on their first date, and A. J. all but crapped his Jockeys.

Feeling a tad nervous himself, A. J. could not keep an overtone of vexation from shading his voice. "Hon," he said, "we're not going to a coronation."

Lightning shot from Lennie's eyes. Spinning on her heel, she marched back into the bedroom. Any other time she would have told A. J. to stuff it, so it was a moment before he collected his wits. When he caught up with her in the bedroom, she had removed her

358

jumper and was tearing at the buttons on her blouse. Moisture dulled her eyes. A. J. tried to embrace her. She pulled away and unzipped her slacks. They fell to the floor, and she kicked them away.

"Exactly what," she said, "do you want me to wear, Alan?" She wouldn't look at him.

A. J. said, "I'm sorry Hon. Anything you damn well please. Honest. I . . . didn't make it clear. Going there isn't a big deal. *Not at all*."

"Good," Lennie snapped, "I'll throw on my work-out jumper."

A. J. stammered, but answered. "Let's both wear jeans. I'll change."

Lennie yanked open dresser drawers and jerked out a pair of black jeans and a loose-fitting pink jersey. She sat down on the edge of the bed and began pulling on the jeans. A. J. owned two pair of jeans, both blue, and he put on the slightly faded pair.

Traffic was still heavy, and it was almost an hour before they reached his parent's home. A. J. tried maudlin conversational remarks on the way. Lennie did not open her mouth until A. J. was pulling into their driveway. "They'll hate me," she said.

Daddy, the whole time they stayed, flirted relentlessly with Lennie. She handled him like the pro that she was, and half way through dinner she was volunteering information about herself. Even A. J.'s mother did not put on airs, her usual manner on the first visit of a strange woman. Evidently Lennie felt her début was a triumph because she was her old self when they said goodbye to A. J.'s folks.

Not much given to idle talk, Lennie nonetheless jabbered most of the drive back; it was almost ten when they got home. A. J. turned on the TV news channel, sat down on the sofa, and kicked off his loafers. Lennie went straight to the bedroom.

Five minuted passed. "What do you think?" Lennie said. Her head was turned and she was fiddling with her earrings, both hands. That was all she was wearing. A. J.'s attention was on the TV, and he did not notice her enter the room.

"Neat," A. J. said, "but you are overdressed for the social activity I have in mind."

She grinned, and as A. J. was rising, removed one earring. "Better?" she asked.

On Monday, June 29th, A. J. reported to the downtown office of Dallas Power and Light to begin the job of liaison between DP&L and the advertising agency that created their local newspaper ads and the cheery, homely pamphlets that were always enclosed with customer bills.

# [49]

Quetsch all along staunchly insisted that he was innocent, and he furiously turned on his lawyer, Lukacs Toth, when he learned Toth was favorably considering Hoover's offer to reduce the murder charge to life in prison – if Quetsch agreed to confess. Lennie, hearing that Toth was open to a plea, figured the case against Hildreth/Quetsch was lead-shielded against any and all nuclear attacks by the defense.

Quetsch's trial began on September fourteenth, a Monday. As Hoover's scheduled fourth witness, A. J. would be called to the stand on the fifteenth. Hoover and a subordinate co-prosecutor prepped him in Hoover's office the preceding Thursday. Lennie accompanied A. J.

Hoover, after warmly shaking A. J.'s hand, introduced his associate, a man named Danny – with a Danish/Swedish (?) surname. Both attorneys, quintessential male yuppies working late, had doffed their suit coats, rolled their shirt sleeves off their wrists, and loosened their neckties.

Flanked by Lennie and Danny, A. J. sat in the middle chair of three leather-padded, wooden armchairs facing Hoover's desk. The room's moldings, door and door frames, window sills, and most of the furniture, were made of dark-colored wood, and the room felt warm and venerable.

Hoover dropped into his chair and pulled up to his desk. "Have you ever testified in court, A. J.?" He looked at his notes.

"No."

"And you, Dear?" he said to Lennie feigning sincerity.

Lennie's answer was swift. "The Full Monte."

Hoover smiled and again turned to A. J., his manner instantly authoritative. "You are currently employed by Dallas Power and Light, Mister MacRae?"

After a second, A. J. realized Hoover was simulating court room procedure. "Yes sir, DP and L."

"You worked at Edgecom Data Corporation when Mister Degeorge was murdered?"

A. J. nodded.

Hoover started to say something but instead glanced at his notes. "Mr. Degeorge founded Edgecom?"

A. J. nodded again.

"Uh," Hoover said, clearing his throat, "in court, A. J., you have to answer verbally – *loudly*."

A. J. nodded. Both Lennie and Danny tittered, and A. J. said, "Yes, Mr. Degeorge did . . . found Edgecom."

"Mister Degeorge was running Edgecom when he was killed?"

"Yes sir. He ran . . . everything."

Hoover turned away thoughtfully. "Uh, A. J., it's best if you just simply answer my questions, 'Yes' or 'No,' if possible. Don't go expansive on me."

"Okay," A. J. said, which word he quickly spoke after reflexively nodding.

"Would you please characterize your association at Edgecom with Mister Degeorge."

The question struck A. J. as irrelevant, and he did not answer promptly.

Hoover noticed. "I'll ask you these very same nothing questions on the stand, A. J. They're warm-up stuff. That's all. So, fire right back." Smiling he added, "*Use* that nervous energy. Hell, sometimes even detectives pee themselves on the stand."

Lennie, defending the starch of cops everywhere, said stonily not that she had ever known.

"He was my boss," A. J. said to Hoover forcefully. "I . . . was in charge when he was away."

Dressed in business garb, a sturdy, middle-aged, dark-haired man stuck his head in the doorway. "Before you leave, Bob," he said authoritatively.

"Your office?" Hoover asked.

The visitor nodded perfunctorily and left.

"That was *the* man," Hoover said quietly.

"Wade," Lennie said softly to me.

"Anyway," Hoover said, cutting his eyes prankishly at Lennie and then back at me, "try not to hesitate when you answer. The jury might think you're trying to finesse a reply."

"Okay."

"Back to work, then," Hoover said. "We're still in the courtroom. How long have you known the defendant, Mister Quetsch?"

"A little over two years. Since the day he reported to Edgecom."

"You did not know Mister Quetsch before he became an Edgecom employee?"

"No sir. Not until after he had hired in."

"Only, you first knew Mister Quetsch as Selig Hildreth. Isn't that right?"

"Yes sir."

Hoover nodded. "The name that everyone else at Edgecom knew Quetsch as. Is that right?"

Danny interrupted. "Objection, your Honor! Leading . . . and iferential."

Hoover glanced at Danny approvingly. "Withdrawn." He looked at me. "It's the way the game's played."

A. J. said, "I've seen it on TV. Reminds me of a quick-pitch in baseball."

Hoover leaned back and smiled. "Exactly! Only a forensic quick-pitch is a strike no matter what the ump calls it . . . what the judge calls it. Know what I mean?

If I ask it . . . and you answer before the judge rules then it's an easy, catchable pop-up to the infield."

A. J. leaned back in his chair. "Right . . . that's what I meant."

Hoover rephrased his question. "Did you ever hear any other Edgecom employee address Mister Quetsch by any name except Selig Hildreth?"

"Hun-uh."

Hoover inclined his head. "Uh, be more positive, A. J. *Convince* the jury. Answer my simple questions either 'Yes' or 'No.' Okay?"

"Then . . . No."

"Now," Hoover continued softly, "I'm getting to the good stuff." Hoover en-quoted the word "good" with his fingers. "How," Hoover asked, "did you learn of Selig Hildreth's real name."

A. J. answer, that he had caught sight of the name Ronald Quetsch stenciled inside Hildreth's briefcase, was pensive and his phrases discontinuous.

Hoover grimaced and slightly shook his head.

Lennie, sensing that A. J. was feeling guilty over fingering Hildreth, interjected. "Keep in mind, Hon," she said, lying her hand on A. J.'s arm, "that Quetsch is a . . . bastard, a heartless serial killer – and worse."

A. J. mumbled something to the effect that they were not yet sure of that.

"Believe me," Hoover said, "the guy is an *animal*."

Danny added his two-bit's worth: "It's a slam dunk, A. J. He's bilge water. Trash."

"Then why," A. J. said, "do I feel like I'm a backstabbing shit?"

Hoover sighed. "You have to understand, A. J., that men like Quetsch are . . . rodents, cockroaches. They're . . . sociopaths. Ronald Quetsch tied his wife to a bed and then . . . harassed her with a red-hot poker."

A. J. jerked his head toward Lennie. "Maybe I should have told you," she said, quenching her face apologetically.

"Terrible," Hoover said, shaking his head. He shared a moment of dismay with Lennie.

"How," Hoover finally said to A. J., back in prosecutorial character, "had you come to provide Detective Deemer with Quetsch's finger prints?" He gestured at a spot in front of his desk. "The floppy disk drive will be on the evidence stand."

"He fixes our floppy drives," A. J. answered, back in character himself, "and I . . . borrowed one when he wasn't around."

"One that you knew had his finger prints on it?"

"Yes. He handled all returns. Fixed most of–"

"Good," Hoover said. "Only, please do not elaborate. Nothing about . . . jurors don't need to know how a clock works, just what time it is. You don't strike me as the type, A. J., but some witnesses go logorrheic on the witness stand."

"Try hard not to rattle on and on, Hon," Lennie said to A. J. sternly. Clearly, brevity of discourse, she wanted Bob and Danny to infer, did not come natural to A. J.

Hoover smiled. "Do you embarrass easily A. J.?"

"Hell, I don't know. I don't think so."

"Okay. You and Detective Deemer are living together. Is that right?"

A. J. looked at Lennie.

Hoover pounced. "The absolute worst thing you can do. Please, A. J., never look around for help when you're on the stand. Your credibility goes right down the toilet."

"I wasn't looking for *help*. I didn't . . . how *should* I answer?"

"A straightforward `Yes'. Or a straightforward `No.' Or whatever. Even if you think it may screw us. Probably it won't. And chances are I can patch over it on re-direct."

"My boyfriend," Lennie said to Hoover, "is a bit of a prude. SMU. Nineteen sixty one. Or, so he claims."

Hoover nodded at Danny. "And a fine school it is. Not in a class with TCU, but it does confer degrees . . . I read somewhere." Hoover clasped his chin as if trying hard to recall something. "Mail order, maybe? I'm not sure."

"Envy," A. J. said to Hoover, "causes baldness, you know."

Hoover scrutinized A. J.'s head. "Evidently."

Hoisted on his own petard, A. J. changed the subject. "I take it, that you're a TCU horny frog?"

Lennie snorted. "More frog than horny."

Hoover pretended to be insulted. "Says who?"

Lennie looked at A. J. "Bob just likes to argue."

"Be that as it may," Hoover said ceremoniously. After a pause he added, "Anyway, *don't* equivocate on the stand, A. J. I know you and Lennie are tight and so will Quetsch's lawyer. We have to provide the defense our witness list and their depositions."

His confidence restored, A. J. said, "Out of curiosity, what does our friendship have to do with . . . anything?"

Hoover answered impatiently. "It doesn't. It is absolutely irrelevant. Of course the defense'll try to make it out as . . . wickedness, as evil, besmirching. Anything to imply that you're conflicted."

"I'm conflicted? How!"

"You're hoping to get Lennie promoted?"

A. J. shook his head. "Ridiculous."

Hoover agreed. "Of course. And one more thing, A. J, don't show anger on the stand. You do, and the defense"– he tossed his head at the window behind him –"will be on you like the bird droppings on that window ledge."

A. J. grinned. "All over me, huh?"

Hoover smiled at Lennie and then looked back at A. J. "Quetsch's lawyer will lay it on. Birds will form up like marching bands do at a big college football game. The clouds will part, and you'll think the sun had never shone brighter than on the days Quetsch humbly strode past. Then, while you're sunbathing supine and naked in that luscious warmth, Toth will knee you right where it hurts. So, be ready."

A. J. answered the rest of Hoover's questions more or less to Hoover's satisfaction. After paging through his tablet of notes one last time, Hoover's gaze swept from Danny to Lennie and then settled on A. J. "You'll do just fine, A. J."

"Who," Lennie asked, "are you calling first, Bob?"

"I'm still tinkering with my witness list. The crime scene's virtually irrelevant, so it won't be you, Darling. I'm thinking . . . Doctor Gisewight. She sure has the balls. "Figuratively speaking, of course."

"Figuratively!" A. J. blurted out.

Lennie and both attorneys burst out laughing.

A. J. stood and flexed his back. "When will you call me?"

"At the moment," Hoover answered, "I'm thinking you'll be my second witness. No later than . . . fourth."

"Can you change the order in which you want witnesses to testify?"

"After I submit my list? Uh, only with the court's permission."

A prosecution's Order of Proof is organized a little like a bowling team: the second witness, like the second bowler, is usually the weakest member of the team. It took a little coaxing, but while Lennie and A. J. were driving home, Lennie finally admitted that that reality would determine when A. J. would appear on the stand.

Lennie also said that it was an article of faith among trial lawyers that jurors, if they did not remember anything else about a trail, always remembered the testimony of the first witness. The prosecution team, therefore, always wanted their first witness to be as self-assured as a politician regaling his supporters with a stump speech. A. J. reflected on the daunting arrogance of Dr. Gisewight and decided that she admirably filled the bill.

We stopped for a traffic light, and while A. J. was fussing over the long wait, Lennie said, "I think Bob would have liked to put Jo Ellen on first, only she's so damned wishy-washy."

"Indeed," A. J. said smugly, an underscored reply for Lennie to chew on.

# [50]

A bailiff wearing a neatly pressed tan uniform beckoned to A. J. from a few feet outside the courtroom's public entranceway. A. J. was one of a half-dozen witnesses waiting to testify – another court on the same floor was also in session – so he assumed he had been chosen from the bailiff's years of sizing up people. The bailiff nodded familiarly at Lennie. Tall, rigidly erect, his holstered side-arm jutting out from his body, he led me purposefully toward the judge's bench. On the way A. J. glanced at his watch. He had no idea why he thought that knowing the time would matter. It was nine twenty-five.

As Hoover had instructed him, A. J. was wearing a dark suit – medium gray, actually – a plain white shirt with a simple spread collar, and a solid blue necktie, the attire of a Dallas-ite of unimpeachable, evangelical integrity. A. J. convinced Hoover that his Texas accent would obviate the need for him to further curry the jury's favor by wearing cowboy boots, which footwear A. J. had never worn in his life and he idiosyncratically detested. A. J. told Hoover jokingly that if he wanted he would utter an occasional inquisitive vernacular Texas remark a "Dew whaaat, now?" or an authenticating, "You bay-ut!" ("You bet.")

The witness box abutted the bench on the judge's left, its location equally favoring the table reserved for the prosecution team and the jurors' box. The jury box was full, and A. J. could feel twelve pairs of ruby lasers boring through his cranium and into his soul. Had someone dropped a pin, he'd have jumped as if an empty garbage pan lid had hit the floor. The room itself, flat, rectangular, and wainscoted in walnut-finished paneling to within five or so feet of the ceiling, was large enough to accommodate several dozen spectators. A. J. could smell the slightly acrid odor of furniture oil.

The bailiff abruptly turned to his right, and they crossed in front of a sturdy dark wood table where Hoover, flanked by Danny, and a woman that A. J. had never seen before, was intently arranging notes. Danny looked up; slight vertical trenches scored the skin connecting his nose to his forehead.

A. J. wondered briefly if Hoover was over his opening-night jitters. Lennie said that he did not share her expectation of a fast and easy conviction – a confidence that had to have been inflated by lab-rat Sharon Rosenberg's discovery of tiny potassium permanganate granules in Quetsch's apartment kitchen – and for two weeks he had telephoned her so often she could hardly get anything done.

Typically, DAs and ADAs, Lennie said, became woebegone antsy as trial dates drew closer and closer. What infinitely irked her was when a prosecution lawyer telephoned and vociferously faulted her evidence as inferior, inadequate, or both and a day later the defendant, faced with that exact same evidence, copped a plea.

Hoover, Lennie explained, was distressed over what he regarded as the make-or-break testimony of Jo Ellen. In his opinion, lab-rat Sharon's discovery – evidence that A. J. had assumed put a smoking gun in Quetsch's hand – was not ironclad, was not the Holy Grail of Lennie's certitude. Bothered over the possibility of the jury buying into the defense's argument of when, exactly, the tiny pellets of permanganate had been spilled, Hoover was beside himself with worry. Did the spillage happen long before Hildreth/Quetsch arrived on the scene? If just one juror bought that defense argument he figured his case was in the dumpster.

Once A. J. was sworn in, Judge Wiggins, in a raspy but friendly voice, ordered him into the witness box, a hemmed-in chair elevated a step above the court's floor.

Judge Wiggins was a large man. Swarthy complexioned, his black, shoulder-padded robe layered extra bulk on his already substantial frame. He combed his brown hair straight back. A Joseph Stalin mustache hung like thick bunting under a long swooping nose, which downward sweep undercut his otherwise formidable presence.

The bailiff switched on the witness stand's microphone; the click was amplified by speakers mounted somewhere inside the jury box. Crossing his arms over his chest, the bailiff took up a watchful stance to the side and behind the jury box. The court reporter, a small, thirty-something, brown-haired woman showing plenty of leg – A. J. was not that nervous – sat at a metal stow-away table standing in front of and to the side of the bench. Her eyes were imperturbably focused on a stenograph machine.

Quetsch and his attorney, Lukacs Toth, were sitting alone at a table ten or so feet to Hoover's left. Toth was staring at me, but his head was cocked as if to better hear his client. A short, dark-complexioned man with a moon face and thick, dominating eyebrows, his hair was brushed into a fifties-style duck-ass.

I looked away quickly, but not before my mind had absorbed an image of Hildreth/Quetsch neatly attired in a pastel blue suit, white shirt, and solid gray necktie. His hands were under the table out of sight – cuffed, A. J. assumed – his head was tilted down, his face was set in a lament worthy of an aged basset hound.

Apparently Judge Wiggins signaled Hoover, who suddenly stood and walked briskly to the witness box where A. J. was waiting. A. J. returned Hoover's greeting, and Judge Wiggins, as A. J. was sure he had done hundreds of times, told A. J. to move closer to the microphone and speak up. A. J. leaned forward and repeated the words "Good morning."

Hoover, after a half-dozen becalming, nugatory questions, virtually the same ones he had used in their preparatory meeting, asked A. J. how long he had known the defendant.

"Two years," A. J. answered heartily.

Hoover nodded. "As I understand it, two years is forever in the computer electronics business. Some . . . novel design comes on the market every month, eh?"

A. J. answered earnestly. "Yes sir, two years in the electronics business is forever."

"Only,"– Hoover turned slightly in the direction of the jurors –"all those seven-hundred-plus days of the defendant's employment at Edgecom you knew the defendant *not* as Ronald Quetsch but as Selig Hildreth. Isn't that correct?"

Toth, turning from whispering something to Quetsch, objected: "Leading."

Toth's intervention, it was A. J.'s impression, was more mechanical than considered. Judge Wiggins sustained Toth's objection. Hoover nodded and said, "Did your fellow workers at Edgecom also know the defendant, Ronald Quetsch, as Selig Hildreth?"

Toth again objected. "What did the witness do, Your Honor, poll his fellow workers?"

Wiggins again sustained Toth's objection, in the process admonishing him for being indirect. "No more circumlocutions," he finished.

Toth nodded. "Poorly asked, Your Honor. I'll be more straightforward."

Hoover rephrased his question. "Did you ever hear anyone at Edgecom address Mr. Quetsch as anybody but Sel? Or Mr. Hildreth? Or ever see him referred to on paper or anywhere else by any name except Selig Hildreth?"

"No sir," A. J. answered confidently.

"Then . . . why, *Mr. Quetsch*? Why Ronald Quetsch? He told you privately that his name wasn't Selig Hildreth, that it was Ronald Quetsch?" Hoover slightly shrugged.

"No sir."

Hoover looked around slowly, allowed A. J.'s "No sir" to resonate a second and then he drew out how I had accidentally discovered Sel's true name. Scripted beforehand by Hoover, our exchange clearly implied that Quetsch was hiding something. Hoover's last question: Did I know why Mister Quetsch was using the name Selig Hildreth sprang Toth to his feet. Judge Wiggins, seemingly as pissed as Toth, impatiently beckoned for both attorneys to approach the bench.

Glaring at Hoover, Wiggins said he was intimately aware of Quetsch's past brush with the law and he would hold any allusion to that part of the defendant's life as prejudicial, inadmissible, and grounds for a mistrial. Another mention along those lines, he warned Hoover, just one more slight, tangential hint, and he'd not only declare a mistrial but would also hold him,

Hoover, in contempt so fast he'd wish the hell he was earning a living mounting bumpers at a Ford factory.

"Move along," Wiggins said to Hoover, waving him and Toth away from his bench. "Right now."

Hoover walked slowly back to where A. J. was waiting, his long face more pretence, A. J. was sure, than veracious.

As A. J. had expected, Hoover's remorse was short lived. "Did the defendant," he said to A. J., back in prosecutorial character, "tell you *why* the name Quetsch was stenciled on the inside of his briefcase?"

Toth's plea, "Relevancy, Your Honor!" buried my answer.

Hoover whirled toward the judge, his visage one of irrepressible disbelief. "Your Honor, surly A. J. can–"

Wiggins ignored both attorneys. "I'll allow it," he said looking past the audience of visitors.

Hoover repeated his question. "What reason did the defendant, whom you knew as Selig Hildreth, give for owning a briefcase with the name Ronald Quetsch printed on the inside?"

"He said he bought the used briefcase at a yard sale."

Hoover mockingly repeated the last part of my answer. "Used, at a yard sale." After a moment of studying the floor, his gaze fell back on me. "And you believed him?"

"Your Honor"– Toth had again scrambled to his feet –"Inferential! Besides, the Prosecution is fishing.

What possible bearing can the witness's answer have on these proceedings?"

Judge Wiggins looked at Hoover. "Your Honor, Hoover pleaded, "Mister MacRae had known the witness over two years. Surely, he's entitled to express his opinion regarding the truth of the defendant's explanation."

Slightly nodding, Wiggins said mechanically to Toth, "Overruled." He canted his head at Hoover. "Relevancy *now* Counsel. Or take up another subject."

Hoover addressed A. J. "You didn't believe the defendant, did you?"

Wiggins was shaking his head even before Toth finished his objection: he would allow it.

As the prick who had fingered Sel, in spite of both Lennie and Hoover insisting his cause was high-minded, A. J. could not help but equivocate. "Actually," A. J. said. "I . . . right away didn't—"

"In fact," Hoover briskly interrupted, "your skepticism led directly to the discovery that the defendant wasn't Selig Hildreth at all but someone named Ronald Quetsch. Isn't that right?"

Toth objected. "Leading *again*, Your Honor! Move to strike *any* answer."

Apparently Toth's objection was irregular because Wiggins's eyebrows shot up. He nevertheless sustained the objection.

By then, however, everyone in the courtroom understood that the part of the game where A. J. was the prosecution's featured running back was over. With Hoover's deft blocking of the defense's objections, A. J. had scampered across the goal line. Could there be any doubt whatsoever in the minds of the jurors that for years Quetsch had been passing himself off as someone else? For, as yet, an unmentioned but obviously sinister reason?

Attorney Toth, in objecting, did not plead, did not even stand; could barely hide his letdown.

Hoover, respecting Judge Wiggins's ruling, in only a few more non-leading questions shepherded A. J. into stating unequivocally that his stumbling on Sel's real name ultimately brought to light his true identity.

After A. J.'s last answer, Hoover turned and walked – buoyantly, it seemed to A. J. – back to the prosecuting lawyers' table. On the way he nodded pleasantly at Lukacs Toth.

# [51]

Attorney Toth, grimly preoccupied, rose slowly from behind the table where he and Quetsch had been dolefully watching A. J. dance to Hoover's carefully scored choreography. A. J. waited restively in the witness box.

"Good morning, Sir," Toth said to A. J., amicably. His scowl had vanished, and he all but offered his hand.

A. J. remembered Hoover's warning: *The golly-jolly set up.* A. J. repeated Toth's neighborly greeting, omitting his respectful 'Sir.'

Toth continued. "You were working at Edgecom Data Corporation when the owner, Mister Degeorge, passed away?"

"That's . . . correct," A. J. answered.

Toth nodded. "What rank did you hold, Mister MacRae?"

"Rank?"

"What was your title? What office did you hold?"

"I didn't have a title. I . . . reported to Mister Degeorge, though."

Toth allowed A. J.'s answer a silent moment of its own. "Mister Degeorge founded Edgecom?"

A. J. nodded. "Uh, yes sir."

"In fact, you were Mister Degeorge's confidant, had his ear on virtually all matters relating to Edgecom's business. Eh?"

Hoover objected. "Inferential, Your Honor."

The question seemed innocuous to A. J. Hoover, of course, knew Toth was not just barking up any old tree, that he glimpsed a fat raccoon of testimonial gain clinging to an upper branch.

Judge Higgins allowed the question, and after the usual back-and-forth courtroom forensics, Toth established that when Degeorge was out of town – often to promote Edgecom products at a trade show – A. J. made Edgecom decisions on all money-matter issues, on virtually all Edgecom trivial and non-trivial spending.

After righteously defining the essence of "Reverse Engineering" as the thievery of another company's proven design – as the "blatant pilferage of a company's sales triumph"– Toth established A. J.'s complicity in Edgecom's constant participation in that common business practice.

A. J. said that Edgecom always refined the design, improved its performance, and typically lowered the retail price. "For all practical purpose," he continued, "we created a new product."

Toth shrugged and tossed his head dismissively. Hoover, I'm sure, covertly agreed with Toth and decided either that the subject was dismissable or that the lameness of A. J.'s answer was harmless. Later, A. J. realized that the feebleness of his counter arguments was likely the reason Judge Higgins allowed his full reply.

Hoover promised A. J. that Toth would try mightily to humiliate him for his collaboration in fingering a putatively innocent man, and one-time friend. The testimony of a remorseful witness, Hoover explained, had as little steel as the bark of a dog hauling butt, looking back, his tail tucked between his legs.

Toth had apparently decided it was time for A. J. to eat a serving of humble pie. His gaze, after glancing at the jury and then at the stenographer, settled on A. J. It was a second before Toth's question. "Did you know Selig Hildreth before he became an employee of Edgecom Data Corporation?" He stepped aside, to where A. J.'s view of Hildreth/Quetsch was unobstructed. A. J. could not bring himself to look at Quetsch, and he was sure the jury noticed.

"No," A. J. answered weakly.

"But, you did become good friends, eh, Mister MacRae?"

"More or less. After he hired in."

Toth bored in. "You *didn't* become good friends?"

"No. I mean, yes, we did not become . . . *good* friends. I wouldn't . . . call it that."

"I see," Toth said, nodding slowly. "Now . . . wasn't it customary at Edgecom for the engineers and technicians to go out and celebrate together every time a new design was released to Manufacturing? Was that not a . . . a *treasured* ritual at Edgecom Mister MacRae?" Toth turned toward the jurors. "I know that it's been a while since you were discharged from Edgecom . . . but isn't that so?"

A. J felt his cheeks coloring, and he barely kept himself from describing the dissolute circumstance of his firing at Edgecom. "Usually we did," he answered.

"And how often was that?"

"I'm . . . not sure."

Toth promptly challenged A. J. "You wrote *every single one* of Edgecom's new-product press releases, but you don't know how often it was that you celebrated those . . . zeniths of Edgecom's business!"

Hoover half rose from his chair. "Badgering, Your Honor!"

Wiggins, his gaze again fast on the back wall of the room, shook his head.

Toth did not wait for my answer. "Wasn't it less than *monthly* that you and your co-workers, including Selig Hildreth – he nodded at Quetsch – met after work, at a nearby cafe, to celebrate the completion of a so-called *new* design? But you say that you and Sel *didn't* socialize? Is that your testimony Mister MacRae?"

"Where," Hoover said, addressing the judge but scowling at Toth, "is this going, Your Honor? It's still badgering!"

"Which is it, Mr. MacRae?" Toth demanded before Wiggins ruled.

Wiggins ordered Toth to begin a new line of questioning.

Clearly satisfied with the trajectory of his questioning, Toth nodded deferentially and took a step toward Wiggins. "If it pleases the bench, Your Honor, I'd like to ask the witness a few questions regarding his very close relationship with Detective Lenore Deemer. Detective Deemer, as his Honor is well aware, is the principal case investigator. My concern goes to motive."

Hoover objected, and Wiggins waved the two attorneys to the bench.

A. J.'s motive in fingering Quetsch, Toth argued, had a hidden impetus, and A. J.'s testimony, therefore, must be recognized as compromised. Toth, it seemed to A. J, was not trying very hard to muffle his voice. Wiggins fulminated. Why in hell hadn't he addressed the charge up front? Hoover, wholly in sympathy with Wiggins, rolled his eyes and shook his head.

A. J. was sure all three men knew exactly why attorney Toth had put off raising the point about Lennie's and A. J.'s cohabitation, knew that he wanted to first savage A. J.'s moral character. A. J. thought, furthermore, that they knew Judge Wiggins was mainly venting his anger over the expansion of A. J.'s insipid, less than crucial testimony. Judge Wiggins told Toth he could proceed to build the case that cast A. J. as a biased witness but only up to a point. "*Don't* dally," he warned.

Toth stepped back to where A. J. was waiting in the witness box. Hoover returned to the defense table, on the way just perceptively shaking his head. Wiggins glared at him, and he did not relent until Hoover was back in his chair stirring through papers. Nor, it seemed to A. J., was Wiggins happy with Hoover's pretence of behavioral innocence.

Attorney Toth's initial questions led A. J. to concisely identifying Lennie, her function, and the fact that they lived together. Then he started in on A. J.'s meandering behavior.

"When," Toth asked, "did you and Detective Deemer begin . . . ah, this exotic life style?"

Hoover, scarcely lifting his head from arranging the mess of papers under his nose, asked Wiggins to rule on relevancy. Toth flashed Wiggins a look of incredulity, and Wiggins, his eyebrows contracted in anger, told Hoover to stop objecting just for the hell of it. Some spectators tittered. Hoover assured Wiggins that it would not happen again.

The court reporter, cued by Wiggins, re-read the question, which was only a word or two different from one Hoover had used in prepping A. J.

A. J. answered promptly: "In December . . . of last year."

Toth, again thoughtfully studying the floor, stopped nodding and fixed his gaze on the corner of the room where in dignified repose stood flags of the United States and State of Texas, silent reminders of the awesome civic responsibility of every Texan – of the personal morality that every citizen juror, not to mention all witnesses, must live up to.

Toth turned his attention back on A. J. "You were still married when you and Detective Deemer began living together?"

Toth, while Hoover was objecting, withdrew his question. Wiggins sharply ordered the jury to disregard the question and simultaneously waved Toth and Hoover to the bench. Staring fiercely at Toth, he said he had warned him not to go too far – one more of his questions about A. J.'s "irrelevant personal morality" and he'd sure as hell hold him in contempt.

Judge Wiggins had lowered his voice, but everyone in the courtroom could tell he was pissed. A. J. was certain every juror, every spectator, the two bailiffs, and the court reporter, contrary to Wiggins' instruction, would carry to his or her grave the notion that A. J. was a callous, unfaithful husband, not to mention that he apparently had little regard for factualness.

Toth's singular objective was to discredit A. J. as a witness, to sully his integrity. He asked four more trifling questions addressing A. J.'s "affair" with

Lennie, before claiming that A. J.'s true motivation in fingering Quetsch was to advance his "new girlfriend's" career. The nexus was so tenuous and so loosely braided A. J.'s alleged motive for his amorous involvement with Lennie that Hoover never once objected to any of his questions. Or, maybe, Wiggins's warning hadn't stopped resonating in his mind.

In any event, on redirect, Hoover led A. J. through a series of questions clarifying that he and Allison had separated long before A. J. met Lennie, and that Allison's self-initiated divorce action was speeding unobstructed through the courts.

Finishing his redirect, Hoover nodded at Wiggins. "No more questions."

Wiggins, after a quick look at Toth, who, in a preoccupied way was shaking his head, excused A. J.'s appearance as a witness, banged his gavel, and declared court in recess until ten a.m. Wednesday.

Hoover, that evening, as he usually did, gathered members of his prosecuting team in his office to evaluate the day's proceedings and plan next day's tactics. Certain that Hoover would not mind, Lennie invited A. J. to accompany her; she drove the two of them downtown in an unmarked police car.

Hoover observed that the trial was moving along about as he had expected. He looked at A. J. and grinned. "Toth kind of made you out a skunk, didn't he?"

A. J. had taken a seat behind and to the right of Lennie, and for a second he did not realize that Hoover was addressing him. Moreover, until he asked, A. J. truly had not understood how badly – at least from the viewpoint of the prosecution – Toth had roughed him up.

"I guess so," A. J. answered sheepishly, adding, as his question sank in, "Yeah, he did."

"Defense attorneys are jackals," Lennie said.

Danny corrected her. "Jackasses."

A. J. asked Hoover if he'd indulge him one question: the relevancy of much of his testimony troubled him. A. J.'s concern amused Hoover.

"Ah, murder trials," Hoover said smiling, a kid eager to explain the Green Hornet ring on his finger. "Why does it matter that Edgecom was into reverse engineering? What in the hell difference did it make if you and Quetsch quaffed a couple suds together now and then? You've been seeing Lennie romantically. Wow!"

"At least," A. J. said, grinning, "he didn't ask if I wore briefs or boxer shorts."

A. J.'s wit was not worth even tiny smiles.

"So," Hoover continued. "Put yourself in Quetsch's shoes. Your life is on the line. Worse – or maybe better – the decision of whether you're going to live or die is in the hands of twelve fellow citizens, at least one of whom is too dumb to masturbate without step-by-step instructions. Now–"

A. J. cleared his throat, "ahemed" loudly in a way to suggest what Hoover had just said was a bit much. A. J. was outvoted by Lennie and Danny.

"So," A. J. said looking away, "some jurors have trouble connecting the dots?"

Hoover answered A. J.'s question. "Hell, some can't tell an ink dot from fly poop. Jurors fill out a questionnaire. All it takes, A. J., is one witless moron to hang a jury. There's at least a fifty-fifty chance one of the woman jurors will question the truth of your testimony because you dated Lennie before your divorce was final! Plausibility, probability, relevancy . . . those words just aren't in some people's vocabulary. That *is* a fact. You see where I'm . . . going A. J.?"

A. J. allowed a second for Hoover's bitterness to fade and then said, "Still, it's hard to believe . . . ."

"Not," Hoover said, mostly to himself, "after you've prosecuted thirty-six cases . . . a third unsuccessfully."

A. J. leaned back apologetically. "I didn't literally mean 'hard to believe.'"

Hoover did not hear A. J. He pulled a briefcase onto his desk, removed a tablet from inside, and thumbed rapidly through it.

A. J. recalled little more of what was said that night. Moreover, being an outsider, he once indifferently wandered off to look for a candy-bar-vending machine.

Riding home, A. J. asked Lennie if she felt Toth had skewered him as badly as Hoover seemed to think. "Naw," Lennie said, "Hoover had way exaggerated the damage done on my cross-examination by Toth. That's . . . defense lawyer think."

Lennie's answer, uncharacteristically flippant, left A. J. wondering if the opposite might be all too true.

# [52]

The red light on the telephone recorder signaled that two calls had been received. Lennie and A. J. had eaten late, their supper delayed because they had met downtown with Bob Hoover, and it was after ten o'clock when they reached home.

Both calls were from Nickerson. He had checked into the Hilton Inn on Central Expressway. "Telephone me when you get in," he ordered. "If you aren't falling-down drunk."

"He's been subpoenaed by Quetsch's attorney," Lennie said, as soon as Nick hung up.

A. J. nodded. "We haven't talked since he moved to Austin."

"He'll testify," Lennie said, with a trace of annoyance, "for the defense. Claim that Quetsch's picture should be on a Wheaties' box, that he is an annointed boy scout leader, that he prays to Jesus nightly, and . . . so on."

"That you Silo!" A. J. barked into the telephone when Nick answered the telephone.

Nick wanted to know precisely why A. J. was out running around after his bedtime. "The sun set two hours ago," Nick chirped, sounding as happy to hear A. J.'s voice as A. J. was to hear his.

"So," A. J. said, "the mayor of Austin ordered your exile, huh?"

"I needed the R and R, Pop. Damn Austin women are sexual predators. Even you could score."

Their banter, before long, tailed off. "I've been subpoenaed to testify," Nick said, sighing unhappily, "on behalf of my buddy, my very innocent buddy."

"Your innocent buddy," A. J. said, not quite so pleasantly, "is a damn monster."

"I'll answer questions honestly. That's all, A. J., that I promise."

In truth, Nick could not have lied to save his own tail let alone another person's. He said he was scheduled to testify Wednesday afternoon. A. J. explained that he likely would not testify until Thursday because the jury had not yet heard from several of the prosecution's witnesses.

The subject of the trial covered, more or less, Nickerson addressed a new topic: "I saw a blurb in Friday's *Statesman.* So, Osgood finally took Edgecom public? I suppose you're a multi-millionaire now?"

"No," A. J. said, in a tone suggesting that the answer was indisputably negative, "But Osgood and Wickersham sure-in-hell are. I don't know of anyone else that became filthy rich overnight. None of Edgecom's Old Guard. Of that, I'm damned certain."

"Yeah," Nick said, sounding downhearted. "So, what else is new?"

A. J. told him to hold on a minute. To Lennie, A. J. said, "We'll be a little while, Dear." She shrugged and removed two bottles of beer from the refrigerator. "Great," A. J. said to her softly, and then into the telephone, "You knew Osgood sacked me?"

Nick answered affirmatively. He did not elaborate, however, and A. J. assumed Quetsch had told him that he had been cashiered by Osgood and that likely he was physically thrown out of Edgecom by Dornhoffer. A. J. badly wanted to know what Quetsch had said of his Judas Iscariot role in Quetsch's his arrest, but he did not have the temper to ask.

A. J. mentioned how everything that he had learned lately about the activities at Edgecom came second-hand from Skip Hardeman. Skip, A. J. said, seemed to have gotten the upper hand on his radio-active libido once he began dating Harriet Muckinhaupt. "He's young," A. J. went on, "like you . . . only much smarter. And handsome."

"You still get everything bassackwards, Pop. Hell, to *you* everyone must seem smart and handsome. And young."

"You knew about MaxWriter?"

"Sunk like a cardboard box of railroad spikes, I heard."

"And ELAN?"

"E what?"

"Edgecom's local area network?"

"Oh, *E-LAN*. No."

A. J. sketchily described ELAN, told him that it was Steen's baby.

Nick reminded A. J. that Edgesales, the data system he and Israel had developed recreationally when they were new Edgecom engineers, was a primitive LAN. His voice trailed off. "Damn, A. J., I know I could have talked Fran into generalizing Edgesales."

"Probably. Anyway, the day Hardeman torpedoed ELAN–"

"*Hardeman* killed E-LANn?"

"Yeah, he didn't sell any of his stock in the IPO, so now he's the half-ton gorilla of Edgecom management."

"Didn't sell any?"

"I guess he figured the price would go up."

"I'll bet Osgood's shitting himself."

"Because Hardeman's the big ape now? Actually, I'd bet he doesn't much give a rat's ass. Skip said Osgood made over four million in the offering."

"That son-of-a-bitch," Nick said disgustedly.

A. J. kept it to himself, but it occurred to him – the expression "son-of-a-bitch" being the second time Nick had bespattered the architect of Edgecom's successful public offering – that perhaps Nick's farewell visit with Osgood had not jelled as he had hoped, that he had learned Osgood's promised "piece of the action" was just more of his non-stop bull.

"Anyway," A. J. resumed, "the day after ELAN's botched premiere, Hardeman, without telling anyone, not even his boy, Skip, hired a consultant to find him a company on the make. I don't think Skip's totally in the loop, but he's pretty sure his daddy is negotiating the sale of Edgecom to some outfit in Oklahoma named TexLine Office Furniture."

"Office furniture!"

"I know, it didn't make sense to me either. Evidently, TexLine plans to resurrect MaxWriter and package it as an option for their high-end office line."

Nick snorted. "It damn well better be high-end."

A. J. said, "My guess is that the men running TexLine know computing like you know women."

"Explain something to me, Pop. What does Edgecom own that's worth a hand of bananas?" (A. J. imagined Nick's eyes narrowing skeptically.)

"Cash. Baskets of it. From the public offering. I wondered myself, so I asked Irickson. Also, Edgecom has full rights to both MaxWriter and ELAN."

Nick reminisced softly. "MaxWriter and ELAN. Ha. One more of Steen's immaculate conceptions and he'd have scored a dumb-engineering hat trick."

A. J. took a long slug of beer from the bottle that Lennie had opened for him.

"Could MaxWriter," A. J. asked, interrupting something Nick was saying, "be re-engineered to make it profitable?"

"I doubt it," Nick answered, indifferent to A. J.'s butting in. "Why? Because it's already obsolete. We're talking *electronics.* Be easier to resuscitate Ford's 1958 Edsel."

"Ah, electronics," A. J. murmured.

"Yeah," Nick said. "In our business, time do fly. What else, Pop?"

A. J. had to think a moment. "Oh. Yeah. A few days after the public offering, Wickersham bailed."

"Wearing a golden parachute, naturally."

"Um, silver, maybe," A. J. said. "You knew he and Osgood had been at each other's throats for months?"

"Yeah, I saw signs before I left. Wickersham was too quick for Osgood. Hummel couldn't stand being backup conductor to his own orchestra . . . especially during his stupid, never-ending meetings. I was there once when Wickersham pissed in his ear."

"Skip told me the straw that broke the camel's back was Wickersham misjudging the opening price of Edgecom stock, that both he and the guy from Nolan and Company blew it. The under-pricing cost Osgood some . . . I don't know, three-, four-hundred thousand bucks. So he blamed it on Wickersham."

"Still," Nick said, "he was a damn smart cookie."

"Wickersham? He was a damn smart *crook.* He cooked the books, Silo."

"For sure?"

"Yes, for sure. That's why Osgood dumped Martha and brought him in . . . to fry Edgecom's books. Wickersham made over a half million in the IPO. I doubt he lost sleep over getting canned, if, in fact, he *was* fired. I mean, if he didn't just tell Osgood to go fuck himself."

"I guess," Nick said, sounding drained, "it's a good thing I cleared out."

"Osgood told Hardeman that *he* booted Wickersham. Over his and Herb's long unsettled disagreement concerning the essentiality of certain of Edgecom's faithful senior employees. Skip was there."

Nick sighed. "That lying . . . garbage"

"The day after Hardeman killed ELAN he fired everyone in sight. Except," A. J. added, chuckling, "Harriet Muckinhhaupt and Miki Vernon. And, maybe, two or three others."

"Is Miki still blowing *Saber Dance* on Hardeman's flute?"

"Well, she's still working at Edgecom. That's what Skip tells me anyway. Both she and Crazy Legs Lou. Whose limbs, incidentally, Crazy Legs has taken to shaving regularly. And they ain't that bad, Silo. Not that you'd know women's legs from rusty stove pipes."

Lennie tilted down the magazine she was reading, or pretending to read, and slowly shook her head. A. J. covered the telephone mouth piece and whispered to her, "It's what he likes to hear."

"Of course," she said, rolling her eyes.

Uncovering the mouth piece, A. J. said to Nick, "Did you meet Appleby? Lee Appleby?"

"I guess not."

"He audited Edgecom's books for the public offering. Now he's . . . I'll put it this way, some relative of his wife owns part of Edgecom. According to Skip."

"*Owns* part of Edgecom?"

"Owns."

A. J. heard the ring of a bell, and Nick said to hold on.

"Room service?" A. J. asked when Nick returned.

"Close," he said. "Jesse? He's gone too?"

"Oh Christ . . . ." A. J. said. Sensing that Nick had turned away from the phone and was listening to someone else, A. J. paused before continuing. "Jesse died in April. I didn't have your address."

After a moment, Nick said softly, "God, I hate hearing that. I knew he was . . . sick"

"Very," A. J. said, "Jesse was good folks, as he would have put it."

Nick said, "I'd have gone to his funeral."

"Thanks," A. J. said.

"No," Nick said. "It was my fault. I should have . . . at least sent a card."

"Let's get together," A. J. said, "after you testify."

"Yeah. Let's do that! You like chili?"

I reminded him that being a native Texan I ate chili for breakfast. He suggested we meet for lunch at the Bowl of Red, a restaurant in downtown Dallas.

As A. J. had surmised, no defense witnesses testified until Thursday, and the three of them, Lennie, Nick, and A. J. met late Thursday afternoon at the Bowl of Red. A. J. was both astonished and pleased when Nick kept his mind off Lennie long enough that they could coherently discuss Edgecom. A. J. thinks Nick was tuckered. As likely, it was just that Nick's back was hurting him.

# [53]

Rosalia Ibanez, one of Jesse's assemblers, was a chunky, sour-pussed *mestizo.* The few times A. J. had noticed her at Edgecom she was sitting, with her arms folded, sequestering herself, at the edge of a group of fellow workers on a coffee break. She had chanced upon Jo Ellen and Quetsch sharing a back-corner booth in a hole-in-the-wall family restaurant on the edge of a Latino community in Garland. A victim of Osgood's first mass layoff, at the time of Quetsch's trial she was no longer employed at Edgecom. Hoover had scheduled her to testify after A. J. As it turned out, no one testified until Wednesday because Judge Wiggins recessed court unexpectedly on Tuesday.

When Quetsch's attorney passed up an opportunity to cross-examining Ibanez, Wiggins immediately recessed court until two p.m. With well over two hours to kill, Lennie and A. J. returned to A. J.'s car, and A. J. aimlessly drove south through Oak Cliff, a large, dry, self-contained section of Dallas, and then to the city of Duncanville, a Dallas suburb. In Duncanville they shared a double McWhatchamacallit and a jumbo Coke at a McDonalds.

Returning to the court house, A. J. left Lennie off at the entrance. He was feeling queasy, a hang-over, he guessed, from his tension of the day before. His nausea, reconstituted by McDonald's big, double McWhatchamacallit, brought on an urge to drive straight home. Lennie insisted she could hitch a ride to A. J.'s apartment in Richardson with Hoover, when he returned to his home in Plano.

Wearing low-heeled pumps, a tight black denim skirt that stopped four inches above her knees, and a majenta-colored, snug fitting, turtle-neck pullover, A. J.'d have given a week's salary for a video tape of the faces of the men in the court room as they either leered or gawked – which he was sure they did – at Lennie's confident stroll to the witness box. Lennie's direct, cross, and re-direct lasted barely twenty minutes. She called A. J. afterward and said that her cross by defense attorney Lukacs Toth was a stroll on the beach, that she'd struggled infinitely harder parrying the wandering hands of dike cops when she was driving a patrol car. (Lennie sometimes used the word "cops," but she screwed on a sour look when others used it, including A. J.) A. J. told Lennie that he would fix each of them a waterball when she got home. A beer, Lennie replied, would be just fine.

A. J. had grown accustomed to Lennie underestimating the time when she expected to arrive home after work, and A. J. was surprised when a little before nine o'clock he heard a car door slam followed by a muffled "Thanks" float up from the street in front of his apartment. A. J. downed a final swig of his beer and opened two more bottles.

They kissed in the doorway. Lennie kicked off her shoes, savored a full-length backward stretch, and then walked to the sofa. On the way she fanned her midsection with the bottom of her pull-over. A. J. knew by then in their relationship that Lennie's stirring of the air was only emblematic, a habit unrelated to the ambient temperature. Dropping onto the sofa, she patted the cushion beside where she had plopped down.

A. J. handed Lennie a longneck and sat down beside her. "So. How'd it go?"

"Nothing to it. Made me wonder why Quetsch hired a lawyer from Fort Worth. Dallas has more lawyers than Baptist ministers. I had expected he'd be a real hard-ass. Hoover didn't say it, but I think he felt Toth never laid a glove on me."

A. J. pretended to toast her with his beer.

Lennie was openly contented. All the same, A. J. sensed an undercurrent of disappointment in her manner, a letdown, he supposed, over her mere twenty minutes in the forensic spotlight.

"Toth tried to make me out a shave-tail rookie. All defense attorneys do. The first time I testified, an assistant DA warned me, me being young and female. I learned a new word then, *con-jex-ur-al*. He said the defense would try to characterize my testimony as purely conjectural, nothing more than feminine intuition. So, for Mister Toth, I dragged out long minutes of concretely itemizing my qualifications. I am *so* considerate."

A. J. leaned back. "Really?" he said, gravely unconvinced.

Lennie capitalized on A. J.'s pretence: "It depends on the company I'm with."

Judge Wiggins, she said, could not keep his eyes off her legs. Lennie's remark reminded A. J. that Wiggins, from his seat behind the bench, towered over witnesses."I *just* could not stop from crossing and uncrossing them. Showed him everything but beaverville."

"Modesty becomes you. Did Toth ask about us?"

Lennie, by then in our relationship, was swearing less, at least around me, and she had almost stopped using the F word. That evening, however, the synergism of her excitement and her worry over the set of Jo Ellen's backbone caused four-letter words to keep bubbling up.

"Yes," she answered. "He tried to make me out a fucking whore."

A. J. cocked an eyebrow. "There are other kinds?"

Lennie out-deadpanned him. "Of course. The ones who're still virgins."

It took A. J. a moment to realize Lennie meant prostitutes who only sodomized their johns: "Your nitpicking is annoying, Detective. What'd Hoover have to say?"

"This evening in his office? This and that. He fished for ideas on how to handle Jo Ellen . . . *if* she denies having left Quetsch alone with your boss. Remember, Hon, for a year she'd been laying this guy who'll be twisting her head off with his eyes from fifteen feet away."

"Even if she does . . . if Jo Ellen does boogie, I mean, couldn't Hoover fix it? Read her deposition back. Or do *something* like that? Isn't she on record as saying–"

"It wouldn't matter. We're toast if she's wishy-washy. Toth would convince the jury – at least one juror – that we had confused the sweet little thing when we deposed her. And Hoover is calling . . . Betty to the stand. She'll sure-in-hell back up her own sister. No matter the truth of Jo Ellen's testimony."

"Yes!" Lennie replied quickly. "Exactly! *Everything* Jo Ellen testifies to."

"Then Betty . . . might perjure herself?" A. J. said.

"For her identical twin sister? You're damn right. Oh, Hon you're so . . . you've got to start fraternizing with real people."

"Meeting more liars? I'll reintroduce you to my daddy. What'd Hoover say about Ibanez's testimony?"

Lennie, mostly from hearing Hoover's account, touched on the action in the courtroom:

"Ibanez," she began, "in spite of mucking up the English language to a fare-thee-well, positively identified Quetsch as the man she had once seen cozily sitting beside Jo Ellen in a restaurant. They were snuggling and sitting closer to each other than she and her marido ever did, she said."

"That's it?" A. J. asked.

"Just about," Lennie answered.

"Didn't Toth cross-examine Ibanez?"

"No. Hoover thinks Toth planned to . . . scape-goat Jo Ellen. So, he let Ibanez smear Jo Ellen's. . . morality, thinking that the collateral harm she did Quetsch, if any, would pay off when he got the jury to at least wondering if Jo Ellen herself wasn't a co-conspirator in Fran's murder."

Hoover said that he figured, if it went too far, he could sway the jury into believing that Ibanez's testimony about her seeing Jo Ellen and Quetsch eating together was little more than her stumbling on a meeting of two friends whining about Dallas's hot summer."

Toth, A. J. told Lennie, would have his work cut out trying to cast Jo Ellen, Fran's torpid, shrinking-violet widow, as the evil co-star of a forensic drama.

Jo Ellen testified after Lennie. Worried that her potentially iffy answers might wrongly sway at least one juror, Hoover moved her up when he revised his Order of Proof.

According to Hoover, that is, according to Lennie's retelling of Hoover's explanation, Jo Ellen, without so much as the blink of an eye, told Toth that she had left Quetsch alone with her husband in the hospital room the night he was murdered, that she had, on that night, walked her sister and brother-in-law to their car, taking as long as twenty minutes to make the two-way trip.

Hoover later told Lennie that he figured Jo Ellen was high on something – likely had popped a couple tranquilizers. She had a faraway look in her eyes, Hoover explained, and there was nothing far away to look at.

Jo Ellen's testimony, according to Hoover, outraged the ever-placid Quetsch. Lennie again transcribed Hoover's account of what took place:

Quetsch, jumping to his feet, screamed that *he* had left *Jo Ellen* alone with Fran, that Jo Ellen's testimony was a damn ass-backward account. Shackled, he accidentally knocked Toth, who had risen to calm him, back into his chair. The collision bounced Quetsch against the edge of the bulky defense table, stopping him from plunging head first onto the floor."

"Hoover's account?" A. J. scoffed. "Frankly, Hon, I can't picture Selig Hildreth in a rage over anything."

Lennie shrugged, said it was how Hoover had seen it: "Quetsch, once he began screaming that Jo Ellen was a lying bitch, wouldn't stop. A few words into his outburst, Wiggins nodded at the bailiff, and the bailiff bull-dogged Quetsch from the room. A door slammed and then another and everyone in the court room could still hear Quetsch intermittently screaming that Jo Ellen was a liar."

Lennie continued transcribing Hoover's account of the courtroom action:

"Jo Ellen never once flinched, never wavered, did not one time refer to Quetsch, the man who had canvassed her naked body for over a year, as Selig Hildreth. Her gaze not only followed Hildreth's wild, involuntary exit, her eyes remained a long time on the closed doorway through which he was dragged from the court room. Her look was either one of sympathy or one of pity, which, Hoover admitted, he couldn't tell."

Toth, on cross examination, could not shake Jo Ellen of her insistence that she and her husband had left Quetsch alone in the hospital room just before Fran died. It helped, Hoover said, that Judge Wiggins – deciding that the testimony would be prejudicial – allowed Hoover's objection to defense questions that might reveal Jo Ellen was the sole beneficiary of Fran's million-dollar life insurance policy.

Hoover's re-direct may have partly offset any damage caused by Toth's unmasking of Jo Ellen's infidelity by letting the jury in on the fact that her husband's wandering eye was not the only part of his anatomy disposed to take random journeys of pleasure. At any rate, that was the thrust of Hoover's questions. At least one juror, he reasoned, would see that two wrongs, contrary to the popular saying, really did make a right.

# [54]

Had Bob Hoover known that Hummel Osgood was an indefatigable blow-hard he would have left him off his witness list. Hoover merely wanted the jury to hear Osgood testify that he only knew Ronald Quetsch as Selig Hildreth, a squid of testimony that would help nail the lid on the casket awaiting Quetsch at an undertaker's in the "Prison City" of Huntsville, Texas. The first prosecution witness to testify on Wednesday afternoon, it was a long minute of Osgood commending his lead technician for everything except his spic-and-span toilet habits before Hoover succeeded in getting Osgood's endless train of verbosity off the siding and back on what he had planned as a two- or three-question express track.

Lennie and A. J. watched from the court room "peanut-gallery," from a small group of seats unintentionally offset from the main spectator viewing area. Hoover had officially agreed not to call us back to the witness stand and attorney Toth went along. It was the first time Lennie watched a trial in which she had personally testified. It was also A. J.'s inaugural observation of an ongoing trial.

Toth, his expression thoughtful, his right hand holding his chin, began his cross examination of Osgood: "You visited the deceased in the hospital the night he died?"

"Yes sir," Osgood answered. "That's correct. Fran, uh, Mister Degeorge, was both my brother-in-law and a beloved friend."

A. J. softly pretended to puke, but not so quietly that Lennie didn't rebuke him with a stern glance.

Toth nodded at Osgood. "And Mister Degeorge's widow is your wife's sister?"

"Her identical twin sister. "Yes sir. They're very close."

"So it'd be fair to say," Toth continued, "that you didn't merely accompany your wife to the hospital for . . . for what, the formality of an appearance? That you're very heart was in it. Is that right?"

"Yes sir that would be a *very* fair way to put it. Fran and I were almost blood brothers."

A. J. felt like faking another upchuck but knew he'd catch it again from Lennie.

Osgood interrupted Toth: "We started Edgecom together, Fran and I."

Toth glanced at Judge Wiggins. Wiggins incinerated Osgood with his eyes but did not reprimand him for speaking out of turn. Ogood smiled timidly and nodded. It was the first time A. J. had seen Osgood express himself timorously, and he knew it was acting.

Toth continued. "Besides yourself and your wife, was there anybody else in the room during your visit?"

Osgood's lips rolled in and his eyes narrowed in thought. "Well," he began hesitantly. "A nurse popped in and out . . . twice, I think. Uh, and an aide, I guess they're called aides, a male in hospital duds." He nodded at Quetsch. "And Selig. He arrived just after we got there. Of course, Jo Ellen was there the whole time. Possibly an ex-Edgecom employee named MacRae stopped by. I'm trying to remember."

"That son-of-a-bitch!" A. J. let slip.

Satan himself would have wet his shorts had he been the object, as A. J. was, of Lennie's glare. Judge Wiggins, however, did not hear A. J., and no one around us stirred, so A. J. mentally upgraded his sociability prowess.

"I see," Toth went on. "And how long did you and your wife visit Mister Degeorge? In minutes, how long were you, uh, actually *in* his room?"

"I'd estimate, oh, fifteen minutes. We didn't want to overstay–

"And you *both* remained there the whole time? Until the two of you left to go home?"

"Indeed. We never once left his room. Not until we, you know, until we left that day for good."

"And how did Mister Degeorge seem to you? Was he in pain?"

Hoover objected on two counts: Osgood's answer would be characterization by a dilettante – and A. J. did not understand the gist of his other objection.

Toth rephrased his question: "Please describe the look on Mister Degeorge's face while you were there. Was it peaceful? Strained? How was he feeling? "

Wiggins shook his head at Hoover, who appeared on the verge of raising another objection.

For several seconds Hoover whispered to Danny, his assistant. Judge Wiggins turned and poured water from a carafe into a plastic cup, an amenity also provided each litigant team. He took a sip, belatedly realized Osgood was waiting, and gruffly told him to answer the question.

"To me, he looked like he was in some pain," Osgood said, his eyes back on Toth. "But, his, ah, hurt came and went . . . you know, welled up and then eased off. He opened his eyes two or three times while we were still there. He didn't recognize me."

Hoover that night told Lennie he thought Toth was spading ground to seed an argument that would put Fran in the stranglehold of death even while his wife and brother-in-law watched from his bedside. He hoped, Hoover explained, to set the jury to wondering if Fran had not already been poisoned. Hoover, in the middle of explaining Toth's strategy, chided himself, pretended to admonish Danny for not yelling "Incoming!" Lennie remembered Hoover's metaphor and asked A. J. to explain it. He did, and she said,

"Well guess what, that damn shell landed squarely in the foxhole occupied by the defense team."

Toth wandered to within a step of the jury box and then abruptly turned back and faced Osgood. "And when you and your wife left for good that evening, you were accompanied by Jo Ellen, by Mrs. Degeorge, the deceased's wife, your wife's twin sister? Is that correct?"

"I believe so," Osgood said.

Toth, colossally astounded by Osgood's answer, spun back toward the jurors. "You *believe* so? You can't say for certain!"

His manner as self-assured as ever, Osgood, with a little shrug, said he was a "mite hazy" on that particular point.

Lennie, her eyes launching thunderbolts, glared at Osgood. "You *bastard*," she mumbled, "that's not what you told *me*."

"Do you mean," Toth asked, utterly aghast at Osgood's uncertainty, "that you don't remember leaving for your car?"

Osgood smiled. "Oh no," he answered hurriedly. "I remember *that*. I don't distinctly recall if Jo Ellen, Fran's wife, was along. I'm not saying that she was, and I'm not saying that she wasn't. It's . . . it's just that I don't specifically recall."

Lennie, through clenched teeth, whispered, "That mother son-of-a-bitch!"

A. J. cut his eyes her way. "Am I forgiven now, Sweet," he said softly, almost under his breath. Lennie, if she heard, did not let on.

"Well then," Toth said, "it's entirely possible that you and your wife returned to your car together *alone*? That you left your sister-in-law behind in the room with her husband? Who was all but . . . unconscious?"

"Uh, we returned to my pickup truck. My Lincoln was . . . to the best of my recollection, Sir, that's correct. However, it could be that–"

Hoover's furor all but obscured the rest of Osgood's answer. He waved a form. "Approach your Honor!" The form, A. J. found out later, was Osgood's typed-up deposition, the words recorded by Lennie's prodding interview.

Wiggins listened to the reasonings of attorneys Hoover and Toth, and ruled in favor of the defense. Clearly unhappy at Hoover for pivoting away angrily, he forbiddingly inclined his head at the highly pissed-off leader of the prosecution.

"So it is entirely possible" Toth said, walking slowly toward Osgood, his face rigidly on Hoover's witness, "that Mrs. Degeorge stayed behind with her . . . ailing husband. When you and your wife left the hospital for home?"

"Leading!" Hoover cried from his table, still fuming. "The witness never–"

"Withdrawn," Toth interrupted quickly. "But it *is* possible, is it not, that you and your wife returned to your car *by yourselves*? You've thought this through and that's entirely possible. Isn't that correct?"

Osgood nodded, he could not, he admitted, could not with absolute certainty, say that Jo Ellen walked him and his wife to their car. "At the time," he said, slightly shaking his head, "we, my advertising agency, J. Hummel Osgood and Associates, were working late every night on a TV spot for a major account and . . . I'm truly ashamed to admit this, but my mind wasn't entirely where it should have been. I know how terrible that must sound, but . . . ."

Toth turned toward the jurors. Nodding self-righteously, he said, obliquely to Hoover, "I have no more questions for *your* witness."

"Christ," A. J. whispered to Lennie, "*Your* witness? Why didn't he just poke a stick in Bob's eye?"

Lennie snuffled. "You caught that, too."

Hoover was on his feet before Wiggins finished his invitation to rebut. Angrily shaking his head, he strode to within a foot of the witness box. "Explain to me Mister Osgood," he demanded, all but leaning into the box. "How it is that both your wife and her sister clearly remember the three of you walking to your car together – *and you don't remember it that way!*"

"Foundation!" Toth barked.

Hoover, his head still wagging vigorously, returned to his chair. "Withdrawn!" he said, mimicking Toth's displeasure.

Glaring at Hoover, Wiggins ordered the jury to disregard the prosecution's last words.

Betty Osgood, following her husband to the stand, stalwartly testified that her sister, Jo Ellen, had walked her and Hummel to their car. Toth was singularly ineffective in discrediting her. Nor did he draw a pin-prick of blood – not that A. J. could tell – when he clumsily implied that the congenital bond between the two women compromised Betty's testimony.

Betty's swearing-in and testimony, both direct and cross, consumed roughly fifteen minutes – less, maybe. Wiggins, after dismissing her, said he'd hear defense motions for a directed acquittal in the afternoon.

As Lennie had assured me, Judge Wiggins found the defense's arguments for a directed acquittal unpersuasive.

Lennie rapped lightly on the open door. "I messed you up," she said, "didn't I Bob?"

Hoover, alone in his office, looked up from his notes and shrugged. "Don't sweat it, Dear," he said. "No big deal."

Lennie stopped behind the middle chair facing his desk. "Bob, I swear, during the dep that that son-of-a-bitch Osgood never once even *hinted* that Jo Ellen may have stayed behind. What . . . can I say."

"Hell, Lennie, like I said, don't sweat it. You couldn't have foreseen that."

Hoover looked at me and smiled.

"Good evening," A. J. said from the doorway. Uninvited, as was Lennie, he had not entered the room.

"I had to see you," Lennie said to Hoover. "Alan warned me that Osgood was a lying horse's ass. I just didn't–"

"Get out of here!" Hoover said jocularly. "Take her home, A. J. She's the best damn detective on the force."

Lennie disapprovingly waved off his compliment, and A. J. gently pulled her away.

That evening Lennie and A. J. tossed together a verbal salad of reasons for Osgood's patently false testimony. They hashed out several possibilities but never were able to combine the ingredients into one wholly palatable dish. The chance that he may have been telling the truth never crossed their minds.

# [55]

Judge Wiggins, after allowing attorney Toth a minute to scrape around in his briefcase, nodded at the docket clerk. A heavy-set black woman, she stood and loudly announced: "The people of the State of Texas call Royce Nickerson to the witness stand."

The door at the back of the court room opened and the bailiff who had escorted me to the witness stand led Nick into the room.

The first witness for the defense, Nick, after answering a few biographical questions, testified that his one-time lead technician was a living saint, a latter-day Gabriel, a Raphael, and an angel congenitally incapable of violent, let alone murderous, behavior. Approximately, that is what he testified to. Toth glanced at the judge, moseyed back to his chair, and Wiggins invited Hoover to begin his cross examination.

Hoover, his mind seemingly elsewhere, approached Nick slowly. "Just to be sure," he began, "would you point out the defendant, please."

Lennie grinned before it dawned on me that Hoover was sarcastically skewering Nick's gilded answers.

Nick pointed but immediately pulled his hand back. "The man in the blue suit."

Hoover smiled. "It's okay to point. This is a court of criminal law. Good manners are not on trial here." Hoover turned back from looking at Quetsch. "You and the defendant became good friends over the . . . what? The two years that you knew each other?"

"I consider him to be a good friend. Yes."

A. J. glanced at Quetsch. His dour expression did not change.

"The defendant," Hoover said, "worked for you?"

Nick shrugged. "Mostly, we worked together."

"Uh-huh," Hoover said. "In any event you came to know the defendant very well?"

"I . . . think so," Nick answered, his expression rigid. "Yes, I did," he added convincingly after reflecting.

A noise in the juror's box caught Hoover's attention. "Then, you generally addressed your good friend by his first name." He whirled to face Nick. "Isn't that right?"

Nick of course instantly saw the intent of Hoover's question and did not immediately answer.

"In fact," Hoover said, walking rapidly toward the jurors, "you didn't even *know* that the defendant's real first name was *Ronald*! You thought it was Selig!"

Toth threw a pencil on his table and showed Wiggins the palms of hands. "Leading, Your Honor!"

"Withdrawn," Hoover said, walking briskly back to the prosecution's table. "No more questions."

Lennie and A. J. exchanged knowing glances: How could any adult, mentally sound juror not infer that Quetsch, sitting cheerlessly in shackles a couple yards from the prosecution's table, was concealing a dark past?

Judge Wiggins looked at Toth.

Toth, his eyes on his client, said he had no more questions, "None at this time, Your Honor."

Dismissed by Wiggins, Nick caught sight of A. J. as he left the courtroom. They exchanged tiny nods, a slight diversion, it turned out, after which Nick could not wrench his eyes from Lennie.

Lennie whispered, "I better tag along when you two meet for chili."

"You think so?" A. J. said softly. "Take a cold shower first."

Lennie pressed her heel into A. J.'s foot. A. J. decided not to ask her exactly why she chose that extreme response.

The two lead attorneys, Hoover and Toth, summoned to the bench by Judge Wiggins – at Toth's behest – returned to their chairs. Hoover, while standing before Wiggins, had slowly and uninterruptedly shaken his head; he may have uttered a few short sentences.

Toth argued fervently the whole time. Grim faced, he trudged heavily back to the defense's table.

The next two defense witnesses, each unknown to me, admitted under cross examination that they only knew Quetsch as Selig Hildreth – after each had recounted Sel's many virtues under Toth's direct.

By ten o'clock, the only person who had not testified was Quetsch himself.

Wiggins, after dismissing the second of the witnesses whom A. J. had rarely if ever before seen, sent the jurors back to the jury waiting room and then recessed court for twenty minutes. Certain that there would be seats when they returned, Lennie and A. J. sauntered into the hall.

Lennie speculated on the reason Wiggins and the attorneys had conferred: Toth, after hearing Nick admit that he did not know Quetsch's other name, didn't want the jury to hear similar answers repeated by other witnesses.

"Evidently," Lennie said, shrugging unconcerned, "Hoover wouldn't agree to exempt either witness, and Wiggins ruled in his favor."

"Seems to me," A. J. said tepidly, "that the defense should have the right to make that decision?"

"Sure," Lennie answered. "Then Hoover would have threatened to call them as prosecution witnesses. It's called . . . I've forgotten the legal term but it happens."

Quetsch, when we returned to the courtroom, was sitting in the witness box quietly concentrating on the slight activity at the prosecution's table. A bailiff was standing alertly two yards away, discretely closer than where he stood during testimony by the other witnesses. The jury was brought back in.

# [56]

Toth painstakingly avoided giving Hoover the opening that he desperately wanted, that is, giving Hoover a bridge spanning the gulf connecting Quetsch to the eight-year-old rape and slaughter of his one-time girlfriend.

After placid routine preliminaries, Toth led Quetsch into testifying that he had left Fran's wife, Jo Ellen, alone with her husband the evening in question. He wanted a smoke, he said, and was gone from Fran's room for twenty minutes. Toth asked him to elaborate, and he said that the number of visitors allowed at one time in a hospital's ICU room was limited. "And," he continued, "feeling like the odd-man out, I likely was away even longer. Besides, Jo Ellen's sister and her sister's husband were also there."

Quetsch vehemently insisted that the traffic of visitors absolutely was not as Jo Ellen had testified, as she had sworn with such utter, unshakeable conviction. Prompted by Toth, Quetsch assured the jury he had no use whatsoever for potassium permanganate and would not know a bead of that chemical from a farkleberry currant – or where to get a sample of either one.

Hoover wearily told Judge Wiggins, when Toth pulled a sketch from his briefcase and began unfolding it, that the prosecution would stipulate that the hospital's designated smoking area was near where delivery trucks unloaded their cargo and thus a good piece from Fran's room.

Quetsch, on cross examination by Hoover, unhesitatingly admitted to his carnal intimacy with Jo Ellen. As readily, he admitted that their affair had begun while Degeorge was still alive – while he was still running Edgecom.

Led by Toth's well-planned re-direct, he testified, that Jo Ellen had aggressively initiated the affair, had "Climbed all over me," was how he put it, late on a Saturday afternoon in the prototyping lab at Edgecom. "Fran," he finished, "was showing Edgecom circuits at a trade show in Chicago."

On re-cross, Hoover, shaking his head skeptically, said, "What in the world was Mrs. Degeorge doing at Edgecom late on a Saturday afternoon?"

"Seducing me," Quetsch answered promptly.

Obviously, the question did not surprise Quetsch. Moreover, Toth's prefatory foresight likely explained why he, Toth, did not instantly object to the question as one requiring an inferential explanation by Quetsch.

Wiggins ruled conjectural any testimony implying Quetsch, in the person of Jo Ellen's paramour, was a potential beneficiary of Fran's million-dollar life insurance policy.

Unfortunately for Quetsch, Hoover managed to shoo that piebald steed into the jury's wide open psychic corral even before Judge Wiggins barred the entryway.

The testimonial part of the trial ended shortly before eleven o'clock. Judge Wiggins, after ordering Toth to give his closing argument at two p.m., instructed the jury on points of the law and recessed court.

Toth, wearing the same rumpled brown suit he'd worn every day of testimony, fervently closed his case. He was surprisingly impassioned, his demeanor fiery in a way that A. J. hadn't imagined possible. Hoover lived up to A. J.'s expectation, that is, to Lennie's opinion of his ability to close strongly if unemotionally.

Wiggins, once Hoover had settled into his chair behind the prosecutor's table, thanked the jury and recessed court.

Lennie and A. J. bucked their way against the departing throng of court onlookers to where Hoover, bent over the defense table, was working papers into his briefcase. "Well," Lennie said softly to Hoover, "Do you still like girls, Bob?"

Hoover discreetly slid his hand across the fly of his trousers. "I'm pretty sure," he said. "But, hell, Lennie, it's a jury trial. Who knows."

"In your gut?"

"Fifty-fifty."

"C'mon, Bob!" Lennie fired back impatiently. "I make it ninety-ten. Nothing I saw . . . . Your worst moment?"

Hoover shoved another clutch of papers into his briefcase and took a deep breath. "This morning. It's always touchy as to what a murder defendant might testify. Attorneys get real creative when their client has killed someone on purpose. I sweat bullets every damn time."

Danny, Hoover's compatriot, sitting and waiting with his hands clasped on top of his briefcase, nodded sympathetically.

"And . . ." Hoover continued, "I worried that one of the witnesses, uh, whats-his-name, Nickerson, would return to swear that he'd chatted with Quetsch at the outdoor smoking area that night."

Lennie and A. J. both nodded to stress that they understood.

"You two were watching?" Hoover said. "I didn't see you."

Lennie preempted A. J.'s response: "From the peanut gallery."

"Nickerson doesn't smoke," A. J. said. "Of course you didn't know that."

"Toth, Hoover said wearily, "might still have had someone waiting in the wings, some clown that he didn't include in discovery, which he'd have claimed, for a good reason, just showed up."

Lennie's manner became tentative. "When you asked Quetsch if he enjoyed his smoke alone? I thought, 'What in the hell is he doing.' I meant, what in hell *were* you thinking?"

Hoover chuckled. "I was thinking," he said, "'Now, why didn't Toth make that point on direct? Yeah. Why didn't Toth hit the floor running? Why didn't he ask Quetsch with whom he had enjoyed his smoke? Judge Wiggins actually fell back at Toth's opening. Did you notice?"

"We saw," Lennie said. A. J. didn't, but he nodded anyway.

"It's what the sidebar was about. Right then, the monkey waved bye-bye to me and hopped from my back onto Toth's."

"Humor *me*," A. J. said. "What *was* the sidebar about?"

Hoover nodded. "Toth told Wiggins he had a witness who'd corroborate Quetsch's testimony about having a smoke away from the hospital. A man he'd personally lodged in a nearby hotel. Only, he had vanished, had checked out and simply disappeared. Wiggins just stared at him. I mean, he looked at Toth as if he was being told that Big Foot had trudged off without leaving footprints. You notice how all the time I just politely listened?"

"Uh-huh," Lennie said. "So Toth wanted a postponement?"

"Exactly. It's what he *wanted.* What he got was the fastest judicial blow-off I've seen in years."

A. J. did not mean it to show, but Danny saw him slightly shake my head. "What, A. J.?" he said.

"I was glad," A. J. answered, "that the judge ruled the way he did, but a postponement, it seemed to me, was a reasonable request."

"In a murder trial?" Hoover said, preempting Danny. "Absolutely. I'll let you in on something A. J., Quetsch's attorney would lose his ass in a poker game playing against demented chimps. First, it was obvious he *wanted* the jury to hear his motion – Christ, you could have heard him in the next courtroom. That's usually how the game's played at sidebars, but he over did it. Same thing when he dragged out that card key and hotel bill. Strictly bush."

A. J. pretended to be convinced, but Lennie knew better. She looked quickly left and then right. "Hon," she said, "do you think for a second Judge Wiggins wasn't aware that Quetsch was once . . . is still a prime suspect in the murder of his last squeeze?"

A. J. hemmed and hawed: "Well, I assumed . . . that . . . he knew."

Lennie looked at Hoover and shook her head. "I have to keep reminding people that my boyfriend is an engineer. He's good with slide-rulers."

Hoover, loosening his necktie, laughed amiably. "Besides," he said, "as I recall he graduated from SMU."

A. J. let on he'd been insulted.

"The system's not perfect, A. J.," Danny said.

"Evidently," A. J. said with a quick glance around. "What's your guess, Bob? Think Toth really had another witness?"

"Oh, hell no," Hoover shot back impatiently. "Not a chance. Wiggins could have given him a year to produce someone – someone credible. It wasn't going to happen."

A. J. was ready to change the subject. "You would know."

Hoover closed his briefcase, snapping the clasps showily. "Let's blow dis jernt"– he glanced slyly at Lennie –"startin' wit da broads."

We followed Hoover toward the double-doors that led in and out of the courtroom. Danny kicked back, crossed his arms on top of his head, and waved goodbye. The bailiff continued staring dully at the jury box.

A. J. moved to where he was walking alongside Lennie, the two of them locking step with Hoover's weary stroll. "I suppose this is another dumb question Bob, but would you hazard a guess as to how long the jury will be out?"

Hoover sighed. "More than an hour, less than a month." Turning and walking backward, he added, "Seriously, A. J., if I had *any* inkling whatsoever, I'd be living in a penthouse suite at the Sahara in Las Vegas."

The jury reached a verdict over the weekend and made their finding of guilt known to Wiggins and the world on Monday morning. Toth consoled Quetsch, a tenderness that his client shrugged off angrily. Hoover and Danny shook hands, and Hoover gave Danny a light pat on the back.

Wiggins set the disclosure of Quetsch's sentence for the following Thursday, September 24th, giving the jury two days to consider testimony bearing on whether Quetsch should die in middle age, succumb to poisoning as had his latest victim, or pass away in old age of natural causes. Or, perhaps, suck in a final gulp of air on an earlier day, the result of a precisely directed shiv to his rib cage.

# [57]

A. J. and Lennie were lazing around in the apartment in Richardson.

"A woman," Lennie whispered, handing A. J. the telephone.

Squinting, A. J. mouthed, "Mother?"

Lennie shook her head.

"Allison?"

Lennie shook her head again.

The caller was Jo Ellen Degeorge. It was four weeks to the day since the jury had returned the verdict that sent Quetsch, her husband's murderer, in an olive-drab bus on a one-way trip destined to end, some day, at the State-run cemetery near Texas's Huntsville Prison. The grave would be marked by a small white cross (most often) with his name, a prison number, and an X indicating the interred had been executed.

About the time her voice became a familiar tone, A. J. realized Jo Ellen was inviting him to an appreciation bash the coming Saturday. It would be a modest "soiree," a handful of "good friends" gathering to memorialize the "avenging" of her husband's murder and the "appropriate sentencing" of the "dastardly" Ronald Quetsch. *"And your onetime lover,"* A. J. said to himself."

"Jo Ellen," A. J. whispered to Lennie.

A. J. accepted Jo Ellen's invitation hesitantly. "There could be complications. "Me and Osgood aren't exactly bosom pals."

A. J. mainly had in mind the day he clobbard Osgood in the mouth for falsely accusing him of lustfully attacking and consequently driving off Pat Brown.

"I'm only inviting members of the old gang," Jo Ellen said, as if slightly annoyed. "Absolutely no one who hired in after Francis died. Not even Hummel. Actually, he and Betty are vacationing in Denver, looking to buy a chateau there. I did invite Skip, Skip Hardeman. He'll be the only one who never worked for Francis."

A. J. mumbled words to the effect that Osgood's absence satisfied his concern.

"You know, of course," Jo Ellen continued, "that Mr. Hardeman let Karl go?"

I looked at Lennie. "Hardeman fired Dornhoffer? No, I didn't know."

"Yes. Betty told me . . . a month ago he quit reporting to Edgecom."

"I'll miss him," A. J. said sarcastically.

Evidently A. J.'s scorn was not obvious. "I will too," Jo Ellen replied. "I finally located Royce Nickerson. He's coming."

"Nick!" A. J. exclaimed. "Great. We almost missed getting together after he testified."

"I'm sure you two have a lot to talk about."

"How about Norman Israel. Is he coming?"

"I invited him. Did you know that he got married?"

"No, I hadn't heard. That's . . . perfect."

"He lives in North Dallas. I've got his address."

"Great," A. J. said genially.

"Let's see," Jo Ellen said after a second. "Who else . . . ."

"How about Sandy?" A. J. said.

"I left a message on her recorder. She hasn't called back."

"She'll show up. You can count on it."

In one of those strange coincidences, A. J. imagined Pat Brown at her Edgecom desk curiously listening to a caller on the telephone, and, simultaneously, Jo Ellen said, "One person who won't be there is that whore Pat Brown."

A. J. flashed Lennie a wide-eyed look and mouthed the words Pat Brown. "That's, ah, understandable," he said into the mouthpiece.

"Can you think of anyone I've forgotten?"

"Ah, Miki Vernon?"

"Miki," she said, after a short wait, "will be out of town."

In other words, A. J. mused, Miki would be spending Saturday and Sunday on Wallace Hardeman's boat, "The Hard Way," cruising the Gulf of Mexico – among other undulating activities.

"The party is this weekend?"

"Eight o'clock Saturday. You can't think of anyone else? That I should invite?"

"The only other person . . . would you care to invite Dolly, Jesse's widow?"

"Probably I should," Jo Ellen said. Her answer was feeble, almost an aside, and A. J. knew Dolly would not be at the party.

"Eight o'clock Saturday?"

A. J. looked at Lennie. She shrugged indifferently.

A. J. said to Jo Ellen that he would bring a bottle of spirits.

"No, no, no!" she exclaimed. "Everything is on me. Just bring yourself. Uh, bring a date too. If you want."

Her amended invitation left A. J. thinking that she knew he'd taken up with Lennie.

A. J. hung up, and he said to Lennie, "You okay with that?"

Lenny said, "Uh-huh. We need to get out more, anyway."

A. J. said that Jo Ellen, if she did not already know, had learned at the trial that Fran was getting it on with Pat Brown.

"She knew," Lennie said. "Admitted it when I depped her. What made you bring that up?"

"Because," A. J. said. "She called Pat a damn whore."

Lennie said, "So?"

"I meant . . . her language. I'd never heard her swear before."

# [58]

A. J was surprised at the size of the Degeorge home. He had expected to pull up to at least a four-bedroom, hundred-thousand-dollar house. Fran was irresolutely opposed to borrowing money for personal use, so A. J. figured that he may have opted for a smaller house and paid for it with cash. In any event, he likely would have thought of his new house as an investment, not a home.

A Corvette, Skip's, A. J. presumed, was parked curbside in front of the house. A. J. parked behind it. The sky had been overcast all day and when Lennie and A. J. arrived a little after eight o'clock it was pitch-black outside. Lennie, neat in a brand new gray and white-trimmed pants suit, and full of herself, waited imperiously for me to open the car door on her side.

The architecture of the Degeorge house, illuminated a fair span to the left and right by a large, suspended porch chandelier, was faux Spanish: the siding was of ochre-colored bricks; arched windows were protected by black, full-length, rough-hewed, cast-iron bars topped with ornamental spearheads; and the roof facer boards were a reddish-brown hue, Spanish red, A. J. suppose, if there is such a color.

Jo Ellen, wearing a red cocktail dress that showed plenty of her slightly chubby legs, met us at the one-step entrance to the slab front porch. Holding a champagne glass, her pinky finger skewed off by itself, she gushed words of greeting that A. J. and Lennie fulsomely returned.

Fran's 1978 Oldsmobile Tornado was parked in the driveway. A. J. assumed his Triumph Classic motorcycle was parked in the garage. Jo Ellen, later that evening, told me that she had sold his motorcycle, that she had ridden it once as Fran's passenger and became "deathly" sick. Knowing Fran, A. J. imagined he nearly scared her to asphyxiation – if she was honest with A. J. about being his passenger. "You likely didn't know," she said, "but Francis took a really bad spill on it when I was pregnant with Joseph."

"No, I didn't know," A. J. said. He was skeptical, however: Fran liked to boast of his misadventures, and he hadn't mentioned a word to him about *any* motorcycle spill, ever.

Skip Hardeman and Harriet Muckinhaupt were waiting alone in the living room. Skip, admiring a figurine sitting on the fireplace mantel, turned and rushed to shake A. J.'s hand. Harriet, sitting by herself on a three-cushion, dusky-yellow, imitation leather sofa, greeted Lennie – rather affably, A. J. thought, considering their infrequent and labored verbal exchanges the night the four of them watched the Los Angeles Lakers basketball team demolish the unhardened Dallas Mavericks team.

Skip released A. J.'s hand. He waved at Harriet, and she waved back.

A. J. said to Skip, "That 'Vette' out front yours?"

"Harriet's. She drives when we party."

"As she should," A. J. said, elevating his eyebrows avuncularly.

Likely, Skip gave her the car outright.

Norman Israel and his new wife arrived. Naomi's oddly modulated Barbados English charmed everyone.

Sandy, on the arm of a bearded dude wearing a checked, flannel shirt, a Wicke's Lumber gimme cap, and one of those quilted, sleeveless jackets signifying that the wearer is a hardy outdoorsman descended straight from Paul Bunyan, arrived next. Either he or Sandy had lain on the doorbell. By default – Jo Ellen was on the telephone – A. J. had to let them in.

An unadorned wall with a double-wide arched doorway in the middle separated the living room from the dining room. The dining room table, leaved out, was set with three large round silver trays of fancily prepared hors d'oeuvres, three large bowls of chips, and a shiny, stainless-steel champagne fountain circulating a red drink that cascaded into a round basin a good thirty inches across the top. There were enough vittles to feed a throng of starving Chinese trenchermen. A rented, folding bar had been placed diagonally across a back corner of the room. Bobbing up and down behind the bar, a mustachioed Hispanic man, wearing a white shirt and bright red bow tie, was busy arranging bottles of booze and different size drink glasses.

After Skip, Norman, and A. J. placed orders with the mustachioed bartender, their conversation turned to Edgecom. Norman and A. J. had questions, and Skip, his father's indispensable advisor – A. J. had belatedly come to realize – cheerily answered every one.

Texline Office Furniture was now Edgecom's principal owner, the fourth in the firm's less-than-five-years of life, succeeding Fran and Jo Ellen Degeorge, Hummel Osgood, and Wallace Hardeman. By mid-1981, Edgecom's working capital had plunged to where the book value of Edgecom stock had stalled at $2.76 a share, while the market price of a share – the influence of the book value on market price is usually tenuous – had fluctuated around the three-dollar mark. Wickersham, of course, was no longer around juicing up the quarterly financial reports. The directors of TexLine bought Edgecom for roughly ten cents a share over its market price – paying not by cashable legal tender, naturally, but with shares of TexLine stock.

Skip guessed that Osgood, if he sold his holdings (the shares of Edgecom Common that as a company officer he could not legally unload in the initial offering) banked another $700,000, nowhere near what he might have made in the IPO, still two or three times what most people earned in a lifetime.

His father, Skip hinted, had doubled his investment. Skeptical of Skip's number, A. J. checked with Irickson. Tom said he'd be surprised if Hardeman *only* doubled his money, having ultimately bought half of Edgecom for (he presumed) around $300,000. A. J. decided Hardeman was not the blustering, dim-witted oaf he made himself out to be.

Edgecom, while Francis Degeorge ran the business, was a going concern providing a good living for some eighty persons, not to mention a fair emolument for Degeorge himself. On the day an express service delivered the certificate of merger from the office of the Texas Secretary of State, Edgecom was brain dead, its pulse, evidence still of some life, was the aimless factory-to-office-to-factory meandering of Osgood, Appleby, and Hardeman's squeeze, Miki Vernon, who was taking telephone calls from what was once Pat Brown's interoffice-room desk.

# [59]

Evidently Jo Ellen had been waiting nearby because once Skip stopped holding forth on business issues currently facing Edgecom Data Corporation, she lightly touched A. J.'s shoulder and asked him to start a fire in the living-room fireplace. "I hadn't planned on one but I've changed my mind," she said. Plainly a bit tipsy, Jo Ellen pretended to shiver. "There's firewood on the patio in back, and a stack of old newspapers in the laundry room . . . the last doorway before the door going into the garage."

"Right away," A. J. said genially, slightly feeling his third margarita. "Did Nick ever call back?"

"Nick?" Jo Ellen said, a blank look on her face. "Oh. No. He did not, A. J."

Norman and A. J. expressed their disappointment, and A. J. said to Skip, "Damn, I wanted you two peckerwoods to meet."

A. J. followed a hallway to the attached garage at back of the house. Skip tagged along and helped him fetch the firewood. Israel, when they got back, was bedding the fireplace grate with compacted wads of newspaper.

"Matches, please," A. J. said to Jo Ellen, who was standing behind him watching. "Also, do you have some kerosene around?"

"I don't know. Check in the garage."

It was apparent that Jo Ellen did not use the garage to shelter their Oldsmobile Tornado: multi-colored plastic toys – several large enough for kids to ride – were lined up facing the closed garage door. A four-foot-by-eight-foot sheet of plywood, the base for a model railroad setting – supported catawampus on a pair of pre-fabricated wooden sawhorses – took up most of the middle of the room.

Fran had built a full-length work bench across the back wall of the garage, and just visible behind a flotsam of household odds and ends was an oscilloscope, a two-voltage DC power supply, a multi-meter, and a sine-wave generator. A wall-mounted pegboard held a half dozen hand tools. Haphazardly situated just inside the garage's double-wide car door sat four large baked-clay planters, each the grave of a dried-up azalea plant.

A. J. circled the interior perimeter of the garage, moving this, tilting that, looking for a blue container, the usual color of a two-gallon kerosene can. He couldn't find one. Standing on the floor to the side of the model railroad base was a two-door metal cabinet, the same size as the ones abutted together to form the interior walls of the corner prototyping lab at the Edgecom plant. Figuring that Fran would presume it to be a safe place for storing inflammables from his children, A. J. looked inside.

A. J. found something even better than kerosene for starting a fire: a one-quart can of barbecue fire-starting fluid sitting on the top shelf. It felt full, and A. J. breezed through the instructions on the can on his way back to the living room. Something, while A. J. was reading the directions, vaguely bothered him. What? Was the barbecue starter too volatile an accelerant for an indoor fireplace? The wording was at best ambiguous, and A. J. shrugged off his uneasiness.

The starter fluid worked fine – if anything A. J. could have used it less liberally – and before long, a semicircle of guests, drinks in hand, were facing a fire on the verge of cutting loose from adolescence.

Norman and Skip plainly found that A. J.'s aptitude for pyrotechnics left much to be desired: Norman asked why he hadn't just rubbed two sticks together, and Skip said he'd kindled more robust flames frying bacon on his kitchen range. Sandy's boyfriend, adding his two bits worth, said he would again telephone the Frisco fire department and advise them that it was okay to go off yellow alert. Had Nick, the once vitally important head of Edgecom Engineering been there, he'd have deftly compared A. J.'s libido to the fire's flickering reach for maturity.

A. J. didn't notice until after the bantering had petered out that he had left the barbecue fire-starting can sitting on the fireplace hearth – formed of the same ochre-colored bricks that were used to side the house – a tad too close to the fire itself. A. J. hurried away with it.

It hit A. J. a step before he reached the garage door: It was not the small skull-and-cross bones pictured under the warning on the can in his hand that had troubled him earlier, it was the same picture, printed larger in bright red on the box sitting on the shelf behind where he had found the can of barbecue fire-starter fluid.

A. J. slowed to a snail's pace, something he was unaware of at the time, but visualized perfectly hours later while explaining to Lennie in the car in front of his apartment. Even before reaching the cabinet in the garage, A. J. could see in his mind's eye, bold as a magazine headline, a title and subtitle on the package sitting behind the barbecue starter fluid: "Kills Pond Varmints" / The Pond Doctor.

For a half-minute, perhaps longer, A. J. seriously considered leaving the can of starter fluid elsewhere – anywhere but inside the tall metal cabinet now standing in front of him. A. J. did not, however, knowing full well that the unanswered question would haunt him the rest of his life.

A. J. returned the can and re-joined the festivities. His knees were so sugar-watery that he stumbled over the four-inch step leading from the garage into the house, where he scrounged a plastic zip-lock bag from Jo Ellen's kitchen. A. J. later stole back to the garage and collected a sample of the contents of the box.

Norman and his wife Naomi were the first to leave. Though A. J. had a buzz on, he could tell that neither Norman nor Naomi had had much to drink. Naomi pledged to mail Lennie a recipe for an exotic Barbados Island chicken salad dish. Likely, if A. J. had not been so thoroughly dispirited, he'd have uttered some dumb-assed remark advising everyone within ear-shot that Lennie would first have to learn how to boil water before tackling anything as complicated as dicing, cooking, and seasoning chicken.

Norman and A. J. promised each other they'd keep in touch.

Lennie, after Norman and Naomi left, hurried A. J. away from the others and down the hall that led ultimately into the garage. Stopping in front of a closed door that had been shut tight all evening, she crossed her lips with an index finger. It was obvious from the non-stop thumping that the persons inside were consumately tripping the light fantastic.

"Who?" A. J. whispered to Lennie.

"Who," she whispered back, "do you think?"

I looked around and decided the ebullient moaning was coming from Sandy. Lennie nudged me, wanted me to barge into the room. At that moment, I would not have found anything funny, including an explicit

devouring of what Jesse used to call Sandy's "Muffin'
Nosh" – always respectfully expressed by Jesse the way
one speaks of a friend on the wagon.

At ten o'clock, Skip, Harriet, Lennie, and A. J.
gathered around Jo Ellen, lavishly told her what a great
time they had, and left together. A. J. helped Harriet
walk Skip to her Corvette.

"Okay," Lennie said finally, breaking the silence.
A. J. had eased onto southbound U.S. 75. Some seven
miles east of Degeorge's home, U.S. 75 was not the
shortest route to Richardson from Jo Ellen's, but it was
free of traffic signals.  U.S. 75 is called Central
Expressway beginning a little north of Dallas itself.

"You're sour because I flirted with Harold. Christ,
A. J. do you think for a second I'd even let that nit-wit
kiss my foot?"

Truthfully, A. J. had not seen her show interest in
any man. He was sober enough, however, not to admit
it, to act mildly put out. After a moment spent fitting
the name Harold to one of Jo Ellen's guests, A. J. said,
"Yeah. Only that's not my problem, Hon."

Lennie waited

"Reach into my pocket."

"Your *pocket*," she said, shaming suspicion of A.
J.'s motive."

"My *coat* pocket."

She exhaled a noisy "Whew."

"This?"

A. J. knew without looking that she was showing him the only item that was inside his pocket, a plastic bag containing a sample of the grist from the Pond Physician box.

"What's that stuff look like?" A. J. asked.

Lennie turned on the dome light. They passed one off-ramp, slowly cruised a mile or so farther southward, and came to another.

"It's crimson or purple . . . grit. Or something. Where'd you get it?"

I answered, carefully enunciating each word separately: "From a box in a cabinet in Fran's garage."

"A box of *what*?" Lennie asked impatiently.

"Some kind of fish-pond treatment. From an outfit named 'The Pond Doctor'."

It was a good half minute before Lennie asked her next question, which really was not a question: "You think it's potassium permanganate."

"I know it is. It said so on the box. 'Permanganic acid'. Same thing. The poison that killed Fran."

"Son of a bitch," Lennie said softly, and then, in her regular voice: "The Degeorge's probably had a need for it. We don't know."

A. J. briefly looked out the side window of the car and then back at Lennie. "There wasn't a pond of any kind behind Fran's house."

"You–"

"I checked. Hell, there wasn't even a lawn, to speak of."

A. J. turned off Central at Arapaho Drive, one exit ramp south of Campbell Road, the west-bound street he had intended to take. Neither A. J. nor Lenny spoke while A. J. backtracked on surface streets to their apartment complex. He parked the car in his assigned space and switched off the engine. Lennie made no effort to leave the car, so after a minute or so A. J. re-started the engine for the heat.

"Christ," Lennie said finally, "Caesar's wife. I suppose she had a key to his . . . to Sel Hildreth's apartment. And scattered some of it around."

Probably," A. J. said spiritlessly. "They'd been seeing each other."

Lennie, for long seconds stared motionlessly out the window on her side. She turned and faced me. The words "Mother fuck!" exploded from her mouth.

"Jo Ellen's just smart enough to be cunning," A. J. mumbled, rehashing an unsettling argument in his own mind.

After a long sigh Lennie indistinctly murmured something. A. J. did not understand exactly what but he knew what she meant: that she would begin at once nudging the pendulum of justice along a different arc.

The door latch on Lennie's side clicked, and A. J. hurried to help her out. She accepted his hand from her seat inside the car, the second time that night – only the third time since they had met.

456

# ABOUT THE AUTHOR

**Hugh McClintock**, coincident with the action of *Murder Light,* was an officer of Dallas, Texas-based Percom Data Corporation (now defunct). Percom manufactured TRS-80 and SS-50 Bus add-on products for the aborning personal computer market.

Hugh also authored *Humor Straight*, a collection of his humorous, one-thousand word newspaper columns that were published in the Meadville (Pa.) *Tribune,* and *Cooper Greens,* an eye-opener about an outwardly quiet nursing home for elders, where calm and implicit decency vanishes amid the uproar of pranks and false rumors orchestrated by bored resident Tom Murtaugh and his black roommate.

Hugh graduated from Allegheny College and Carnegie Mellon University. Retired, he lives in Meadville, Pennsylvania.